SONS OF NEPHI

MARK H. DuMOND

A special thank you to my wife Kris for her love and support. I would also like to thank our family, as their love and strength make all things possible. Another special thank you goes to Penny and Charles; the help, encouragement, and hours of editing performed by Penny cannot go without a special mention.

TABLE OF CONTENTS

PREFACE

In the two-year window leading up to the events told in this story, much had occurred, some of which had been in the works for many years. The American people had their flat screen TVs and cell phones; they had no desire to know how bad things had become. The US government was in debt, but to what extent, few knew. The collapse of the dollar, the loss of faith in a nation, and the power-grab of a desperate president may lead to the destruction of a nation, yet could also result in the salvation of a people.

Starting in the fifties with a post-war boom, the American public became used to a constant rate of growth; families became wealthier and wealthier. During the nineties and early in the twenty-first century, the push for economic equality produced a false economy. The economy was that of homes owned by banks and children graduating from college with hundreds of thousands of dollars in debt and an education of little more value than a high school diploma. A new definition of poor emerged: people with huge debt loads, high quantities of material goods, and little to no equity. Low-income housing was regularly outfitted with flat screen TVs and satellite dishes; every home had a laptop, and the poor were no longer without material goods. It would not take long for the housing and credit market to collapse once the market paused. A few key men and women spoke out against the decline that was so clear to them. "Our house of cards is due to fall," presidential candidate Ron Paul said. Pundits and talk show hosts who spoke out were marginalized by the hard news media.

They were called kooks or conspiracy-theory crazies. When a well-known economist pointed out that the interest due on our national debt was nearing balance with the nation's gross domestic product, most of the country, even the world, ignored his warnings. In fact, he lost his position at Stanford University and was labeled a "conspiracy theorist" by his peers.

The truth was that the American people were enjoying the benefits of all of the borrowed money and ever-increasing stock market values too much; doing without was no longer acceptable. Like any system, a leveling and reset was inevitable. The nation could survive if the attitude of a spoiled, entitled population would tolerate any form of hardship or loss of wealth. The inevitable hardships and failing markets were seen by a select group as a great opportunity. President Prescott was quoted, "Never let a good crisis go unused." Prescott was a student of history. Like many historical figures—such as Hitler, Mussolini, and Pol Pot—Prescott saw opportunity in a crisis. To some degree the blame that then-candidate Prescott placed on the opposition was deserved; yet the true blame belonged at the feet of an entitled and lazy population, a series of generations that sold their freedoms for material goods. Prescott was elected by a disgruntled electorate, one that was tired of foreign wars, and an electorate that was easily convinced that big business was the cause of all of their woes. The age-old game of class and race warfare was used with great skill by the Prescott campaign.

Once elected, it was not much of a stretch for the President to transfer the blame from big business to big religion. The truth was that the politics of the religious tended to be balanced; yet President Prescott saw strong churches as a threat to the power of the government. Prescott was not just a power-hungry politician; he was much more dangerous than that. Prescott believed his words; he was a man of ideals and convictions and a student of Noam Chomsky. Prescott truly believed that the ends justify the means, and he truly believed that the capitalist-based power and economics were evil. Prescott believed that equal opportunity was not enough; equal results were the only true equality. The only way to make change on this level was collapse, complete and total collapse. Prescott would govern not to save a nation; he would govern to change a nation at any cost, even if that cost was the nation itself.

With all of these events, wars, poverty, unemployment, and near-depression levels of misery, the American people had little time or ability to react. The American people were fighting so hard to save their lifestyle that they did not see what was happening around them.

The world economy was in a state of decline; election fraud and political battles sparked rioting in the streets. The sitting president attempted to outlaw several churches. The US dollar collapsed, and inflation hit. Rural areas became isolated. Most of the military walked off the job. Fifty thousand troops were stranded in the Middle East, and another seventy-five thousand were stranded in Asia. The sitting president attempted to hold office at any cost.

CHAPTER ONE

Walking down the street in dark suits, two young men made their way from home to home. The two young men were dressed alike, with one exception. Looking closely, one could see they had on different ties—one red and one blue. They both carried books. The young man in the red tie had a large, older, leather-bound book, nearly four inches thick. The young man in the blue tie carried several smaller, blue, paperback books. The books were the tools of the trade for these young men, young men living out their calling of serving a Mormon mission. On their bikes, or walking with backpacks, or even knocking on doors, teams like these were seen in almost every town in the world.

Mormon missionaries are always referred to by their titles: *Elder*, or *Sister*, if female. Often they are ridiculed or scorned; some see them as religious fanatics. The truth is that most young men and some women who are raised in the Mormon Church would spend up to two years on a mission. This was a rite of passage of sorts, a responsibility that families feel toward their faith. These young men and women go out into the world and share their faith, often at their own expense. They don't come home to be preachers or theologians; they return home to be accountants, doctors, and mechanics. Often missionaries are sent overseas; they receive special training and go to language school to give them the tools they would need in a foreign land. The skills and experiences these missionaries gain is often life-changing, maybe explaining the high rate of achievement seen in Mormons.

The two young men walked down the street in a small town. One nineteen years old and the other twenty, both were from typical LDS families, one from Southern California the other from New Jersey. In high school they both played football; they were average kids. Most people who knew them did not even know of their Mormon faith.

On their mission, the two became companions. They struggled through the occasional criticism and taunts from the uninformed; they gained real-world experience with a safety net. Being on mission was more to the two young men than a religious experience. Like many others, for these young men, it was the first step toward manhood. With all of this in mind, the two walked down the street joking and laughing. The day had been tough with doors slammed in their faces and taunts from passing teens. Now it was time to use their ace in the hole. Missionaries worked off a system of grids: they planned neighborhoods and areas to knock on doors, often saving a special neighborhood or apartment complex for days just like this one.

The building they were coming up on was the favorite of such places. They saved it for rough days or days when they just needed a little pick-me-up. This building on the west side of the street is a retirement apartment complex, an assisted living unit for the elderly. The elderly most frequently enjoyed the company of the missionaries. They often had small tasks they needed help with, and they loved to talk. After a day or a week of slammed doors and little success, such a reprieve from the harsh realities of the world was always welcome.

The elderly would talk and share stories. Conversations with experienced, educated people would bring a smile to the face of even the most discouraged missionary. Today these two young men had had mixed results, with the larger part of the mix being negative. They felt that visiting a few old women with cookies or an elderly couple that needed someone to take out the trash would be a great way to end the week.

Over the years the job of being a Mormon missionary had changed little: spread the word, help those who will accept help, and provide service where it's needed. Many non-Mormons did not know that serving and helping others was the Mormon missionary's charter as much as converting the willing.

"No more slammed doors today," the shorter and younger of the two young men said with a smile on his face,

The two young men were much like any other two missionaries one would see across the country. The older was tall, maybe six foot two, and slender. He had dark hair, thin and neatly cut, and his face had very chiseled features. His accent was clearly rural, but it was hard to discern from which area of the country. He was confident, standing tall and somewhat authoritative in stature.

The younger of two was about five foot seven with sandy blond hair, some might call it light brown. Neither thin, nor fat, he was very non-descript in features and stature. His voice was quiet and deliberate, not shy, but quiet. When he spoke, he made clear and constant eye contact. His demeanor would make one think he was raised in a strict, yet loving, home.

"Bet you we get cookies, too," responded his companion, the tall dark-haired young man.

The two looked forward to this afternoon. Tomorrow they would be at a stake meeting, so no door-knocking. Today they would end their week on a positive note.

The first door they knocked on was apartment 101. A small placard on the door read "M and L Scott." In this building the missionaries knew to wait a few minutes for the door to be opened. The average age of the residents was in the nineties, and it took most residents some time to answer a knock. The two young men stood tall. They adjusted their ties and straightened their hair while they waited.

The door opened slowly, and a thin, gray-haired man stood in the threshold with a smile on his face. From inside the apartment they heard the words of a woman.

"Who is it, honey?"

"Missionaries," he responded over his shoulder. A soft, loving response, unlike so many older couples—this was the response of a man still very much in love with his bride.

The gray-haired man turned to the missionaries and smiled the kind of smile you see on a parent when a child comes to visit. It was clear he was happy to see them.

"Come on in, boys." He turned and walked into the living room as though expecting his young friends to follow.

As the two followed the elderly man into his apartment, they closed the door behind them. Looking into the neatly kept living room, they saw a woman sitting in her chair. She was frail and aged but had a light in her eyes and looked excited to see the young men. The room was lined with family photos. On one wall was a framed box with a folded American flag and Marine Corps flag. The young men also saw several framed documents and a photo of a man in his forties with a general and a man in a suit. It was familiar to the two missionaries; they had seen this photo when they had visited this couple before.

On the bookcase below the picture was a scrapbook full of newspaper clippings. The two young men focused on the scrapbook and photos, hoping today might be the day.

"Go ahead; you can look at it," the man said to the young men, pointing to the scrapbook.

The elderly man had settled into his chair, an overstuffed recliner, and seemed a bit self-conscious of the fact that he was the only one sitting, as his wife had gotten to her feet and started walking into another room.

When the young men made no move towards the scrapbook, he slowly returned to his feet, picked up the book they had been eyeing so longingly, and went to the dining room table. Sitting down, he gestured to them to join him. "Let's take a look at this old book, I will tell you all about it."

The two young missionaries had a bit of an anxious look; they followed the direction and walked toward the table.

From the kitchen they heard a voice call, "You boys hungry? I made manicotti and chocolate chip cookies." She spoke in a tone only a grandmother could muster.

For a moment the two were just hungry teens; they joined in a quick high five.

"Score," said the younger of the two with an ear-to-ear grin.

Before anyone could respond, she finished with, "It will only take a few minutes to heat up."

The two had asked about the pictures on the wall before, and the old man had always told them, "Oh, you wouldn't be interested in that old stuff." The old man had always directed conversation away from this subject as long as they had known each other.

"Is this about the picture and flags on the wall?" asked the taller missionary. The old man smiled, nodded, and glanced at the table, clearly directing the young men to have a seat.

The three were now seated at the table, and the scrap book was opened; the first pages consisted of newspaper articles, yellowed and old. "This is how we used to get the news," he said, pointing at the yellowed paper clippings as if he were talking to small children.

"The headlines went unnoticed by most people back then. People were hungry and frustrated; they had little time or will for complicated political matters," he explained.

"Most people did not pay too much attention back then," his wife interjected as she walked back into the room.

"Excuse me, Elders, I need to go to the restroom." The old man got to his feet and slowly made his way toward the other end of the small apartment. The two missionaries flipped through the pages, continuing to read, fascinated by what they saw as real history.

NEW YORK TIMES

US deficit reaches all-time high; debt ceiling debate rages in Congress. Can the United States survive?

CHICAGO TRIBUNE

President Prescott calls for the end of religious tax exemptions. The President seeks the wealth of churches to solve debt crisis. A bill is introduced that places a 60% tax on the holdings of all churches and removes any future tax-exempt status. "It is an all-out attack on religion," states the opposition leader. "The President and Congress have spent all of the nation's wealth. They have taxed business out of existence, and now they attack our faith." The line is drawn in the sand. LDS church authorities hint that they will no longer recognize the authority of President Prescott.

USA TODAY

Can we afford four wars? A question for President Prescott, the anti-war president.

War rages on in Libya; US presence grows as ground troops take Tripoli. Air strikes in Syria. Damascus under siege Afghanistan, Iraq, and Iran combat continues. What happened to the man who was going to bring the troops home?

WALL STREET JOURNAL

US dollar collapse? Prime rate dropped to less than 1%. Gold over $2500.00 an ounce. Unemployment 18% President Prescott calls it "a bump in the road to prosperity." Opposition claims White House is not telling the truth and economic collapse is imminent.

LOS ANGELES TIMES

President losing support in his own party. Congressman Davies says, "The truth about the economy must get out; this administration is playing with the numbers." Davies claims things are much worse than the Prescott administration will admit. Davies puts unemployment at 28%. Davies calls for investigation of CBO. "The Congressional Budget Office is bending the numbers at the President's will," he says.

CHRISTIAN SCIENCE MONITOR

President Prescott calls for the arrest of Church leaders and other outspoken critics, calling for the subversion charges. The President calls the Mormon Church a subversive group and demands a congressional investigation. Catholic Archdiocese asks, "Are we next?"

Neither young man spoke; they were absorbing the information like sponges.

When the elderly man returned, he found the table set and a plate of hot manicotti sitting in front of each of the young men. His wife sat across the table, waiting for her husband. The two young men were so engrossed in the clippings and photos that they barely noticed her bringing food to the table.

As the elderly man settled into his chair, he asked, "Will you say a blessing? Then we will eat, and I will tell you how it all happened. You know, what really happened, not just the stuff you read about in history class." The younger man said a brief grace. Then the elderly man began to tell a story of events that occurred long before the two young men were born.

CHAPTER TWO

Like so many days for Matt, it started with the beeping of the 5:00 a.m. alarm. When Matt Scott was a younger man, he woke before the alarm. Now a little older, and maybe a bit more tired, Matt snoozed the alarm clock a couple times each morning. By the third alarm he was up and out of bed at the urging of his new bride, Leanne.

His time by himself in the morning before work had always been his favorite moments of the day—a cup of coffee in hand, and his ass parked on the couch. This ritual, minus the snooze button, was one that had gone on for the last twenty-five years. Now in his forties, he had finally been able to cut his workdays down. The sixty-hour work-week had passed with his youth, yet the need to get up and be moving early had never left. Matt was feeling the run from the day before while walking across the cold hardwood floor toward the kitchen. The cold felt good on his feet, as his knees popped loudly for the first few steps. The popping of joints was accompanied by a quiet moan. The popping knees and aching bones had slowed him down quite a bit, but generally Matt was a fit man—he ran and went to the gym. The gray hairs out-numbered the brown now, and his neatly trimmed goatee was all silver at this point in life. Some mornings, like this one, the pain in the knees and back reminded him that he was no longer an eighteen-year-old marine. Matt still felt young inside, but some days his body disagreed.

Leanne looked very fit but had never been one to go out of her way to exercise. She loved to swim and play in the pool with the grandkids, and she enjoyed long walks. Leanne never understood Matt's obsession with running or exercise. Matt ran as a young man—all Marines ran— but that was not what started his love of running. He found sometime in his thirties that he could clear his head when he ran. Relationships, business, and politics could sometimes gang up on a man. Matt would run to escape the things that overwhelmed him. This morning's groans and cracking joints were just more indicators that soon Matt would only be remembering a long morning run. The act of aging often stole away some of the joys of life; running was a joy Matt would soon lose.

This morning, like most, he made a cup of coffee, put a single piece of toast in the toaster, and then sat on the couch to watch the news. Eating toast, sipping coffee, and grumbling at the state of the world was the usual beginning to his day.

His wife, Leanne, would often tell him, "If you just shut off the news, you wouldn't be so damn grumpy."

Matt knew this was true, but it was sort of an addiction. Matthew Scott had always been interested in politics, but this year it seemed to be more intense. The reelection bid of the current president and the fighting of multiple wars, combined with the state of the world's economy, left him in a bit of a political rage. He worried about his son-in-law, a young marine fighting in the Middle East. He worried for his two daughters, and his wife's two children and their families. Often his worry turned to anger toward the current administration.

Matt made sure to turn the volume down low; he didn't want to wake Leanne, as she didn't need to get up for work for another hour or so. Leanne was in bed, pretending to be asleep, as she knew how much Matt loved his morning time. The familiar noise of his popping knees accompanied by a quiet groans made Leanne worry quietly from their bed. Leanne also worried about Matt's stress level. They were not young when they married, and she was not going to lose her new husband to a stress-induced heart attack. The stress or anger that came from politics was not helping, and he needed to avoid the news a little more often. Leanne tried hard to avoid talking to Matt about politics. It wasn't a lack of interest, or even that she disagreed with her husband, but she would much rather enjoy life than get worked up over things she had no control over. Matt, on the other hand, had it in his blood to see the big picture, often to his own detriment. Leanne worried about the sound of the popping knees and the painful moans, but she worried more when she heard Matt turn the news on. The TV was down low, but she could hear it. "Why is he watching the news again?" she thought with a bit of irritation.

Instead of the usual news, the station was airing an ad. Since it was an election year, it was one of those scare-tactic ads that showed a picture of a presidential candidate while in the background a concerned voice says, "They want to take away your Social Security, they want to ban abortion, and they will starve the poor." In this day of left- or right-leaning news and biased coverage, it was hard to tell the attack ad from the news coverage. Frustrated and a bit angered by the ad, Matt clicked the remote to change the channel, and again the same message was on, so off went the TV. Political or not, there was nothing Matt liked less than sensationalism and scare tactics. It would be good to take a break from this crap anyway, he thought.

Enjoying the quiet for a moment, Matt found himself unable to break from his routine. He walked to the office and picked up his laptop. He returned to the couch and opened it. He quickly checked Facebook for a message from his kids, and then posted a song of the day, something Matt had done every day for the last two years. A scan through the posts of friends showed more political messages than normal, some nasty things about right-wing religious nuts, and some equally venomous statements calling the president and democrats a bunch of Marxists. Matt did not want to start his day with all of this crap, so he firmly closed the laptop and loaded it in its case to take to work. Through Leanne's influence he was learning to put the politics aside at least for the moment. The words of his wife made sense; Matt was working on avoiding those things that made him so angry. He made his way to the master bathroom to get ready for work.

The master bath had a door at each end. Like every other morning, Matt entered from the hall, shaved, and then brushed his teeth in the shower, another one of those old habits of a type-A workaholic. Matt never felt like there was enough time. In many ways he had learned, with Leanne's help, to slow down and enjoy life, but on occasion the old Matt was evident. The simple act of multitasking by brushing his teeth in the shower showed old traits of living life in a hurry. He left the bathroom and entered the bedroom, where he saw Leanne lying quietly in the bed. She watched him as he put on a dress shirt, jeans, and a pair of Rockports, the same thing Matt had worn almost every day of his adult life.

Leanne sat up and the two exchanged a long embrace, followed by the ritual morning good-byes. "Have a good day. I love you," Leanne told him.

"I will, and you don't work too hard. I will see you at dinner." Matt kissed her one more time on the cheek, they exchanged one more "I love you" and he quickly strode out to the garage and his car.

Only after Matt had come back into the bedroom for a good-bye kiss and then left for work would Leanne be up in her usual flurry of housework, bill paying, and the other things that she magically got done every day. Leanne was the soccer coach and Cub Scout leader, yet she still found time to make cupcakes for open house at the school. During her first marriage, she was also the primary breadwinner in her household. Much like Matt, Leanne often had difficulty breaking old habits; her need for order combined with an overdeveloped sense of responsibility kept her moving at the pace of a teen. The unspoken pride Leanne felt knowing she took care of her family was one of the things that attracted Matt. The couple had their baggage, they were both a bit OCD and type A, but overall it worked very well for one simple reason—they loved each other very much. The couple respected each other's space and needs. But most importantly they trusted and supported each other, something neither had experienced in their first marriage.

Matt ran an auto repair business in the neighboring town of Port Smith. He had purchased the business from a friend some ten years before. The business did very well over the years, and had grown to become the largest auto shop in the county at its peak. Between Matt's divorce and the declining economy, things had slowed down substantially, but the business was holding its own. Matt's shop was no longer the cash cow it once was, yet the slower pace was somewhat of a relief. Leanne worked for an insurance agency in the same town—the insurance agency that Matt had used for years. Long before they were divorced from their first spouses, Matt and Leanne had known each other on a business level.

Matt and Leanne had only been married a year; they were both divorced two years prior and had started dating right away. A charity dinner, a mutual friend's wedding, and a few drinks on a Friday night led to dating and eventually getting married. It did not take long for them to see what friends and family already knew: they belonged together. Matt and Leanne had a way of communicating without words that was almost scary to some. Leanne, a few months older than Matt, actually looked five or ten years younger than he did. She was thin, with red hair and light skin, and stood five foot seven inches tall. Leanne was one of those confident women who did not need to raise her voice to be assertive; a simple word in her quiet, confident tone got things done. A glance from her green eyes seemed to have a controlling effect on most. This strong nature intimidated some and had left Leanne with a bit of a reputation of being a bitch, but nothing was further from the truth. Leanne got things done, yes. She held people accountable, true. But most of all she was fair and kindhearted.

Leanne had been married all of her adult life. She had married young, and like so many young marriages, the marriage became troubled as the children grew up. Leanne often stated, "I accepted my lot in life. What a fool I was." She would then say, "If only I knew how happy I could be, I would have left him years ago." This was said with a smile at Matt. The truth was that both Matt and Leanne were proud parents, and they had stayed married to their previous spouses for many years for the sake of the children. Both of them still had their children in their lives, but the children were grown and self-sufficient, for the most part. Children do sometimes challenge their parents' second marriages, but Matt and Leanne had promised each other that they would always put each other first.

Matt drove a Cadillac CTS—a sports sedan—his midlife crisis car. It was overpriced, a little too sporty, and impractical, but he loved it. Black, with tinted windows and black leather seats, it was just what he had wanted the day he said, "What the hell" and bought his first ever brand-new car. Leanne would often tease him about the car, but it did make Matt smile to drive it.

As the Cadillac pulled out of the garage and off the cul-de-sac on which he and Leanne lived, the satellite radio came to life. Annoyed by what seemed like repeat programming from the day before, Matt switched to a CD. Jimmy Buffet's *Banana Wind*, his favorite CD, soon poured from Cadillac's stereo. Jimmy Buffet sang the type of music that fed a desire for a cold drink and a hot beach. Singing along to "Boat Drinks," Matt smiled and thought of sailing or maybe just sitting on a beach in the sun, a mental game of removing himself from the Pacific Northwest. This was a game often played out by those living in such climates.

Something about the lack of news and the tone on Facebook that morning had left a bit of an uneasy feeling in Matt that even Jimmy Buffet could not wash away. By the time he made it to work, the feeling had grown. Matt always got to work first—he opened the shop and did some paperwork. The mechanics and service writers would show up by 8:00 a.m., then he would go back to his office to prepare for the day.

The office was modest—just a room with file cabinets and a large oak desk. The office housed several computers. Matt spent much of his workday on a computer, so when he arrived in his office, he booted up his computer and attempted to log in to Facebook, Yahoo news, and his company web page for e-mail. It seemed the Internet was down, so it was going to be a tough day. As strange and unnerving as it was to not have news, Facebook, or e-mail, work had to be done, cars needed to be fixed, customers needed to be talked to, and employees needed to be counseled. The process of running a small business would distract Matt from the uneasy feeling he had come to work with. By the day's end, most of the strangeness of earlier seemed to be lost in the every-day tasks of making a living.

Matt drove home listening to more of his favorite CD, and then went into the house and started to prep dinner. That night it would be Caesar salad. Most days, Matt would get home by 3:30 and prep dinner, and then he would go to the gym to work out and shower. By the time he was back, Leanne would be home, and the couple would cook dinner together. This day Leanne was home by 3:45, and she did not appear to be very happy.

Leanne had been working for a large national insurance company for years; it was a great job with good hours and amazing benefits. Sometimes the office politics were a bit much, but the pay and hours made it worth it. In the economy they lived in, any full-time job with real benefits was a godsend.

"What's up, sweetie? Why are you home so early?" Matt asked.

"Not sure what's going on. They closed our office." Leanne said with an air of frustration. She tossed a canvas carry bag and briefcase onto the kitchen table.

"What?" Matt was actually not sure he understood what she was saying. It was a question often asked, as years in a loud repair shop had left his hearing a bit lacking. Today it was a lack of understanding: he had heard the words correctly, yet he was unsure of their meaning.

"Some suits from the head office showed up and sent us home. They said not to come back until we got a call," Leanne answered. "Not like we could work anyway—we had no phones or computers all morning. They locked up the office, and we all went home. I am not sure if I still have a job." Matt could hear the concern in her voice. They would be fine without Leanne's job, but she needed to contribute to the family finances. It made her feel whole.

At that point the strangeness of the day was really starting to sink in. Matt had remembered his problems with the internet at work. Without even responding to her concerns, he went straight to the TV and turned it on. Matt and Leanne had a way of working as an unspoken team; it was one of the things that sometimes made others uncomfortable. They were always on the same page, and it explains why, instead of feeling ignored at that moment, Leanne instantly pulled her laptop from the canvas bag and booted it up. The feeling of unease Matt was projecting left Leanne worrying about the well-being of her kids.

"Internet is down," she said.

"So is the satellite," Matt replied.

Without another word, Matt tried to call his daughters. First he dialed Sam. Samantha was his oldest and was married to her high school sweetheart. She was living in San Diego while her husband was serving in the Marine Corps fighting in the Middle East. Riana, his youngest, was away at college attending the University of Connecticut.

Both were a long way from their home in the Pacific Northwest. As Matt dialed his cell phone over and over, Leanne was frantically texting. Leanne's son, David, lived in Seattle; he was married, had two kids, and was her absolute pride and joy. Totally out of form Leanne was starting to become a bit agitated. Leanne's daughter, Sarah, was twenty-two and lived in Portland with her boyfriend and two children. Sarah and Leanne talked at least once a day and spoke more like sisters than mother and daughter. Sarah was the stability that helped Leanne through her divorce. Leanne could not talk about her kids without a smile bursting out. Today there was no smile, just the face of a worried mother.

"What the hell is going on? Nothing is working!" Leanne asked. Her tone was clearly anxious Matt could tell by the elevated pitch and speed with which she spoke.   Leanne was snapping her words out sharply and quickly.

"I know, baby, I am trying." Matt responded his words seemed monotone and almost unrelated to the anxiety in Leanne's voice; he was answering but not clearly listening. Becoming vaguely aware of her intensity, Matt fought back the urge to tell Leanne to calm down. That was a mistake he had made once in their relationship, and was one he had vowed to never repeat. Matt was trying to speak with more composure than he was feeling, hoping to calm Leanne a little. Of course Leanne could see through his facade. Matt was feeling some genuine stress, something he never could hide from his wife. The couple continued to dial, text, type, and operate a remote with no success. After some time, the two sat down beside each other on the couch. Leanne had her phone in her hand, and Matt was staring at the silent blue screen on the TV. The tension was extreme: two very worried parents, who didn't know what to do or how to check on their kids and grandkids, sat quietly on the couch.

It was now pushing 5:00 p.m., and all of the sudden the TV came to life, startling them both. "A message from the White House," the news anchor stated. The screen showed a picture of the White House seal and the words, "Stay tuned for instructions from our President." Both Matt and Leanne had a disdain for the current president, and instinctively Leanne reached for the remote to change the channel. She changed the channel over and over, but every channel had the same screen.

It was clear that they needed to find out what was going on sooner rather than later. Matt calmly walked to the bar and poured a glass of his favorite scotch for himself and a glass of red wine for his wife. He returned with the drinks and sat on the couch. In the quiet they sat and watched, waiting to see what was coming next. Considering the political climate in the nation, combined with a collapsing economy, Matt did not know what to expect.

The ongoing presidential campaign was unlike anything anyone had seen before. The Republican ticket was clear—the front-runner was so far ahead in the polls that a primary was just an exercise. He was a conservative, a Mormon, and his vice presidential candidate was also a Mormon and a moderate. Now in the grand scheme of things this may have seemed strange to some, having two Mormons on the ticket, considering only two percent of Americans are baptized Mormons. The truth was that neither man was running on a religious platform. The nature of the election had gotten very ugly. The incumbent was way behind in the polls, and there was an all-out attack on the religious beliefs of the challengers. The divide and hatred, fueled by the political attack ads, had gotten so bad that the local LDS Church had found it necessary to post armed guards at their church to protect the building and members. There had not been a local incident of violence, but there had been some attacks on Mormon churches across the country. The news had played it as a small group of fanatics attacking a church now and then over social issues. The media tried to identify the attacks with gay rights or atheist groups, even linking the attacks to some fundamentalist Christian groups, all without any evidence. Leanne and Matt felt that the media were portraying the victims of violence as the villains, as the news so often did. Some news stations blamed the Muslims; some blamed Evangelists. Many newscasters thought it was a very leftist faction of the Democratic Party, a splinter group. In Seattle, Los Angeles, and New York, a few LDS churches had been burned. In Chicago, the Temple building had been ransacked and two people were killed. The President claimed it was terrorism and that he would get to the bottom of it. Many, like Matt, believed President Prescott might be closer to the top of it.

To a man like Matt, the religion of the candidate really did not mean much. Though not widely known, there were many Mormons in the Senate and House on both sides of the aisle. Matt was baptized Mormon and had joined the LDS Church some five years earlier, only to leave it after his divorce. He had a good understanding of the Mormon faith, and was often caught defending it to critics and naysayers. Leanne was raised Catholic and had not been back to church since childhood. Both Matt and Leanne believed in God and were somewhat religious, yet they both had a dislike of the culture of churches. Even though they didn't attend a church regularly, Matt and Leanne often spoke of their beliefs and found they had more common ground than either had expected. When they were first dating, both had worried secretly that their different faiths would bring conflict.

Leanne would often tease Matt and say, "Don't you ever think I am going to convert and be one of those good Mormon wives." This was said as a joke, but like many jokes, it was rooted in her truth.

Back at the manicotti meal, the two young missionaries looked to the elderly man telling the story with some degree of confusion. It was clear that they had not learned about the events surrounding the story in high school history.

"I don't understand," the younger missionary said with a pause. "Why did the Internet go down? Why didn't the phones work?"

"Boys, it was bigger than that. The country, the whole world, was a mess. Let me explain." Pushing away a plate half full of manicotti, the elderly man stood to stretch his legs. Then he sat back down and continued.

"For several years, in the early years of the twenty-second century, the state of the American economy—in fact, the state of the whole world—had become more and more desperate. The United States was involved in four wars. Israel was fighting for its life. Most of Europe was in a state of decline, and the governments and economies of Greece and Spain had totally collapsed. Sometime in late September of 2019, the Chinese government had made a deal with OPEC and had taken all financial control of the world's oil reserves." He was explaining complex events as simply as he could. The young missionaries had only learned of these events as names and dates in history class.

"It was so simple. The Chinese had spent most of the 1980s and 90s buying US and European bonds and treasury notes. Next they convinced the Saudis to start selling oil to them in exchange for American and European bonds and T-bills. Finally, the Saudis called some of the debt due. So the Euro collapsed first, and then the dollar. The United States and most of Europe had no conceivable way to pay back their debts. OPEC had destroyed the currency they used to back their own oil. To the rescue came China, buying oil with Yuan. After years of being devalued, the Yuan suddenly jumped up in value. In September the Yuan was worth sixteen cents on the dollar; by January the Yuan was dead-even with the dollar and worth more than the Euro. Some people made a lot of money, but most lost everything."

"Why didn't anyone stop it? Didn't anyone see it coming?" the quiet, younger of two missionaries blurted out. The volume of his question made it clear how confused he was. "Those who warned of the possible ramifications of these events were labeled "conspiracy nuts" by the US administration and blamed for the economic collapse," he explained to the boys.

"Do you understand?" he asked them. Without waiting for a response, the old man continued with his tale as though he was determined to finish his story whether they understood or not. "It was a different time. With all of the dramatic world events such as wars and entire currencies collapsing, it seemed amazing that Matt and Leanne had been doing so well. They had managed to keep their home, pay for college, drive new cars, and generally live well. If you had a job or viable business, those times were not so bad. But the unemployed and chronically poor—*they* had it bad."

As Matt and Leanne leaned toward the television screen with extreme interest, the President walked up to the podium. It was clear there were no reporters in the room. This was an announcement, not a press conference. No camera flashes, no questions, not a sound.

President Prescott was in his mid-sixties. He was about six feet tall and carried himself with a lot of self-confidence. This man was either loved or hated, not much between. President Prescott ran as the anti-war, liberal candidate, yet he had done little to make his base happy, and even less to appease his critics. The man had a tight gray Afro and was very neat. President Prescott looked presidential; he spoke with an orator's confidence and always would command a room.

"My fellow Americans," the President began. "I speak to you today with sorrow in my heart. As you all know, there has been a series of attacks against some religious groups in our nation. My administration has been investigating this as a first priority. Over the past weeks, some alarming information has come to light. The FBI has uncovered plans that lead to the highest levels of the Republican Party, and to the leadership of the Church of Jesus Christ of Latter-day Saints. I cannot divulge the sources of this information at this time, but let me be clear, we will not tolerate terrorism by any person, organization, or political party. As your elected leader and commander and chief, I am suspending all campaigning at this time. I am postponing the upcoming elections until further notice. By executive order I am temporarily closing all wards, churches, and temples affiliated with, supported by, or loyal to the LDS church. I have put a freeze on all assets of both the RNC and the LDS church. I have taken actions to secure the airways, and to control any social media that may be used by these organizations. I will be addressing the public again through a series of announcements over the next days, as the investigation and subsequent actions continue."

At this point the President left the podium and the screen went to a scrolling text of the address.

"My God, he has done it," Leanne said with tears in her eyes.

"I'm not sure what this means." Matt said. "Did he just say the Mormons are attacking themselves?"

Leanne Scott had absorbed the gravity of what she heard instantly. Matt Scott, on the other hand, had that surreal feeling a person gets when he doesn't believe what he has just seen with his own eyes. This was a moment much like when someone hears of a death in the family or some other unbelievable event. To some degree, Matt and Leanne's reactions seemed subdued. They looked at each other, sipped their drinks, and sat quietly. In a way, Matt was not surprised; he had distrust for President Prescott that went back to his time as a junior senator. Prescott had a history of moving up very fast. He would shut down any rebuttal of his arguments by calling anyone who dared to dissent a racist. Matt was far from a racist, but had not found one thing President Prescott stood for that he agreed with.

With no communication from family, Matt tried instead to contact his employees. Jeremy, his longtime friend and the manager at Matt's shop, was the first he tried to text, then call, with no luck. Jeremy lived near the shop in town and was a single dad. A loyal employee, he was someone Matt trusted without question.

"What do we do?" Leanne was looking to Matt for reassurance, maybe not an answer. She was just scared.

"Let's keep trying to get the kids on the phone. Maybe the Internet will come back online soon." Matt did not believe his own words, but he knew that there wasn't much that could be done, at least not right now.

"I am sure something will be working by morning, the Internet at least, and if not, then maybe we should go to town," Matt said.

Leanne leaned in and laid her head on Matt's shoulder. She was scared and she was confused, yet there was a sense that everything would be all right. Leanne had always been the optimist. It was easy for Leanne to be positive; it was her nature. Yet she did worry about David and Sarah and the grandchildren. It was going to be a long night. Matt locked all the doors and windows, and checked them several times. Matt checked the pistol he kept in the nightstand on his side of bed, and he even pulled out an old shotgun and loaded it. Matt and Leanne lived in a very safe and quiet neighborhood, and they would often forget to set the alarm or even lock the door, but tonight it felt like all of that might be changing. Leanne changed into some sweatpants and a loose sweater, brushed her teeth, took a vitamin, and went to lie down in bed. Matt followed her lead. He put on pajama bottoms and a shirt, and he pulled his slippers out of the closet and set them by the side of the bed. Matt usually slept in nothing more than his shorts, but tonight he needed to feel more prepared. Matt and Leanne lay down in an embrace and attempted to sleep. Thoughts of their children and worry kept both of them awake into the small hours of the morning.

Finally, sometime around 2:00 a.m., Leanne fell asleep. The last thing Matt wanted to do was wake her, but when he heard a knock on the back door something inside said danger. "Wake up," Matt said as he nudged his wife.

Leanne, who sat up quickly, said sleepily, "What, what? What's going on?"

"There is someone at the door. I'm going to check who it is." He put his slippers and robe on, walked to the gun safe, and pulled out a small revolver. He put the pistol in his robe pocket. Matt then pulled the automatic pistol from the nightstand, chambered a round, and handed it to Leanne.

"My God, what is this for?" Leanne said.

"Just in case. Who would be at the door this late?" Leanne saw a bit of fear in Matt's eyes, something she had rarely seen.

Leanne looked at Matt, nodding and agreeing, yet not really wanting to hold the gun. She was never a fan of guns. Sitting up in bed, looking a bit like she had been crying, Leanne tried to look confident. Her red hair was over one shoulder, and Matt could see mascara that had run down her cheek and been wiped off. Her chin quivered just a bit.

Matt had taught her to shoot soon after they were married. He had been a marine, had hunted for years, and was generally fond of guns. He had quite the collection of pistols, rifles, and even a civilian version of an M4 rifle, similar to what he used as a marine. Leanne used to think of them as a waste of money and a bit scary, but she indulged his hobbies. Tonight she was unsure if they were such a good idea. As Matt walked toward the bedroom door, Leanne said, "What about you?" To reassure her, he quickly showed her the small pistol he had stashed in is robe pocket. She nodded.

When Matt got to the door, he pushed aside the blinds to see a young man in a suit. The young man looked disheveled, scared, and he was bleeding from the left eye. Instantly, Matt recognized him. It was Elder William Black, a Mormon missionary. Elder Black was about five foot nine, a bit heavy, and very blond. Even though Matt was no longer an active member of the local LDS church, the missionaries would often visit Matt at work. Young men like cars, even Mormon boys on mission, and Matt's shop often had hot rods and vintage sports cars in it. Elder Black and Matt had become friends during those visits. Elder Black could see past Matt leaving the Mormon Church. He just saw Matt as a friend he could trust.

Instantly Matt opened the door, but before he could say a word, two more young men came up out of the dark, startling him. He reached into his pocket and grabbed the revolver. One of the young men was in bad shape—his white shirt was stained with blood. The other looked like he was in another place—he was thin and tall, and stared into space, as though he was not all there. His black hair was matted down on one side, maybe from blood.

"Get in, quick." Matt helped the bleeding missionary into the house and put him on the couch. Before a word could be said, Leanne came into the room. Leanne had the automatic pistol in her hand as she strode up to Matt. She handed off the pistol to her husband and was instantly at the side of the injured boy.

"What happened? Who did this to you?" she demanded. She turned quickly and looked at her husband in alarm. "Matt, this young man has been shot!"

Elder Black started telling the story in his strong south Texas accent. He explained they had stopped door knocking, something the missionaries call tracking, about a month ago. With all of the trouble, church leaders thought it best to keep the missionaries in. For several weeks they had only been helping the families of church members in need, cutting wood, doing chores, and staying out of the public eye. That day they had been at a member's home, and when they finished all of the chores that needed to be done, they decided to go the church to see if anyone else needed help. Back at the church office was a list of people in need. When they arrived in their little Toyota Corolla, *the standard car of the Mormon missionary*, they were met by a mob. The missionaries got out of their car and attempted to calm the group of fifteen or twenty angry people gathered in front of the church entrance. The group was yelling something about Mormons being traitors and saying that they should be arrested. Several people had anti-Mormon slogans on signs and were chanting vulgarities at the young men. "Through the commotion, we heard a loud bang," Elder Black said, shaking his head in disbelief. "That's when we realized somebody had shot Elder Jones."

Leanne looked up from caring for the young missionary, a bit of confusion on her face. Like many others, she was often taken aback by the term *Elder*. In Leanne's world, and most of the world, the Elders would be the senior members of the congregation. A Mormon or any-one with any LDS background referred to all missionaries as Elders.

"It happened so fast," Elder Jones said in a weak voice. Leanne was trying to get a look at his wounds. The wounded missionary was named Nick Jones. Nick Jones had an average build and was twenty-one years old. Although he was from Georgia, his southern accent was barely noticeable. He was a missionary near the end of his service. He had brown hair, was about five foot eleven, maybe one hundred eighty pounds, and very clean-cut. His once clean and pressed black suit was tattered, and his white shirt was almost all red with blood. Elder Jones was obviously in pain and frightened, but he was being strong. He of-ten referred to himself as a "Soldier of the Cross", and today he was going to be a brave one. Nick Jones had planned on entering the army after his mission; like many young LDS men, he would first serve his church, and then his country. The soldier of cross comment referred to an old country western song that he loved. Elder Jones was definitely a country boy, and it was reflected in his attitude and taste in music.

"Somehow we managed to get into the car; we were driving away when someone threw a big rock through the windshield. That's how I got this," Elder Black said as he pointed to his eye. He had a cut on his eyebrow that had bled a lot but was not bleeding now. While Elder Black was telling the story, Matt had cleaned it thoroughly with a damp washcloth. Leanne had left the room to get some first aid sup-plies. When she returned, Matt took some medical tape from her and taped the wound shut. Leanne started cutting the blood soaked shirt from Elder Jones and wiping his side with a washcloth, looking for the source of the blood. Elder Jones winced and lay back, not wanting to see. Leanne brought a sense of calm to the room, which was something that Matt very much admired about her.

Elder Black continued. "The car died about five miles down Highway 2. We walked from there. Ran out of gas, I guess," Elder Black said in what seemed like a very nonchalant manner, considering all of the blood and violence they had just experienced.

Elder Jones had been shot in his side. It was a grazing wound that hurt, and there was quite a bit of blood and bruising, but no broken bones and no wounded organs. Leanne left the room with the dirty towels and went to the kitchen. She washed up, and within a few minutes she was back with a plate of food and several glasses of milk. Leanne had habit of feeding everyone that came to the house. In some strange way, offering food was her way of taking control of a situation—something she had done her entire life.

"You boys eat something," Leanne said as she set down the tray of cheese, crackers, and cut vegetables. Then she walked to Matt's side and whispered in his ear, "We need a doctor."

"I will make some calls as soon as the phone works," Matt whispered back with a bit of sarcasm. Leanne had forgotten about the lack of phones or Internet. "No need to be a smart ass," Leanne responded. For now it was up to them to take care of the wounded young man.

Once the wounds were treated and the young men had a bite to eat and drink, Matt realized that the third young man had not yet said a word.

The tall thin missionary ate and drank he followed the lead of Elder Black—but never seemed to initiate anything or even make a sound. Matt and Leanne had almost forgotten he was in the room. Noticing him in the corner, Leanne had looked at the small cut on his head. She gave him a washcloth to clean up and returned to check Elder Jones's bandages.

Matt turned and spoke. "What's your story?" he directed at the unfamiliar missionary in an almost accusing manner. For some reason this young man made Matt very uncomfortable. Matt knew most of the missionaries and had never met this young man before. The strange mannerisms and almost eerie calm attitude made Matt suspect.

Elder Black interrupted. "That's Elder Miles. He doesn't talk much." Elder Black then quietly asked to join him in the kitchen, out of the ear shot of the others, and explained that Elder Miles had Asperger's syndrome and he regressed as events around him got out of control. Elder Miles added that Asperger's syndrome was a form of autism that affected people's social abilities. This young man was closing the world out. He looked physically fine, but he seemed to have no expression on his face. His mannerisms did not indicate any emotion or awareness of what they had just gone through. This explanation did not sit well with Matt for some reason. Something else seemed out of place, but there was really no time to worry about an awkward missionary.

"He is OK; he hasn't talked much since he got here a month ago. Elder Miles was sent to us direct from Salt Lake." Elder Black wore his responsibility for this young man like a badge of honor. "He is a special missionary; Elder Miles is close to God." This response from Elder Black seemed to reinforce Matt's unease.

When he returned to the room, Elder Black sat down on the L-shaped couch next to the three young men. Matt and Leanne sat in two easy chairs facing them. Rising up from her chair, crossing the room and kneeling in front of the injured young missionary, Leanne checked the eyes of Elder Miles, looking for signs of concussion. Miles would only allow this after prompting from Elder Black. Matt looked over Elder Jones, who had a bandage taped to his bruised side and was lying on his back, fast asleep. Within moments all three young men were asleep; their exhaustion, combined with the safety they had found, had given them a chance to relax. She did her best to make them comfortable. Elder Jones lay on one end of the couch, and she covered him and inspected his dressed wound. By now Elders Black and Miles were leaning to one side as they slept. The tall boy looked like a little brother, taking reassurance and comfort from Elder Black. Leanne covered them with a blanket and softly touched their cheeks. "Sleep well," she said quietly, as a mother would.

The next morning, after the couple had made an attempt at a night's sleep, the sun peeked over the trees. Leanne and Matt sat quietly, both wondering what was coming next. Neither wanted to speak for fear of waking the injured and sleeping young men. Both had a mix of fear for their own children, questions about what had happened, and a bit of rage over the injury to the missionaries resting in their home. Lack of sleep, shock, or something else had placed a sense of calm over them and all in the room. Everything was wrong, nothing made sense, and the world was a mess, but for some reason Matt and Leanne felt a bit of control and peace. Maybe the presence of three young men of such strong faith helped, or maybe it was Leanne's way of making even the worst day look wonderful. It did not matter why, what mattered was they knew everything would be OK.

CHAPTER THREE

In Portland, Oregon, Sarah was loading her two children into her minivan. Sarah, Leanne's daughter, had spent the previous night alone; her live-in boyfriend had gone east to look for work and left Sarah and their two children in their downtown apartment. She did not sleep a wink, and by 4:00 a.m. she was on the phone with her big brother David.   Sarah had an old fashioned land line in her house and David's house was equipped with internet phone.   This strange combination was working while most people had been counting on cellular phones, cellular phones that were now rarely working, if at all.

"David, Jeff has headed east toward Colorado; he's trying to find work in the oil fields," Sara explained to her big brother.

"Are you OK?" asked her brother in a concerned voice. David could hear Sarah's stress in her tone and hurried words.

"I'm scared, and there is a lot going on down here. I'm not used to being alone," she replied.

"Well, sis, load up the kids and come stay with us for a while. We would love the company, and maybe we can get over to mom and Matt's house. I'm sure mom would love it." David was talking with a degree of normalcy. He did not want to scare his little sister, yet he knew she needed to get to someplace safer. He had just watched the announcement from the president, but it made no sense to him. David was worried about his family, and this was the perfect opportunity to get them all in one place so they could take care of each other.

After the brother and sister spoke of kids, family, and how they would make ends meet, the decision was made. Sarah spent the rest of the early morning packing bags for the kids and herself, and by 8:00 a.m., she had the van loaded and was buckling the kids in.

Portland, Oregon had become the center for a large movement of violent Anarchists and Marxists. The ongoing protests and news of riots had Sarah in a bit of a state of frenzy and worry. She knew if she could just get to her brother's house, she would be safe. Oddly enough, Sarah had not seen or heard about President Prescott's announcement, yet she still had a sense that she had to get her children to safer ground.

After pulling out of the apartment building parking lot, and turning onto Belmont Street, Sarah headed toward Interstate 5. It was only a matter of blocks before the traffic started to build. Traffic had stopped in front of her. She looked in the rearview mirror to see cars behind her boxing her in, with no way to back up or turn around. Ahead of her she heard a chanting crowd. A large group was protesting loudly. It was unclear what the people were protesting, but to Sarah they were frightening. The street was blocked, and the group was standing with arms locked. Hearing her baby cry, Sarah quickly reached behind her and pushed a bottle into her youngest baby's mouth. Little Leah quickly grabbed the bottle and started to drink before she fell back asleep. The little boy in the seat beside Leah, David, named for Sarah's brother, was already sleeping soundly. Sarah was afraid for her children and for herself. She turned the radio up a little and pushed the door-lock button twice, just to be sure.

After sitting for maybe three or four minutes, things got very strange. The protesting crowd seemed to be just standing and chanting, "Hell, no, we won't go," or something to that effect. The chants were then interrupted by screams; some of the screams came from the protestors and some from people in the cars in front of her. Sarah saw people running through the cars, and some were actually running and jumping from roof to roof, smashing hoods and caving in the roofs of the cars as they ran toward the protestors. The people running ahead were mostly dressed in black. Almost all were wearing black-hooded sweatshirts with black bandanas over their faces. All accept one—a thin, dark-haired girl that Sarah recognized instantly. It was Naomi, David's ex-girlfriend from college.

David had gone to school at the University of Oregon, where he had met Naomi. Naomi was studying environmental sciences. They dated most of their freshman year until David broke it off. He had noticed that something was changing in Naomi; she had become more radical and political. Naomi started attending on-campus protests, and then she would take bus trips to Seattle, or San Francisco, or wherever she could go to protest. David broke off their relationship. He tried to explain that he was not into being an extremist. About this time she went over the edge. Within a month she had dropped out of school, and within two months, David was being questioned by local law enforcement, and then the FBI. David used to say, "Wow, dodged a bullet with that one." He had no idea how true it was.

The FBI and the Portland police looked for a reason for Naomi's behavior. The truth was no one knew. There was not one clear reason why this normal young girl had transformed from protestor to activist to revolutionary to psychopath, but she did. By the time Sarah saw Naomi on the roof of the white Chevy truck, Naomi was wanted by the FBI. It would make Naomi mad if she knew she had not made the ten most wanted. She was only number eighteen. Sarah had heard that Naomi was in trouble, but it did not seem to be a big deal until now. Naomi was wearing a black sweatshirt and jeans, but she was not covering her face. Naomi was acting as if she wanted people to see her face. She stood on a truck ahead of Sarah. She was pointing people out, and the others were attacking each in the order in which Naomi pointed to them. An Anarchist leader, a bit of an oxymoron, but it was clear she was in charge. The driver's door of the truck opened and a large man got out, yelling and reaching toward Naomi's leg as she stood on top of the cab. Without hesitation, she swung around with what looked like a dark stick or piece of pipe and hit the man in the side of the head. The sound was horrifying. Sarah heard a crunch of breaking bone and then a huff of air as he exhaled and slumped to the ground.

"Trash them all!" Naomi yelled. "Just trash them all!" She jumped from the roof the truck to a small SUV to her right. Standing on the hood, she started smashing the windshield out with the pipe in her hand. She moved from car to car toward Sarah. Sarah started to shake; she turned and put a blanket over the faces of her children. In the commotion, the two started to cry. Leah was screaming loudly. "Quiet, baby, it's OK," Sarah said to the little one in the car seat. The children could feel their mother's fear and were now were screaming louder and trying to uncover their faces.

Boom! The top of the van dented in and the van shook. There was someone on the roof.

Sarah screamed and spun around. She started the van and put it in reverse. Quickly backing up, she hit the car behind her and heard the person on the roof fall and roll off the driver's side. As Sarah looked out the driver's window, a very angry Naomi stood up and looked her in the eye. Her expression changed as recognition flashed across her face and froze for a moment. Sarah was paralyzed with fear. The van was still in reverse and pushing against the car behind her. The babies were screaming, but all Sarah could hear was her own heartbeat. Naomi continued to look at Sarah. Then she dropped the pipe, and for a moment the psychopath must have felt something, maybe a moment of compassion, if that was possible. She stepped back until she bumped the car behind her. Then she smiled at Sarah, a crooked little smile that made the hair on the back of Sarah's neck stand on end.

Jumping up onto the hood of the car behind her, she yelled, "Enough, enough, let's go!" The group stopped, except for an occasional kick of a car or punch thrown at a fallen protestor. "Go! Go!" she yelled. Within moments the group was gone. Naomi turned and looked at Sarah one more time, and she cracked a smile and then disappeared into the crowd of parked and smashed cars. It was not quiet: the children were screaming, and there were moans from people in their cars and lying in the street. Ahead of Sarah, where the original protest line was, several women were on their knees wailing, the kind of scream that only comes when someone had died. Dead and wounded bodies lay scattered about on the ground, and blood and glass was everywhere. All Sarah wanted to do was get out of there, get to David's and be safe. Sarah wanted to get her children out of the city, out of Portland, away from all of this.

The sound of sirens filled the air. Within a few moments, the police and aid cars had arrived. The police were working to move cars to allow access for the ambulances. Sarah watched closely. When an officer came up to the man lying on the ground in front of her, he just gave him a kick. "This one is dead." The callousness of his words took Sarah's breath away. She watched as two officers stood over a dead protestor. "Looks like the Anarchists took care of business for us this time," one officer said to the other.

"Move it!" yelled a tall black cop, directing cars ahead of her to move to the side of the road to let an ambulance through. Some of the cars moved without much incident, others the police had to remove a wounded driver to move the car, and others required breaking the shattered windshields out with nightsticks to allow the drivers to see. Sarah saw an ambulance drive to her right, so close it clipped her passenger side mirror. The path ahead of the ambulance had been cleared. Without a thought she threw the van into drive and forced her way in behind the ambulance and up onto the lawn to her right. In the process of getting the van out Sarah hit two other cars, which caught the attention of the tall black policeman. Ignoring the yelling police officers and the screaming babies, she pushed the throttle to the floor and drove her minivan through a yard, over a curb, and onto a cross street. As the van careened to the right up the lane, she saw a road closed sign and barricades that must have been put in during the protests the night before. Without a thought she crashed through the barricades and headed for Morrison Street. She turned left through a red light and sped to the freeway on-ramp.

Sarah made it to the highway and never looked back. Heading north on Interstate 5, the traffic was fairly light. She tried to drive as normally as she could, not wanting to draw attention to herself. Amazingly, she stayed calm until she crossed the bridge into Washington State. When Sarah drove off the bridge and could see the Columbia River and downtown Portland in her rearview mirror, she started to cry. Driving at more than seventy miles per hour, she continued to drive for a good twenty minutes. With tears streaming down her cheeks and two small children crying in the back, Sarah pulled over and turned down a dirt road off the freeway. The young mother got out of the driver's seat and climbed into the back with her two children. Sarah took both kids out of their car seats and hugged them; she calmed them and held them as only a mother could until all of the crying had stopped. It had now been almost two hours since she left home. She knew that she needed to get to her brother's house where they would be safe. She buckled her children back into car seats and then backed out of the dirt road and onto the shoulder of the freeway. Sarah was back on the road, and in a few short hours she would be in Seattle with her brother and his family.

Later that morning, back at the Scott house, Leanne was unaware of what her daughter and grandchildren had just gone through. She was watching her husband interact with the young missionaries and laughing a little inside. The talk between Matt Scott and the missionaries had awakened Leanne, who was sleeping in her recliner. It was a bit strange watching them bounce from friend to father figure to religious teacher and back. Leanne thought, "This is the strangest relationship I have ever seen." She smiled as she laughed a little internally.

Elder Black asked, "Brother Scott, could I lead a prayer?"

Matt quickly said, "Of course." The oddness of this would be lost on most, but in the Mormon traditions, the eldest man, the leader of the home, leads or directs all prayer. Matt's response had the tone of annoyance; he was trying to be the man of the house, yet he was not a fan of protocol and tradition. This was clear from the tone in his voice. Now usually Mormon missionaries were known for their never-ending, on-and-on prayers, but not this time.

"Heavenly Father, please bless this home and the Scott family. Please help our wounds heal and guide us to do right." He paused for a long moment and then finished, "In the name of Your Son, Jesus Christ. Amen." As the prayer was ending, the sound of a cell phone ring interrupted them.

Leanne jumped to the phone so fast that no one else had a chance to react. It was David; Leanne talked for ten or fifteen minutes. During the conversation it was all Matt could do to not interrupt. Leanne was wide-awake, bright eyed, and deep in conversation; her smiles were ear to ear. The call ended with, "I love you, hug your sister for me, and call me when she gets there."

As Matt realized what was happening, he grabbed his phone and started to dial. He had been so interested in his hearing the one side of his wife's conversation with David that the reality of the phones working had not sunk in. Before he could complete the call a text came in from Riana.

"All safe. The college is telling us to stay on campus and not to worry. I love you."

Matt texted back, "Call?"

Riana replied, "Can't, can only text. It's OK; I am safe, Dad, like Mrs. Kitty is at Grandma's."

Matt instantly smiled because that was code. Riana was sending a signal that it was she, and she was telling the truth. Riana knew that Matt worried about her safety. He was a bit over-protective, but then again, his baby had moved three thousand miles away. When Riana went away to school, her cat, Mrs. Kitty, went to live with Grandma. No one else would know this fact beside Leanne, Matt, and Riana, except maybe Grandma and Mrs. Kitty. Being a smart young woman, Riana knew that Matt would not trust a text without hearing her voice, unless she could prove it was her. This little code went a long way toward calming a worried father. Matt knew she was safe, and that was enough for now. Worries would continue, but the good news was she was safe. She had family nearby—cousins and aunts and uncles. Matt could breathe concerning Riana.

Now he must get ahold of Sam. After dialing for about five minutes, he reached her.

"Sam, are you OK?"

"Yes, Daddy, I am good," she said.

"I think you need to come home," Matt said with concern in his voice.

"I may get to," Sam replied positively. "The Corps is telling all the families that we may get to go home soon."

"Do you know how you are getting home? Or when?" Matt was feeling relieved in a sense, but he was unsure he believed his daughter would be home anytime soon.

"I can't talk about it, but I am safe. I have marines taking care of me, Daddy. I will be fine." Sam was definitely a military wife. She took pride in her husband's service and sounded very sure that she was being protected by the best. Just then the phone went dead. Matt knew that Sam saying she had marines taking care of her was her way of reassuring him. Matt would worry about his children, but he knew they were alive in and safe places. With Riana on campus and Sam on a Marine Corps base, he could breathe a little easier.

It took some time for Leanne and Matt to explain their conversations to each other, and during that time the three missionaries were off in a corner. Elder Jones was uncomfortable. He was in pain and needed attention. Elders Black and Miles were praying over him and trying to comfort their fallen comrade. Leanne saw from across the room that Elder Jones needed her. She gathered fresh bandages, some warm water, and rubbing alcohol. Leanne also went to her medicine cabinet and found a bottle of codeine. She would buy over-the-counter medicine when they went to Canada because it was much stronger then the American stuff—it had codeine in it. Living in a rural area, both Matt and Leanne always found a need to be prepared, each in their own way.

As Leanne tended to Elder Jones, she explained that Sarah and the kids were going to Seattle to stay with David, and that they would all be together soon, safe and having fun. She answered Matt's questions about Jeff, Sarah's boyfriend, and explained that he was off trying to find work. The kids had seen the news about the local church, and they saw the national news, but they were a bit less affected in David's neighborhood. David was worried about his mother. Being aware of Matt's linkage to the Mormon Church, David was concerned Matt and Leanne would be involved in the nation's unrest. Leanne convinced David not to worry through a few white lies only a mother can get away with, small lies that would keep her children from worrying about her. Leanne knew that David would keep Sarah and the babies safe. David explained that Sarah had checked in by cell phone and that she was only a couple hours away. He neglected to tell his mother about Sarah's ordeal in the streets of Portland or about Naomi. Leanne knew that David would not worry his mother any more than necessary. He might not tell her how bad things were, but then again Sarah could not be in a better place than with her big brother. The mother and son had equally deceived each other, both out of love.

After tending to Elder Jones for a few minutes, Leanne walked back to the kitchen table where her laptop was set up. "The Internet is back," she announced.

Matt checked and then announced, "TV is back on too." He started to click through the channels, and it seemed normal except for the absence of the BYU network and Fox News.

"Well, my mom will be happy, Fox News is finally gone!" Matt said as he laughed out loud. Matt's mom was a hippy in her young days. She was so far left, she cried when Matt became a marine. They loved each other very much and would tease each other regularly about their political views.

Matt stopped on a local news channel that was showing smoke rising over Portland and talking of riots in the streets. Leanne walked toward the TV without blinking. "Thank God Sarah and the kids got out." Then Matt heard Leanne gasp. There was a picture on the screen of a dark-haired young woman. The caption read, "Armed and dangerous. Avoid contact and alert the authorities if you see this person."

"Naomi?" Leanne said, a bit confused.

"You know her?" Matt asked.

"That's David's ex-girlfriend from college." She paused. "We knew she had gone a bit nuts, but this is crazy." She paused again. "You know, the one Sarah calls psycho?"

As they watched Naomi on the flat screen, Matt wondered if his family's situation was the worst of it. Could it be that people would have a day or two to catch their breath? Maybe people would calm down and the world could get back to normal. Maybe Sunday would arrive like every other Sunday, the church would open, and the missionaries could go back to their work. Matt was thinking these things, hoping that the whole nightmare was just a strange day or weekend. But he knew better; things had changed in a huge way. Matt's small bout of wishful thinking was quickly put in its place by reality.

Seeing Naomi on the screen was a reminder of the days of WTO protests and Occupy Wall Street, but it was clear this was much bigger. This was big, and it was being orchestrated by some very powerful people. Matt firmly believed it was being directed from the White House. Like many people, Matt was hoping things would blow over, but inside, he knew this was a life-changing event. All of these thoughts where rushing through his head as he quietly stared at the TV, not actually paying attention to what was on at all.

Elder Black was making phone calls, Elder Jones was looking a lot better, and Elder Miles just sat in the corner and read from a small book. It was pocket-sized, leather-bound book, maybe a Bible or the Book of Mormon.

"We need to get you to a doctor, Elder," Leanne said in a firm but kind voice. She spoke in a way that everyone knew this was something that was happening, not just being discussed.

"We also need to call the police," stated Matt.

Elder Black quickly argued. "They won't help."

Matt sternly responded, "OK, that's not the right attitude, Elder, and you know as well as I do that they already know what happened at the church and are most likely looking for you three. These local cops are good people."

Matt's lack of sleep, stress, and the fact he had not eaten in some time was starting to take its toll. Leanne learned early in their relationship that if Matt missed a meal or two he became a bit more than a grump. She would look at him and say, "Blood sugar, sweetie," Leanne's way of saying, "You're being an ass." This was one of those times.

Leanne was in the kitchen cooking eggs and potatoes. The smells and sounds of eggs, bacon, and fried potatoes wafted through the house. Leanne's use of food to comfort or control a situation was a bit ironic, as Leanne was so thin and fit. One would think she rarely ate.

Matt picked up the phone and called the local sheriffs' office.

"Yes, they are here, and yes one is hurt pretty badly. When? Yes, we will be here."

Matt hung up the phone.

"Leanne, sweetie, come here." Matt and the Elders all sat down in the living room as Leanne came in carrying a cup of hot coffee in each hand, one for her and one for her husband. As she handed a cup to Matt, Leanne felt a moment of awkward panic, "Oh, I am so sorry," she said, looking toward the Elders.

Elder Black laughed out loud. "We are not going to get upset if you drink coffee. " Leanne knew a little about Mormons—no coffee, no drinking—but she was not really sure how far they took things.

It was clear that the presence of coffee was not something that bothered the missionaries.

"Really, who cares about a cup of coffee?" Matt said, clearly irritated by the distraction.

Matt stood up, and in a very serious manner, began to speak. "Leanne, have a seat." She sat down next to him. "So, I have spoken to a friend at the sheriff's office. They have arrested two people—one admits to shooting you, Elder Jones. He claims it was an accident. They are sending an ambulance for you boys, and a deputy to take your statements. "

"Then what?" asked Elder Black. "Then where do we go?" His tone was a cross between fear and insolence.

"Well, I am sure the church members have a place for you, and if not, you are always welcome here." Matt looked at Leanne with a questioning glance, hoping he had not overstepped.

"You can stay with us until we find a solution," Leanne said with a bit of unease. Leanne was not so comfortable with the missionaries, as she tended to feel judged by them.

Leanne would often tell Matt, "They blame me for you not being a Mormon." Matt would tease her in response, "Who said I wasn't a Mormon? Maybe I'm just really bad at being Mormon." Leanne loved Matt's faith, yet was always a bit confused by his leaving a church he spoke so highly of. His retorts often left her with mixed messages.

Within moments the smell of bacon filled the house. Leanne jumped up and ran to the kitchen to remove the pan from the burner before the bacon went from crispy to blackened. She then fixed plates and carried them two at a time around the bar to the dining room table. Each plate was covered with eggs, hash browns, bacon, and slices of apple.

"We need to wash up," said Elder Black, looking at his companions

"Sorry, Elder, but I think you should wait until the sheriff gets here, then you can have a shower, and I will even get you some clean clothes, if you like," Matt said.

Matt wanted the police to see the state of these young men. They had received first aid and cleaned up a little, but they looked rough. The effect of dirt, torn clothes, and dried blood might gain some empathy from the sheriff. These boys were victims, and deep inside Matt was afraid they would be treated otherwise. It was the history of religious persecution—Mormons, Jews, Catholics, it didn't seem to matter.

"If you insist," Elder Black said as he and Elder Miles made their way to the table. The young men were very hungry, and the smell of bacon and eggs had them excited.

Elder Jones sat up and was actually looking very well; his color was coming back, and his eyes showed some energy. He tried to stand, and

Leanne gave him a quick glance. "You sit. I will bring food to you," she said in a stern voice. Leanne knew that keeping the young man still would keep the bleeding to a minimum.

Elder Black again said a quick prayer, and Elder Miles said "Amen" out loud. This caught everyone's attention, as it was the first sound anyone had heard from him. Everyone in the room looked at Elder Miles for an uncomfortable moment, then Leanne flashed him a smile and a wink. This broke the tension, and Elder Miles began to eat after smiling back at her.

Leanne took her plate and Elder Jones's plate and put them on a tray. She added a glass of orange juice and her cup of coffee. She walked carefully across the hardwood floors, making sure nothing spilled.

"Can I get a hand?" Leanne asked Matt, as she nodded toward a TV tray rack in the corner of the room.

"You sit," Matt said to her as he stood up. He set up two trays, one in front of Elder Jones and the other across from him in front of Leanne's favorite chair. He then returned to the dining room table, which was at the other end of the long room that served as living room on one end and dining room on the other.

As soon as they had settled down to eat, the sound of multiple cars and a diesel truck were heard in the driveway.

"Keep eating, I got this," Matt said to Elders Miles and Black. Matt stood up and looked toward Leanne. She took a quick bite of bacon and moved the TV tray forward. Looking at Elder Jones, Leanne took two pieces of bacon off her plate and put them on his.

"Eat up," she said and walked to her husband's side. Matt and Leanne together walked to the front door. The young missionaries were eating as if they had not eaten in weeks. Maybe they thought this might be their last chance at a meal for some time. Matt feared the same for them.

"All the guns put away?" Leanne asked Matt.

"In the safe," he replied.

The front door to the Scott home was an extra-wide door; it opened onto a large landing with a single step down into the center of the room, to the left the living area, to the right the dining area and the kitchen. From both the dining room table and the living room everything and everyone coming through the front door could be seen.

Matt and Leanne stepped out onto the front porch; it was sunny and warm for so early in the day. The two stood together watching as police cars and an ambulance lined up in the driveway. Leanne grabbed Matt's hand and gave it a squeeze. Matt leaned over and kissed her on the cheek.

Once the couple was outside, Matt realized he had left the young missionaries alone. "Will you go in and make sure they keep calm?" Matt asked Leanne, and his tone made it clear it was a bit more than a request. Leanne kissed Matt and said, "I love you." Then she quickly stepped back into the house and closed the door behind her. Leanne would much rather have been at her husband's side, but she understood what she needed to do.

As Matt stood at the door, first a deputy walked up, and behind him was Sheriff Chow. Chow was recently elected, and even though Matt did not support him or vote for him, he did respect him. Chow was short, maybe five foot two, but he obviously lifted weights and was quite muscular. Chow had spent ten years in the Navy before being hired as a deputy. After only two years as a deputy, he ran against the good-old-boy sheriff, and had won by a landslide. Matt did not trust Chow's lack of experience, and he had less trust in the wave of elections that brought Chow to office. When President Prescott was elected, it was followed by many upsets in local elections across the country. Matt and many others had figured Prescott attracted a new group of voters to the polls, and this group upset the norm. Many voters were voting on emotion, some were just plain radicals, but most of all, people wanted change. The problem was they had no idea what they were changing to. The wave of incumbent losses left cities, counties, and states being run by inexperienced idealists, people with no idea how to keep government working. It was strange to see a Communist elected Mayor or a Socialist in the County Commissioner's seat sitting next to a Libertarian. No one could agree on anything, and even worse, no one knew what they were doing. Chow may have been elected in this landslide, and Matt may not have been a fan of his politics, but at least the sheriff was competent; he knew his job and would get it done. This was something that Matt had seen over the last three years, changing his overall impression of the man.

The younger deputy looked very military, and Matt did not recognize him. This was no surprise, as Chow had replaced several deputies with young men and woman returning from one of the current wars. The young man stood quietly by, just watching.

Behind Chow was an ambulance; in it were two volunteer firemen. Matt recognized them but did not remember their names.

Chow asked, "So, what's the situation?"

Matt replied, "My wife and the three young men are in the house; they are all scared. One has been shot and received a grazing wound. He got lucky. The other has some abrasions, and the third, well, it's emotional."

"And the neighbors?" Chow asked. For a moment Matt thought, "What about the neighbors?" And then he realized Chow wanted to know if they were involved.

"Neighbors keep to themselves in this neighborhood," Matt assured the sheriff. "Besides, I'm not sure if any of them are even home."

Matt and Leanne had moved to this community for its quiet nature. Most of the neighborhood was made up of snowbirds or retired people. Several of the homes on the street were vacant—a sign of the economy—and others were weekend and summer homes, not used much in a declining economy.

Chow turned and talked quietly to the deputy, who promptly went to his patrol car, pulled out an M-16, and positioned himself behind the ambulance. Then Chow went and spoke to the fireman, who quickly jumped to action. A man opened the back doors from the inside, and the other two men jumped from the cab and grabbed a gurney. Within moments they had what looked like a small hospital stacked on the gurney and at the front door.

Matt stopped them. "Let me go in first. No need to panic anyone."

Matt entered the room and looked at the concerned group. "They are here to help." He paused then added, "I trust them." Inside Matt was not so sure that what he was saying was actually true.

Within moments the gurney had been wheeled and lowered to the area of the living room beside Elder Jones. Two firemen started first aid and an IV. They had him on the gurney in minutes. Leanne stood to one side and held the Elder's hand to keep him calm.

One of the firemen turned to Leanne. "You did a nice job on his wounds. Are you a nurse?" he asked.

"Nope, just a mom," Leanne answered back with a bit of pride in her voice.

Elder Black was receiving some treatment as he was giving his statement to Sheriff Chow.

During all of the commotion, Elder Miles sat quietly next to Elder Black. Matt could see Elder Black take a moment every now and then to assure Elder Miles. On occasion he would reach out with his bruised and bandaged hand to put a hand on his friend's shoulder. The bond between these two was becoming very apparent. It was strange—at first it looked as if Elder Black was watching over Elder Miles, like an older brother. After watching more closely, Matt noticed something else was going on. Elder Miles would look at Elder Black. After making eye contact, he would nod or give signs of approval or disapproval. As Matt studied their interactions, it became less evident who was in charge. Elder Miles was giving approval to Elder Black's words and actions. Matt was a bit confused by what he saw. Elder Miles gave an approving look to Elder Black, who then, and only then, turned to finish giving his statement to Sheriff Chow.

Within a few moments, another ambulance arrived with two more patrol cars. Two more firemen came in and attended to Elders Black and Miles. After Sheriff Chow was done taking notes, he looked up and asked Matt to joint him outside. During this time, Leanne was speaking with deputies and firemen.

As soon as Matt and Chow stepped out the front door, Matt noticed more officers with shotguns and M16s setting up what looked like a defensive perimeter.

"You think it's a bit much?" Matt said to Chow, pointing at the officers

"It's for your safety. I'm not so sure this was such an isolated incident," Chow responded. It was clear to Matt that Chow was uncomfortable. Chow must have felt he was in a bit of an indefensible position as Matt noticed him shifting awkwardly from foot to foot. Since Chow didn't know who was behind this incident, or how his actions would be perceived, he must have wanted as much back-up support as he could muster. This was made clear by the fact that the normally confident and secure man was clearly nervous and uncomfortable.

"I thought you had someone in custody," Matt mentioned with a bit of concern in his voice.

"We do, but I am still investigating." Chow made it clear in his tone that the questions from Matt were no longer welcome; he also made it clear with body language by stepping slightly forward and almost puffing up as if to say "I'm in charge here," combined with a stern look. Chow had taken control of the house, driveway, and street; he was not taking any chances, and he apparently did not have time to answer Matt's questions. In some ways this offended Matt, yet in other ways Matt knew he would do the same. Someone had to be in charge, and Chow was that someone.

Chow handed Matt a notepad and pen. "Give me an account of the last twenty-four hours. Get it to me by tonight." He walked away and began speaking into the radio mic on his shoulder, leaving Matt standing on the porch, and not giving him a chance to answer, question, or respond in any way.

Matt sat on the step and began to write. Suddenly the door opened behind him, startling him. Two firemen wheeled out Elder Jones. The young man looked up and said, "God bless you, Brother Scott," and then lay back down. Next the two other young men came out with a fireman attending each.

Elder Black said, "Thank you and God bless you. And please don't worry. We will be OK."

Matt replied, "Please call and let me know what happens. Stay in touch." Elder Black nodded.

The young men were loaded in the ambulances, each accompanied by an armed deputy. The procession of patrol cars and ambulances left, lights flashing but no sirens.

Matt walked back into the house, realizing how exhausted he was—emotionally, physically, and mentally. As he closed the door and latched it, Leanne came bounding up the landing and wrapped her arms around him. "I love you," was all she could say as tears poured down her cheeks. The in-charge, strong, almost stoic woman that the world knew was gone. The sometimes-fragile human being that Matt loved so much was now sobbing in his arms. Leanne was free now to feel the fear, anger and emotions that she could not earlier. Now her world was safe.

Matt held his wife for a good ten minutes. The two then walked into the bedroom. Leanne went into the bathroom, closing the door behind her. This gave Matt a chance to go about the house to check doors and windows, and set their alarm. When he returned to the bedroom, Leanne was standing in a robe, hair up in a towel.

"You should take a shower; it will make you feel much better," Leanne said to her husband, smiling.

Matt went into the bathroom and looked in the mirror. His face looked tired—he needed a shave and to brush his teeth. The truth was he looked like hell, and then he realized he didn't smell much better.

After a good twenty minutes of shaving, teeth brushing and showering, Matt came out of the bathroom wrapped in a towel.

Leanne was lying on the bed sound asleep. She was curled up on her side. She looked so peaceful and safe that Matt did not have the heart to disturb her.

Matt kneeled beside the bed, something he had not done in years. "Heavenly Father, please give me the strength to meet the challenges placed before me. Bless the Elders. And please, Father, keep my family safe." He paused for a long time—fear or a moment of desperation took his words away. Then he ended with, "I ask this in the name of Your Son, Jesus Christ. Amen." Matt pulled a silver crucifix from his chest, a cross he wore on an old tarnished chain. He kissed the cross and stood up. Mormons don't wear such iconic jewelry; it was a Catholic symbol, something he had embraced since his days as a young marine. When asked about it, he always just responded, "It's personal." Matt's loved ones may not have known why he wore it, or what it meant, but they knew it was important.

Matt then pulled the blanket back on his side of the bed, climbed in and fell asleep within moments. Usually Matt would lie in bed contemplating the day or maybe the upcoming day and take a few minutes to unwind before he fell asleep. This time he was asleep by the time his head hit the pillow. Matt and Leanne were sound asleep. It was late morning, or maybe even early afternoon. Exhaustion had made time of day a non-issue.

CHAPTER FOUR

Back at the small apartment, one of the missionaries spoke out, interrupting the elderly man's story.

"But what about the Church? I am confused. The Bishop, the Mormon Church headquarters, what did they know? Why were the missionaries on their own?" The young missionary was confused because in his belief system and life experience, the Church was all-powerful. He believed no chain of events or misguided politician could possibly be more powerful than his church.

The elderly man smiled. "Getting to that. I will explain." He looked across at the other missionary. "The Church, the Prophet, and all of the leadership had their own issues to deal with." He diverted his story to events in Salt Lake City, Utah.

Nine hundred miles away, in Salt Lake City, Utah, a meeting was taking place in a spacious office in a big stone building. The room had mahogany walls and large, ornate lights hanging from the ceiling. A long table was the centerpiece of the room, a horseshoe-shaped table with room for at least twenty or thirty. An oversized large chair occupied a place of prominence at the center of the table. Around the outside curve of the table sat twelve men. All appeared to be between the ages of sixty and eighty, or even older, all in suits and ties. At the center seat sat a very distinguished-looking man with dark hair, who was clearly in charge of the meeting. The man was in his late sixties or even early seventies. The meeting resembled a board meeting, but it was not. This was a meeting of the presidency of the Church of Jesus Christ of Latter-day Saints and the top twelve advisors. This group was known as the Quorum of the Twelve. Members of this church believed the president was a prophet with a direct line to God. Meetings of this group were secret. They were not for public review or discussion. Within the walls of this building, in this room, many decisions concerning the membership of the Mormon Church had been made for many years, yet the events of this meeting would affect every American.

"This young man you speak of… Elder Miles. With all due respect, may I ask what his role in our future is?" a man from the end of the table asked. The speaker was an older man, bald and slight of frame, a very weathered man in his nineties. His voice rang like that of a younger man, but visually he was very old and fragile looking.

The question was phrased in such a way as to avoid disrespect. It was clear that the men set at each side of table were somewhat subservient to the dark-haired man at the center seat. This man was the president of the Mormon Church. He was the Prophet, and according to the beliefs of all in the room, he received direct prophecy from God. How could they dare question him? Yet they wondered what their leader was doing.

"Elder Miles, this young man you speak of is much more than a simple missionary." The president's voice, although aged, was clear and very authoritarian. He had no need to speak loudly. The Prophet's tone and pitch sent a message, and the message was clear: "Don't question me." Few details of the actual meeting were known by anyone outside that room until the history of these was uncovered from notes and memories of the few who survived. One thing was certain, the general subject was Elder Miles.

Back in the small apartment, the elderly man said, "I'm getting ahead of myself." He paused, stood up, and walked around the table. The two young missionaries sat tall, watching his every move, waiting to hear more.

"Yes, I am getting ahead of myself," he repeated as he sat back down.

The elderly man began to speak again. With his words he took the young men back to the wounded missionaries and the Scott family. His wife was leaning on the counter in the kitchen, listening intently.

She knew the story but was clearly enjoying hearing it from her husband's perspective once again.

Sarah was tired. She was driving up Interstate 5 past Olympia. She had handed a bag of animal cookies back to each of her children and was trying to remember what turn to take to get to her brother's house. Sarah had made this drive before, but she wanted to be sure. Getting lost or ending up in the wrong neighborhood was not an option today.

After driving past the Seattle-Tacoma Airport, Sarah noticed her fuel gauge was reading less than a quarter-tank. She remembered that the exit to her brother's house had a Chevron station. Once she arrived at the exit, Sarah drove off the freeway and pulled into the gas station and up to the pumps. A handwritten sign read, "Cash Only." She opened her purse and started to dig for cash, finding six dollars and some change. She knew this was a problem. Sarah had a Visa Card, a debit card, and an American Express Card, but apparently none of these was going to get her gas. And at over five dollars a gallon, what good was six dollars and some change? As Sarah dug through her purse frantically, she heard a knock on the window. She was so startled that she let out a quick short scream. Turning quickly to look as she reached for the ignition, she saw a young man. He was clean-cut and in a dirty black suit and tie. The name tag on his jacket read "Elder Boeticher," and under his name where the words, "Church of Jesus Christ of Latter-day Saints." He was a missionary. Sarah rolled down the window about four inches, enough to talk, not enough to let him reach her. "Can I help you?" she asked.

"I am so sorry. I did not mean to scare you." He looked and sounded very sincere.

"It's OK. I'm just a bit jumpy," Sarah responded.

"I think we can help each other," he replied.

Sarah was not so sure, but she was willing to listen. What choice did she have? She was pretty sure she did not have enough gas to get to her brother's house, her cell phone battery had died, and she had forgotten the charger back in Portland.

"My friends and I need a ride, and, well, it looks like you need gas," he said with a nod toward the gas pump.

"Go on," Sarah said, a bit curious and concerned.

"You give us a ride, just a few miles, and we will fill your tank. We won't hurt you or your kids. We are missionaries," the young man reassured her.

Now Sarah new better than to pick up anyone, but what was she going to do? And they were missionaries, so it should be OK. That's what she told herself, anyway. Sarah was thinking of her stepfather Matt. He had told her to trust missionaries. She quietly said under her breath, "*God, I hope he is right.*"

"OK, I guess," Sarah said as she hit the fuel door button and then unlocked the door. The missionary looked back over his shoulder. "Come on, we have a ride." Four more young men came out of the woods beside the gas station. Two of them were dressed in similar suits, and the other two were in jeans and T-shirts. For a moment Sarah second-guessed herself, as she had no way to defend herself and her children. Before she could change her mind, the other two in black suits were in the van and sitting behind the children. Elder Boeticher started to pump gas as the two remaining young men had gone into the store, she assumed to pay the clerk. They did as promised and pumped nearly nineteen gallons into her tank; the dollar amount on the pump was over a hundred dollars. That was a lot of money for a two-mile ride, she was thinking.

When the tank was full, they all got in. Elder Boeticher sat in the passenger seat, and the others entertained the children, singing children's songs and playing peekaboo. Sarah was feeling very uncomfortable, and it was showing.

"Don't worry. You will be okay, I promise. We would not let anything happen to you or your kids. Where are you going, anyway?" asked Elder Boeticher.

"To my brother's house. He is expecting me," Sarah pointed out, trying to ensure her family's safety.

"Well, then, we had better get moving. Would not want to keep him waiting," he said with a smile.

Sarah pulled back onto the road and followed directions from the young man in the passenger seat. After a couple of miles, she turned into a gated parking lot, stopping at the locked gate.

"Can you find your way back?" asked Boeticher.

"Yes, I think so," Sarah responded, as the four in the back of the van piled out, saying good-bye to the kids and smiling.

Elder Boeticher walked around to Sarah's window. As she put the window down, he placed his hand on the door of the minivan and looked at Sarah in a very serious manor.

"Don't stop for anyone. Drive straight to your brother's. You understand?" His voice was very stern. He then continued, "If you get in any trouble, you start honking your horn. Don't stop honking."

"Then what?" Sarah asked

"You just do what I say. If you need us, we will find you," Boeticher reassured her.

"Who are you?" she asked. "Are you cops?" Sarah was confused by the whole encounter.

"They call us the Sons of Nephi. Just missionaries trying to help." He smiled at her, turned and winked at the kids, spun on his heels, and walked away. Sarah watched as the group of young men scaled the chain-link fence and made their way into what looked like an abandoned warehouse. She quickly put the van in gear, backed out and sped back in the direction that she had come from. In less than twenty minutes she was pulling into her brother's driveway. David saw her coming and opened the garage door so she could drive in. Once she was in the garage, where David and his wife were waiting, Sarah broke down in tears and slumped over the steering wheel. She was safe; her kids were safe. This day had been the hardest thing Sarah had ever done, but she had made it.

Over the next hour, the families reunited. Sarah told her brother all about her day. She spoke of Naomi, about watching Naomi kill a man, and about Naomi letting her and the kids go. She told David about the missionaries and the Sons of Nephi. The entire thing seemed surreal to David and his wife, Tami. They had heard that the Sons of Nephi were a gang of sorts. They had heard of violence and protests in the streets, but the truth was they were somewhat insulated from it all. They lived in a safe, affluent neighborhood and had protection from the police and military. They had food and utilities. To David and Tami, the stories from the other cities and neighborhoods seemed like exaggerations. Sarah made it real. While the children reunited with their cousins, Sarah got her phone charged and called her boyfriend,

Jeff. Then she called her mom and some friends from Portland. Then the families settled in together in the big house.

Back at the Scott home, Saturday passed with a lot of sleep and a few moments of worry. On several occasions, Matt or Leanne would wake up and sit for a moment and then go back to sleep. It was not until almost 3:00 p.m. that they both got out of bed. The couple had a light dinner and spent a little time cleaning up some of the mess from the night before. Leanne did a couple loads of laundry, and Matt cleaned the kitchen. By 5:00 p.m. Leanne had talked to Sarah and David. Sarah didn't tell her parents the details of the drive and the encounters with the Sons of Nephi and with Naomi. "There is no need to freak Mom out," David said before Sarah called. It took some convincing—Sarah shared everything with her mother, and she hated to lie or even leave anything out.

Sunday morning came, and both Matt and Leanne needed answers to several questions. Matt awoke early and decided that a trip to town would be in order. They needed to know what had happened to the missionaries, and to stop by the office and get some idea of how the rest of the world was reacting to the events of the last few days. The two were alone and isolated to a degree; they had no idea how widespread the violence and chaos was. Leanne had not shared the events of the missionaries with David or Sarah for the same reason the kids kept things from her. None of them wanted to alarm the others.

Matt and Leanne decided to go to town early. After some coffee and toast they were out the door by 7:30 a.m. After all of the sleep of the day before, the couple was a bit eager to get moving. The drive to town took about twenty minutes, and it was a quiet drive. It seemed strange that there was no traffic; even on a Sunday morning they would expect to see a car or two. Neither of them had much to say, at least not until some questions had been answered. The two rode in the car in silence.

During the drive Leanne did make a phone call to her daughter Sarah; it was not a long call, but they caught up a little more. The mother and daughter talked about kids and meals, and the usual sort of things mothers and daughters chat about. They spoke about things as if nothing had changed. For Matt, it was nice to hear Leanne laugh. It was nice to know Sarah was not just OK, but that she was happy, at least as happy as someone could be in this situation.

David's wife came from old family money. No one in David or Leanne's family knew how much, but they knew it was a lot. David and his wife lived somewhat modestly considering the sizable trust fund. The family lived off of David's income and saved the rest. David's love of his sister and her children made it natural that Sarah and the kids would stay with David and his family during hard times. Leanne seemed very satisfied that her children and grandchildren were safe. For the first time in her life, their lack of interest in politics and religion seemed like a godsend. Maybe they would be immune from what she had witnessed the night before. Leanne knew in her heart that the world was changing, but at least they were together. Leanne saw her son David as Sarah's protector, and it gave her peace.

Just over half way to town, they passed the LDS church. The church building was set back away from the road. It looked like every other LDS church built in the 1980s. It was brick and had a symmetrical design north to south. The front of building had a rarely used large set of doors. The south side of the building serviced the south side of the county; the north serviced the north side. Bill King was bishop of the North Ward. In an effort to control costs and not waste resources, most LDS churches shared space with multiple wards, or congregations. Most of the non-Mormon population was unaware of the huge growth rates of the Mormon Church. Planning ahead and using resources efficiently made this growth manageable. The practice of sharing space made sense.

Matt clearly remembered seeing all of the empty church buildings of other denominations and thinking what a waste it was to only use a building a couple days per week. His business sense was always trying to figure out things like cost per square foot, per member. If nothing else, the Mormon Church was run with a good business sense. Other areas that seemed to make sense were the use of regional food storage warehouses that sold bulk foods to members. There were many things Matt liked about the Mormon Church, yet he could not get past a few key problems he had with Mormon teachings and culture.

When Matt joined the Church, he had learned much and enjoyed the open discussions with some of the other members, but he had little patience for literalists. Nothing annoyed him more than people who lived the literal word. Matt used to argue to no end that God gave us free agency, and following a church blindly was ignoring that gift. Over the past years many friends were made, and some were lost. Matt's view that religion was a guideline, not a set of specific directions, created friction between him and some of the Mormons. Matt's faith was strong, yet it did not seem to mesh cleanly with the modern Mormon Church. More than once Matt was heard saying, "If you don't think God was involved in the making of a good single-malt scotch, then you're just daft." Matt joked about this, but it was part of why he left the Mormon Church. The hypocrisy of being told not to drink coffee by someone who made regular stops at McDonald's, or drank energy drinks, was more than he could take. Matt's religious and political views did have some common ground with the Mormon faith, yet he had little patience for those who were unable to think for themselves and take responsibility for their own well-being. Matt Scott maintained a special place in his heart for the Church he had left; he believed in many of its teachings and in some way would always think of himself as a Latter-day Saint.

Bishop King and Matt had had many long discussions on these matters before he left the Mormon Church. The Bishop finally conceded that maybe Matt just needed to live his life as he saw fit. It had all come to a head one day in a meeting when Matt was asked what he thought Joseph Smith would think of the current-day Mormon Church. Matt thought for a moment and said, "Well, I think if Joseph Smith was praying and asking which church was the true church today, he would get the same answer he got back then: none of them." This was taken as blasphemy by quite a few, and it was Matt's last meeting at the church up to this day. If he had been given a chance to explain, he would have told them that maybe this was the closest thing to a true church. But Matt truly believed man corrupted anything and everything he touched, and the LDS church was no exception.

As Matt and Leanne passed the church building, they were both amazed to see that the parking lot was not just full but overflowing. Two sheriff cars and a black Chevrolet Tahoe were blocking one entrance, all with flashing lights of one form or another. Matt pulled into a side road, turned around, and drove back to the church parking lot.

Leanne immediately protested. "What are you doing?"

"We will just be just a quick minute," Matt responded.

Matt spotted familiar faces among the people standing out front. Many of the people were milling around as if it was just another Sunday before church; others were looking more distressed.

Stopping behind a green suburban, Matt recognized the vehicle as the Bishop's family car. He stepped out and greeted several different people, none of whom Leanne recognized. Across the lawn and beyond a group of children milling about, Matt spotted Sheriff Chow. The sheriff and two deputies were talking with two men in dark suits. Now at a Mormon Church, suits are the norm, but these men were obviously not churchgoers. As Matt walked up, he heard Sheriff Chow speaking very sternly to the two men.

"I don't care who you are or who you work for. I don't care what the President said. These people can and will worship as they see fit. Do you remember that thing called the Constitution?" Chow was nearly yelling with anger.

It was obvious that Matt had walked in on a showdown. He quickly turned away, but not in time.

"Matthew, over here," said Chow. "This is the man I was telling you about. If you think those young men brought on what happened to them, maybe you should talk to Mr. Scott. I am sure he will set you straight."

Not wanting to be involved with what looked like federal agents, Matt was put out by Chow's words. The two federal agents looked like something out of a movie. The taller one had dark hair cut very short and was so tan it almost looked like he had painted the tan on. He wore the typical mirrored sunglasses and what appeared to be an off-the-rack black suit from JC Penney. The shorter man was mostly gray, slightly less athletic, and quite a bit calmer. He appeared to be in charge, yet he said nothing. He was wearing what was obviously a very expensive suit. Matt looked at the man's shoes. He had learned a long time ago that a man can fool you with his clothes, but his shoes tell the truth. Funny, you will find a man in jeans and a T-shirt with quality on his feet and you know who you are dealing with. Conversely, a man can put on an Armani suit and K-mart shoes, and you also know who you are dealing with. This was something Matt had learned from his father; it had served him well in business over the years.

"Let me make this clear: We will be back. This church will be closed, and anyone in our way will be arrested," said the taller of the two suited men. He had quite the attitude. The two walked toward their car, and the shorter man pulled a satellite phone from his belt and made a call. Matt had a bad feeling that this call was going all the way to the top. Why did this little church on the Olympic Peninsula mean so much? Matt was not sure why, but he did have a sense that someone, someplace, with a lot of pull was going to make all their lives a bit rougher.

"Matt, it seems you are in the middle of this, whether you like it or not. I plan on meeting with Bishop King this afternoon, and I would like you to be there." Chow was not really giving Matt much of an option, and his comments were more informative than inquisitive.

"Now wait a minute, I helped some young men in need, and I did not sign on to be some kind of leader, or even worse, a martyr." Matt was getting defensive.

"I am truly sorry, but Bishop King said he did not trust anyone from the police or anyone in the government. He said he would only meet with me if you were there. I am afraid of what might happen if he doesn't go underground and get his congregation under control."

"You act like they did something wrong. All they want to do is go to church and be left alone." Matt was becoming very irritated with what he saw as Chow placing blame. "You don't believe that crap the President spewed on TV do you?"

"I don't know what to believe. I do know that right now *why* doesn't matter; what matters is protecting these people." Chow was being very logical, and this was reassuring to Matt. Chow was also making it clear he was worried about the safety of all involved, which went a long way toward mollifying Matt.

Matt was in deep, and not sure how he had gotten there. Two days ago Matt and his beautiful wife lived quietly and anonymously. They ran a small business and enjoyed their new home with a view. Today he was aiding in what could be perceived as sedition by some, or even treason by others.

Why me? He thought. It would be up to him to convince the Bishop that he was not needed. *Why would the Bishop want me? I left the*

Church; I am not one of them. All of these thoughts ran in Matt Scott's head.

After a few minutes of small talk and greetings with the people entering the church, Matt found the Bishop.

"Bishop King, can we have a word?" Matt was interrupting a conversation.

"It's Bill. Call me Bill. And, of course."

The bishop was trying to ease some tension. Bill King was a devout man, and he was very strict in his protocol. For him to ask to be referred to as Bill in the presence of church members was very telling. In a normal situation, the proper salutation or address would be Bishop King.

"Matt, come with me. We can meet in the North Ward office." Bishop Bill King led the way.

Bishop John Riley led the South Ward. The South Ward would meet in the afternoon following the services and meetings of the North Ward. The two men entered the north side entrance, and the Bishop's office was immediately to the left. Ahead of them was a common chapel, and to the right was a long hall, lined with classrooms, restrooms, and a small kitchen area. The hallway wrapped all the way around the building to the South Ward's Bishop's office. One could walk through the chapel as a shortcut, but this was rarely done, as the chapel was quite often in use. The chapel was also to be treated with reverence at all times.

Bill and Matt walked directly to the office; there were several men waiting inside. Chow and his men waited outside, because Chow said that having uniformed, armed men enter the church during times like these would be disrespectful. Sheriff Chow had little understanding of the Latter-day Saints, but he was making an effort to be respectful. The spiritual energy one feels in a cathedral, mosque, or synagogue was not missing in this building. Chow seemed to be aware of it, and in some ways he was acting a bit humbled by it. Matt thought maybe Chow would not quite understand his feelings, but he did seem to give in to them.

Matt had a feeling this was pre-arranged and that he was a bit of a pawn at the moment. The question was who put him in this spot? The Bishop? Chow? Who? Either way, it seemed he was in deep even if he wanted out.

"Can someone go tell Leanne I am going to be a minute? She is waiting in the car." Matt spoke over his shoulder in the direction of Sheriff Chow.

"No problem," said Phillip, one of the men in the room. "My wife and kids would love to see her." He left the room in a hurry. Phillip was a short, round man, yet he moved quickly. Phillip and Matt were friends, but when Matt spoke up and left the Mormon Church, they became estranged. Like many religious men, Phillip had a hard time socializing with people outside the Church. It took time for Matt to understand that it was not a matter of Phillip judging him, but it was purely a matter of culture. Matt figured out that people surrounded themselves with that which makes them comfortable. Matt did not live within the guidelines that made Phillip comfortable. This did not mean they were not friends and did not respect each other as men; it just meant they were living in different worlds.

Within moments, Phillip returned to the office. There was a total of seven men in the room: Bishop Bill King, Phillip, a man Matt knew as JR, three other men that Matt recognized but could not recall their names in the moment, and himself. The three men whose names Matt couldn't recall were part of the group that had been offended by Matt's questioning. They did not look too happy to see him. When Matt left the Church, he had openly questioned the direction the Church had gone. Matt felt the spreadsheets and organization had become more important than the faith. Matt made it clear that he would not worship a church or an organization, and he felt that many in the room were doing just that. A group of families saw Matt as a bit of a lost soul. Some saw him as an apostate; it was those who saw him as an apostate who were throwing stares and even glares. In their eyes, Matt had committed a sin, the sin of forsaking his religion. For a man or woman who lived their life in the Church and knew nothing else, it was hard to understand Matt's point of view. Matt understood this. He never held it against his former friends, and he always left the door open for a re-kindling of the friendships lost. Matt never lost his faith in God; he lost his faith in the Church, and in some ways he lost faith in humankind. Much of Matt's life left him questioning his faith in people, from his days as a young marine to his divorce, and even his dabbling in local politics. Matt, as a man, had little faith in any group. His favorite quote was, "A person can be smart, but people, they are always stupid." He saw this group as the stupid.

Bill King quickly called the meeting to order and opened with a prayer. Matt was expecting a long, drawn-out, never-ending prayer, but the Bishop was quick and to the point that day. Matt recalled one meeting that opened with a prayer so lengthy that the one-hour meeting never commenced. This was something that would grate on Matt's nerves, and he was very grateful that the men in the room seemed to be ready to get to the point.

Matt's thoughts were interrupted by the words of Bishop King. "Heavenly Father, we ask You to bless the men in this room and the work they are about to do. We ask these things in the name of Your Son, Jesus Christ. Amen." That was the *shortest* prayer Matt had ever heard in these walls.

Before anyone could speak, Phillip piped up, "Matthew, the Church needs you. We need you."

"Wait a minute, I am not..." Bishop King quickly interrupted Matt, "You may not be active, you may not consider yourself a member," he said, "but we trust you, the Ward trusts you, and Sheriff Chow trusts you. You and Leanne did God's work for our young boys, and now we need you more than ever. It's a calling, and you can't say no. The calling comes from much higher than this ward or even this stake." Bishop King was insinuating that Matt Scott had been called upon by Mormon Church leaders in Utah, and maybe even by the Prophet.

"What do you want from me?" Matt was feeling a bit trapped. He knew the words and what they meant to this man: a *calling* or *direction from God*. Matt knew he would never reason his way out of this, and while he actually felt somewhat honored by it, he also felt drafted or conscripted.

"We need you to be an intermediary. We are afraid for the safety of our wives and families," Bishop King said very forcefully. "It's much like the days of persecution." The Bishop was referring to a part of history Matt would understand.

Most people did not know of the persecution in Mormon history, but the truth was Mormons were hated, and even killed, not so long ago. Recently there was still a law on the books in Missouri that made shooting a Mormon missionary legal, just for the crime of being a Mormon. This is what Bishop King was referring too.

People who think of Mormons bring to mind Donny and Marie Osmond, or the TV show *Big Love*. The truth was that the Church had a deep history, some of which brought shame, like the Mountain Meadows Massacre, or the actions of the FLDS Church, a breakaway group that made headlines in the 1990s. Yet most of the history was of achievement and perseverance.

The history of the Mountain Meadows Massacre was rarely taught in the Mormon Church, and it was rarely spoken about publicly. In 1857 a group of settlers were attacked by what was believed to be a group of Mormon men. By most accounts nearly one hundred fifty people were killed, and the attackers attempted to make it look as if Indian tribes had been to blame. There was never any evidence of official church sanction, yet many believed this stain on LDS history was the work of Brigham Young, the namesake of Brigham Young University. It was widely believed that the attackers were a breakaway group, but that the Church also did nothing to prevent the inevitable violence.

The violence and persecution the church members suffered had forced them to continue to move east until they settled in Utah in 1847. Many, like Matt, believed that retaliation was inevitable. Even godly men are just men and can take only so much before they act out in an inhumane way. Matt often wanted to speak of such events in church when he was a member. "Exploring one's weakness only leads to strength," was his argument. But like many organizations, the black marks were often ignored and even covered up.

Matt found the history of the Church of Jesus Christ of Latter-day Saints fascinating. The LDS, or Mormon Church, was the only church in the history of the United States to have had the United States Military attack them, with the exception of David Koresh and the Branch Dravidians in Texas in 1993. The history of persecution and rebellion was one that few were aware of, but it was a history that left many devout Mormons fearing government and other Christian denominations, and it was a fear that is based on real events. Many pioneer families, families with history back to the founding of the Church had a deep fear of religious persecution, and justifiably so.

Matt enjoyed studying the history of the Church; he learned about Mountain Meadows, the pioneer trail, and other events. Although plural marriage, breakaway groups, and rebellion were part of the Church's history, it was far from a defining part of its history. Much like Catholicism, which was tarnished by sex scandals or the Crusades, Mormonism was commonly identified as a plural marriage cult, which was far from reality. With the ensuing attacks on the Church, it seemed clear to a man like Matt that history was repeating itself. Maybe his perspective on these events was the reason for his conscription.

"I told you he wouldn't do it," said one of the other men in the room.

"He will," stated the bishop calmly. "He will."

Matt was very unsure of the whole situation. He had a wife who had nothing to do with this church; he had kids, step kids, and grand-kids that didn't have any linkage to the Church, and it was becoming clearer by the minute that a Mormon was not a very safe thing to be right now. The question that Matt had to face was whether he could risk being identified as a Mormon even if he was not. Could he even risk being identified as a Mormon sympathizer? Or was it too late?

"I have to think of my family first," said Matt.

"I know. We would expect nothing less," Bishop King said. He paused, and then added, "And that's why I know you will help." It was clear that the word *family* was being used to mean the whole church. Bishop King apparently felt that Matt had never left his church. Matt was just following a temporary directional shift.

The meeting ended as quickly as it started. The three men whose names Matt could not remember hustled out, each shaking his hand. But none of them thanked him, and they all looked a bit angry.

Matt was put out. "I did not agree to anything." Matt was speaking out loud to anyone that would listen.

Bishop King and Phillip walked out of the room with him.

"Be here in two hours," the Bishop stated firmly.

Leanne walked up to Matt. He tried to explain what was up, yet it seemed that maybe Leanne already knew. Leanne could tell they were in deep. She had a feeling that whatever was coming was meant to be and all she could do was to go along with it. Sally King, Bill King's wife, had given some indication to Leanne what was happening.

"Sally told me what was going on. Matt, I know you," she said. Then after a pause, she added, "I know you can't say no. Please, let's go someplace and get out of the public eye. Whatever we are going to do, let's be smart about it." Leanne was very aware of the possible consequences of her husband's actions.

As Chow walked up, he looked at Matt in an unsure way. "Here in two hours?" he asked.

Matt thought for a minute. "No, not here, let's meet at my office at the shop in town. Tell the Bishops to come in the back way. Two hours, and don't bring the whole damn sheriff's department with you. Just you, the two Bishops, Leanne, and myself."

Leanne piped up. "I want the Bishops' wives to be there, or at least Sally King. Why do you men always ignore the wives?" Leanne saw value in the wives' perspectives. Inside she knew the women might bring calmer heads to the table.

Before anyone could object, Matt and Leanne Scott walked away toward their car, climbed in, and drove out of the parking lot toward town, toward their auto repair shop and his office.

Leanne leaned across the center console and kissed Matt. "It will be OK, right?" questioned Leanne. Leanne trusted Matt more than anyone, but she was in an unfamiliar situation, with a group she knew little about, and she needed just a small bit of reassurance. She had put herself out there so often with Matt's family and Matt's kids that by this point it was old hat. But this time it was way bigger, this time people could get hurt or even killed.

"I don't know, I don't know," Matt responded in a very subdued tone. This was probably not what Leanne wanted to hear, but it was the truth. If he tried to sugarcoat it, she would see right through him.

The couple drove the rest of the way to town in silence, both pondering what they had been dragged into, both wondering if life would ever be the same. Leanne reached across the car and rubbed the back of Matt's neck. Leanne was a nurturing woman, and she could see the weight of the world building on his shoulders.

When Matt turned the corner into his shop parking lot, he opened the first roll-up bay door with a garage door opener button on the sun visor. He pulled the Cadillac into the shop and closed the door behind him. Turning the car off, he looked to his wife. "I love you," he said. There was not much else to say. They both knew very well that Matt would never refuse to help. This was something he had to do.

The Scotts' shop was one of those super clean, almost sterile garages. Matt would say, "If I have to be here half of my life, I want it nice." The floors were painted a light gray; the lighting was like daylight. There was not a drop of oil or grease to be found; the toolboxes were neatly aligned down the wall. The workbenches were all empty except for one—an engine was in pieces on a bench in bay three, and there was a bright yellow hummer sitting in the bay with no hood on and no engine inside. Besides that, you could have mistaken this repair shop for a show room.

Matt and Leanne made their way to Matt's office at the back of the building on the ground floor. The lobby was in the front, and five repair bays were to one side. Between Matt's office and the lobby was a bathroom and shower area, and then some stairs heading up. From the office, Matt could see if anyone drove up on the security cameras. Matt and Leanne would know if the Bishops and the sheriff agreed to the meeting place in an hour or two if they saw the arrivals turn off the highway and drive to the back of the shop.

The office was a busy-looking room. One side was lined with file cabinets; the other had a small desk facing a window. Matt's desk, an old military surplus oak desk, was positioned so he sat with his back to the shop. Behind him was a one-way mirror—Matt could see out, but no one could see in. Across from him, the wall was covered with bookcases, each shelf filled with trade magazines and technical manuals. All of this was silly to most, as in this day and age all information could be found on the Internet. Few people understood why Matt kept old technical books and such. Matt did not trust the Internet; he wanted books so they could work in the event the Internet failed. In a storeroom upstairs, Matt had a library of repair manuals dating back to the 1940s. It was his way of being prepared. In the remaining upstairs area was one large room made into a break room with a TV and kitchenette. Off of this room was a small alcove with a trundle bed and a nightstand. Beside that was a small bathroom with a shower and sink.

Prior to his divorce, Matt had seen the handwriting on the wall. He remodeled the upstairs to a state he could live with if he ever had to move in. The divorce went much better than that for Matt. The courts gave Matt custody of Riana, who was sixteen at the time. He got the house, the business, and, of course, the bills. For some time he was bitter about this, but Leanne helped him see what a blessing it was. Yes, he had lost his retirement, he lost his daughter's college fund, but he had kept his ability to make money. Leanne would tell him, "It's only money, and you got everything of real value." She was right. If you looked in Webster's dictionary for *optimism,* you would see a picture of Leanne. She made lemonade out of lemons in her sleep. Matt was never super-wealthy, but at one point in his life, he had no money worries. Matt had come a long way from his childhood days of free lunches and food stamps. Over the last year, working together with Leanne, he was able to put some money in the bank. It wasn't easy, though. Riana's college did not come cheap, and Matt took great pride in making sure she had what she needed to finish. In Matt's family, Riana would be the first person to go to a four-year school and get a degree. She was on the dean's list, and he was very proud.

Leanne asked Matt, "What should I be doing?"

"The safe—get all of the cash except the till and put in my satchel." Matt paused for a minute, then said, "Let's make sure we set aside enough for Jeremy—a couple paychecks worth."

Leanne moved a framed poster of a vintage Jag off the wall and opened the antique safe Matt had installed. She moved some documents, a Colt 1911 45-caliber pistol, and pulled out a box. It was a cowboy boot box, which was odd, as Matt had never worn cowboy boots a day in his life. One of those silly mysteries—nobody knew where the box came from—but Matt had been using it for about eight years.

Leanne put the box on the smaller of the two desks and opened it up. Inside was cash, quite a bit of it, actually. She started to sort and count the twenty-, ten-, five-, and one-dollar bills arranged like a till. Each stack was at least three or four inches high. Then she pulled up a cardboard divider from beneath the bills. In the bottom of the box was a sandwich bag full of coins. In the bag were twelve South African Krugerrands; at a quarter-ounce of gold each, this little pile amounted to a lot of money. Matt had been buying one coin at a time, when he was ahead, since high school. There were also some Canadian twenty-dollar bills and a banded stack of American fifty- and one-hundred-dollar bills.

Several years before, Matt had gone to the bank to withdraw ten thousand dollars to buy a motorcycle. The bank did not have enough money on hand and took a week to gather up enough currency. This event ended what little trust he had in banks. Matt felt a need to keep a large part of his company's money in cash. This made Leanne nervous. She always was afraid he was going to get robbed. Then as the economy was spiraling down over the last two years, and the dollar was losing value, Matt kept every bit of Canadian cash he received. There was a time in recent history when businesses in the Pacific Northwest had to struggle with saying "no" to Canadian money or had to discount it at a high rate. Now Matt welcomed Canadian money and would offer a ten percent rebate to anyone paying with Canadian currency. American currency was losing value by the day.

While Leanne counted, Matt looked at his schedule of upcoming jobs.

Over the last several years, the economy had been getting worse. Matt's staff had gone from ten employees down to four. Although this was bad, it was not as bad as it could have been. Port Smith had a population of just over twelve thousand, and Matt's Auto was the only repair shop still in business. Of the shops that had gone out of business over the last two years, many owners were now working out of their homes. But as a traditional business, Matt's Auto was the only repair shop left.

Matt picked up the phone and dialed his friend and manager, Jeremy.

"Yeah, I'm at the office. You heard. Good. I have a meeting in a few with some people, but I will call you when I am done, and we can talk." Jeremy had heard of the events at the Scott house and was happy to hear his friends and employers were okay.

Matt was making arrangements for Jeremy and his daughter. They had been having issues with housing, as his divorce had not gone well. Jeremy was living in a one-bedroom apartment, and he was not feeling like his daughter was very comfortable or safe there. He was an amazing dad, and his love for his little girl was what kept him going. Matt respected Jeremy for this and would give the shirt off his back to help his friend.

Leanne looked up and spoke. "Well, we have one thousand Canadian dollars, fifteen thousand US dollars, and the gold coins."

"Yeah, good." Matt pulled his laptop and some books out of his satchel to make room for the money. Then he handed the satchel and two file folders to Leanne. "All of this will stay with us for now, except for what Jeremy needs." He handed Leanne an envelope, and she wrote "Jeremy" on the front, then she put thirty-five hundred dollars in it and sealed it up. She set the envelope on the keyboard on the small desk and proceeded to put everything else in the satchel, or "man purse," as she called it.

Leanne had little to do with Matt's business. He had it before he met her, and she had made an effort to stay out of it. This did create some issues for Matt. He loved her very much and was about as committed as a man could be. Matt and Leanne had not been together that long in the big picture, but Matt did not care. Leanne was his wife, and that's all he knew.

"Hand me that gun and box of shells, sweetie."

Leanne put the satchel on the desk, which was filled to the limit, and handed Matt the gun and box of ammo.

Matt quickly put the box in his coat pocket. He chambered a round and laid the pistol on his desk. The gun lay across his desk in clear view. Matt was setting the tone for anyone who entered the room.

A large monitor hung on the wall across the room from the desk, which was fed by a series of security cameras. On the monitor they saw a car pull up, an unmarked patrol car, and right behind it was a green suburban, very familiar. Out of the driver's side stepped Bill King, and from the passenger's side Phillip stepped out. Sally King and JR climbed from the back. As soon as they stepped out, Sheriff Chow opened his door and stood up. He was out of uniform but carrying a shotgun.

Matt hit a button on an intercom panel behind his desk. "I'll open a door. Come on in. I am in my office," he told the arriving visitors. Matt then pushed a second button, and the bay door behind the Cadillac opened up. When Matt saw all five were in the shop, he pushed the button again to see it close.

"Leanne, come back here with me." Matt gestured for Leanne to get behind the desk. She took the satchel and empty boot box and placed it under the desk at Matt's feet. Leanne then closed the safe and placed the poster over it. She walked back and stood behind her husband, one hand on his shoulder. This made Matt feel good. It was more than symbolic, as Leanne always had Matt's back.

As the door opened, Matt looked Chow in the eye. "You can leave that gun in the hall," he said. Chow did so, but looked unhappy about it. He glanced at the pistol on Matt's desk and shook his head.

When everyone had entered the room, it was clear that the Bishop from the South Ward, John Riley, was not present.

"Seems we are not all here?" Matt stated questioningly.

"Mr. Riley has been detained. Seems the Feds did not like the fact that he would not let them into his office," said Sheriff Chow. "They came back after you left and arrested him. Last we knew, he was being taken to the Federal building in Seattle."

"What did they want to get in his office for?" Matt asked. Matt knew the answer, but he hoped he was wrong.

"They are looking for records: the schedules for home teaching, the names and addresses of members, tithing reports. I am really starting to get worried about the families." Bill King had a slight tremble in his voice.

Sheriff Chow stepped forward. "This is much worse than I thought. I am not sure what is going on, but I have reason to believe that I won't be able to protect you or your families much longer."

JR angrily blurted out, "Like you protected the missionaries or Bishop Riley and his family?" It was clear from his fuming that JR could go off the handle if not for those with calmer heads in his presence.

Not acknowledging the outburst, Chow continued, "We need to disperse. We need to get the missionaries someplace safe, and we need to warn all of the Mormon families that they are in danger." Chow turned and looked into the eyes of each person in the room, "There are groups starting up, vigilante groups." He took a deep breath, "Anti-Mormon groups," he said.

Bishop King, looking overwhelmed, said, "We need to go underground before it gets any worse."

"We need to arm ourselves," JR said with anger in his voice.

Matt and Leanne sat quiet; they were waiting for their place in the discussion.

"This is where you come in, Matt. We would like it if you would put up the missionaries for a short time. We will supply food from food stores."

Leanne blurted out, "They can stay with us, but we will take none of your food. We can provide." Leanne took pride in her ability to be self-sufficient, and she was not going to be taking food from someone who needed it more than she and Matt did.

Bishop King placed his hands on Matt's desk and leaned in, looking at Matt closely. "We will need you to do more soon. I hope you understand."

"What does that mean?" Matt asked.

"It means just that. We will need your help, Brother Scott." Bishop King was quite serious.

Matt then stood up. "OK, let's make this quick. Chow, you and the others need to get back to the church and get rid of the records. This will buy us some time. And then get the missionaries to my house tomorrow. We need some time to get things arranged. Bishop King, you need to warn the families, make sure they stay under the radar."

"You know the Feds will find everything at the stake office, and everything we have is also there," Bishop King pointed out.

"They will, but by then maybe we can get the word out, people can blend some and maybe protect themselves."

Matt was clearly taking charge at this point, and this seemed to make Chow somewhat uncomfortable, Chow was opening and closing his fists, almost like a young boy backed into a corner, but he was going with it. In some ways Chow was relieved. He had a wife and brand-new twins at home, two little girls. He wanted nothing more than to be relieved of this responsibility, yet his sense of duty kept him in the mix.

"Leanne and I need to get some shopping done before things get any worse, so we are going to leave first thing tomorrow morning for Seattle to stock up. When we get back, you have the missionaries at our house. After dark would be best."

"We should get going," said Chow. "I have work to do, and you all have to get busy. I don't want to know any more. Just do what you need to do to take care of each other." Chow must have felt like an outsider since he was not of their faith, but Matt knew Chow was a good man and obviously believed deeply that bad things were in the works. Chow was not a Mormon—he was really not religious at all—but Matt saw through Chow's actions that Chow had a deep belief in peoples' right to religious freedom. The line between military man and sheriff was getting cloudy. Chow had sworn an allegiance to the Constitution, and he was now going to have to step up.

Bill King asked JR to say a prayer. After a short blessing, they all left the room. Leanne looked at Sally and said, "What can I do to help?"

"If I need you, I will call. We have much to pray about." Sally was trying hard to be strong in front of all of these men. "Mormon women are strong," she said with a laugh. "Just read your history."

The meeting broke up and everyone left but Chow and Matt. Leanne walked out with Sally, arm over her shoulder. They were talking about kids and trying to make life a little more normal.

"Chow, how bad is it?" Matt asked.

"Days, I guess, just days, and martial law will be in effect. They called out the National Guard in Utah, and they broke ranks. Rumor is that the commander at Camp Pendleton ordered all of his marines to ignore commands from Washington. It's a mess." Chow seemed genuinely scared. "The local base is locked down—no one in, no one out. I'm not sure what I am afraid of more, the military following President Prescott's orders, or the military going out on their own."

The men shook hands. Matt slipped the pistol into his belt and picked up the overflowing satchel. "Is there anything you and your family need?" Matt asked Chow. These two were never friends, but events had forced them to trust each other. Chow and Matt often would disagree on the little things in politics, but the big ones, the things that mattered, they agreed on more than they knew.

"No, we are okay. " Chow lived on an old farm out in the county, and if anyone could fend for his family, it was this man. Matt knew Chow and his young family would do OK. Chow went to his car, got in, and sped away. Matt loaded the satchel in the Cadillac, then walked to the back door where Leanne was waving to Sally and the three men in the Suburban.

Matt reached behind him and handed the pistol to Leanne. "You drive the caddy home. I am going to take the shop van." Matt's shop had a Ford Club Wagon that was their courtesy van.

"Why?" Leanne asked.

"Tomorrow we will go to the city to buy food and water and ammo, if we can. I talked to Chow, and he is pretty sure it's going to get much worse very quickly," he told her. "The feds started to call up the National Guard and the Army. Chow said they are refusing to follow orders."

Leanne hugged Matt and gave him a kiss. "Seattle, huh?" she questioned, "We need to stop and see David and Sarah, to see if there is anything they need."

"Yes, I was going to see if you could give them a call, let them know we are coming," Matt replied.

Leanne seemed a bit put out by Matt's making plans without talking to her first, but she knew he had no choice. She climbed into the Cadillac, opened the garage door with the overhead button, quickly started the car and backed out. Matt went back to his office and called Jeremy.

"I am going to be gone for a while, and I would like it if you and your daughter would stay upstairs. Come up here, and bring clothes and whatever else you need." He explained, "There is an envelope on the small desk in the office with some cash in it, so use whatever you need. I need you to take care of the shop. If you could stay here, it would be great. I will make sure I stock the fridge for you and Holley." Holley was Jeremy's daughter, fourteen years old. She was trouble before her parents split, but now she had grown up a bunch, maybe too much.

Matt ended the call. Jeremy had welcomed the chance to move into the upstairs at the shop. Holley would most likely protest, but the free housing and lack of utility bills might give him a chance to catch up financially. Jeremy liked the thought of Holley not being in such a rough neighborhood. Not that Port Smith had really rough neighborhoods, but the apartments they were living in were definitely not in a very nice part of town, and if there was a place in Port Smith that could be called the "ghetto," that was it.

Jeremy had always treated Matt's business as his own, and Matt took care of him when he could, as a friend and a boss. They had a good thing going. Jeremy had fallen on some hard times lately, but a more loyal employee and friend did not exist. Matt locked up the shop and drove off in the Club Wagon knowing that his business and life's work was in good hands, one less thing to worry about in a world falling apart. When he returned home, Matt parked the van around back— not visible from the road—locked it up, and went into the house. Matt really did not want the neighbors involved. The strange thing was, of the few neighbors Matt thought might be home, he had seen none. Come to think of it, Matt and Leanne had not seen any neighbors in a week or more. To some this may seem strange, but when you live in a retirement community, it's not so unusual, especially a community like theirs, full of seasonal residents. Port Smith and the surrounding area had a relatively high cost of living; anyone with multiple homes might opt to stay someplace cheaper with more built-in infrastructure.

Leanne greeted him with a hug and kiss, and then she said, "I called the kids, told them we might be over, but did not want to promise until I knew what you were planning. You did leave me in the dark." Matt had a bad habit of sometimes making plans without first clearing things with his wife.

"Sorry babe, I didn't mean to. It just came together pretty fast."

"Don't let it happen again," Leanne said, smiling as she said it.

Bill King and JR drove by the church slowly and saw a black SUV parked on the south side of the building, most likely the same car that they had seen earlier that day, the one with the federal agents. They drove one block past and pulled down a dirt road, an old access road to the large property behind the church building. This road, or driveway, was often used during church events, as it had access they could use to bring in sports equipment or barbeque supplies for events like Founder's Day. Bill King saw Elder Black leaning against a tree, watching the church.

"Elder, what are you doing?" JR asked, leaning out of the window.

"Waiting for them to leave, and then we can go in," Elder Black said.

"We?" questioned JR, "Who is the *we*, and do you really think that's such a great idea?"

"Elder Miles is across the street with Elder Jones." Elder Black motioned across through the woods.

"Elder Jones? Why isn't he in the hospital?" asked Bishop King with a sense of amazement.

"We left the hospital. Elder Jones is okay." The young man explained that earlier that day, Elder Jones had been moved from the third floor of the hospital down to the first floor. Elders Black and Miles had been sleeping in the lobby, not really knowing what to do. When they had arrived at the hospital with Sheriff Chow and the others, Elders Black and Miles were quickly treated and then told to wait. They had been waiting for hours, maybe even a day. They were hungry and tired, and as time passed, they realized no one was coming to question them, help them, or feed them. Sheriff Chow had left as soon as he saw they were receiving treatment, and then the others left gradually, first the deputies then the EMTs. It seemed as if no one knew what they were supposed to do with the young men.

When Elders Black and Miles saw the nurse had put Elder Jones into a different room, they followed and listened. A nurse was telling an orderly that all of the patients were being moved to the ground floor because most of the staff was not showing up to work. Elder Black had noticed that there were fewer and fewer staff members in the hospital every hour. Apparently, when payday had come and gone for the second time and no one received a check, most of the staff just quit coming in.

Initially, the Sheriff's Office placed a guard on Elder Jones, but the guard had left earlier that day. After the nurse left the room, Elders Black and Miles entered, found Elder Jones's clothes, less his shirt and jacket. They got him dressed, and then Elder Black found a coat closet down the hall, where he found a jacket for Elder Jones. The three of them just walked out of the hospital, and no one seemed to care. Elder Black felt that the fewer people knew where they were, the safer they would be. The hospital was in such a state of disorder and so short-handed that the fate of a couple of Mormon missionaries was apparently not very important to the staff. The young men hoped they could find someplace to go or get some help from the church before anything bad happened. Elder Black was not totally sure what was going on, but he did not trust anyone that was not a member. Even Sheriff Chow, who seemed to be helping them, had left and offered no answers or protection.

The decline in service and employees walking out on the job was really nothing new. It was such old news that it actually seemed odd to the young men that the hospital had any staff at all. To many, the thought of receiving pay or compensation from any government entity was really laughable at this time. Over the last four months, the economy had taken a turn for the worse. The dollar had dropped in value at alarming rates, inflation was nearing hyperinflation, and those who were getting paid were not getting enough to even get them to and from work. When the price of a gallon of gas was higher than the average hourly wage, the decline accelerated; it was a tipping point, of sorts. Attempts at propping up wages with new minimum wage laws just created even more unemployment. The news reports kept telling citizens it was a bump in the road, and that this was the beginning of a great recovery. When Congress could not approve a budget, and the majority in the Senate walked off the floor, it became clear things were going bad. No budget, no continuing resolutions, no funding for any part of the government.

Every day the news seemed to be getting a little less factual in its reporting and adding lot more fluff, such as stories about the President's dog and stories of sex scandals in Congress. Many stopped reading the news, stopped watching the news, and generally stopped believing anything they heard from the government or the media. Survival was the primary concern for most: food, shelter, and safety. It became dangerous to live or work in the cities, as many had little to no law enforcement, and areas in Seattle and Portland had become no-man's land. Cities like Washington, DC and Los Angeles had actually attempted to bring in National Guard, but most did not report for duty. Some Guard units became criminals and looters. The truth was, there was no leadership coming from the top.

Much of the news media had a strong bias toward the President and his administration. The few who had spoken out and questioned what was happening seemed to disappear quite quickly. Very little about what was happening was being reported. Even small towns like Port Smith had a Wild West feel to them. Those who had guns carried them, and those who didn't rarely went out after dark or risked the bad parts of town. Matt was a bit of a news junkie, and he was not a dumb man, but the truth was that the information had become so distorted and so obtuse that even he had almost given up.

When the President gave a press conference, the questions were about his golf game, and rarely was he challenged. In one instance, a reporter deviated from the rule of only previously submitted questions. When Sheppard Smith asked the President what he was going to do to get Congress to work together, he was quickly escorted out of the White House pressroom and subsequently fired from his job. With the exceptions of Fox News, which had gone into a full-out attack campaign and had been banned from the White House, and MSNBC.com, which had gone on a full-out "support-the-President-at-any-cost" campaign, there was little news. The news from the esteemed sources was far from trustworthy. The truth was that there was no real Press, no journalism, just detractors and supporters. No one would cover the dangerous stories. Why risk one's life only to get fired, or worse, disappear, when someone in power did not like what you had to report?

"You walked all the way from the hospital?" Bill King asked the young man.

"Yes, Bishop, it seemed like the best thing to do," responded Elder Black.

Bill sent JR across the street to get the two young men, and then he put Elder Jones in the back of the Suburban. He was doing much better, but it still made sense to keep him down. His wounds needed to heal. Elder Jones was a strong young man, and Bill knew this would lead to his overdoing things. Earlier in the year, Elder Jones had gotten very sick—a bad case of pleurisy had put him in the emergency room. He had gone back to his duties way too early and had a terrible relapse. As Bishop, Bill was responsible for this young man, and he was not going to let him overdo it again. Bill King, if nothing else, was a man with a sense of responsibility. He felt personally responsible for every man, woman, and child in his ward, sometimes to a flaw. Bishop Bill King was exactly what a Mormon Bishop should be: devout, strong, and willing, with a sense of purpose and duty.

JR stayed in the car with Elder Jones. Elders Black and Miles went with the Bishop; they went to the north entrance through the woods and into the Bishop's office.

Stopping at the tree line, Bishop King turned to the two missionaries. "Boys, if anything happens, if anything gets strange, you get out of here, you find your way to Brother Scott's house. Do you understand?"

"Yes." Elder Black seemed to know the Bishop was not kidding around.

Bishop King had a tone neither boy had heard from him before. In fact, it was a tone that Bill King had not used in many years. He was a decorated war veteran, something few people knew and something he never spoke of. Bill King was a young lieutenant in the first Gulf War; he drove tanks as a Marine Corps Reserve officer. It was supposed to be a way to pay for college. Saddam Hussein and President Bush changed that. In 1990, a young Lt. King was sent to war. He understood what it was to be responsible for other people's lives. The young Lieutenant lost several of his men—five, to be exact. His unit was responsible for capturing the airport in Kuwait City. Lieutenant King's M60 tank and the three others in his platoon destroyed over fifty Iraqi T-72s.

He never spoke of these days; there was little pride in his accomplishments. Between his lost marines and the countless numbers of Iraqis he killed or had ordered killed, Bill King had little peace. This was an area that haunted him; he knew in his mind he had done the right thing, that he had done his best. His commanders knew it, too, and awarded him the Silver Star, yet the man who came home to his family never could justify the lives he took. Matt Scott was one of the few people Bill had confided in. Matt had a great respect for the Bishop, and his war service and his feelings about the lives lost was one reason. Some men came back and wallowed in their troubles. Bill King started a family, lived in his religion, and spent little energy on things he could not change. This approach to life and the demons that men have was the same for Matt Scott. "It was what it was," was both men's answer to questions about their past. Once, when questions about their pasts were asked in a church meeting, Matt Scott said clearly, "What I did as a Marine is between me, the Corps, and God." This ended people's questions of Matt Scott. After that meeting, Bill King asked Matt, somewhat in jest, if he could use that line. The two men had an unspoken understanding; details were not needed as so often occurs with men of similar pasts.

Bill King's previous life as a Marine was showing its value again today. Bishop King and the two young missionaries followed a line of trees to the narrowest part of the parking lot. "Just act casual and follow me," the Bishop told the two as he turned and walked toward the building. When the three men crossed the parking lot, they walked with purpose. They did not run, or sneak; they just walked to the side door. Bishop King inserted a key in the door, and the three men entered. As they entered the foyer, the Bishop took a second key and opened his office door. During this time, the sound of people rifling through files and slamming file drawers was coming from the south side of the building. Bishop King entered his office and turned to the two missionaries. He put the index finger of his right hand over his lips and nodded. *Quiet* is what that meant, without a doubt.

Elder Black was feeling energized. His life thus far had been limited to the mission by a promise he had made to his mother. Elder Black had dreamed of becoming a Navy Seal, but his loyalty to his church and family came first. To some degree he welcomed these events. Maybe he could not be a Navy Seal, but he could show he was capable. Elder Black felt alive; he felt like he was making a difference.

Bishop King and Elder Black started by trying to unload file cabinets, quickly realizing that they had little time and too much to move. They looked at each other without a sound, but they were looking for answers. What to do? This was too much to deal with in such a short time. The files would be more than the Suburban could hold, and how could they move them all without being seen?

Elder Miles was watching quietly, studying the actions and words of the other two, much like a cat watches a bird. To some degree this made both Bishop King and Elder Black nervous. Very quietly, and deliberately, Elder Miles slipped out of the room and went down the hall toward the front of the church building. He quickly returned with a green-colored gas igniter, the kind one buys for a fireplace or gas stove. The young man had gone to the kitchen and returned with a solution.

"Yes, yes," said the Bishop very quietly. "We will burn the files. Elder Black, get the hard drives out of the computers. I will go shut off the water to the sprinklers." Bill King then went outside to the main water control valves inside a small area surrounded by a chain-link fence. He knew this system well, as he had helped work on it when the church was built. The Bishop then did something he never thought he would do. He turned off the water to the fire suppression system, returned to his office, and proceeded to prepare for arson. Bishop King loved this church, not just the LDS Church, but this building. When the building was built and later renovated, he had put in countless hours. It was a home away from home, one he had part in building in many ways. Bishop King had worked for years not only to build a structure, but a congregation, a community of sorts. The idea that, of all men, Bill King would burn this building seemed very wrong, but much like a retreating army, he was not going to leave anything in his wake that would benefit his enemy. The safety of his congregation was much more important than bricks and steel. This would be the Port Smith Ward's own scorched earth campaign, like the Czars against Napoleon or Saddam Hussein in the Kuwaiti oil fields. Bishop King would sacrifice fire damage and maybe even the whole building for the good of his community.

Elder Black had three hard drives and a box of CDs. Elder Miles was quickly and quietly pulling file drawers open and placing handfuls of shredded paper on each one. Within two or three minutes, they were ready. Bishop King went to the supply cabinet, pulled out a large bottle of toner, and poured the dark powder on the piles of shredded paper and into the file drawers. He took the igniter in his right hand and turned to the boys. "You two, get to JR and Elder Jones, and I will be right behind you."

The two young men made their way across the parking lot and back to the tree line, and then they stopped and watched for the Bishop. Elder Black was disobeying his Bishop, but he wanted to be able to help him if needed.

Bill King looked around, and then he dropped to his knees and said a prayer. Not realizing how loudly he was praying, he poured his heart out. "Heavenly Father, please guide me. Please, Father, forgive me if that which I am about to do is against Your will. Heavenly Father, I do these things for Your children. Please grant me grace. I ask these things in the name of Your Son, Jesus Christ."

As Bill King rose to his feet, he had tears streaming down his face. He paused for a moment and then began to light each pile of paper in each file drawer. It seemed like it took forever, and by the time he lit the last drawer, the smoke was pouring out of the office door and the alarm was sounding. The sprinkler head clicked loudly and dripped one drop of water. Bill king dropped the igniter and backed out of the office. The toner not only flashed with heat, but also created a dark, caustic smoke. Bill was coughing and choking as he stepped back toward the door.

It did not take long for the two agents in the south office to realize what was happening. They quickly left the office and headed through the chapel to get to the other side of the church, where Bill King was barring the chapel doors with a coat rack that had stood by the front door since the church opened. He watched the two federal agents for a split second as they ran toward him. He could see them through the small window in the left door, and he noticed they each had a fire extinguisher in hand. He ran out of the north entrance a moment later and headed toward the trail in the woods. Smoke poured out of the doors and windows behind him, and the loud bell of the fire alarm was ringing. The two missionaries turned and ran toward the green Suburban as soon as they saw him. They could hear the agents yelling in the background over the sound of fire alarm bells. The black smoke was rolling out the doors and roof vents. It looked much worse than it was—the smoke and the fumes from the toner gave the office fire the appearance that the entire building was burning.

"You can't do this; we know who you are. We will find you!" This was the first time anyone had heard the shorter man. The shorter, more in-charge man had yet to speak, and the sound of his voice seemed to bring fear to those around him.

Bill King did not have long. The agents were backtracking and going around the building; and by now they did not have fire extinguishers in their hands, they had government-issue Berretta 9mm pistols, and they were intending to use them.

Elders Black and Miles came bursting through the woods onto the gravel road; they opened a rear door on the Suburban and dove in.

"Start the car, now!" yelled Elder Black.

Bill King came bounding out of the woods on the same trail, and then he jumped into the open passenger door and slammed it behind him.

"Go, go!" Bill was coughing as he yelled, black soot covered his face, and he smelled of burnt chemicals.

JR dropped the Suburban into gear and sped away, spraying the trailhead with gravel as the two agents came out of the tree line.

"Get down, boys," yelled the bishop.

As JR navigated the Suburban around the corner to the highway in a full power slide, the sound of pistol fire was heard behind them. Right or wrong, it was done, and now they all were in some serious trouble if they got caught. There was a feeling of jubilation in the car; no one wanted to celebrate. They acted somber, but each of them felt a sense of victory. Elder Black cracked a little smile and said, "Now that's *my* kind of mission." The Suburban roared off toward the north end of town. Looking out the mirror, JR could see a cloud of smoke billowing up from the church. He was confident that the brick building would not burn and that the fire would be contained to the office.

CHAPTER FIVE

Matt and Leanne spent the early evening at their house, planning their trip for the next day. They had plenty of cash and a van to haul supplies, because if they were going to be housing three teenage boys, they would need to stock up. Matt and Leanne also had a feeling that things were only going to get worse; it was not possible to be over-prepared. Leanne had come to realize that Matt had an internal need to always be prepared, especially when it came to food. Matt's desire to stock up or, as some would say, hoard food, was not a product of his days as a Mormon, but a product of his childhood. When Matt was young, he and his brother and sisters where raised by a single mother. During hard times they often went hungry; years later it was his own baggage that kept the cupboards overfull. Matt had long ago vowed that he and the people he loved would never go hungry again. He also kept water, ammunition, fuel, and other supplies. Some thought him strange, maybe a survivalist or a doomsday planner. The truth was that he had done without; he had been homeless and hungry and would do whatever it took to prevent these things from happening to his family. Was it pride or fear? Even Matt did not know, but either way, it was how he lived his life.

With all of the stress of the past days, a little time alone together was long overdue. In some strange way, the sense of adventure and danger was exciting and made the couple feel young and alive—a touch of a Bonnie and Clyde syndrome, maybe. The couple was missing their quiet time, their alone time. Matt and Leanne enjoyed spending their spare time together—girls' night out or guys' poker night seemed counterintuitive to them. It had been a few days since the two of them could just be at home with no outside world encroaching on their happiness.

The two had been making an inventory in the kitchen as Leanne started to prepare dinner. Leanne was mixing ricotta cheese with fresh spinach and her secret blend of spices. She was standing at the bar with her hands deep in a large glass bowl, kneading and mixing. Matt always teased her that she had every kitchen gadget known to man but still did things the old-fashioned way. Matt had bought a pasta machine for Leanne last Christmas, the best machine he could find. But to his dismay, she still made her pasta by hand, and the machine sat in its box in the pantry. The KitchenAid mixer sat clean and unused at the end of the long counter, a drawer was full of spatulas and cutters and assorted cooking tools, yet Leanne's hands seemed to be the only tool needed.

"Get me some manicotti out of the pantry, would you?" Leanne asked Matt, as she had cheese, spinach, and various contents of the filling she was making all over her hands. Matt brought a box of manicotti shells; he opened it and laid each tube-like piece of pasta on the counter. Then Matt pulled a large glass baking dish out and coated it in olive oil. The two loved to cook together. When they started dating they would often just go to each other's homes and cook meals together. The time would pass, and before they knew it, a three-course meal was prepared, and only the two of them to eat it, neither with much of an appetite by that time. The freezer was always full of dinners, desserts, and snacks. When kids or family would visit, they always left with boxes of food. Neither Matt nor Leanne had mastered the art of cooking for two. When work ran late, or the gym or needs of a child or friend interfered with their schedule, it was nice to have freezer food, as Leanne called it. This explained why a home with only two occupants had to have two freezers in the garage.

As Leanne stuffed the pasta, Matt arranged it in the pan and poured sauce over it. Everyone thought Leanne had some secret sauce recipe; the truth was they used sauce from a jar with a few added seasonings.

"Three fifty?" Matt asked Leanne.

"You ask every time, and every time, yes, it's still three fifty," Leanne said with a laugh.

They put dinner in the oven and Leanne washed up. While the pasta was baking, Leanne worked on laundry, dishes, and the other household chores that got left for the end of the day or even end of the week when life got busy.

As the last load of laundry was put away and the smell of Manicotti wafted through the house, Matt went to the wine rack in the dining room and picked out a bottle for dinner. Matt loved wine. He was not trained, was no expert, but he knew what he liked and made a habit of having plenty of it around. This was one of many things that were at odds with his Mormon background. Matt often said that good wine and good scotch is proof that God exists.

Leanne pulled the dinner from the oven and dished up two plates, which she carried to the table. Matt uncorked a nice domestic Cabernet, and they sat down to dinner. The house was quiet, and the two felt at ease. Much was happening in their lives, but tonight things would be as they should—just the two of them, a nice dinner, a glass of wine—a romantic evening. The two rarely prayed, but tonight Leanne reached across the table and put her hands in her husband's. She bowed her head and sat quietly, a smile on her face. Matt bowed his head and spoke aloud. "Heavenly Father, we give thanks for the blessings You have bestowed upon us." *Simple and to the point.* "Amen," the couple said quietly in unison. Leanne pulled her hands back slowly and looked up at her husband. "I love you." She paused for a moment and then with a slight giggle said, "Let's eat, I'm starved!" Before Matt could respond to the moment, forks and knives were rattling. Matt just sat back and smiled, for a moment looking at his wife as she dug into her meal.

She looked up at him suddenly. "What?" she asked.

Matt smiled. "I love you, too." Not much else to say.

During dinner they talked about the kids and the future. There was no talk about the craziness that had gone on the previous days or the extreme changes they saw on the horizon. Matt and Leanne dealt with stress by living their lives as they chose. When life got stressful, they had a habit of retreating to an evening of just the two of them—it recharged their batteries. Leanne called it "compartmentalizing," Matt just knew it was a good way to live: when life was hard, live in the moment. The moments were good and helped put perspective on the big picture. A happier or more in-love couple would be hard to find, and this may have been why the Church picked the Scotts to help. It sure was not the full wine racks or fully stocked bar or the gourmet coffee machine. The Scotts were definitely not a poster family for the Mormon Church.

After dinner and a second glass of wine, Matt cleared the table and washed the dishes. Leanne took the leftovers and started to package them up in small portions.

"Honey, maybe we should just put it all in the fridge. Remember, missionaries are coming, and they will want more than that."

"I forgot for a moment. I was going to make lunches." Leanne smiled. "Not like I'm going to work soon, or you either."

She placed foil over the pan and put in the fridge.

"Enough food to feed an army, an army of missionaries," Leanne said with a smile.

Matt had been cooking for the young men of the Church for some time. Before Matt and Leanne became a couple, back when Matt lived alone, cooking and meals with the missionaries was therapeutic for him. Matt Scott did not like living alone and enjoyed the company. The presence of the missionaries softened the transition from marriage and children to empty nest and divorce. When Matt and Leanne were married, the missionary dinners became less frequent for Matt. In some ways Matt missed them. He was looking forward to having the young men at the dinner table once more. After reviewing past year's expenses, Leanne said Matt should have written off those costs on his taxes, as it seemed he spent more on groceries than a family of five. After dinner he would usually send them home with a cake, a pie, or a batch of cookies. Matt often joked that when you saw a fat missionary you knew he was just transferred from Port Smith.

The kitchen was clean, the chores were done, the sun was down, and the two went off to their room. The world was falling apart outside, but in the Scott house life was perfect, or at least it was for the night.

Again the morning started with the beeping of the alarm clock, but this time Leanne was first up. She brought two cups of coffee when she came back into the bedroom.

"Sweetie, we have to get going."

Matt growled a little, sat up, and reached for the coffee. After five or ten minutes of sitting on the bed, drinking coffee, and watching the sun come up, the two got up and headed to the shower, but only after Leanne pointed out that they were on a schedule. "No lazy bones today. You need to get up and moving." The couple showered and got dressed. Leanne packed a road-trip bag, and Matt put some things in his satchel.

The drive to Seattle would take about three hours if all went well. Leanne had her little bag of snacks and bottled water. Matt had put a large amount of cash in his satchel, and he'd put his colt 1911 in a shoulder holster and two extra magazines in the carrier on his belt. Leanne had put her pistol in her purse. "Look at us, we are just like Bonnie and Clyde," Matt said.

"Keys, wallet, phone," Leanne said like she did every time they left the house, ignoring the Bonnie and Clyde comment. Matt touched his wallet, looked at his phone, and rattled his keys. They walked out the back of the house, and Matt locked the door and set the alarm. Matt got into the van with a cup of coffee. Leanne climbed into the passenger seat, and the two were off. The auto repair manager and insurance administrator were armed like cowboys and off to town to get supplies. They both saw the humor in it. Humor was a good way to avoid the uneasy feeling they had that made it necessary to leave the house armed. Matt maneuvered the van up the driveway and out of the cul-de-sac, heading for the city.

The drive was quiet. It was early, and there were very few cars on the road. As they crossed the Hood Canal Bridge, they noticed a black Chevy Tahoe parked at either end. Both SUVs had smoked windows and US government plates.

"Wonder who they are looking for?" Leanne asked Matt, but she knew the answer, and it was a bit unsettling.

Matt never acknowledged her question; he just drove right on. There was a sense that things would not go as planned.

After crossing the bridge and turning right, Matt noticed another dark SUV following them. "You think they could drive something other than a black Tahoe," Matt said with concern in his voice, trying to make light of an increasingly concerning situation.

As they neared the next town, traffic was picking up, and by the time they had traveled another four or five miles, they were in a true traffic jam.

"I wonder what's causing this." Leanne often spoke her thoughts out loud when stressed or worried.

Within moments they could see. There were at least four or five of the black SUVs parked along the road, several county sheriffs' cars, and a tow truck. They were stopping every car and asking questions; occasionally they would open a trunk and search a car.

Matt pulled up in the line of cars, and a man in khaki uniform shirt walked up to the window. Matt rolled it down.

"Can I help you?" Matt asked.

"Where are you headed?" The man in khaki asked.

"The city, Costco, and a few other places. Why?" Matt was trying hard to not be short, but he felt seriously violated by the whole thing.

"Well, we are looking for some people; I think we need to check your van."

Matt looked at Leanne. He was worried that if they searched him and Leanne they would find the guns. Both Leanne and Matt had permits, but he did not think that would matter. The police often did not care about a concealed carry permit. Matt had had a gun taken from him during a traffic stop once. Only after hiring a lawyer was he able to retrieve his gun and get an apology from the sheriff's office. Matt had little trust in the protection of his rights, and he knew that if they found the guns, legal or not, it would mean trouble.

"Who are you looking for?" Leanne asked.

"Just open the van, ma'am," responded the deputy. He walked around the van and opened the sliding door. He climbed in and looked under the seats and in the back between the seats. It was clear he was looking for a person or people and would have no reason to look in a purse or under Matt's coat.

"All clear!" he yelled out.

"You two should get home. You never know, they may close the bridge," the deputy said, looking at Leanne with concern.

Matt took this warning to heart. "We will be heading home as soon as we can," Matt responded.

The young officer waved him through the checkpoint and immediately went about searching the car behind them.

"Wonder if we should make a change of plans?" Matt asked Leanne. "Maybe we should not go so far as Seattle."

"But the kids, I was hoping to see the kids," Leanne sadly responded. She knew it was not going to happen; she knew that it was not a good idea to travel so far today.

"Call them. They will understand." Matt was genuinely concerned for their safety, and Leanne could hear it in his voice.

Leanne called David's house. She spoke for a few minutes to both David and Sarah, and spent a few additional moments on the phone with each of the grandkids.

"They are fine; David did not want us to risk driving that far anyway. He said the gas station down the street is only selling gas for cash, and the others in town are closed or out of gas, so we might get stranded." Leanne could feel at ease: David and Sarah were safe and had everything they needed.

"So that means we get everything we need here." The town they were nearing had a Costco and a Wal-Mart. Matt first pulled into Wal-Mart. The parking lot was full, and there seemed to be a run on the store. There was chaos, people were yelling and running about, fights were breaking out all across the parking lot. The noise from the crowd was amazingly loud, and people were pushing and shoving at the front door.

"Maybe I should go check to see what's up." Matt parked the van and walked toward the front door, leaving Leanne in the passenger seat.

As he got close, Matt saw what looked like chaos going on inside, people were stocking up on everything, and the shelves were nearly bare. Matt did not want to waste his time in an empty store, so he turned and walked quickly back to the van.

"Well, we are too late, and I bet Costco is just as bad," he told Leanne as he buckled back into the driver's seat.

"What about the restaurant supply store—you remember—the wholesale place we found?" Leanne had hosted a large event for work earlier that year. When they went to buy the food they needed, they went to a wholesale food supplier that one of her clients had told her of.

"Good idea," Matt said, wondering if the place would even be open. Matt was worried it was their last chance to stock up.

Matt started the van and drove away from the chaos at Wal-Mart, turning down a side road. It was about three miles to an industrial park between Bremerton and Silverdale, Washington. They had only been to the warehouse once before, but Matt was confident he could find it again.

"There it is on the right." Leanne pointed at a group of warehouses.

In the warehouse parking lot, he saw a van similar to his being loaded at the back door. There were a few delivery trucks on the far end of the parking lot, but overall the place looked abandoned, with the exception of the one van being loaded. Matt drove up beside it and rolled down his window. Before he could say a word, the young man spoke.

"We're closed," he said as he tossed boxes into the van. The young man looked to be about eighteen, fairly tall, and fit. He was a redhead and was acting as if he had a chip on his shoulder.

"We just…" Matt tried to speak, but was interrupted immediately.

"I said we are closed!" The young man turned and faced the van. "This is private property, and you need to leave."

Matt and Leanne had not eaten breakfast, and Matt had only had a piece of a cookie from Leanne's snack bag. The blood sugar issue was starting to show its face, combined with worry and frustration. Leanne could see Matt's fuse was short. Matt backed the van up twenty feet and stopped; he put the van in park and shut it off.

"Let me talk to him," Leanne said. She unhooked her seat belt and stepped out of the van as she spoke. Before Leanne closed the door, she turned to Matt, smiled, and said, "Blood sugar, sweetie."

Matt was not happy with the situation. His wife should not be out there dealing with this rude young man, but Matt also knew that she was a strong woman. Besides, Leanne was not one to back down when she had made up her mind. This time he would have to bite his lip and let her try to talk to the young man.

Leanne walked over to the young man quickly; she was talking to him as she walked. Matt could not hear a word but could see they were exchanging words; he was very uneasy. Matt slowly pulled his colt 45 out of the shoulder holster and laid it on his lap. He watched as Leanne spoke. The boy spoke and then pointed into the warehouse. The conversation between Leanne and the young man seemed to be coming to end. Leanne was looking slightly frustrated as she turned and walked toward the van. Matt saw what looked like empathy in the boy's face, but he still felt very uneasy about the entire situation. Leanne walked up to the van, opened the passenger door, and climbed in. She closed the door soundly and looked at Matt.

"It's no use. He said his dad has him picking up stuff for the family, but that they are closed down. He made it sound like they are out of business," Leanne said. Her statement sounded almost like a question, as if she was confused by the whole thing.

Matt picked up his pistol and handed it to Leanne, and then he opened the door and stepped out of the van. Leanne wanted to say something to him, but Matt closed the door and walked deliberately toward the young man before she had a chance. Now Leanne was worried. Matt had that look—he was not taking no for answer. She was worried but was grateful he had left his gun behind.

"I told the lady we can't help you," the young man said to Matt, and then he reached for a box and tossed it in the van. Studying the young man, Matt noticed a ring on his left ring finger. The ring was a familiar, a CTR ring. The CTR ring is a ring worn by young, devout Mormons. The letters on the ring mean Choose The Right. This was an in; Matt knew could use his knowledge of the ring to get the young man to open up.

"Little risky wearing that ring nowadays, brother," Matt said.

The young man looked shocked and a bit scared. "Why do you say that? It's just a ring."

"It's not just a ring, I know what it means, and I know it could be dangerous in this day and age." Matt was trying to sound fatherly as he responded, but the frustration and anger was coming out in his voice instead, scaring the young man.

Now Matt had a bit more control of the situation. The young man was LDS; that was without a doubt. It seemed to be his parents' business, so that meant their family was LDS. Matt knew if he played his cards right, he might just get what he needed.

"Son, we are looking for food stores to take care of some missionaries." Matt was playing all of his cards at once. This was either going to get him in with the young man or make matters much worse.

"Wait here." The young man went into the warehouse. Had he scared him away? Had he gone for help? Or had Matt made matters worse? The young man returned in moments with a tall, bald man in coveralls.

"My name is Earl Kimball, and this is my son, Levi," the older man said. "And you are?"

"Matthew Scott, from Port Smith Ward." Again Matt was playing the Mormon card heavily.

"And your businesses here?" Mr. Kimball asked firmly.

Now Matt had to make a decision: Should he tell the whole story? The more people that knew about the missionaries, and that the Scott home was a sanctuary of sorts, the more danger everyone was in. Matt needed this man's help; maybe it was time to take a chance.

"Brother, I am here for supplies, food stores. I would rather not give you the details, but I have cash." Matt was buying time.

"You use all the right words, but how do I know I can trust you?" Mr. Kimball asked.

"You know my name and where I live; that puts me and my wife at risk enough. There are others, and I don't know if I can share too much information. It's not that I don't trust you. I just can't risk it." Matt was hinting but had decided that they would do without supplies before he risked the missionaries and his family any further.

Earl Kimball nodded his head; he put his arm around his son and looked Matt in the eye. "Brother, I am not sure why, but I think I need to help you. Son, you open up number two loading dock and get this man what he needs."

Matt was taken aback. "I have money. I will pay," Matt stressed.

"Money means nothing to me anymore. We are leaving. The government froze all of my accounts, and they put a lock on my business. The only reason I am here is they had a local policeman guarding the place and he left yesterday, told me he had not been paid in a month. I filled his patrol car with food, and he quit his job." Earl Kimball then reached into his pocket and showed Matt a badge. "The young man tossed it out the window of his car as he drove away," he said, shaking his head.

Matt gestured to Leanne. He pointed at the roll-up door that was opening one down from where the men were standing. Leanne slid over to the driver's seat, started the van, and backed it up to the door.

Leanne climbed out of the van, and Matt quickly introduced her. "My wife, Leanne. Leanne, this is Brother Kimball." Matt was hoping Leanne caught the need to be church-like. Matt felt a little uneasy leading Earl Kimball to believe he was an active Mormon, but in truth Matt had not lied, maybe misled, but not lied.

"Sister Scott, you tell my son Levi what you need. If we have it, he will load it up."

Leanne looked at Matt. She caught on very quickly and she was not going to confuse matters. "Thank you, Brother," she said a bit unsure. Leanne almost played the part too hard; she bowed her head slightly and acted a bit subservient. Not Mormon-like at all, Matt thought. More like an Amish or Quaker wife.

Leanne and Levi went into the warehouse and disappeared into aisles of shelves filled with food and boxes.

Matt turned to Earl and asked, "Is there anything you need? Anything we can do for you?"

"Just pray for us, Brother, just pray," Earl responded.

Levi and Leanne returned, each pushing a hand truck loaded with boxes and number-five cans of food.

Earl and Matt quickly loaded the van, not even looking at what was in the boxes. Leanne and Levi returned five or six more times. Cases of dry goods, large fifty-pound bags of flour, and more cases of dry pasta and canned sauces kept coming until the van could hold no more.

"Let me pay you something," Matt said to Earl as he reached into his pocket and pulled out four gold coins. "Not necessary," said Earl.

"Look, you have a family to take care of, and you may need these to get past a checkpoint. They are stopping people on the highway, you know?" Matt was genuinely concerned. While they were loading the van, Earl had let it slip that he and his family were heading for Utah as soon as he and his son returned with provisions. Earl looked at Matt as he considered, and then he reached for the gold pieces. Matt dropped three of them into his hand.

"I will keep one, just in case we get stopped on the way home," said Matt.

"God bless you," said Earl. "Levi, let's get going." Levi rolled down the loading dock door, slammed the back door of their van, and climbed into the driver's seat. Earl rolled down the loading dock door behind Matt and Leanne's van and turned toward the couple.

"You two be careful, and stay off the highways." Earl paused with emotion on his face and in his voice. "God bless you."

Earl looked sad, but determined. He had a family to tend to. "God bless you and your family," Leanne blurted out as he walked away toward his van. "God bless you," she said again in a quiet voice.

Earl Kimball was leaving a life's work, his business, and his community; the loss could be seen on his face.

Matt and Leanne closed the side door on the van and climbed into their respective seats.

As Matt started the van and put it in gear, Leanne asked, "Now what? How do we get home?"

"Back roads, luck, and the grace of God," Matt responded with a smile on his face. "I don't think we should risk heading back toward the bridge. If we get stopped again, we might not be so lucky," he continued.

There was one primary way to get from the mainland to the peninsula, and that was across the Hood Canal floating bridge, and the route was already plugged with roadblocks. The other option was to drive 101 around the Hood Canal, and that route would most likely have less activity, as there was little to no population in the area. Matt also knew that he could take old forest service roads and logging roads to stay off the main road if he took this route. Matt knew the area well; he had hunted deer and also ridden his mountain bike on many of the old roads off Highway 101.

"The canal road; that's our best bet." Matt was thinking out loud.

Leanne knew this meant three hours of driving at least. This was not a good thing, but it seemed the best option.

The drive back was long, but pretty much uneventful until they hit the town of Lilliwaup, a little town on the Hood Canal. As Matt and Leanne drove up the canal, traffic started to appear sporadically. Up to this point an occasional car or motorcycle passed them, but overall no traffic. In Lilliwaup there was a motorhome pulled over by two police cars—one state patrol car and one county sheriff's car. As Matt went by, the state trooper turned and made eye contact with him. The state trooper was a short Hispanic man, and he looked like he was not very happy, his Smokey Bear hat tipped down over his scowling face.

Matt drove on. "That looks like trouble," he said to Leanne.

"I hope not. We are so close," Leanne responded.

Matt rounded another switchback corner a hundred yards down the road, and as he did he slowly pulled off the side of the road into a driveway.

"What are you doing?" Leanne asked, slightly panicked.

"Just buying some time, and making sure," Matt responded without looking up from his side-view mirror. Matt was watching to see who would come up the road behind them.

Within moments they heard the sound of a roaring engine. Matt pulled forward and paralleled the road on the side driveway; there was a line of cedar trees between him and the road. Matt shut off the engine and sat watching his mirror. A few moments later, the state patrol car came around the corner, quickly followed by the sheriff's car. Neither had sirens on, and both were moving very quickly.

"How did you know?" Leanne asked once they were past.

"Eye contact. That trooper looked at me like he wanted something. I don't think those two cops were on the up and up. How often do you see a county mounty and a state trooper working together?" Matt asked.

Matt started the van and backed out of the driveway. He turned and headed up the canal, following the route taken by the two patrol cars.

"Now what?" Leanne asked.

"There is a forest service road about a mile north; we should make it before they turn around." Matt was planning out loud.

In the middle of a long, straight stretch, Matt slowed the van and turned onto a dirt road. This road would be missed by most; it was not clearly marked and had grass growing in the median between the highway and the road. Matt made an effort to drive the van as slowly as possible so the van wouldn't kick up dust. Leanne sat quietly watching her mirror, worried about the two patrol cars.

Matt was right. No sooner had they turned onto the forest service road then the two patrol cars came back down the highway. The state patrol car was leading the way as the two went by at high speed, light bar on, again with no siren. They were looking for the van; with local knowledge and luck, Matt and Leanne had avoided the confrontation.

The rest of the drive was long. Matt and Leanne had left the house early that morning, and now it looked like they would be lucky to get home before dark. Matt was driving slowly, and Leanne had fallen asleep in the passenger seat. Matt turned the radio on and was scanning the AM band. Nothing but static until finally he came upon George Noory, the radio host, and Matt turned it up.

Leanne woke up and said, "Not that nut," with a smile.

George Noory was doing a show on the influence of space visitors on the White House, "That explains everything," Matt said with a laugh. Of course, it was a rebroadcast of a show from sometime in the 90s. The radio host was talking of a past president, one that was not only out of power but dead at this time.

"You must be starving," Leanne said with concern. "Stop for a minute, and I will get us something out of the back."

Matt stopped the van long enough for Leanne to rustle through a box and come out with a large can of Chef Boyardee ravioli.

"Now to open it." Leanne used the P-38 opener that she kept on her key chain, a gift that Matt's mother had given Leanne for their wedding. Matt's grandfather served in World War II, and this was the only memento he had kept to remember the war. Grandpa had given it to his daughter when she got married. "You never know when you're going to need to open a can," he said. To most this seemed strange, but to a man who lived through the depression, he was giving his daughter a survival tool. It meant a lot to Leanne that her mother-in-law had gifted her small but important piece of history. And grandpa would be proud. He was right; you never know when you're going to need to open a can.

Leanne unfolded the small tool and pressed the sharp edge into the can. Matt started driving slowly as Leanne sawed at the can lid. When the can lid was successfully removed, they took turns dipping into the can and pulling out raviolis. Eating with their bare hands was messy, and before long they were both laughing hysterically. After about fifteen minutes, and some well-needed nutrients, Leanne pulled out a large bottle of water. They shared the first half of the bottle and then stopped the van again to use the rest to wash the red sauce from their hands. Both had managed to get sauce all over the front of their shirts, but neither seemed too concerned. They just wanted to get home. The steering wheel was sticky, and they were a mess, but their bellies were full and they were heading home.

The van they drove was not very comfortable and was not very fast. But it had what they needed: it carried a lot of weight; it had good ground clearance for the rough roads; and it had a forty-gallon gas tank, which was the only reason they made it home. It was after 10:00 p.m. when Matt turned the van off a gravel road and onto the county highway. They were less than a mile from home, and it looked like they were going to make it.

"I wonder if Earl Kimball and his family are OK," Matt thought out loud.

"I am sure they are. What a wonderful man," Leanne said with a very tired smile.

Matt turned the van down the road toward their home, and the low-fuel light blinked on the dash. Matt pulled down the driveway and stopped in front of the garage. He could see a young man waiting in the dark, and then he saw two more. It was the missionaries; they had been waiting outside all evening.

"I'll get the garage door," Leanne said as she stepped from the van. She opened the side door with her key and turned the alarm off. The door opened, and Matt pulled the van in beside the Cadillac.

"Come on, boys, get in here," Matt said as he stepped out of the van.

The three missionaries stood inside the garage, Leanne was at the front of the van, and Matt stood beside the driver's door as the garage door closed. As the door went down, the room illuminated, as the raised door no longer blocked the fluorescent light hanging from the ceiling. The look on the missionaries' faces was that of horror.

"What happened? Are you OK?" Elder Black asked in a panicked voice.

Elders Jones and Miles just stared at Matt and Leanne. And for a moment, neither Matt nor Leanne had a clue what was going on. Then Matt turned to his wife and saw that she had red sauce all over her shirt and on her face. Matt looked down at his shirt and started to laugh.

"Ravioli," he said out loud. Leanne started to laugh too. The three young men stood there, horrified, until Leanne went around to the passenger side, opened the door, and produced an empty ravioli can from the floor.

"Ravioli," she said, pointing at her shirt.

Elders Jones and Black broke out into laughter; Elder Miles managed a small, crooked smile.

They had made it home. The missionaries were safe, they had reason to believe their kids were safe, and now it was time to get some rest. They could collapse after they washed the ravioli off. A hot shower would feel good after such a long day.

Leanne went through the house to the back bedroom. The Scotts had a two-bedroom house. The spare room was fairly large and had a queen-size bed and a twin with a trundle bed under it. Leanne made the beds up, and then she set out towels and other things the young men might need. Not knowing how long their stay would be, she wanted to give them a sense of safety and belonging.

In the garage, Matt started to unload the van. Elders Black and Miles helped him.

"Elder Jones, you need to go in and have my wife check out your wounds," Matt said. "Let's make sure you're OK before we work you too hard."

"Brother Scott, I can't go in there alone. You know the rules. We can't be left alone with a female. We are on mission."

"Elder Jones, the church rules may not apply right now. We need to take care of ourselves, and I am going to be damned if I have to chaperone you every time I leave any of you alone with Leanne." The statement was firm enough that it was not to be questioned.

LDS missionaries have some very strict rules pertaining to being alone with the opposite sex; the Church does what it can to avoid scandal. They also have rules pertaining to water sports, boating, and entertainment. Matt Scott was fairly aware of the rules, but he also felt that rules have a time and a place, and this was neither.

"OK, boys, we need to have a sit-down meeting, all of us," Matt said with a sigh. "Let's all go in and get this figured out."

The three missionaries and Matt went into the dining room; Matt sat at the table and directed the others to do the same. Leanne came out to see what was going on, putting a pillow into a fresh pillowcase as she walked.

"Leanne, we need to figure some stuff out." Matt pointed at the empty chair at the table.

Elder Black asked, "May we open in prayer?"

"Rule number one: in this house we pray when we choose. You do not need to ask my permission," Matt said.

Elder Black smiled and looked toward the other two missionaries. Elder Black was clearly acting as the leader in this small group.

"Heavenly Father, please direct us in your works, guide us through our troubles, and give us the strength required to persevere. Father, bless the Scott family and all the families affected by these times of trouble. We ask this in the name of Jesus Christ, Your Son. Amen."

"Now, let's get down to business." Matt took charge and set the tone. "First, boys, we cannot live by the rules of your mission, we will be in close quarters for who knows how long. When it comes to rules of the house, well, Leanne can you take this?"

Leanne leaned forward placing her hands onto the table, pushing the pillow she was carrying aside. "Well, OK, it's simple. You clean up after yourself, we all respect each other's space, you eat at meal time, and you do the chores Matt and I ask you to do." It's no different from when the kids were home, Matt thought.

Matt chimed in. "As far as religion and Church rules, well, Mrs. Scott has never been a Mormon. So I ask that you understand that this is our home. We will try to respect your needs, and you respect ours."

"So do you think we should just ignore our mission?" Elder Black stated the question quite seriously.

"Your mission has changed, Elders. We have no idea what is coming next, but I can assure you that your mission has changed. You must live within your beliefs. But again, being a missionary may have a whole new meaning now."

It was clear that Leanne was fine with things. She had work to do, and she was acting much like a doting mother. Matt was OK with things. It was the young men who seemed unsure. Elders Jones and Miles were looking to Elder Black for direction.

Elder Black stood up at the table, looking sad. "I am senior on mission, so I can say, Brother and Sister Scott, this is your house and we will respect that. All we ask is that we are given a place to worship and study, a place with as little outside influence as possible. "

"It's simple. We communicate, we respect each other, and this will all work out," Matt interjected.

Leanne got up. "Enough talking. We have work to do." She picked up the pillow and headed back toward the back bedroom.

"Leanne, honey, can you take a look at Elder Jones? I am worried about that wound."

"Elder Jones, I wish we could use your first name." Leanne paused, looking at the young man. "Come, take your shirt off and sit on the couch. I need to see that bandage." Elder Jones did as he was told, though he blushed a little from embarrassment.

Leanne took several trips to the master bathroom, returning with gauze, hydrogen peroxide, and Q-tips. She removed the dressing and cleaned the wound, and determined that it was healing quite well. Leanne then redressed the wound with gauze and surgical tape, and then she gently wrapped an ace bandage around the young man's middle to ensure the gauze would stay in place.

While Leanne took care of the wounded young Elder, Matt and Elders Black and Miles unloaded the van. They took boxes of food and stored them in the pantry until it was full. Then they began storing food in the hall closets and even under the stairs. The stairs led down to the back of the garage to a patio and small office/sunroom. It seemed like it took the three of them an hour or more, as Leanne had managed to acquire much more food than Matt had realized. No wonder the van felt so heavy when he was driving back home.

As the three finished in the garage, Matt opened the overhead door and pulled the van out. He parked the van around the back of the house again and locked it up. When Matt returned to the garage, Elders Black and Miles were waiting. "I hate to ask, but we have not eaten today," Elder Black said.

"Let's go get you fed. Don't ever be afraid to ask, Elder. Come on, boys. Chop, chop…" Matt was trying to keep the mood light. It was amazing that none of the three missionaries had fallen apart. Elder Miles had gotten very quiet, but that was to be expected. They had been through hell. They should be a mess by now.

When the three entered the dining area, Leanne was just finishing in the bedroom. Elder Jones had put a large pot of water on the stove to boil. It was obvious that he was following instructions from Mrs. Scott.

Leanne came into the kitchen and began giving directions to Matt and the three houseguests. Before long, a large bowl of spaghetti was on the table, along with a spinach salad and a pitcher of juice. Matt opened a bottle of wine and set out a glass for each.

"We can't drink that," stated Jones.

"It's for the juice, silly. You three will have juice," Leanne pointed out.

Two of the three missionaries looked relieved by the fact the wine glasses were for juice, but Elder Miles looked a little disappointed.

This time Matt said a prayer before the meal, something he had only done maybe two or three times since he and Leanne had been together. It was a bit awkward, but he felt good about showing his wife that he still had faith.

After dinner, Matt and Leanne cleaned the kitchen and tended to the dishes. They were not surprised that there were no leftovers.

The three missionaries went to their room to clean up and get settled in. On occasion, Matt and Leanne could hear Elder Black speaking to the other two. It seemed clear who was in charge of this threesome. Matt went to his closet and dresser and gathered enough clean clothes for each of them to wear for a couple of days. Leanne had found extra toothbrushes, toothpaste, and other bathroom items. Matt took the whole pile of things into the bedroom and set them on the larger bed.

Elder Black was coming out of the bathroom wrapped in a towel, and Elder Miles was sitting on the floor reading from a pocket-sized book, most likely scriptures. Elder Jones was in the bathroom getting washed up, avoiding the shower to keep his fresh bandages clean and dry.

"You guys OK?" Matt asked with genuine concern.

"We are good. We have each other, we have you and Sister Scott, and most of all we have God on our sides." The unbreakable faith of these young men was very evident. It was inspiring, yet hard to understand at times.

Elder Black turned to Elder Miles. "Take a shower, get cleaned up, and you can have the big bed," he said. This puzzled Matt. He was sure that Elder Black, being the leader, would sleep in the big bed. This was not the first time that Elder Black showed that Elder Miles was revered or given special treatment. As he gave direction to Elder Miles, he did it in a sort of respectful, almost questioning way. He often spoke to Elder Miles as one would to a grandparent who was confused—respectfully and with care.

"Good night, boys. You get some sleep, and we will see you for breakfast." Matt walked out of the room and closed the door behind him. Matt found himself referring to the missionaries as boys, which struck him as odd, as they were very much young men. In reflection, Matt realized it was his way of being fatherly. He was trying to put them at ease when he called them boys, but often it would actually seem to make them less comfortable, or little less sure of their standing with the Scotts. Missionaries are young men with a calling, being referred to, or treated, as boys may have felt like it undermined their religious authority. Leanne was sitting at the kitchen table, looking at her laptop and drinking a glass of wine. "Well, the Internet works. Sure is a lot of strange crap going on," she said without looking up.

"Like what?" Matt asked.

"Well, none of the bank web pages are working, so we can't do any banking or pay any bills. Oh, and Google crashed. It's just gone. I have to use MSN. Wonder what's up with that? Funny, never thought you would catch me using Bing," Leanne chuckled.

"Any news? Kids, Facebook?" Matt was starting to worry about his girls.

"I sent them messages, but chat isn't working. I hope they are OK." She paused for a moment, and then said, "I wish we could be with them." Leanne knew that Matt was thinking of Riana and Sam. She could not get her kids off her mind either. David and Sarah lived closer; they often seemed to be more present in their lives. But Matt missed and loved his girls.

Matt and Leanne had no time to worry; they had to deal with reality. Matt poured himself another glass of wine and sat on the couch. He turned on the TV but kept the volume way down so he wouldn't disturb the three in the back bedroom. The news was on. Local law enforcement had lost control in several major cities, and the Military and National Guard had instituted martial law. The East Coast was suffering rolling blackouts; New York City without power was a dangerous place to be. Generally things did not look good, and clearly the news was being controlled to some degree. The news anchor talked about the blackouts as if they were weather related—"solar flares" was the explanation given. The martial law was being blamed on over-active religious protesters. One thing was clear: nothing was clear. As Matt watched the news anchor read from a scripted page, it was very evident that even he did not believe what he was saying. There was news, there was information, maybe cause and effect had been misrepresented, but Matt was able to get a sense of how bad things were getting. Just as Matt was trying to get an understanding of the big picture by flipping channels from broadcast to broadcast, the picture changed to a solid message on the screen.

"EchoStar communications has suspended transmission at this time; you may check Channel 100 for messages pertaining to the state of emergency."

Before Matt could say a word, Leanne chimed in, "Damned Internet is down again."

"I think it's all down," Matt said pointing at the TV.

Leanne and Matt looked at each other, both exhausted. They stood up and walked toward each other and met in the center of the room. After a long embrace, the two of them walked hand in hand to the back bedroom. They quietly opened the door and peeked in. Elders Jones and Black were sleeping soundly on the twin and the trundle bed. Elder Miles was sitting on the floor next to the queen bed. He had a flashlight and a large book of scriptures. Elder Miles was studying, and did not even notice the door had opened.

"Elder, you need your sleep. God will understand," Leanne said to the young man.

Elder Miles slowly marked his page, set the book on the foot of the bed, and turned to the couple. "Pray not to be blessed, but rather to see and understand the many mercies and blessings that our Father puts in our lives." Elder Miles said this with a look that passed right through the two of them. He then stood up and pulled the covers back. Without saying another thing, he climbed into bed and lay stoically on his back.

Matt and Leanne backed out of the room and closed the door.

"Creepy," Leanne said.

"Not sure that's the word for it," Matt countered. The two walked toward their room, shutting off lights and setting the alarm.

Matt took a hot shower as Leanne wrote in her journal, something she did often. When Matt came to bed, Leanne went to take a shower.

When morning arrived, Leanne was by Matt's side in bed. Matt had no recollection of her coming to bed, so when he moved he made an effort not to wake her; she obviously had been up later than he was.

It was early, and the sun was not yet up. Quietly heading into the kitchen, he flipped the light switch, but nothing happened. For a moment Matt was confused. He looked at the microwave and the screen that normally showed the digital time was dark. The clock on the wall was working. And then it made sense. They had no power. The old clock ran on batteries. When Matt tried to make his morning coffee, not only did the coffee machine not work, but the lights were dead. This would be a challenge, Matt thought. He then heard the faint beep of the house alarm; it had a battery backup. This alarm system seemed like overkill, but Matt kept guns and some cash in the house, and he wanted them kept safe. He hurried over to the alarm panel, knowing that if the battery neared the end of its life, the audible sound would wake Leanne and the young missionaries. With a quick tap, tap, tap of the code, the alarm was off.

One thing worse than low blood sugar was no coffee, so Matt went to the garage and found a propane cook stove in the camping gear. Matt did not camp, and neither did Leanne; they joked that camping was a hotel with bad room service. Matt camped as a marine; they called it being in the field. Matt called it misery and would make a point to avoid camping at all costs. Having camping gear in the garage was a bit ironic, but it was part of being prepared. It did not take long to get the stove set up and running, and then coffee was brewing in an old aluminum percolator on the propane burner on the kitchen counter. Matt was trying to be quiet, but he made quite the noise when Elder Miles startled him.

Matt had been in and out of the kitchen, in and out of the garage, and had not noticed the Elder sitting at the kitchen table. He looked as if he had been outside; he had some dirt on his face and was fully dressed in his black missionary suit. He wore a blue striped tie and white shirt. He was sitting at the table reading from a pocket-sized book and making notes in the margins.

"Have you been up all night?" Matt asked.

"Can I have some breakfast?" was the response.

Matt was not sure what to do or say; it was a strange situation. He went to the pantry and pulled out a box of Cheerios. Then he got a gallon of milk from the refrigerator, closing it quickly, as he remembered the lack of power when the light did not come on. He took the cereal and milk to the table and returned with a bowl and spoon.

"Thank you, Brother," Elder Miles said as he poured some cereal.

If Matt did not know better, he would think that the young man had been out all night. But the house alarm system had been on and Matt hadn't heard it go off. And why would the Elder go out alone? Where would he have gone?

Elder Miles finished his cereal and rose from the table. He washed his bowl and spoon in the sink and dried them with a dishtowel. He put everything away and walked quietly into the back bedroom. Water ran in the bathroom for a moment, and then it was quiet. Matt sat at the table wondering what was going on and how to react. He had found a newspaper from last week in the recycling and proceeded to read the articles he had missed. He sat with his back to the window at the kitchen table, reading in the morning sun and drinking a cup of what could only be described as campfire coffee. The coffee was bitter, but it was hot, and it was coffee.

The paper was full of news about the upcoming election, but it seemed strange, as there would be no election as far as Matt knew. The front page had pictures of the challengers and the words *cult or church*. Matt wondered what had become of the challengers. Had they been arrested? Or were they in hiding? Matt knew that the story the president was pushing about the Church and Republican Party conspiring was a load of crap. It was clear that there was some type of a coup going on, and the real question to be asked was whose side the Military was taking. But no one was asking that question, as far as Matt could tell. Matt's son-in-law, a young marine, would he be friend or foe? Matt wondered what he would have done if this had happened when he was a young marine. Loyalty was a strange thing and was not always predictable. One thing Matt was sure of: the soldiers, marines, airmen, and sailors in question were the ones with hard choices to make. Would they follow the President? Or would the generals and admirals do their duty and refuse unlawful orders? Based on Matt's experience, and his knowledge of military history and customs, the people being followed would not be the generals, it would be the lower level officers, and it would be the NCOs. Marines and soldiers are loyal to their unit, not necessarily to a commander they had never met who issued orders from thousands of miles away.

As Matt read the paper and sat and contemplated the events around him, Leanne came into the room. She looked at the coffee on the counter and said, "Camping, are we?"

"No power," Matt said without looking up. He was engrossed in the article. He was reading a story about the Speaker of the House and his attempts to mediate between President Prescott and the Republican Party.

"Oh, glad I got a hot shower last night!" Leanne realized Matt was not listening so she walked over and pushed the paper down and gave Matt the look—the "Me, not the Paper" look—that she had perfected.

"Sorry." Matt realized his inattention and gave Leanne a kiss.

Before the morning greetings could progress past a quick kiss and a few words of conversation, Elders Black and Jones emerged from the back bedroom. Matt quickly remembered his strange encounter with Elder Miles.

"Did you sleep well?" Matt asked in a bit of an accusatory fashion, earning him a jabbing glance from Leanne. Leanne had not seen Elder Miles this morning and had no idea why Matt was acting this way.

"Yes," Elder Black answered quickly.

Now Matt never dreamed one of the missionaries would lie to him, but he had the feeling he was not getting the whole truth. Yet before Matt could push the issue, Elder Miles came out of the bedroom. The young man was looking strangely refreshed to Matt, not at all like he did less than an hour ago. Elder Miles made very direct eye contact with Matt, then walked to the sink and poured a glass of water.

Leanne went into the kitchen and started to cook on the camp stove Matt had set up. She pulled a dozen eggs from the fridge and a package of turkey bacon. Elder Jones asked, "What can we do to help?"

"Grab some potatoes from the pantry and wash them up," she told him. "We can make cottage fries with our eggs." Leanne rarely ate breakfast when it was just she and Matt. But when she had a chance to feed others, she was all over it. Matt watched Elder Miles for a reaction. He just had breakfast; would he eat again? What was going on with this young man? In a strange way, Matt trusted that Elder Miles was not doing anything wrong, and that maybe it was just not Matt's business. This young man was a mystery. Yes, he was strange, but there was something not tangible about his presence that kept Matt from mentioning what he had seen earlier. Neither Elder Jones nor Elder Black had yet realized that the power was out; the northeast wall of the Scott home was lined with windows and the blinds were open. The room was brightly lit by natural light, and they did not seem to think the two-burner camp stove was out of place on the counter. Being raised Mormon and not knowing about things like coffee in the morning, maybe they thought it was normal to make it this way.

Elder Jones was washing potatoes, Elder Black was dicing them up into small pieces, and Elder Miles was back at the table reading and making notes in his small book. Suddenly, loud beeps came from the oven and the microwave. The power was back on. Elders Jones and Black looked around in surprise, as though they just realized they had been in the dark. Elder Miles never looked up.

"I think we should shut off the breakers to the office and the TVs," Matt said as he headed toward the garage. "We are not going to use them until the power decides to stay on." Matt was concerned more with the unstable power; his TVs, computers, and other electronics would be damaged if the grid was unstable. The only thing worse than no power was low power. The flickering lights, beeping, and toning of different electronics was annoying, at the least. Matt turned the breakers off to the office and living room.

"Why was the power out?" Elder Black asked.

"Not sure, but I figure people were leaving the hospital, the sheriff and most of the deputies walked off the job, so maybe the people at the power company were not getting paid either." Matt was thinking out loud more than answering. "Better save the propane, though. We might not be so lucky to have power at breakfast time tomorrow," Matt said with a laugh.

Leanne agreed. She had already started the camp stove and was getting ready to cook breakfast on the kitchen counter, but she switched to the stove once she knew the power was on for good. She had a cast iron pan on the burner, and the smells of breakfast were already starting to waft into the room. She was in a cooking frenzy, dicing onions and seasoning. Elder Jones tried to help, but he quickly found it best to stay out of her way. As the five sat down to eat breakfast, Elder Black opened with a prayer as always, as he had become the one in charge of such things. This time he did not ask; obviously he remembered the discussion that Matt had with them.

"So, today I need to go to the shop and see what is going on," Matt announced to the group.

"Will we all go?" asked Elder Black.

"Well, let's discuss this; I think maybe you three should lie low. Leanne and I can go to town and get a feel for what's going on." Matt had a plan. He was going to check on the shop, catch up with his friend Jeremy, and Leanne could check on her office and maybe go to the local coffee shop to get some news. "After breakfast, we will drive to town and get some gas in the van, and then we can check on the shop. You three could maybe take care of the dishes and clean up a little, but whatever you do, stay low. If someone comes to the door, you are not here. I am serious." There was a degree of concern mixed with sternness in Matt's voice. The three gave a conforming look with eye contact and a small nod and went straight back to eating. At this moment Leanne's cooking was much more important than any threat from outside.

CHAPTER SIX

Two thousand eight hundred miles away in Washington, DC, much was happening. The President's postponement of the election had created a chain of events few could predict. The Senate and the House were locked down, with the exception of thirteen senators who were extremely loyal to the President. The US Senate Building and House were locked down from the inside, and a contingent of heavily armed marines guarded the building. Neither the senators nor the marines were sure if they were keeping the senators in or protecting them. But maybe it was a combination of the two. Earlier that morning, the Commandant of the Marine Corps was in his office in the Pentagon when two Supreme Court justices and the Speaker of the House walked in.

"General Siebel," the Speaker of the House, Congressman Davies, a young man for his position, spoke first. "We have a problem, a very big problem, and we need your help."

"I am listening," the General replied.

Judge Holloway, a judge known to be a strict constitutionalist to the dismay of President Prescott, was leading the discussion. Not unlike many Supreme Court justices, he sat the bench with a much different tenor than the man who appointed him desired. Judge Holloway had been appointed many years prior by a very liberal administration. After a hard-fought confirmation and approval, this judge had shown himself to be quite a different judge than he had been on the Ninth Circuit Court. When Judge Holloway was on the Ninth Circuit Court of Appeals, he was known for extremely liberal interpretation of the constitution; on the Supreme Court, he was a strict constitutional advocate. President Prescott spoke openly about his distrust in the judge, and Judge Holloway had spoken often of his concerns about the President's actions. He was quoted once as saying, "This man runs roughshod over the Constitution."

"We need to stop this thing that's happening, and we are looking for a constitutional solution," the Speaker said. "Impeachment is the next course, but we may not have time."

"Politics. What does that have to do with me?" General Siebel spoke clearly and questioningly. This was an inaccurate statement, as any military man who makes it to the rank of general is truly a politician, not to mention to the status of Commandant of the Marine Corps.

"We are asking the Commanders of all of the Armed Forces to act in a neutral manner, to keep the peace and not take sides," Speaker Davies explained. "If this election dispute turns violent, it will get out of control very quickly."

"Sounds to me like you are asking me to disobey the President and his staff," the General said with a smile. "That's not really being neutral, now, is it?"

It was well known that General Siebel had no love for President Prescott or Vice President Gillard. During Prescott's first election campaign, he referred to the Marine Corps as "thugs" and "assassins." President Prescott was elected as an anti-war candidate, but after three years in office, the country was now engaged in four wars, not just the two he inherited. The President had gone to war in Angola and Syria without Congressional approval, and this lost him much support, even from his own party, in both houses.

Before the justices or the speaker could answer, the General asked, "Who is with you, and who is on Prescott's side?"

"We don't know yet. We have people meeting with the Secretary of the Navy, the Army Chief of Staff, and the Undersecretary of the Air Force. We would like all parties to get together as soon as possible," responded Speaker Davies.

"And what is Prescott doing?" asked the General. He was weighing the odds. The Commandant of the Marine Corps is a powerful man, but he still needed to get a feel for the odds. This could be seen as treason to many, and a serious decision was at hand. General Siebel knew that he must pick a side, and he must pick the winning side. Being a man of ideals and principals was important, but he also had nearly three hundred thousand marines under his command, and his decision would affect each one of them and their families.

"The President has called his key supporters to a meeting at the White House. He has thirteen senators and twenty-four congressmen, along with the Secretary of the Air Force and a large group of cabinet members," Davies continued.

"That explains the Undersecretary of the Air Force and not the Secretary himself," commented the General.

"I think you know why." Speaker Davies responded, his eyes squinting and lips pursing, showing irritation with the general's question.

The Secretary of the Air Force was appointed by President Prescott and had not been confirmed. There were some questions about his actions in the Balkans. Some had labeled him more loyal to the UN than the US, and General Siebel believed this. The general also knew full well that Speaker Davies had led the effort to stop this appointment.

General Siebel had a deep-seated distrust of the man who was acting as Secretary of the Air force, and his siding with the President was swaying the General's thinking on the entire matter at hand.

"So here is the problem. We need to get control of the White House. We need to block any press conferences and outgoing transmission. And we need to do it fast. We can't trust the Secret Service or the CIA. We could use the Army, but the public likes you, General. They trust the Marine Corps. We need men in dress blues to contain the President and his supporters until we can get an impeachment hearing started." Davies spoke as if he were reciting a rehearsed speech.

The speaker of the house had thought this through from a political stance more than a tactical one. "The image of a marine in dress blues will give the public much more confidence than a soldier in camouflage," Davies concluded out loud.

"You want me to order my men, in dress uniforms, to lay siege to the White House?" the General asked with a snicker, as the idea was beyond ridiculous to him. General Siebel even let out a chuckle at the thought.

"And, don't forget, control the crowds out front, and keep order in the area in front of any cameras," the speaker interjected.

"I will guarantee you immunity if it goes bad," Justice Holloway said. Yet everyone in the room knew he was promising something he could not deliver.

"You really want men and woman in dress uniforms?" The General was confused.

This question gave relief to Speaker Davis and Chief Justice Holloway. The general was speaking of *how* it was going to get done, not *if*.

"General, it's as much about image as force, they need to be in blues," Davies said, getting a nodding approval from Justice Holloway.

"Hypothetically speaking..." The General paused as if he were unsure for a moment, then he continued, "Marine Barracks Washington could take the White House within the hour. I could move an MEF (*Marine Expeditionary Force*) up from South Carolina within the day. This is treason; there's no going back. And what if the Army doesn't go along?" The General was moving chess pieces in his head. "You know the Army outnumbers the Marine Corps almost five to one," the General pointed out.

"We have the Army. We may have some rogue units, but we have the Pentagon." Speaker Davies seemed very sure of himself.

"If not, this could get ugly." The General had no desire to see American soldiers and Marines fighting each other. "I can put some commanders in blues, but my Marines will not sacrifice safety for image." This statement by the General was what the Speaker needed; the General and the Marine Corps were on board.

"Take the White House. If we can't get a deal within twenty-four hours, you and your men are free to walk away," Davies continued.

"Let me explain something to you, Congressman. We will walk away or not walk away when I say." The General paused, and then continued, "I am on the side of the US Marine Corps. I will make my decisions based on the good of the Corps." General Siebel was flexing some political muscle, and it was something that neither Davies nor Holloway took too seriously; to them it was political ass-covering.

The room sat quiet for what felt like ten minutes to Speaker Davies and Justice Holloway, though it was probably less than ninety seconds. The stress was thick enough to cut with knife. General Siebel was tapping a letter opener on his desk; it was a miniature Mameluke Hilt, a copy of the coveted sword every Marine Corps officer earns upon commission. On the wall in a case, behind his large oak desk, was a broken and damaged full-sized sword. It was hanging in a case with a picture of the Syrian Embassy. This was a ceremonial sword that had been used in hand-to-hand combat when the embassy was overrun last year. A young lieutenant in a dress uniform fought off intruders with no more than this sword until his unit could give him backup. This was the beginning of the war in Syria, and the lieutenant was the first war hero the people had seen in years. His heroics were caught on security camera and then broadcast worldwide by Sky News. Later, when he was awarded the Congressional Medal of Honor, Lieutenant James Merrill presented the sword and medal to the Commandant of the Marine Corps, who happened to be his father in-law. The case had a gold inscription on it: "To those who fell before me." The young Lieutenant was killed three months later by a car bomb in London.

General Siebel made his decision—he had prayed to God for guidance, he had looked to his education and experience, but most of all he asked himself, what would Jim do? Lieutenant James Merrill, his son-in-law, the father of his grandchildren, and a hero was always in the General's thoughts. The General turned to the framed picture and looked at the face of the young man he lost, he looked at the sky blue ribbon on the medal hanging in the case, and he looked at the broken sword, blood-stained.

The General turned slowly, in an almost ceremonial about-face, with what may have been a tear in his eye. He spoke quietly and clearly.

"Our Country needs us, gentlemen. I will have control of the White House by 1:00 p.m. today, you have my word." He then sat and picked up the receiver of the old corded phone on his desk. He barked through the phone at his secretary, "Get me Colonel Luke right away," hanging up instantly.

He looked up briefly at the others in the room and said, "Gentlemen, if you would excuse me, it looks like I have some work to do."

"Can we count on you to meet on the House floor at 6:00 p.m. tonight?" Justice Holloway asked.

"I'll be there; just let me get to work." The phone rang and General Siebel picked it up. He waved the visitors out of the room and went about the business of overthrowing a government.

The mission went well with no shots fired; the General delivered on his promise. The Secret Service agents were relieved of their weapons and of duty, and a contingent of 135 of the Marine Corps' finest took control of the White House and everyone in it. The streets around the White House and the Congressional buildings were cleared, and some two hundred Army Rangers were called in to keep the peace. Overall, things went as planned. The sight of Marines in dress blues with M4 assault rifles on the front steps and roof of the White House was something to see. This image was burned into the mind of anyone who witnessed the takeover. It was an image of pure power.

Later that night, the Commanders of all branches of the military, the majority whip from the Senate, the Speaker of the House, the Director of the FBI, and the heads of the CIA and the NSA met in a room with seven current Supreme Court Justices. Chief Justice Holloway directed the meeting.

Justice Holloway had made it clear that he was calling on the House to start impeachment proceedings. He stated that, in his legal opinion, any order given by President Prescott at this time was to be considered unlawful. The opinion was shared by five of the seven justices present, enough to sway any doubts of its constitutionality. The men in the room justified their actions with the President's breach of his oath of office. They walked a fine line when it came to defining their actions as either a treasonous coup or the rescue of Constitutional law and order.

The Speaker of the House quickly recognized General Siebel when he walked into the room. "It is our intent to put General Siebel in charge of domestic military affairs; all other branches shall maintain their current duties," the Speaker said to the crowd. He was standing at a podium at one end of the room.

"The question is, what about our troops overseas?" asked the Secretary of the Navy. "No one has been paid, and we are running out of reserve supplies. We need fuel and food to get them home."

The politicians did have a problem on their hands. If at any time any of these military men felt they or their troops, sailors, or marines were being abandoned, neglected, or mistreated, the potential for a military takeover was great. The Speaker of the House knew this, and as much as he needed the Military to stay neutral, he needed them to feel secure in their place in the government, or what was passing as a government. By the end of the meeting, everyone agreed that the Air Force would mobilize to return the troops to the United States as soon as possible. The strategic oil reserves would be under Army control, and the Marine Corps would keep the peace at home. All reserve units would be activated as soon as possible.

The Speaker of the House looked at each of the generals in turn. "It is your mission to keep the peace, help feed and protect people, and provide medical services when possible. It is not your mission to install or facilitate a change of leadership." The Speaker was trying to keep the generals in check. "We will need the military to run elections, but we will maintain civilian control." Speaker Davies was laying out something that sounded good on paper, but he was worried that reality may be much different. He needed the Military, but he feared them very much.

The plans laid out during this meeting would not work if the President could keep control of the media. With this in mind, Special Forces units were quickly ordered to take control of several key broadcast media centers. Any media center that supported the removal of this president had already been put out of business by the administration. The men in the room figured that if a media outlet was still broadcasting, it was a Prescott supporter. The Congress and Senate were placed under Marine guard. Air Force One was grounded, and the president, vice president, twenty-three representatives, and twelve senators were placed under house arrest at the White House. The process was quick and smooth, to the shock of many involved; there was a contingency plan on file. General Siebel and the Joint Chiefs did not have to do much planning. The plans had been made years ago and were updated on a continual basis. The Speaker of the House had some idea of plans for civil unrest, domestic terrorism, or maybe even for a coups but he had no idea that the Military had a plan for an out-of-control executive branch. To a constitutional scholar like Justice Holloway, it was disturbing that there might be a plan on file to overthrow the Commander in Chief. Even more alarming was that there had been a plan on file since the days of FDR. The politicians in the room all wondered what else could be done with just one phone call from a Marine Corps general.

When General Siebel noticed the shock on the faces of the men in the room, he responded as only a Marine general could. "You really didn't think we did not have a plan for this, did you? Do you have any idea how close we came to overthrowing JFK during the Bay of Pigs?" The General gave a bit of a smirk. "Gentleman, don't make the mistake of getting power hungry yourselves. We have plans for every possibility."

This was a warning. This would not be a revolution; it was going to be nothing more than a course correction.

"Congressmen, we are not overthrowing our government. We are stabilizing it." The General was letting these men of suits and ties know that when it came to power and control, he had it, not them.

The Speaker of the House was taking the lead, and he would be recognized as acting president of the United States. This was tactical, as he was of the same political party as President Prescott, and was even a supporter of his before the economic collapse started. General Siebel and Justice Holloway made it clear that this was to be a temporary solution. The Speaker's position in the coup, course correction, or constitutional uprising was temporary. There would be no possibility of his continuing as leader of the nation once elections were held. The generals and justices went as far as making the Speaker put in writing that he would never run for any office again. The Speaker would be required to step down from public office once a new administration and congress were elected.

As much as the politicians wanted to work out the details of chain of command and authority, it was not up to them anymore. The plan, the previously unknown and unnamed plan that the Pentagon had for such an event, was put into motion quickly.

The government had changed drastically, but there was some form of order. Now it was time to address the nation and the world. The small group moved under armed guard to the House chambers. They all entered through a mahogany paneled door that opened onto the House dais.

General Siebel and Speaker Davies approached the podium. The House floor was full, and all eyes were on the two men. Even the address of the nation was specifically laid out in the plan: who and when. Davies stepped up and pulled the microphone down toward his mouth. As the Speaker took a breath, the TV cameras positioned around the large room came to life.

"My fellow Americans, I am speaking to you from the floor of the House of Representatives. At 1:00 p.m. today, I, Speaker of the House of Representatives, Congressmen Davies, with the authority and consent of the US Supreme Court, have ordered the house arrest of President Prescott and his cabinet. Several of the President's key supporters and campaign officials have also been detained. This is in reaction to unconstitutional actions taken by the President, to include the canceling of an election and the persecution of a political party and a religious faith. It is my intention to call for a nationwide election as soon as possible. I will be working with the leadership of both parties, as well as the military, to achieve this goal. Law and order will prevail, democratic elections will take place, and our nation will once again hold the position of the greatest democracy on earth. I ask you, the American people, to be patient, help one another, and be Americans." The Congressmen paused, then continued, "Pray for our great nation." Again he paused, before stating, "I would like to introduce you to General Seibel. I have appointed General Seibel Commander of Homeland Defense and Security. It is the General's charge to protect the people and provide assistance when possible. General," he said, nodding toward Seibel, "a few words, if you would."

Davies stepped back, and General Seibel stepped to the podium. He was bald, lean, and in his mid-60s. He wore a perfectly-pressed set of Marine Corps dress blues, white gloves, and a high collar. His medals covered his chest and included the Congressional Medal of Honor, which hung around his neck. The General stepped up and cleared his throat. He placed his white hat on the podium and placed a hand on each side.

"I am General Stephen Siebel, Commandant of the United States Marine Corps, and I would like to say a few words about my mission and what it means to you." The General cleared his throat again and took a deep breath. He was speaking off the cuff, as there had been no time for speechwriters and he had no teleprompter. He was nervous, and he was sweating. Under his breath, the General muttered, "God save us."

"It is my mission," he continued, "to keep the peace, to provide protections and assistance to the population whenever possible, and to facilitate a resolution to all matters political. By order of the act-ing President of the United States, Speaker Davies, these actions were taken with the support of both houses of Congress and the Supreme Court. "

Four teams of camera crews recorded the event for broadcast. General Siebel had one chance to get this right, and he knew it. Soon the world would know that the United States Government was not only broke financially, but was now in a state of coup.

"In the days to follow, you will see a military presence in your towns and cities. We will support local law enforcement, local hospi-tals, and help with local infrastructure. The men and women you will see are there to help you. Over the next weeks and months, we will be returning troops to the United States from each of our four areas of engagement. As manpower increases, the operation of power grids, water, and sewage systems, along with other infrastructure needs, will be supported by the Armed Forces. I will remind you: these men and women are trained soldiers, sailors, Marines, and airmen. Treat them with respect, and stay out of their way when you can. It is our goal to return to civilian control as soon as possible. Until such time, a state of martial law exists." The General stepped back a half a step and said, "Thank you."

The General then reached for the bright white Marine Corps hat and placed it firmly on his head. He performed a perfect about-face, and two armed marines in digital camouflage utilities stepped up to each side of him. General Siebel turned to Speaker Davies and said, "Sir, I have work to do." He saluted and stepped quickly out of the room. The General and the two Marines marched in step with a loud report from the heels of their boots as they left the room. The sound of the marines' heels hitting the floor in perfect har-mony left Davies out of sorts. He wondered for a brief moment if he had opened Pandora's Box. Their precision and military bearing put a firm reality on what had just been done; there was no going back now.

Speaker Davies stood beside Justice Holloway as a flurry of questions came toward them from the members of the press. Several of the members of Congress were yelling, and several were applauding. It was clear that there was not going to be a question-and-answer session. Davies and Holloway stepped back, looking at the crowd, and then they turned and left the room in the same direction as General Siebel.

Back at the Scott house, Matt and Leanne had loaded up the Cadillac and prepared to go to town. Elders Black and Jones had been given specific instructions on dealing with the alarm system and to stay in the house.

"Elder Black." Matt called the young man into the office adjoining the master bedroom. "Seven, fourteen, three. Don't forget those numbers, the combination to the gun safe." Matt opened the safe and pointed to a pair of .40-caliber semi-automatic handguns, both loaded. "Only if you have no other option," Matt said calmly.

Elder Black and Matt Scott had talked about guns and hunting in the past. Matt trusted the young man's judgment; he had no idea of the experience of the two others. Matt was hoping that there would be no reason to need a gun, yet somehow he knew deep inside that things were only going to get worse. A missionary with a gun was a strange thought, but these were strange times.

"Seven, fourteen, three," Elder Black repeated. "You can trust me."

Matt and Leanne loaded what they thought they might need for the visit to town in the Cadillac. They locked the house up tight, to make it look as if no one was home. The Scotts had no neighbors to snoop, but Matt was not so sure that someone wasn't watching. Better safe than sorry. Matt walked around back and started up the Club Van. The low-fuel light flickered, and Matt wondered if he could make it to town. In the garage, Matt grabbed a five-gallon gas can he used to fuel his lawn mower. The can was half full. Matt put the two and a half gallons of gas in the van. At ten miles per gallon, he thought that should get him to the shop with no problem.

Matt backed out and motioned to Leanne, who was sitting in the driveway in the Cadillac. The two drove away, van following Cadillac, heading towards town.

The three young men had cleaned the kitchen and were all sitting on the floor in the living room. Elder Jones was reading from the *Pearl of Great Price*, and they were discussing the significance of Joseph Smith and his belief in authority. The question was, were they following the teachings they had dedicated their lives to? Could they be true to their calling in a world so confused? Looking to Church-specific teachings like the *Pearl of Great Price*, a book of scripture exclusive to the Mormon faith, was an act of searching. These young men needed to know they were not violating the terms of their mission.

"We can only pray for guidance and trust that God gives us the strength and judgment to prevail." Elder Black may have been trying to convince himself more than his companions, but either way, he was taking the lead.

The three were deep in contemplation and prayer when they heard a sharp knock on the door. Elder Black froze in fear for a moment. Looking at the other two, he whispered, "Be quiet." He then made his way quietly toward the front door. Peeking through the blinds, he saw a sheriff's deputy and the two Feds that he had seen at the church. The deputy was a young man they did not recognize.

"Scott! Matt Scott!" yelled out the deputy.

"They are not home," the deputy said to the shorter of the two.

Without hesitation, the shorter fed nodded to the larger man, and the larger man instantly started kicking the front door. Elder Jones had made his way to Elder Black's side, and when the kicking started, they backed away from the door. By the third kick, the door was open.

"What the hell?" the deputy said. "You can't just kick the door open!" He stood on the porch looking at the two Feds, knowing he was in way over his head. The two Feds marched into the house, but not before drawing their guns. Elders Black and Jones had managed to make it back into the master bedroom. Elder Miles sat still on the living room floor and almost seemed unaware of the commotion, or maybe he just did not care. He calmly prayed in a soft voice as if nothing had happened. He sat cross-legged on the floor, his head bobbing slightly as he offered his devotions.

"Seven, fourteen, three," Elder Black said to himself under his breath as they found their way to the office. He quickly and quietly opened the gun safe, removed a single pistol, and locked the safe again.

Elder Jones watched in horror. Elders Black and Jones then slid under the desk and listened. Elder Jones stared at the pistol with wide eyes and wondered how his companion had known the combination and what he planned to do with the gun.

"You over there, put your hands up!" the taller man yelled at Elder Miles.

Elder Miles said nothing and just kept reading from his book of scriptures. He even took a moment to highlight something with a scripture marker, as though no one else was in the room. The tall agent walked up and shoved him. "Take it easy," said the deputy, "this one isn't all there." The younger deputy had tentatively followed the two in and was standing back watching what was happening. Elder Miles fell forward when he was shoved and tore a page in his book; he sat back up and continued reading and praying as if nothing had happened. He carefully placed the torn page back in place as he read.

"Where are your friends?" demanded the tall agent.

At this time the shorter man, the one who seemed in charge, was calmly making his way around the house. He had made his way into the bedroom used by the missionaries. From the other room he heard a thud and a groan. The tall agent had quickly lost his temper with Elder Miles's lack of response and had hit him in back of the head with the grip of his pistol. Elder Miles was now on the floor, bleeding and out cold. Elder Miles had fallen onto his right side; there was a large gash on the back of his head and a puddle of blood was growing around him. The entire time the deputy was standing back, just inside the front door on the landing. He was in shock and kept uttering phrases like, "You can't..." and "Why?"

"Would you shut up?" the tall man said, looking over his shoulder at the muttering deputy.

The older agent looked around the corner. "Morris, you idiot, what the hell did you do that for?" This was the first time he had used a name; he was obviously very angry. Either the Feds believed no one else was home, or they had just stopped avoiding the public use of names. Prior to this point, in town, at the church, and in any other public setting, no one had heard a name; no identification was displayed long enough to be read. It was as if they were trying to keep their identity secret. After all of that effort, for some reason unknown, they were using names. Apparently they were no longer concerned with concealing their identities.

"He wouldn't talk." Before he could say another word, the deputy spoke up, "I tried to tell you, this one is retarded or something." The young deputy had a sound of fear in his voice. "You did not have to hit him."

During the verbal sparring in the living room, Elders Black and Jones scurried out from under the desk that was in the office beside the bedroom and sneaked into the walk-in closet. They positioned themselves behind the clothes on Leanne's side of the closet. The walk-in closet was over-full, it was easy to hide behind the packed-in clothes. The shorter man and the young deputy walked into the master bedroom.

"Agent Lamphier?" The deputy was very thin, and tan. His blonde hair and tanned skin made him look more like a lifeguard than a cop, and the tremble in his voice made it clear he was not very sure of himself. Hearing the deputy's quivering voice made Elder Black even a little more uneasy. Elder Black was remembering his grandfather's stories about the Vietnam War. His grandpa made a point of getting the young boy to understand the power of fear. The older man explained that fear makes people unpredictable and dangerous. "Always avoid the fearful," he'd say, "and don't confuse fear with anger. Anger can be reasoned with, but fear defies reason." Elder Black was thinking of those discussions now. When he first heard the stories, at the time he thought of them as the ramblings of an old man. In a way, he wished his grandpa were with him now; grandpa would know what to do. The voice of Agent Lamphier broke his train of thought, and brought Elder Black back from the memories of grandpa to the situation at hand.

"Morris...keep looking!" Lamphier yelled toward the living room as he scanned the master bedroom for clues.

"They're not here!" the deputy blurted out as though he desperately wanted to get out of this house before anything else happened.

"Look for the other two; they must be close, "Agent Lamphier said as he went into the office and started to turn the dial on the gun safe. Once he realized he was not going to open it, he rifled through the desk drawers. Between the gun safe and Elders Jones and Black was a thin wall; every sound the searching agent made could be heard clearly by both missionaries. *If I can hear them, they can hear us,* thought Elder Black. Elders Jones and Black did their best to keep quiet as the deputy looked under the bed, in the bathroom, and even in the linen closet. When the deputy stepped into the walk-in closet, both missionaries froze in fear. Elder Jones bit his lip so hard he could taste blood. The sound of their breathing and heartbeats seemed to be deafening, and Elder Black could not figure out how the deputy did not hear them.

The deputy carelessly pushed through the clothes. He looked through Leanne's things, holding up some of her negligées and giving them a disturbed look. Elder Black suddenly became full of rage; Leanne was like a big sister, or even a mother to him. As the deputy worked his way down the closet, he moved closer and closer to the two missionaries. He was acting like he was sure he was alone in the closet.

Elder Jones's racing heart banged in his ears, and the taste of blood and his locked knees had him close to blacking out. Elder Black was regretting picking up the gun; when they caught him he would wish he did not have it. *Why had he gone for the gun?* He wondered. He had no intention of using it. Elder Black's mind was racing: what to do with the gun, how to explain the gun if or when they got caught. There was no question in his mind that he could not use it, and it would only make matters worse. Elder Black slipped the pistol into the pocket of a coat hanging to his right. The coat moved just enough to catch Deputy Miller's eye. The young deputy slowly walked over and parted the clothes right in front of Elder Black; their faces were less than a foot apart. Elder Jones was watching from a few feet away, not yet discovered.

"What are you doing in there?" shouted out Agent Lamphier from the other room.

"Nothing, just looking," Deputy Miller said as he looked Elder Black in the eye. "Nothing in here but clothes and shoes," he said. The entire time neither one broke eye contact, and neither one blinked. Elder Black could see a small silver chain around Deputy Miller's neck, and on this chain was a two-inch silver crucifix. The young blonde man reached for his crucifix and not his gun. Elder Black watched as the deputy squeezed the cross so hard that a small drip of blood came from his closed hand. "Nothing in here," he said again and turned and walked out of the closet. During the few seconds this took, Elder Black did not breathe, and neither did Elder Jones. When Deputy Miller left the room, they both gasped a little. Elder Black felt like throwing up; it took all the strength he could muster to stay still and quiet. Elder Jones sagged to one knee, trying not to breathe loudly as he caught his breath. Elder Jones was very close to passing out; he was seeing stars. The room was spinning a little, and the young Elder had one knee and a hand firmly planted on the carpeted floor as if he were keeping from falling. The room was tipping. Fear, lack of oxygen from holding his breath, locked knees, and maybe some residual weakness from his injuries had the young man fighting to stay conscious. Elder Jones knew if he fell they would be discovered.

Elders Black and Jones stayed in the closet without moving for what felt like an hour. They listened intently, prayed quietly, and waited. They listened as the three men searched the house, occasionally hearing Agent Lamphier give a direction or an order, like, "find the attic access" or "leave it be; we are not thieves." They heard the sound of the outside garden shed being opened and closed, the garage door opening, and even trash can lids banging. Agents Lamphier and Morris were thorough. If not for Deputy Miller, the two Elders would have been discovered for sure.

Elder Jones was pretty sure he heard the sound of the black Chevy Tahoe driving away. They waited in the silence for about ten minutes, and then, looking at each other, without a word, they stepped out from behind the clothes. Elder Black reached into the pocket of the jacket and produced the pistol, which he then placed into his beltline on his back. The fear of being discovered was overpowered by the concern they felt for Elder Miles. They had failed Elder Miles, and they had failed to protect their charge. Elder Black made his way to the broken front door and peered out, looking for anyone or anything. He could see nothing out of the ordinary, with the exception of the splintered wood of the broken door jam. Then he noticed blood; red spots lead out of the house, down the steps, and to the side of the road. They ended where he assumed the Tahoe had been parked.

"They took him, and he's hurt," said Elder Jones. He was trying not to be loud, but his emotions were getting the best of him. Elder Miles had fallen, there was quite a bit of blood on the floor, and the familiar pocket scripture was lying on the floor with blood on the open pages.

Elder Miles's large Quad (a book containing all of the scriptures of the LDS church), lay open with a page torn. Elder Black returned to the living room where Elder Jones was standing, and both young men fell to their knees. They looked at the blood and the book and prayed. Elder Jones looked over to see tears streaming down Elder Black's face.

"Not him, not him." Elder Black knew there was something very special about Elder Miles; he knew it was not a disability. Elder Miles had a gift—his spirit was pure—and Elder Black had the responsibility to keep him safe.

CHAPTER SEVEN

Matt and Leanne had stopped at the gas station on the way to town. A cardboard sign in the window read, "No Gas, No Food, No Water. Closed."

This store was normally very busy, but it was empty. The hoses on several of the pumps had been cut, and one of the glass doors leading into the convenience store was broken. From the van, Matt could see the shelves were tipped over. The store had been ransacked.

Matt pulled out of the parking lot and back onto the highway. Leanne followed closely behind him. En route he saw a couple cars on the side of the road, abandoned. Two cars passed going the other way, and that was it. Throughout the twenty-minute drive, it seemed as if things had been abandoned. The traffic light at the entrance to town was not working. It wasn't blinking red; it was just completely off. Matt drove up the hill and turned into the parking lot of his shop. Leanne pulled the Cadillac around the back of the shop as Matt parked the van beside Jeremy's truck. It was good he had found the gas can; he would not have made it all the way to town on the fumes that he had in the tank. Jeremy's pickup was parked on the side of the shop. One of the roll-up doors was open, and Jeremy was under the hood of an old Chevy van. Across the parking lot, the coffee shop where Leanne and Matt had spent many hours was dark. But there was some sign of life inside—several people sat around a large, round table, their outlines visible due to a dim light that could be a candle or small lantern.

Jeremy walked out of the shop while wiping the grease from his hands on a blue shop towel.

"Boss, it's good to see you. You too, Mrs. Boss." Mrs. Boss is what he had called Leanne ever since he was the best man at their wedding.

Leanne stepped out and gave Jeremy a hug. "How is your daughter? Do you have everything you need?"

"We are great; all is good," he responded with a smile. "We are doing very well here."

"I am going to see what's up at McGinn's." Leanne pointed at the coffee shop. Jeremy responded with a smile and nod.

Leanne made her way across the parking lot and entered into the coffee shop while Matt watched her from the open bay door. As Matt looked down Main Street, he could see that most of the businesses were closed. A few had open doors, and a few people walked from shop to shop. Matt was also very concerned about Jeremy and his daughter. "You doing OK? You and the kid got what you need?" Matt asked Jeremy in a very serious tone.

"We are doing fine, and I can't thank you enough."

Before Jeremy could continue, Matt quickly said, "Don't thank me, just keep this place going."

"Well, as you can see, no one came to work, and there's not many customers," he said. "I have some small jobs I can do with the spotty power. Not sure how they are paying, though. Mrs. McNulty tried to give me a credit card for putting a fan belt on her car this morning. I couldn't run it—no phones or power at the time—so she gave me three jars of canned peaches and some frozen salmon." Jeremy looked at Matt nervously then, as if he wanted approval for his decision to help the longtime customer.

"Do what you can, Jeremy. Do what you can, and don't worry about me." Matt tried to reassure Jeremy with his soft tone.

"You?" Jeremy suddenly blurted out. Then he paused before asking his boss the hard question. "Are you part of this whole Mormon revolt thing they talked about on the news?" He looked away, as though he was worried that his question was crossing the line.

Matt laughed out loud. "First of all, you know me better than that, and second of all, what Mormon revolt? All the Mormons I know are in hiding."

"Thought so," Jeremy said. "You know the priest from the Catholic church on the hill? Shit, can't remember his name. Well, he was at McGinn's this morning telling everyone to help the Mormons. And he said it was all a lie, and that if we let this happen, the Catholics and Jews would be next. He was pretty upset. I think he is still over there."

Matt did not want to share any details with his friend; he did not want to involve him in any trouble. Jeremy had it bad enough, and his hands were full taking care of the shop and his daughter. Matt directed the conversation away from the political and religious events.

"I need gas?" Matt said in the form of a question.

"Well, the Chevron has a sign up that says they will be pumping gas from 3:00 p.m. to 5:00 p.m., or until they run out."

"Can't stay that long. What about the shop? Do we have any gas?" Matt asked.

"Out back, your boat. I filled the tanks before I brought it up to do the trailer bearings." Matt had a twenty-three-foot speedboat, but he rarely used it. Matt raced sailboats and loved sailing, but recently he had sold his sailboat to try something a bit faster. It wasn't much to his liking, so Jeremy used the speedboat more than Matt did. The good news was the boat held 120 gallons of high-test fuel, and Matt needed gas if he was going to make it back home.

Jeremy and Matt went out back and proceeded to siphon some fuel into the Cadillac. When it was full, Matt pulled the van around and started to fill it. Matt then set two gas cans beside the van to be filled next.

"Told you this damn thing was a gas hog," Jeremy teased his boss about the boat.

While they waited for the van to fill up, they discussed what was happening in town. The churches were open. Most of the stores were opening for a couple hours a day, mainly when the power came back. Not much left on the shelves—no food or vital supplies, as they had sold out in a day. In a small town like this, in a very rural area like the Olympic Peninsula, stores often sold out. If a snowstorm was predicted, or maybe even a big windstorm, people would buy out the stores for fear of no resupply. This time they were right.

"Matt, I know that some terrible things are happening, but it's strange. The people of this town seem to have a sense of calm about them. They are helping each other and just lying low until this blows over. It will blow over, right?" Jeremy looked at Matt with eyes full of hope and fear.

"I hope so." Matt wasn't feeling so positive about his answer. The truth was he was afraid it had just begun.

At McGinn's Coffee Shop, there was a meeting going on. When Leanne entered the room, she saw Father Flarraty, Sheriff Chow (out of uniform), and a couple other people she did not know by name. Leanne was extremely uncomfortable as soon as she saw the group of men. A rush of unease, bordering on panic, swept over her. She stepped back, hoping to back out the door without being noticed. Leanne never was one to be afraid of anything, so the feeling made little sense to her, and that in itself was scary.

"Mrs. Scott, come join us," said Father Flarraty in a calming voice.

Leanne froze, knowing she'd been caught. She took a deep breath, forced a smile, and turned around. "I've only got a minute. Matt's waiting for me at the shop." She had not been to church in a long time, but the instinct to trust a man wearing vestments was strong. Leanne looked at the priest and made extended eye contact. The fear and momentary panic was set aside.

"Sheriff Chow, I see you're out of uniform," Leanne said. "Is this get-together business, or social?"

"A little of both," Chow said, responding directly to Leanne. "I have been relieved of duty by a Fed named Lamphier. There wasn't much left of the department. Most of the deputies quit coming to work, as I had had no way to pay them for over a month. Jeff Morris and State Trooper Richie are working with the two Feds in town, but the rest just went home."

Across the table sat a large man. Leanne recognized him from town, but did not know his name. He glanced up at her and then looked sternly at the priest. He leaned across the table and asked, "Who is bringing the food?" He was obviously annoyed at the interruption of the conversation they'd been having prior to Leanne's arrival.

"I don't know," responded the priest, getting back to the subject at hand.

"Last night, someone brought food to several families out in the county. We are thinking it might be the missing missionaries. You wouldn't know anything about that, would you?" asked Chow, looking at Leanne. His piercing stare and stern tone was clear; it was saying, "If you do know, don't say a word."

"And the Johnsons are gone. Word is they left for Utah." The large man's frustration was evident in his raised voice and clenched fists. He was looking for information, and it was clear he was not very friendly toward the Johnson family or the idea of missionaries. Leanne quickly determined that being a Mormon, being a missionary, or even moving to Utah makes one an enemy to this man. His bigotry was as clear as the nose on his face. Looking at Leanne, he snapped, "What do you know about the Johnsons, missy?"

"Why would I know anything about missionaries or food?" Leanne was feeling cornered. She knew damn well that Chow knew where the missionaries were, and she was not happy with the situation.

"There are lots of people who left, and a few who showed up. We need to watch out for squatters," said a thin man with dark hair who had a hunting rifle leaned against the chair next to him.

"Fred, someone is bringing food and supplies to people in the night," the large man said as he stood up, his pauses and deep breaths between words made it clear he was trying to control his anger. "We're not talking about squatters, we're talking about Mormons. Damned hoarders!"

"What's the problem if someone is helping a neighbor?" asked Leanne.

"The problem is this." Fred held up a flyer that read, "Wanted! Hoarders, Looters, and Mormons. Wanted dead or alive."

"This is a wanted poster put out by some vigilantes," Chow spoke up.

"Or maybe just concerned citizens," said the large man.

"That's another way to put it, isn't it?" The priest stood up and looked sternly at the two men. Fred the hunter and the large man were standing side by side at this time. "Just a matter of semantics, isn't it?" the priest continued.

"We will find these hoarders and put a stop to it," retorted the large man.

"With the help of Lamphier," said the priest in a bit of a condescending tone. It was clear to Leanne what was happening here, and she was sorry she had not walked out when her instincts told her to.

"We don't know if the Feds and vigilantes are working together."
Chow seemed to be evoking the blue code of silence.

"Apparently, Agent Lamphier had some document that made him
the acting authority in this side of the county. Lamphier was judge,
jury, and executioner. He was the President's representative from
Washington, DC," said a man sitting across the room. He had obviously been there for some time, but in the dark, Leanne had not even noticed him. She was so startled by his interjection that Leanne stepped
back toward the door only to step into the path of the large man and
the rifle-toting hunter. For a moment things were very tense. Leanne
stepped back to her left quickly. She saw the look in the eyes of the men
leaving the café, a look that sent a cold fear clean through her. Leanne
was wishing Matt were by her side; she would feel much safer with her
husband. Father Flarraty turned and placed his hands on the table in
front of him. He leaned forward and looked straight at Leanne. He
waited, watching out of the corner of his eye and listening for the two
to be out of sight and sound.

"We want to help; we are all in this together. If you know anything,
if you know where they are, warn them, hide them, and tell them we
are praying for them." The priest spoke slowly, quietly, and clearly,
looking directly at Leanne.

Over the last month life had become stressful, but over the last
week it had gotten crazy. Over the last day Leanne hadn't been sure of
anything, but this was the first time she was really afraid, afraid for her
life and the lives of her loved ones. Leanne had been through much
over the last five years, but nothing prepared her for what was happening now. Grabbing one of the posters from the table, she turned and
walked out the door without saying a word. Tears streamed down her
cheeks as she headed across the parking lot toward the shop. Leanne
was walking fast and with a purpose. Was she running from McGinn's
or to her husband? A little of both, she decided. Leanne looked forward. She was afraid to look back. The look she got from the large man,
a look that had her very afraid, was imbedded in her memory.

Leanne was suddenly startled by the sound of vehicles. She let
out a quick, high scream, almost a squeak like one would release at
a scary movie. This was so out of character for Leanne. A convoy
of twenty or more Humvees and a few trucks were coming down

the road at high speed, all filled with heavily armed men in camouflage uniforms. They drove straight through town without slowing. Leanne thought that they must be headed for the small naval base on the other side of town. It was a storage facility, very secure, but had never been very busy in the past. Stopping her quick walk, she turned to watch the vehicles speed by for a moment. It was surreal to see what appeared to be the military rolling in to take over a small town, her town. The lone woman stood in the center of a parking lot, poster in hand, watching in awe, as though she was suddenly an actor in a movie. Leanne could have been Jennifer Grey in *Red Dawn*, watching the Russians take her town, or any other character in a Cold War saga from the 1980s.

Matt drove the van around the shop and stopped quickly at Leanne's side. Leanne climbed in the passenger seat and closed the door. Not saying a word, she handed the poster to Matt.

Matt did not even look at it. He reached into the back seat and retrieved a duplicate, showing Leanne he had one too.

"Jeremy gave this to me. He said there are some men claiming to be the law now, vigilantes," Matt said.

"I just met some of them at McGinn's." Leanne responded. The tone in her voice had some pride; she had faced some scary people and come out OK.

"Father Flarraty was trying to warn me. We have to get home; it's not safe." Leanne was speaking calmly, but her words struck Matt deeply. His wife was afraid.

"Did you see all of those army guys?" Leanne asked.

"Yeah. Let's check out where they are going." Matt drove the van toward town, not toward the house. He received a very disapproving look from his wife as he tried to explain. "I'll just drive through and then we can stop and pick up the Caddy." Matt said as he drove. "Oh, and Jeremy is doing OK. He and the kid are staying at the shop full-time now." Matt and Leanne both knew it was the best thing for the shop and the best thing for Jeremy and his daughter.

"I am happy for them, but, honey we have to get home. We left three young men at our house, wanted young men, who are in serious danger." It was clear Leanne wanted nothing to do with driving through town.

Matt turned the radio on in the van, and they heard the tone of an emergency broadcast message. He pulled the van over quickly and turned up the radio. Leanne was feeling a unheard and frustrated. She knew that they needed information, but she was just eager to get home.

The two sat quietly and listened to the Speaker of the House, a Marine general, and a Supreme Court justice make announcements about the President being arrested, an impeachment, and martial law. This sure explained the Military rushing into town. They listened for about fifteen minutes. Matt had shut off the van to avoid using up gas, and Leanne was sitting back with her eyes closed. Matt was not sure if she was overwhelmed, tired, or praying. The truth was she was getting very frustrated with their situation and was just trying to stay calm. The announcement repeated itself; it was a continuous loop and was playing on every station.

Without opening her eyes or moving, Leanne asked, "Can we please go home now?" Her voice sounded near tears.

Before Matt could respond or they could discuss what they just heard, or even digest the gravity of it, there was a knock on the passenger-side window of the van. Leanne opened her eyes and turned toward her window. Two people dressed in full combat gear stood by the door.

Leanne thought they might be Army, but Matt recognized the rank.

Matt opened the window from the driver's door control and spoke to the young Hispanic woman. Speaking across his wife, he asked, "Can I help you, Lance Corporal?"

The young lady looked at Matt and Leanne then asked, "Do live in this town?"

"No," Matt responded.

"What's your business in town?" the young lance corporal asked accusingly.

"Checking on my shop, trying to get some news." Matt was not letting on that they had heard the announcement on the radio.

Leanne sat in the passenger seat quietly. Out her window she could see another young marine standing beside the van but further back. He was watching and covering the female lance corporal.

"Just keep your hands were we can see them," he said when he realized that Leanne had seen him.

"We don't want any trouble." Leanne spoke up in a hurry.

The young female lance corporal handed Leanne a document, one that explained the rules of martial law. "I suggest you go home," she said as she stepped back from the van.

"Can't we go to the store?" Leanne piped up, fishing for information.

"The stores will be open tomorrow. Come back tomorrow," the female marine replied.

"Yes, we will," Matt agreed. He wanted out of this situation. There were way too many guns in the hands of scared young men and women. Matt saw these young marines as people. He knew they had families at home who must be worried sick. Matt could tell these people were away from home, scared, young, and inexperienced. He did not see them as a threat, but he did see them as dangerous.

"Excuse me." Matt leaned across his wife toward the lance corporal. "Any word on Seattle? We have kids there."

"Secure, sir. We secured the larger cities and towns first. I am sure they are fine. Now time to get moving, sir."

"Yes, ma'am." Matt pulled the van onto the road and proceeded to drive toward the heart of town.

"Look at that." Leanne was looking at the stores on Main Street; each one had an armed soldier or marine at the door. It was very intimidating.

The elderly man paused in the telling of his story, and reality returned to the small apartment. The two missionaries looked on helplessly as the elderly man suffered a coughing fit, which interrupted his tale. His wife quickly tended to him with a medicated nebulizer, a kind of breathing machine.

After a moment or two of breathing through a steaming tube, the elderly man caught his breath and began to speak again.

"Sorry boys, lungs." He paused and took a deep breath. "Getting old, boys, is hard work," he said with a chuckle. As he sat back, his loving wife brought a glass of water to him.

"Honey, maybe we should call it a day?" She rubbed his shoulders and furrowed her brow with worry.

"I'm OK, if you two aren't bored by the ramblings of an old man," he responded.

"No, sir," the two responded in unison. "We can come back tomorrow if you are too tired," continued the taller of the two.

"Tomorrow? Who knows if I will even be around tomorrow?" the old man responded with a smile. He sat forward and continued explaining, not giving heed to his wife's worries or the young man's suggestion of returning tomorrow. It was history, and someone had to tell it. The old man knew he did not have many days left to tell the tale; he was going to take advantage of the youth sitting at his table.

He sat up tall, fought off a cough, and began to speak again. He spoke in the tone of a narrator.

So the Marines and the Army were in charge in little towns like Port Smith. What was it like in the cities? You may wonder. Food shortages, energy rationing, and a general lack of resources led to martial law in almost every major city in the US. Some cities had it worse than others; San Francisco had been quarantined as diseases started to run out of control. A lack of sanitation workers and failure of the water system brought typhoid in medieval levels to the city. The death rates in San Francisco were only rivaled by those in New York. In New York City the military and police had given up on whole areas: Queens was in a state of anarchy, Brooklyn was close to falling, and there were all-out street battles being fought in Jersey City.

Los Angeles was also a mess—riots and gang violence had taken its toll, and now the major street gangs had control. To the surprise of many, the gangs were keeping some level of peace and providing some basic necessities. Many of the Latino marines that returned from the wars in the Middle East had returned to gangs or joined gangs. The young veterans came home to a society with little help or support for them and even fewer jobs. The discipline and loyalty that one learns in combat actually improved life for many in these gang infested cities. Good or bad, the gangs were now much more efficient, more organized, and overall running like military units. Street gangs were in charge, and for the time being that was better than having no one in charge. The military could use their resources elsewhere.

Some cities like Charlotte, North Carolina, were running smoother than ever, with just occasional power interruptions. Seattle was not *doing so badly—riots had taken place, and downtown was not a safe place for anyone, but the outlying areas, the suburbs, were self-policing to a degree. There was a system of block committees growing, and they would meet with neighborhood committees, which answered to the military commanders. It was not the freedom and prosperity that Americans had become accustomed to, but it was working. It was becoming evident that the way people governed and interacted was going to be different in the cities than in small towns and the country. And both would be very different from the way folks had lived in the past.*

The elderly man's explanation moved back into the events of Port Smith.

After a drive through town, Matt and Leanne stopped in the parking lot of the shop. They discussed what it would take to keep the business alive. The repair shop was the only source of income and security of the Scott family, as well as the lifeline for Jeremy and his daughter. They agreed that for now Jeremy was their best hope and quickly ended the discussion so they could head for home. Leanne got out of the van and walked over toward the Cadillac parked in the back of the shop. Stopping for a minute to give Jeremy a hug, she quickly got into the car and started to drive toward the highway. Matt put the van in gear and followed closely behind.

The morning progressed, and the little town of Port Smith came to life. It was strange having armed guards at stores and walking the streets, but the military was doing well to stay out of the way and to keep neutral. Matt and Leanne were glad they lived out in the county. It would have been hard to live in a town that felt under siege whether it was or not.

Matt turned onto their street a few hundred feet behind Leanne in the Cadillac, and as he approached the house, he saw the broken front door. Leanne had not noticed the door and had turned down the drive and pulled the car into the garage. When Matt saw the damage, he hit the accelerator hard and turned the van into the drive, tires squealing. He then slammed on the brakes halfway down the driveway and threw the van into park. The sound of the van accelerating into the drive brought Leanne out of the garage in a hurry. She saw Matt jump from the van and run toward the front door. Matt had retrieved his colt 1911 from its holster as he approached the front door. Leanne had run up the drive and was close behind him. She looked down the side of the house and across the yard to be sure they were not walking into a trap. Matt could hear Elders Black and Jones talking quietly from the inside of the house. They were praying. Matt slowly entered the house, gun drawn and hammer back. The rage was building. Matt had spent many years avoiding rage and anger, something that he was proud of, but today, it was starting to take root again.

"If anything has happened to those boys…" Matt spoke out loud.

Seeing the anger in her husband and sensing the possible danger, Leanne stepped back toward the van, watching in every direction. Although she had a desire to run into the house, Leanne knew that watching her husband's back would be the right thing to do.

"Brother Scott," Elder Jones spoke out as he caught a glimpse of Matt coming across the living room. "They took him." He was crying as he pointed at the blood on the floor.

"They took him," Elder Black repeated. "They did not see us, but they got Elder Miles." He spoke without looking up, as though he felt ashamed. Elder Black reached down and picked up Elder Miles's book and handed it to Leanne, who had entered the room after she heard the missionaries. Leanne saw a look on her husband's face. It was one she had not seen before. She was concerned, and his look said it all. Matt was angry, and Matt was planning in his head; Matt Scott was going to make this right.

Leanne quickly went to Elders Black and Jones, checking the two missionaries for bruises or blood.

"We are fine. They did not find us," Elder Black reassured Leanne.

Matt Scott left the room and went straight to his office off the master bedroom. By the time Leanne and the two missionaries entered the room behind him, there was an M4 lying on the bed with four loaded magazines, a Winchester 300 magnum with a large scope, a box of shells, and two pistols.

"What are you doing?" Leanne said as she looked at the array of guns on the bed.

"I'm not sure yet." Matt was putting the tools together. The tools were needed to rescue, exact revenge, or just defend—his plan was not formulated yet. But it was clear Matt was ready to start playing rough. A part of Matt Scott that had been stored away for years was showing its face. This part of Matt was a stranger to Leanne, and it scared her. Leanne stood back. She looked at her husband, and she watched as he arranged guns and ammunition. When Matt saw her, he stopped for a moment. Matt walked to his wife, hugged her, and said, "It's going to be OK." He stepped away from her but kept his hands on her shoulders. "Trust me."

The two young missionaries stood in the doorway. Elder Black was not sure what to think. He was impressed by the macho nature of what he was seeing, yet knew that violence was not the answer. Elders Black and Jones watched and silently prayed.

CHAPTER EIGHT

They weren't aware of it, but events of the prior week in Salt Lake City had put the residents of Port Smith, the Scott family, and Elder Miles in serious danger. When the Secret Service arrived at the LDS Church and offices in Salt Lake City, many were caught by surprise. The President of the Church and several other leaders, seven of the twelve, had been arrested and taken away. No one knew their whereabouts. The buildings were searched by NSA and Secret Service agents, and an odd but important document was found. In the office of the presidency was a notepad with the name Francis Miles, and Port Smith, Washington. On the back page, there was a list of Biblical references and the words *Restoration of Israel* written in red across the top of the page. Agent Lamphier guessed that this document was important—it was handwritten and on the desk of the President of the Church.

Agent Lamphier was searching the office when a spontaneously formed local militia drove the agents out of the church buildings. At this point the president ordered the National Guard to take and secure the temple, the church offices, and the surrounding blocks. After a refusal to follow presidential command, the Governor of Utah ordered the National Guard to take control back from the Federal agents. Guard units worked with small bands of local men to drive the agents not just out of the church and temples but also out of the center of town. This was the first time since the Civil War that American soldiers fought American soldiers or agents. The National Guard units took the buildings back within a couple hours, but not without major losses to both sides. The gun battles left civilian soldiers and federal agents wounded and dying in the halls of the Great Temple.

Agent Lamphier was one of the agents who escaped by helicopter, and he escaped with the notebook. Lamphier did not know what this meant, or why one man in Port Smith, Washington, was so important. Lamphier took the notebook with him back to Washington and turned it over to the White House Chief of Staff. Later that day he was ordered to get to Port Smith, find this young man, and hold him for interrogation. He also had orders that authorized the killing of this young man if capture was not possible. The administration was afraid of this young missionary, and Lamphier did not know why. Lamphier actually knew very little of his mission. He knew that Miles was a missionary, and he knew that Miles was important to the President of the Church, who was the leader of his enemies, and to the President of the United States, his boss. He also knew that it was up to him alone to catch or kill this young man.

It was now Friday evening, and Matt and the two missionaries had just finished repairing the front door. Matt's thoughts of rescue or revenge were put on hold for a short time while he secured the house for his wife. Leanne was preparing dinner in the kitchen. The power came back on, and there was a flurry of things getting done, as no one knew how long it would be before it went off again. Matt came into the living room and turned on the TV. The large flat screen came to life, and to his surprise an episode of *Leave It to Beaver* was on. Matt flipped through the channels slowly, seeing old reruns and test screens one after another. Leanne had walked up behind Matt and handed him a large glass of ice water. The two young men came into the room.

"Any news?" Elder Black was getting worried about his family back in Texas.

"Looking," Matt snapped a bit impatiently, the stress of the week was showing itself on Matt's face and in his attitude. This time it was not blood sugar, Matt was feeling like it was time to take some action. Not sure what step to take next, he was searching for more information. He was still unsure of what was going on; he had no idea why they would take Miles.

"Sweetie, let's try the local channels," Leanne said. Matt had been looking only on the national and international news channels and only finding test screens. Leanne was right. When the channel was changed to a Seattle-based station, they saw a familiar face. The broadcaster was reading from a sheet of paper. "Remember, the Military is here to keep the peace," he read. "If you have needs—food, medicine, or other needs, contact your neighborhood leaders. Do not take your request to the Military, as they are only going to respond to the block leaders."

The four of them watched in shock. It reminded Matt of September 11, 2001. Matt had been watching the news when the planes hit the towers. Much like that morning, there was a feeling that they were watching a movie, not the news.

"I'm getting word of an announcement," the news broadcaster put his left hand to his ear, holding in an ear piece, and listening as if his life depended on it. The screen immediately went blank and then came back with the image of a man in a black suit standing at a podium in what looked like the House of Representatives, or maybe the Senate floor.

"My fellow Americans, I am speaking to you from the floor of the House of representatives, At 1:00 p.m. today, I, Speaker of the House, Congressmen Davies, with the authority and consent of the US Supreme Court, have ordered the house arrest of President Prescott and several of his supporters. This is in reaction to unconstitutional actions taken by the President to include the canceling of an election and the persecution of a political party and a religious faith. It is my intention to call for a nationwide election as soon as it becomes possible. I will be working with the leadership of both parties as well as the Military to achieve this goal. Law and order will prevail, democratic elections will take place, and our nation will once again take hold the position of the greatest democracy on earth. I ask you, the American people, to be patient, help one another, and be Americans.

He stopped, took a deep breath, and then continued.

"I would like to introduce you to General Seibel. I have appointed General Siebel Commander of Homeland Defense and Security. It is the General's charge to protect the people and provide assistance when possible. General, a few words."

Davies stepped back, and General Siebel stepped to the podium. He was bald, lean, and in his mid-60s. He wore a perfectly pressed set of Marine Corps dress blues, white gloves, and a high collar. His medals covered his chest and included the Congressional Medal of Honor hanging around his neck. The General stepped up and cleared his throat. He placed his white hat on the podium and placed a hand on each side.

"I am General Stephen Siebel, and I would like to say a few words about my mission and what it means to you. " The general cleared his throat again and took a deep breath. He was speaking from the cuff, there had been no time for speechwriters; he had no teleprompters. He was nervous, and he was sweating. Under his breath, the General muttered, "God save us."

"It is my mission to keep the peace, to help feed and protect people, to provide medical services when we can, and to generally protect our population until such time as resolutions to matters political are found. My orders come only from the acting President of the United States, Speaker Davies."

The four of them stood together in the living room of the Scott home, listening to the message and looking at each other.

Elder Black stepped forward and said, "Church on Sunday. We will have church on Sunday." To Matt it seemed like a random statement until he realized that seeing some authority gave the young missionary a moment of security.

"Do you think that's a good idea?" Leanne was worried about the poster she had seen; she had not shared it with the young men. "Do you really think you should be out in public?" Leanne's voice was shaking with worry.

Matt was still planning in his head; he had not even heard the statements by Elder Black or his wife. "We need to find Elder Miles," Matt said in a commanding voice. It was like the four in the room were all caught in their own reality. They made statements without hearing the others.

Leanne had gone back to the kitchen and started to tend to dinner when she realized she needed something from the pantry in the garage. When she reentered the room empty-handed, she looked at Matt and said, "Honey, we need to talk," and motioned toward the garage.

Matt was still deep in thought, but he did follow his wife's lead. The two entered the garage and closed the door behind them.

"We are missing quite a bit of the stuff we got from the wholesalers." Leanne pointed at the stacks of boxes they had brought back from Bremerton.

"They could not have eaten that much. Maybe the feds took it." Matt said.

"Too much for them to have eaten, and, look, the boxes are put back empty," Leanne said. She was thinking about the questions at McGinn's—the food and supplies. Leanne did not want to think the missionaries had taken it.

"I need to tell you what I heard at McGinn's," Leanne said to her husband. "Two men, they wanted to know who was bringing food to the Mormons. They were very angry and said something about hoarders." Leanne was sure there was a connection to their missing supplies.

Matt looked through several boxes. He found cases of pasta with half of the contents gone and several cases of canned goods missing. After about five minutes of sorting through empty box after empty box, the two of them walked into the house and sat at the table.

"Elders, come over here." There was a tenor of parental discipline in Matt's voice. Leanne sat up tall at the end of the table; she wanted to know what was going on.

"We need to trust each other," Matt said to the two young men after they approached the table.

Looking confused, Elders Black and Jones looked at each other blankly.

"The food," Leanne said. "Did you take the food?"

Again the two looked confused and questioning. Elder Black spoke up. "I don't know what you are talking about."

"The food in the garage," Leanne said. "The food you helped us unload from the van that night, it's almost all gone." The four of them sat quietly for a moment, and then Elder Jones spoke up.

"I think I know." Elder Jones was holding the small book that Elder Miles had carried with him. He opened the book. "There are some strange notes and highlighting in this book." Elder Jones opened a page and pointed to writing in the margin. "Rankers, two need seven," it said.

"What does it mean? And what does that have to do with the food?" Elder Black was getting angry. His face was flushed and his voice was rising, not only in volume, but also in pitch.. Leanne could tell he didn't like being accused of stealing, especially after the stress of losing his friend.

"It's notes," Elder Jones said. "Look. Rankers, the family out on Mountainview Road, Rankers two needs seven. The Rankers have seven kids. They have two. Maybe they have food for two and need seven. You think that's where he was going?"

"What do you mean, where he was going?" Matt asked, remembering that odd morning when Elder Miles was up looking disheveled.

"Elder Miles would go out at night sometimes," Elder Black said. "He has always done this. He can't sleep indoors sometimes. Actually, he hardly ever sleeps."

"Look," Elder Jones opened the book to another page and showed Leanne one, and then another.

"My God, he has been feeding half the congregation!" Leanne said.

"Ward," Elder Black corrected her.

It was clear that Elder Miles was much more capable than Leanne and Matt had thought. His book was full of notes, and much of it seemed to be in some form of code that made little sense to Matt or Leanne.

"We need to get the word out. We need to find him." Elder Black was showing his concern for his friend, but it was more than that. Elder Black knew this was proof that the strange boy was special. There was something about him that made many uncomfortable, but he was special. Dinner came and went in relative silence that night. The two missionaries went to their room. Matt set to cleaning and tending to the weapons he had laid out earlier. Matt double- and triple-checked the guns and ammunition, and then he locked them back in the gun safe. This left Leanne alone with time to be worried and to cook, what she did when she was upset. The power stayed on most of the night and did not go out until sometime long after they had all gone to bed.

In the morning Matt awoke early as always. When he went into the dining area, he saw the table covered with baked goods. A smile broke out on his face. Leanne had warned him in the past, "You will know when I am upset or mad—I bake." And it was true. The few times they argued, Leanne would end up baking enough to feed an army. He knew she was upset, not with him, not with the Elders, but upset. She should be—the world as they knew had ended. Now her husband was arming himself to go rescue some strange young man they had been taking care of. Leanne was feeling out of the loop and alone. Matt was not including her in his planning; she knew this but also knew there was little she could do about it.

Matt was dressed, had made coffee, and had put together a backpack and his motorcycle gear. In the garage was a dirt bike that he rode on occasion. Matt's Yamaha yz 460 was something he had traded some work for; he was doing a friend a favor and ended up with a toy out of the deal. Quietly, Matt put his gear in the garage on the bike and then returned to the house.

Matt stood at the kitchen counter and wrote a note to his wife. Leanne was still sound asleep in the bedroom. He wrote quickly, as he did not want to have to explain this in person. "When you read this, know that I love you and will be back as soon as I can. Do not follow me or let the missionaries follow me. I will be back soon with Elder Miles. I love you." No matter how he handled this, he was going to make her mad, but keeping her safe and mad was a better option than to include her and put her in danger. Matt laid the note on the table next to his empty cup of coffee. Then he went into the missionaries' room. Elder Jones was sleeping; Elder Black was awake and staring at the ceiling.

"I am coming with you," he said. Apparently he had been listening or watching.

"No you are not. I need you here. I need you to make sure Leanne is safe." He knew if he gave Elder Black responsibility he would honor it. "Give me your word." Matt looked sternly at the young man. "Promise me you will keep my wife safe." Matt left the young man no options.

"My word, Brother Scott, but you had better get back soon." Elder Black sounded very sure of himself.

Matt went to the garage and put on his backpack. He had a pistol holstered on his side and an M4 slung on his shoulder. Matt opened the side door and walked the motorcycle out to the side of the house.

Then he walked it to the end of the driveway, uphill. Matt was breathing heavily and sweating by the time he had pushed the bike to the top of the driveway, but it was downhill out of the cul-de-sac, so he jumped on and pushed off. Matt coasted to the bottom of the hill before he started the engine. This was an old two-stroke motorcycle. It would be hard to start, and he needed to be clear of the house before it made any noise. He was sneaking away and felt bad about it. But Matt needed to do this, and he could not risk Leanne stopping him, or even worse, following him.

The Yamaha crackled to life, and Matt pulled up with his toe, shifting into third gear. With the front wheel off the ground, he roared off toward town. After about five miles, Matt reached a dirt driveway on the right. The driveway had a large sign over it that said, "Chow." Sheriff Chow joked about his Asian ranch often. Matt turned onto the driveway and rode up to the large, white, two-story house at the end of the drive. Shutting off his engine, Matt pulled off his helmet quickly; he wanted to be recognized.

Chow walked out on the front porch with a shotgun in his hand.

"Matt, Matt Scott, is that you?"

"Yes."

"Put that damn thing around back and get in here." Chow waived at a small barn beside the house.

Matt pushed the bike to the garage and put his helmet on the seat. He closed the barn door behind him and walked to the back of the house, where Chow was standing on the back porch.

"Not very smart, riding that noisy thing around and carrying guns," Chow said. "Between the feds and some trigger-happy soldier or marine, you could get shot."

"Least of my worries." Matt looked at Chow and paused before he stated, "They took one of the boys. They broke into my house and took one of the boys. I don't even know if he is still alive."

Matt proceeded to tell Chow about the missing missionary, the blood, and even about the food and the book with notes in it. By now Matt needed someone to trust. Right or wrong, Chow was it.

"I know where they are," Chow explained. The day before, Chow had gone back to his old office and had spoken to a marine captain there who explained the situation and wanted Chow to take charge of the sheriff's office again. When Chow arrived at the office that day, he saw the black Chevy Tahoe parked in his spot. Chow saw Agent Lamphier talking with Deputy Miller. Pretty sure he had not been spotted, Chow drove right by and went back home. "I planned on going back with a few marines if they would help," Chow said with a chuckle.

"Miller is working with them?" Matt questioned.

"I think so." Chow liked Miller, and he was a little disappointed. The thought of his young deputy turning against the people in the community felt sickening. Miller was someone that Chow had trusted, and now he did not know what to think.

"Did you talk to the military?" Matt kept up the questions. He knew he was pushing Chow hard, but he needed information and Chow's help. He didn't want to do this alone.

"Not anyone in charge, just keep hearing that it's not their business." Chow's response sounded weak to Matt. Matt felt maybe Chow was trying to justify his not fighting to keep his job as the elected sheriff.

"The way I see it, Lamphier does not have any support left in Washington or locally, except maybe whoever put those anti-Mormon posters out." Matt was trying to talk himself into confronting Lamphier, and more importantly trying to convince Chow that Lamphier was vulnerable.

It was clear that Matt was going to take some action—he was going to find a way to get the young man back—but it was also clear that Chow was becoming less and less committed to the idea.

"I am going to get him back," Matt let Chow know his intentions, "with or without your help."

"I will go with you to check it out, but we are not going in half-cocked and get ourselves killed," Chow finally said. Matt needed Chow because he knew his way around the office and could maybe turn Deputy Miller and any other officers that had sided with Lamphier. Matt knew that without Chow's help he did not stand a chance of finding or helping Elder Miles.

"You know I am not going to let that young man get hurt anymore." Matt was very concerned. The thought of Elder Miles being interrogated was horrifying. Matt didn't believe the young man had the ability to tell them what they wanted to know.

Sheriff Chow and Matt Scott worked out the details, and then they loaded up in Chow's pickup and drove toward the sheriff's office. Chow had brought a spotting scope and some binoculars. They agreed that they would take a look and devise a plan. Chow was afraid Matt was going to go in guns blazing.

Back at the Scott home, Leanne was up and she was mad. How dare he go out on his own? It was dangerous, and he was leaving her with the missionaries. By the time Leanne had gotten up, read the note, and had a cup of coffee, she had calmed down very little. Matt had done the wrong thing for the right reason. She could forgive this, but she still was not happy. She went to bed the night before half expecting something like this. Even so, she was angry and worried.

Elder Black was avoiding Leanne this morning. First of all, he was quite uncomfortable with being left in the home with a woman. Mormon missionaries are not allowed to be alone with someone of the opposite sex without supervision, and this was the second time the Scott family had pushed his comfort zone in this area. The changing or breaking of the rules did not seem to affect Elder Jones; he was more of a go-with-the-flow type than the type-A Elder Black. Second, Leanne knew that Matt could not have left without the young men knowing. They had deceived her, and Elder Black was feeling some shame over the whole thing.

The two Elders had been in the living room, and Leanne was sitting at the kitchen table. Anyone who knew Leanne well would have expected her to have whipped up breakfast for the two by now, but not today. A confrontation was in the making, and Leanne was not going to act like nothing was wrong. As far as she was concerned, they had been keeping a secret from her, and Leanne hated it when people lied or kept secrets to protect her. It made her feel weak and insignificant.

Elder Black walked quietly past Leanne to the bathroom and returned a few minutes later. As he approached the kitchen table, Leanne put her arm out straight. "Not so fast," she said, "what were you thinking, letting him leave alone?" Leanne knew this was a stupid thing to say. Matt was going to do what Matt needed to do, and he was going to try to protect everyone he could while he did it. His strong will and sense of chivalry was part of what she loved about him.

"Sister Scott, I couldn't..." but before William Black could finish his sentence, she said, "I'm sorry, I know." Leanne had a tear running down her cheek. The young missionary had no idea what to do. Most men have no idea how to react to a situation like this, let alone someone as young and sheltered as William Black. "I swear, if anything happens to him, I will be so pissed off." Leanne cracked a smile at William Black.

Leanne had never seen her husband truly angry or violent in any way, yet she knew from long talks they had that Mathew Scott had the ability to become something he did not like. Matt and Leanne had discussed the fact that he had moments of violence in his past. Not unfettered or unchecked violence, maybe not even unjustified violence, but nevertheless, he explained that he was capable of hurting people. The truth was Matt had never lashed out or been out of control. He had a period in his life in which he was called on to do things that were contrary to his upbringing and his nature. Matt's mother was a pacifist, and as a young marine, pacifism was not an option. Leanne was afraid, but not that he would get physically hurt. She was afraid that he would be forced to do something he would regret, something he could not live with later on in life.

"He isn't stupid, Sister Scott. He will be careful," Elder Black reassured her.

"OK, no more Sister. My name is Leanne," she said with exasperation. "And I'm sorry, but I can't do the Elder thing anymore. It's weird because you are so young. So what else can I call you?"

William Black looked mortified. "Elder Black," he said.

Elder Jones piped up. "Leanne, my name is Nicolas. My friends and families call me Nick." Elder Black threw a glare in his direction.

"Come on, loosen up, William." Now Nick Jones was getting out of line, and the looks from Elder William Black showed it. "We have not been released. We are on mission, and we will continue to act like missionaries." Elder Black was getting angry, not very becoming of a missionary.

"OK, so I will call you Nick; you will call me Leanne," she said. Then turning to Elder Black, she said, "I would like to call you Bill or Will if it's okay, Elder." Leanne was showing respect to the young man and was hoping it made a difference.

"Bill is my dad's name," he replied.

"OK, Will or William?"

He paused and looked a bit conflicted. "I am a missionary, and my title is Elder Black. But I guess Will would be okay. Just please don't ever call me…" As he finished, Nick piped up, "Willie."

The three broke out into laughter. "Don't ever call me Willie," Will said as he laughed.

Leanne got up from the table and went into the kitchen. "Will, what is your favorite breakfast?"

"Crepes," Will said and smiled. "My father would make me crepes most Sundays before church." He suddenly realized how much he missed his family.

"Nick, what is your favorite breakfast?" Leanne asked.

"Bacon, eggs, and corned beef hash." Nick was smiling. This young man had lost contact with his family, had been assaulted and even shot, but the thought of someone making his favorite breakfast seemed to bring a new level of joy to him. It seemed that in times of the greatest turmoil, the simplest things would bring happiness.

"When was the last time you two talked to your families?"

"It's been over a month," Will responded. His answer seemed to pull the smile right off his face.

Leanne went to the kitchen table, picked up her cell phone, and handed it to Will Black. "You call your father, and you tell him that I am making crepes for you tomorrow before we go to church." Leanne had never been to an LDS church and was not sure what she was getting into—she was not even sure there would be a service—but either way this young man needed this and she was going to make the best of this situation. "When you're done, you let Nick call home. I will be making corned beef hash and eggs for breakfast this morning, if you can live with canned corned beef." Nick Jones wanted to hug Leanne, but he knew that would be crossing the line.

"Thank you," both young men said simultaneously, "Thank you." There was not much more to be said. Will reached his father on the cell phone and they talked for about ten minutes. When he was finished, he looked at Leanne. "God bless you, Leanne." It was difficult for him to call her Leanne, but he did it. He respected her wishes, and he respected her.

"So, what's the news, the gossip with your family?" Leanne was trying to lighten the mood.

"They are okay; they are at the hunting cabin with another family. My little sisters are safe, too, and my mom. She thanks you and said she wants to meet you someday," he replied.

"Little sisters?" Leanne asked.

"I have four little sisters, Jovi is two, Anna is nine, Elizabeth is fourteen, and Stephanie is seventeen," Will said with a smile.

Nick had the phone at this point, and he was across the room talking and pacing. He had dialed several times before he got someone on the phone. Nick's conversation did not look like it was going as well as Will Black's did.

"Everything OK?" Leanne asked as Nick closed the phone and handed it back to her. She was afraid of the answer. Sometimes not knowing is better; it leaves room for hope.

"Yes, I think so. I could not get in touch with my family, but I did get in touch with the neighbor," he said with a frown. "He said that they had gone out of town, that they took the boat, and that they would be gone for some time."

Nick Jones was from Georgia. His family—two brothers, his dad, and stepmom—lived in the Richmond Hill area. Nick's father owned an old sailboat, and they would often take trips to the Barrier Islands.

"I'm sure they are fine. Dad probably took everyone to St. Catherine's, his favorite island. I just wish I could have heard their voices." Nick was feeling a sudden and strong dose of homesickness. His voice had the vibrato one gets when holding back tears.

The three had a large breakfast together. Elder Nick Jones said a prayer, and they talked and laughed as breakfast dragged on for over an hour. After breakfast they cleaned up and did chores. The three worked in a flurry, because keeping busy would cut the worry and the sadness they each felt.

CHAPTER NINE

Back in Port Smith, Chow and Matt were driving down a gravel road through a thick patch of woods. Matt was eating a granola bar he had packed in his pocket before he left. Chow was eating a Hostess fruit pie.

"Those things will kill you," Matt said to Chow, pointing at the apple pie.

"I know. But, man, they are good." Chow pointed at the glove box of his 1970 Chevy. "There's more in there."

Matt smiled. "Thanks." Opening the glove box, he found it packed with junk food. Chow had restored his old four-wheel-drive truck, and he kept it in mint condition. Matt was a bit surprised that Chow allowed anyone to eat in it, let alone hide junk food in the glove box.

"You don't tell Laurie, and I won't tell Leanne," Chow said with a laugh.

"Deal," Matt agreed.

Laurie was Chow's wife. She was a nutritionist at a clinic in town, and she would not be happy with hostess fruit pies. Actually she would be furious. This was funny to Matt. Leanne would be a bit less bothered, but Matt played along. Maybe it was a way of bonding and getting past the tension.

Matt was sure Chow had a first name, but he had never known what it was. "What's your name?" Matt inquired as he polished off his apple pie. Talking with a mouth full of sweet crust and sugary apples, it almost seemed like a childhood schoolyard question.

"Chow," he said with a questioning voice. "What kind of question is that?"

"Your first name, you idiot," Matt said as he laughed so hard he almost spit the remaining pie across the truck.

"You couldn't pronounce it. Just call me Chow."

"Try me," Matt challenged.

"Huizhong," he said quickly with a very strong accent. Matt had always thought of Chow as a very Americanized man, so the accent and name caught him by surprise.

"OK, you're right. I'll just call you Chow," Matt said with a chuckle.

They were approaching an old gravel pit that was gated and locked. Chow pulled the truck over to the right side of the road. He handed a key to Matt and said, "Hop out and get the gate, and lock it up once we are in."

Matt stepped out and unlocked the bright orange metal gate made of what looked like a piece of eight-inch pipe. It was clear no pickup truck was going to be breaking through anytime soon. He swung it open, and Chow drove through. Matt then closed and locked the gate and got back in the truck. Chow drove another hundred yards or so without saying a word, and then he turned the truck down a short spur road and shut it off. Chow was making sure no one saw the truck; he parked behind a large patch of blackberry vines, far enough down the spur road that it could never be seen from the other side of the gate. The two men got out of the truck; Matt reached for the M4 he had put behind the seat.

"Just looking today, Matt," Chow said as he put his hand on the barrel of the assault rifle. Matt Scott was out for blood. Without the cooler thinking of Chow, things could go from bad to worse.

"OK." Matt slid the gun back behind the seat, and the two gathered binoculars, a spotting scope, and a water bottle each. "We can do it your way for now." They locked the truck and walked around the back toward the road they had arrived on.

"Over that hill, and then we will be less than a hundred yards from the sheriff's office." Chow pointed at what looked like it used to be a trail. The brush was thick, and there was a thin trail snaking up the hill. The two men went up the hill slowly, pushing the brush aside and trying not to leave an obvious path behind them. The two occasionally stopped to untangle the underbrush, or to catch themselves as they tripped on an unseen root or blackberry vine. As they arrived on the top of the hill, they slowed and surveyed the area. There was a clear area, what looked like an old campfire pit that had not been used in years, and a couple of chairs fashioned out of stumps. Chow sat down and gestured Matt toward the other chair.

"What now?" Matt asked.

"We watch and we wait," Chow said.

Matt looked around the area to see old beer cans and an occasional empty shell casing—the type of things one would find in a rural campsite. The beer cans were mostly Budweiser, but Matt found a few old Rainier beer cans, the kind with pull-top lids. The age of the cans made it clear that generations past had used this spot. No signs of youth—not one modern aluminum beer can or energy drink can. The trash of a modern campsite would look much different, just as the beer aisle at the local Jackpot convenience store looked so much different from Matt's youth. The two men watched, Chow with a spotting scope and Matt with binoculars. They could see the Tahoe and a patrol cruiser parked in the sheriff and undersheriff's parking spots. There were three other patrol cars parked in a chain-link enclosed parking lot. Matt could see nothing through the windows. He wanted to go down and look around.

"Patience. Let's just see what they are going to do," Chow said to Matt. Chow was not itching for the fight that Matt Scott was looking for.

The time passed slowly. Other than the mosquitoes and the occasional bee, nothing happened. They watched the metal back door and the gray cinderblock building. An hour or so after they arrived, the back door opened, and they clearly saw the silhouette of a large man in a dark suit. Although they were some distance away, they could hear what was being said quite clearly. This was a bit alarming; could they be heard as clearly? Matt knew that often in the woods, especially when on a hill, sound traveled much farther and clearer than people would think. Matt looked through the binoculars and recognized the agent. Elder Black had filled him in on everything he had heard at the house, and Matt recognized the man from the church. This was Agent Morris.

"Lamphier, are you coming or what?" Agent Morris turned back toward the door as Agent Lamphier came out of the side door. He was walking quickly and straight for the Chevy Tahoe.

"Get in, you idiot." Lamphier sounded very frustrated and was obviously getting tired of Agent Morris.

The two men got into the Tahoe, backed up, and drove out of the parking lot in a roar.

"Now we go down and look," Chow said.

"I count three cars in the yard, and one in the parking lot." Matt was trying to formulate a plan. It was clear his initial idea of going in with guns blazing was not going to happen.

"Those three are always there; I think Miller is the only one still in the office. The three in the yard are back-up cars, and two of them don't even run," he explained. "The one parked by the door, that's Deputy Miller's car. It's the only car we had with the traffic logo on the back." Chow was showing his value. This type of information was priceless. Matt was calming a little internally. He knew from the beginning that Chow was right, but he just was too angry to want to hear it. The two men arranged their gear and proceeded to make their way down the short hill toward the sheriff's office. They would have to cross a large lawn, exposing them to being spotted. The good news was that there were no windows on this side of the building, and as long as Deputy Miller stayed inside, they would be safe. Miller had a definite advantage if he was paying attention, but why would he think anyone would be coming for the young missionary?

They walked across the lawn side by side; they walked like they belonged there, deliberately and with purpose. Often, if you just look like you belong, people won't notice you, something Matt learned long ago as a young marine. As they approached the door, the offices appeared to be deserted. It was a strange feeling for Chow, as this place had been a hub of activity for the past four years for him. Chow had spent more time at these busy offices than he did at home, and now they were quiet and empty. Chow pulled a key chain from his pocket and opened the door. The two men stepped in, and Chow closed the door softly behind him and then locked it. Chow was trying to be as quiet as possible, as surprise and stealth were the only chances they had.

"Lamphier, that you?" Miller was calling from the jail area of the building.

Chow and Matt walked toward the voice, peeking into every open doorway and window on the hall. As the two men walked down the hall, a figure appeared from the last door, which was thirty or so feet in front of them. The figure stepped out into the hallway in plain view.

"Oh, shit," Miller voiced, realizing it was not Lamphier or Morris.

"Is that all you have to say?" Chow scolded Miller. The boss in Chow was very disappointed in the young man he had recruited.

"You don't understand," Miller said.

"I understand; you picked sides," Chow stated clearly.

"The wrong side," Matt added.

The three men looked at each other, none quite sure what was coming next.

"Now what?" Miller asked, expecting Chow to have an answer. "What do they want with this kid, anyway?" The look on Miller's face was a cross between fear and shame. Miller was still thinking of the two he left in the closet. If Chow only knew the truth, he might not be so upset.

"If I give you the kid, well, Lamphier will come after me." Miller knew he had made a mistake back at the Scott house; he just could not find a way out of the mess he was in. Miller's true loyalty was with Chow, but in a situation like this, misplaced loyalty could be fatal.

"Is he OK?" Matt was worried about Elder Miles.

"I think so. He won't talk, just stares out the window. "

"Can I see him?" Matt Scott was intent on getting the young man to safety.

"I don't know," Miller said. He stepped back a step and rested his right hand on his pistol. Miller carried a .45-caliber Glock on his service belt. Like many police officers, his first instinct when feeling threatened was to place his hand on the pistol.

"You are going to shoot us?" Chow asked with a bit of disdain in his voice. Miller did not respond; he just stood still, looking confused.

"You can just walk away," Chow said. "Just leave. You go home or take a trip, and I will forget you were here, forget you were with Lamphier."

"Where could I go? They are with the Government; they will find me." The young deputy was afraid and had no idea what to do. He was loyal to Chow. He had already lied to the feds about the two missionaries back at the Scott home. The young deputy had broken the trust of Chow and of Lamphier, and he felt cornered.

Chow saw fear in the young deputy's face; both Matt and Chow were watching him closely. The pitch in the young deputy's voice indicated he was feeling trapped or desperate. They needed to calm him down.

"There is no government anymore. Haven't you seen the news?" Matt said in a condescending tone.

"I'm not sure who to believe—you, the news, or Lamphier," Miller said with a bit of a shake in his voice. His hand was now wrapped around the grip of his holstered pistol. Matt stepped forward slightly ahead and to the left of Chow. He was standing less than ten feet from Miller with both of his hands elevated chest high.

"We did not come in here guns a-blazing. I don't have a problem with you. I just need to see Elder Miles and make sure he is OK." Matt was done waiting. "So you can either shoot me or get the hell out of my way." He slowly moved forward but stopped after two steps.

Miller was lost and unsure of what to do. Chow and Matt knew it wasn't a good combination to be armed and unsure. The three stood in silence. Matt looked at Miller, and Miller looked at Chow. The standoff was getting a bit more tenuous.

"I am not going to stand here and wait for those two thugs in suits to come back," Matt said as his impatience, worry, and temper got the better of him. Matt stepped forward again, this time with authority, and pushed Miller aside. As he did, Deputy Miller took his hand off his gun and just fell back against the white-painted cinderblock wall. Miller had no intention of drawing his gun; he just wanted out of this mess.

"Which room is he in?" Matt yelled at Miller, walking down the hall.

Leaning back on the wall, Deputy Miller once again put his right hand on his gun.

Chow made his way up to Deputy Miller and firmly grabbed Miller's right wrist. He was not going to let Miller pull that gun from his holster.

The two men stood there, Chow with his hand on Miller's wrist, and Miller now resting his hand on his gun. It was like a game of standoff. Matt was regretting the fact that they had left their guns in the truck, yet Chow did seem to have complete control of Miller at this point.

"Last door on the left," Miller said as he lifted his hand off his gun. Miller's tone and attitude was lightening by the moment, and he was obviously not going to try to stop them.

Matt ran to the door and pushed it open. Elder Miles was sitting in a metal office chair, and his hands were handcuffed to the chair on each side. Dried blood matted his hair down on one side, and he had a large bruise over his left eye. Elder Miles looked at Matt Scott and smiled. Chow and Miller followed behind and quickly went to work taking the handcuffs off. Elder Miles didn't look too good. He had obviously been beaten; the closer Matt looked, the more welts and bruises he could see. Lamphier or Morris had done a number on him.

"We have to get him out of here," Matt said as he helped Elder Miles to his feet.

Elder Miles put his arm around Matt's shoulder and stood up. Miller dipped under Elder Miles's other shoulder, and the two men started to walk Elder Miles out of the room and down the hall. Chow led the way, opening doors ahead of them. Elder Miles looked at Miller and cracked a small smile. He then looked at Matt and said, "This one, he is OK." Matt thought this was a strange thing to say, because if Miller had not stopped the beating, why would he be so forgiving? And worse, if Miller had done the beating, why wasn't Elder Miles angry or afraid? Matt looked around the battered young man at Deputy Miller. Without words, Matt Scott gave a look, the look of warning to the young deputy.

"You wouldn't understand," Miller said, only to be interrupted by Matt, who said, "Not a word." Miller was clearly not going to justify his actions to Matt Scott, not now. They had no choice; they had to trust each other at least for now.

As the three men and the beaten missionary stepped out of the rear door of the cinderblock building, the sun popped out from behind the clouds. Elder Miles looked up and squinted into the sun. "Thank you, Father," he said very clearly. Matt shook his head. Just when he least expected it, Elder Miles had something to say.

"Put him in my car." Miller pointed to his cruiser.

"I don't think so," Matt said with anger in his voice.

"Surely, you don't expect him to walk." Chow said.

"I will carry him before I let him go again." Matt was not playing; he was angry. He did not trust Miller as much as Chow did, and he actually was not sure he trusted Chow at this point.

"We will get back to the truck, and then we can get him back to my house," Matt stated with some degree of authority. The problem was even Matt knew that he was not going to be able to get this injured young man up that trail.

"Look, you can't do it alone," Chow told Matt. "Deputy Miller can take him back to your house. We can get the truck and your bike, and meet him back there. It's the only thing that makes sense."

"Brother Scott, I will be fine." Elder Miles tried to calm Matt down.

Matt stopped for a moment; he knew it was his only option. Matt and Chow could not get Elder Miles up the trail in time to avoid the Feds. Miller had already helped them, so he had to be trusted. Miller had not turned in Elders Black and Jones, Matt was reasoning in his head. He knew he had to go along with Miller taking the young man, but he did not like it.

"OK, that's the plan. But Miller, if anything else happens to him, it's on you. Don't underestimate me." Matt was threatening the deputy, and it was clear he meant it. "Whatever happens to him, I will make sure you get twice."

"Are you threatening me?" Miller asked.

"Not a threat, a promise." Matt Scott was very angry.

Miller and Matt turned to the left and helped the missionary into the back of the patrol car. Deputy Miller closed the door after buckling him in. Miller climbed into the driver's seat and started the car; he instantly rolled down the back window from the driver's seat, buckled his seat belt, and closed the door.

"It's OK. He will take you to Elders Black and Jones, and Sister Scott will be there too. I will see you soon." Matt was hoping he wasn't lying to the young man. There was a lot of doubt in Matt's heart. How could he let this young man out of his sight after all that had happened? He would never forgive himself if it went wrong. Chow walked over and leaned in. He said something quietly to Miller, something Matt Scott could not hear. Miller responded with a nod and a, "Yes, Sir," and then Chow turned and started to walk away from the car. Chow was already heading for the trail and Matt stood watching as the patrol car pulled away.

"You coming?" Chow yelled over his shoulder. He was jogging quickly.

"Yeah, yeah," Matt turned and jogged to catch up with Chow. The two men walked up the trail to the top of the hill. At the top they took a moment to pause and survey the area below them. Matt asked, "What did you tell him back at the car?"

Chow responded, "Nothing for you to worry about; just know he will take care of him. You have my word." This gave Matt some peace of mind. When the two men reached the cleared-out campsite, they turned and looked back at the jail and sheriff's office. Chow could see the Tahoe making its way back up the road toward the jail, and he could see Miller's patrol car heading away on the same road. He pointed, and Matt lifted the binoculars to his eyes. "Oh shit." Matt sucked in a deep breath of air. "No." It was very out of character for Matt to cuss, but this was a genuine moment of panic. As they watched the two vehicles heading toward each other, they knew that at any moment the Feds would figure out that Miller was turning on them. Chow looked at Matt, and then he looked back down the hill through the spotting scope he had taken from his jacket pocket. The Tahoe was speeding along the road at high speed; the patrol car was driving much slower. They saw brake lights on the patrol car, and then Miller stopped in the road.

"What the hell is he doing?" Matt said. Then they saw a flash of white, the reverse lights. Miller backed the car up and into a side road and stopped. The two men watched, holding their breath, as the Tahoe rounded the corner. The patrol car was just off the road, and if either man in the Tahoe looked to the side, they would see it. From this far away, it looked as if the two vehicles were just feet from each other. The Tahoe passed by the side road without slowing a bit, rounding the next corner with a cloud of dust coming up from behind. Once the

Tahoe was past, Miller's patrol car pulled out and headed away from the sheriff's office at top speed. This time, dust billowed in the wake of the patrol car as it roared toward the paved road ahead. The two men on the hill watched—one through a spotting scope, the other through binoculars—until the patrol car entered into the section of the road covered by tree canopy. They lost sight of the car. They turned their attention to the jailhouse as the Tahoe pulled up. They could hear the two men talk. They had found before that sound carried in this little valley.

"Where the hell is that idiot?" Morris yelled loudly. He jumped from the driver's seat, leaving the door open, and stormed toward the metal door at the end of the building. Lamphier stepped out of the passenger's side and walked slowly but deliberately. He pulled a satellite phone from his jacket, methodically swung the antenna up and dialed, then began talking to someone as he walked. Morris had opened the door and gone inside. The sound of yelling could be heard, but neither Matt nor Chow could make out the words. Lamphier went in and closed the door behind him. The two agents were then out of sight and sound. Matt and Chow looked at each other for a second and allowed a quick moment to feel victory.

"We had better get going," Chow said and then turned and put the scope in his pocket. He headed across the open area and started down the trail. Matt took another moment to look and see if he could spot Miller's patrol car off in the distance, with no luck, and then followed behind Chow. The two men arrived at the truck at the same time. Matt took the key from Chow and walked toward the gate. He was not quite ready to get into the truck, as adrenaline, combined with worry, had his head spinning.

Matt opened the gate as Chow pulled up and drove through. Then he locked the gate, climbed into the truck and slammed the door. Chow drove down the dirt road until he hit the highway, driving at sixty and seventy miles per hour. Chow wanted to get back home as soon as he could. Both men were thinking of their families. They needed to get back to them. How could they protect their loved ones if they were not home? Matt opened a bottle of water and handed it to Chow and then opened a second bottle and drank continuously until it was empty. The drive back to Chow's house felt like it took forever, and little more than niceties were said. When they got back to the Chow farm, they put the truck in the barn. Matt got out of the truck and arranged his gear and slung the rifle he had retrieved from behind the seat over his shoulder.

"Tomorrow they will all go to church, you know," Chow said with a degree of worry.

"Yes, as they should," Matt responded.

"And you?" Chow asked, "Will you go?"

"When was the last time I went to church?" Matt said with a crooked smile. Matt got on his bike and gave it a kick. Three attempts later, the motorcycle started. Matt turned to Chow, "Will I see you there?" he asked. He pulled the helmet off the handlebars, put it on, cinched the chinstrap, and threw the bike into gear. Out of the barn and to the end of the drive, Matt sped away, leaving Chow standing beside his truck in a cloud of dust.

Back at the sheriff's office, Lamphier was on the satellite phone again. Someone in Washington was giving him direction, but it wasn't the White House. "I know, sir, at any cost. Yes, I will bring him in." Lamphier folded down the antenna and closed the satellite phone. Walking calmly over to Morris, he took his pistol from its holster and put it directly in the temple of his partner. "You mess this up," he said threateningly, "if you get out of line one more time, I swear to God I will blow your head off." Lamphier then lowered the gun and holstered it. Morris looked at him with a degree of disgust. "You point that thing at me again, old man, you had better pull the trigger." The two men got up and left the room. They made their way to the waiting Tahoe, doors still open, and climbed in. "Where to?" asked Morris. "The Scott house," Lamphier replied. The Tahoe left with tires spinning.

Matt was riding down the highway at nearly sixty miles an hour, quite fast for a dirt bike on pavement. When Matt left home earlier that day, he was ready for a fight. In some ways he was grateful that Miller had given in without violence, yet his adrenaline was up. Like a police officer in a high-speed pursuit, or a soldier storming a beach, Matt Scott had prepared for battle. The lack of combat had left his adrenaline in a dangerous state. He was riding hard, and the events of the last few hours were bouncing around in his head. The possibility of confronting the two agents in the near future was an inviting idea.

Just then something broke his train of thought; something looked out of place. The house he just passed, the house he knew to be Bishop King's, had several cars and trucks in the driveway. This was strange, as it had been rare to see a car lately, let alone a group of them. There was little gas to be had, and most people were staying off the streets. So if a bunch of cars and trucks were together, something was up. Since Matt had been riding so fast, he couldn't be sure exactly how many cars and trucks he had seen, but something else was just not right. He also saw what he thought was smoke. Matt pulled the bike to the side of road and turned around to get a better look. Seeing black smoke above the trees, Matt put the bike in gear and headed back toward Bishop King's house. He had no idea what he was getting into, yet to some degree Matt was still looking for a fight.

As he turned off the pavement onto the gravel drive, Matt pulled in the clutch and killed the engine, coasting to a stop along the side of the tree-lined driveway. There were twenty or so men and teen boys there, some with hunting rifles in hand, about a seventy-five yards down the drive. On the porch of the house was Bishop King, and Matt could see his wife and children peeking through the window from the inside. Matt then saw the fire. The group had filled a truck tire with gas and lit it on fire. One of the younger men was yelling, "We told you Mormons to get out of here." He was lighting a branch on fire by dipping it in the burning tire. Now most people would think that this would feed Matt's already aggressive mood, but it seemed to do the opposite. Just for a moment, the thought of riding away crossed his mind. Was this his business? And if so, what was one man going to do against a horde of well-armed men? The thought was fleeting and quickly overpowered by a need to defend, and maybe a bit of the "looking for a fight feeling" he had left the house with this morning.

Matt instinctually pulled his rifle off his shoulder as he dismounted his motorcycle. This type of mob was something he had dealt with in the past. During Matt's time as a marine, he had handled civilian mobs on several occasions. Facing a well-trained military unit would have always been preferred to an unorganized group of civilians. This group was no different from any group of Islamic extremists in Baghdad or

Egypt. Group-think and mob mentality knew no race or religion. It was dangerous, and it was real, and Matt had seen how quickly it could become inhumane. The media called them "insurgents" or "protestors", but in Matt's experience they were little more than bullies with guns, rocks or Molotov cocktails. It was amazing to Matt how the oppressed could become the oppressor given just one little bit of authority or power. Matt pulled back on the charging handle of his rifle as he stepped behind his motorcycle. He now had a round in the chamber. Using the seat as a rest, he started to aim at each armed man and then pass over to the next. A technique called target-spotting—Matt would find each target, one at a time. There was no need to think at this time...it was an exercise, a habit or instinct, trained in from days long past. Each target was identified and mentally noted, each was assessed for threat and risk. Then he would move his sights to the next, all the time building a mental threat map. This technique was taught to young marines heading into urban combat, and it was proven to be brutally successful.

Matt was about seventy-five yards away from the targets, and the optical sight on the rifle was set to one hundred meters. So Matt reached up and made an adjustment without stopping his spotting process. The sound of his breath and heartbeat were deafening to him. He must take deep breaths and force himself to relax, he thought. Slowing his breathing, in the nose and out, he calmed down. Now that the targeting was done, a more in-depth assessment was next. Watching each man or boy, he recognized a couple of the men from town, and one was a customer of his auto shop, for sure. Matt did not want this to escalate, but he had a feeling things were going to get worse very quickly. With the thumb of his right hand, Matt switched his rifle from safe to fire mode. One older man, maybe in his fifties, walked up to the porch holding a poster, the same poster Matt and Leanne had seen in town. "We gave you all day to get your stinking Mormon asses out of town. No more time!" he yelled as the Bishop stood his ground. Matt could hear his wife trying to comfort a crying child.

Everything from this point happened quickly. A young man, one of the bishop's teenage sons, came out the front door with a shotgun in his hands. "Get out of here! Leave us alone!" he yelled. He stepped out the door, raised the shotgun, and pointed toward the man with the burning branch. This man had been walking toward the house as if he intended to burn the family out. When the man saw the boy with the shotgun, he ran toward the house and threw the burning cedar branch onto the porch. The Bishop ran toward the branch and kicked it off, and as the branch fell down the stairs, one of the men in the front row raised a rifle in the direction of Bishop King. Before the rifle came level, the teen with the shotgun turned and fired two times, hitting the other gunman in the chest, and the man beside him in the leg. One man was thrown off his feet backwards and was dead before he hit the ground, and the other crumbled to the ground with a blood-curdling scream. Bishop King had turned his back to the mob and was stomping out the fire as his son took aim at another man with a rifle. Two shots were fired. The Bishop went down, and another man in the crowd fell backwards and dropped his gun. In a matter of moments, the mob had lit the King home on fire, the young King boy had injured one man and killed two, and Bishop King was either dead or seriously wounded on the porch.

Matt had to choose sides. Right or wrong, there would be no turn-ing back. As the young teen ran to his father, he dropped his shotgun. Matt's sights found a man lifting a gun; he fired three rounds. Through his sights Matt saw one round hit the gunman in the middle of the back, the second round hit the shoulder, and the third round hit the head. The three rounds were fired so quickly that many thought it was only on shot. Yet to Matt Scott, things where moving slowly. He felt he had time to think between impacts. As the first target fell to the ground Matt was scanning for his next target. The crowd turned to-ward Matt, many of them taking cover in the trees or behind their cars. Matt moved quickly from behind the motorcycle to the tree line. He stood behind a large fir tree, never looking away from the crowd.

Gunfire erupted, and Matt watched as four or five rounds hit his motorcycle, knocking it off the kickstand. Matt dropped to one knee and returned fire with another quick three-round burst, and another man was dead. The bark on the tree around him was exploding; rifle rounds impacted the tree nonstop. Matt stood quickly, his back to the tree, as he waited for the hail of bullets to stop or slow.

The Bishop was dying on the porch, four men from the crowd lay dead on the ground, and some fourteen or fifteen more were taking cover behind their cars. The teen picked up the shotgun again and trained it on a group of four men with their backs to him; these men were looking over the bed of their truck, looking for Matt. With the shotgun up in the firing position, the young man reached into his right pocket and slid three more rounds into the magazine well of the shotgun. The young Mr. King had hunted ducks and grouse with his father, and he was good at reloading quickly. Shotguns for hunting could only carry three rounds by law, but a good hunter could reload so quickly that it was not uncommon to get five or even six shots off at a flock of geese or ducks.

"Drop your guns!" the teen yelled in warning. Matt knew that young man was in trouble, three shotgun shells was no match for fourteen or fifteen hunting rifles.

"You don't all have to die!" Matt yelled, trying to distract everyone from the teen. He even went as far as exposing a shoulder as he peaked around the tree. "You can drop your guns and drive away!" Matt yelled again.

Several men stood up and looked at the area where Matt was standing. Matt was worried the young man on the porch would fire again.

"Son, drop the shot gun!" Matt yelled. "No one else needs to die."

"Who are you?" yelled a voice from behind a red Chevy pickup.

"Your worst nightmare if you don't drop those damn guns and get the hell out of here," Matt responded, not thinking that many would recognize his voice or even his motorcycle.

The young man on the porch walked backwards into the house. His father was dead, and his mother and sisters were in hysterics in the house. The standoff continued for a few more minutes. Matt spotted targets—feet under cars, a shoulder leaning out from a tree. His efforts paid off: the King boy was in the house. Now Matt was the target. The entire time a small fire was building on the porch. Bishop King had managed to nearly extinguish the fire before he was shot, but some burning rubber and gas was still flickering away beside the man lying dead on the porch.

"Don't shoot," a young-sounding voice said. The red dodge four-by-four truck started up, and several men climbed into the back.

"Drop your guns on the ground!" Matt yelled. "You are not leaving with your guns."

It ended as quickly as it started. Most of them complied and dropped their rifles. Some were unarmed, and some managed to toss their guns into the back of a truck or the car they entered. Matt watched, continuing to pick targets, as all but two cars pulled out of the driveway. There were four bodies in the yard, so two of them must have driven these cars. One in a white Dodge diesel truck was a customer of Matt's, and he lay dead just feet from the dead Mr. King. As the cars and trucks came down the driveway, Matt worked his way around the tree so as not to be seen. He could hear them roar past but could not see them, as he was keeping hidden.

Matt stayed in the tree line until he heard the last car drive away. The sound of crying and screams of sorrow were coming from the house. The family had come out onto the porch, and they were leaning over the dead father and husband. Matt noticed the teen on the porch and recognized the young man, but Matt could not remember his name. The youth was sobbing on his knees and looking out at the two men he had killed. "God forgive me," he repeated over and over. One of the Bishop's younger sons had managed to put out the small fire that was still burning on the porch. The tire in the driveway was now burning hot, and black smoke was billowing into the sky.

The day was getting long. Matt had left Leanne asleep hours ago, and he had no idea how or when he was going to get back to her. Would he go to jail for killing these men? What would happen to the King family? It was no time to break down; he stopped, closed his eyes, and took a deep breath. Never had he imagined things would get this bad. It felt like minutes, but it was probably less than thirty seconds before Matt had regained some composure and stepped out from behind the tree. He made his way to the porch and helped Mrs. King to her feet.

"The kids. We need to get the kids inside," he said to the crying woman.

"Yes." Mrs. King took a breath and found some instant composure, the kind a person can only find during a major trauma. Shock, maybe, but either way, the kids had to be taken care of. Matt walked over to the teen and put his arm around him. "You had no choice, son," he reassured him. The boy stood, still sobbing, and Matt walked him into the front room of the house.

The porch of this house was large; it ran all the way across the front of the home and had steps to the yard. The steps were eight to ten feet wide, and there were six of them. Standing at the top of the steps, Matt had a dead friend, Bishop King, lying to his right. At the bottom of the steps lay two bodies that he didn't recognize. To the right he saw his customer, the man with the white Dodge, who was also dead. Ten or twelve feet away was another body, not identifiable, as most of the head was gone. The carnage was something no one should ever experience, especially in her own front yard.

Matt had been carrying his rifle in his left hand; he slung it over his shoulder as he went into the house. "Blankets," he said to no one in particular. "I need blankets." He went toward the hall and what he thought would be the linen closet. He opened it and started to grab blankets and sheets and anything he could find. Then he went back outside and placed a large woolen blanket over Bishop King's body, trying to cover as much of the blood pool as possible. Matt then went down the porch stairs and covered each body with a blanket. When finished, he walked to the front door. Noticing the sticky blood on his shoes, Matt unslung his rifle and leaned it against the wall, and then he took off his shoes and walked into the house. He looked at the family. Not knowing what to do next, he asked, "Do you have a fire extinguisher?" A young girl got to her feet walked into the kitchen, opened the cupboard under the sink, and got out a large red fire extinguisher. Matt took the extinguisher to the front door and calmly put his shoes back on before walking across the porch and down the steps to the burning tire, which he quickly extinguished in a cloud of hissing white dust. Matt then dropped the extinguisher and walked back to the house. He took his shoes off and reentered the front room of the house. The air was filled with the sounds of sobbing children and an occasional outburst from Mrs. King. Matt was in a fog; he heard no words, just the sounds of shock, mourning, and grief.

Inside the King house, things were starting to calm a little. The children were crying quietly. Mrs. King was starting to act as if nothing had happened and her husband was not dead on the porch. She was cleaning and fussing about the house. Matt was starting to feel like the fog he had found himself in was beginning to clear. He looked around at the King family and wondered what to do next.

"Dinner, who wants dinner?" Mrs. King asked. "Footprints on the floor, kids you need to wipe your feet," she added, looking at bloody footprints on the beige carpet.

Matt knew she was in shock, but he also knew he was not equipped to deal with what this family was going through. He sat down at the end of the couch, head in his hands, and tried to think. What to do? Who would help this family? *I killed them*, he thought. *My wife is home without me. The King family, who will take care of them?* Matt was starting to realize that he needed help, even if it meant getting arrested for shooting the men that lie dead in front of the King house. He was surrounded by young children who would need help in so many ways—they had witnessed unspeakable violence, they had lost a father, and their mother was in shock. Matt sat on the couch, thinking and watching as the family reacted around him.

At the Scott house, a patrol car pulled up to the front driveway. Leanne looked through the blinds in the kitchen and watched Deputy Miller get out of the car.

"Get in the back room. Quick, hide," Leanne hissed loud enough for Nick and Will to hear. The young men quickly and quietly followed her instructions and made their way to the couple's bedroom master closet.

"My God, he is with them." Leanne had no idea how loud she said it this time, but it was loud enough for Deputy Miller to hear as he opened the back door to his patrol car and helped Elder Miles out of the car. Leanne scanned the street for more cars; she saw none as the two came to the front door. Before Deputy Miller could knock on the door, Leanne pulled it open about a quarter of the way. Standing behind the door, she peeked her head around and looked outside.

"Get in." Leanne was concentrating her attention on the young missionary; he was bruised and had several abrasions on his face. Elder Miles was walking with a slight limp and holding his right side.

"What did you do to him?" Leanne asked as she looked sternly at the deputy.

Before Elder Miles could answer, the two heard the sound of a car or truck coming at high speed. It was in the distance but was getting closer quickly.

"That should be Matt," the deputy said.

"What? He was on his bike when he left," Leanne said with a question in her voice.

"Oh, shit. Get inside now." The deputy pushed the young man through the doorway so hard he fell to the ground. Then Deputy Miller turned and ran toward his patrol car. He slammed the back door of the car just in time to see a black Tahoe come sliding around the corner and enter the Scott's road. There were people in the yard of the first house on the street, and they ran toward the house. It was clear to the neighbors that things were not looking up for the Scott neighborhood. This was the first time in weeks Leanne had seen any of them.

As the Tahoe slid to a stop, the driver's door opened and out stepped the tall agent. His suit looked like it had not been cleaned in days; he was wrinkled and a mess. The normally neat Agent Morris had a couple days' growth of beard and messed-up hair. Morris's general demeanor was that of a man who had been working too long and had had enough.

"What the hell are you doing?" Morris stormed toward the smaller deputy. He grabbed him by the shirt and slammed him up against the side of the police cruiser.

"Get off me, you…" But before Miller could finish his sentence, Morris had thrown a punch, hitting Deputy Miller in the stomach and dropping him to his knees. Around the side of Tahoe came agent Lamphier. His suit was neat, he was clean-shaven, and he walked very deliberately.

"OK, so you have a choice. Tell me the truth, or I let this gorilla have his way." Lamphier looked at Morris with a grin.

"What the hell are you talking about?" Deputy Miller said in a weak voice, gasping for air. "I came here looking for the kid. He escaped." He paused to catch his breath. "I checked, and he isn't here."

Leanne was listening from behind the front door; Elder Nick Jones had helped Elder Miles into the back room. Will Black retrieved two pistols from the gun safe—one for himself, and one for Leanne.

Without a word, he walked up to Leanne and handed her an automatic pistol and a full magazine. It was her .40-caliber Smith and Wesson.

"Where is he?" Leanne mumbled under her breath. She was worried about her husband, yes, but she sure would like him here to deal with this mess. Leanne needed Matt, but she wasn't angry. She knew that if he was not here, then he couldn't be. This fact worried her even more than the situation in her driveway.

Out front, Lamphier turned and walked toward the front door. Agent Morris kicked the deputy as he tried to get to his feet, and he slumped to the ground.

"Open the door," Lamphier said. This time his voice was not calm; he was angry. As he approached the door, he pulled a revolver from under his jacket without breaking stride. Leanne motioned to Will, and he moved behind the hinge side of the door and leaned back against the wall. The door was framed in fresh lumber and did not close quite right since the repairs made following the damage done by these two the day before. Elder Black chambered a round into the 9mm Taurus pistol he had in his hand. Quietly, in his head, he prayed, "God, guide me and give me strength." William Black was trying to decide whether or not he could kill a man if he had to. He was not going to let them hurt Mrs. Scott, and he would not let them take Elder Miles again.

Leanne Smith also chambered a round, and then she put the pistol in her left hand, opened the door about four inches, and peeked around.

"Can I help you, sir?" she asked as if nothing was out of place, almost in a condescending voice. When she spoke, Will Black almost burst out in laughter, Leanne's statement seemed almost like an insult to the approaching federal agent. Before she could finish her question, Agent Lamphier lifted his right foot and kicked the door open, sending Leanne against the back wall of the entryway. Her gun fell from her hand and slid across the hardwood floor. In a moment, without thought, Will Black kicked the door as hard as he could, slamming it back into the face of the already angry agent. A loud thump was heard as agent Lamphier hit the ground. Will Black picked up the pistol Leanne had dropped and handed it back to her. "Get up. We have to move now," he said as he helped her to her feet. Still stunned and bleeding from her lip and the back of her head, Leanne stumbled to the master bedroom, where the other two were now out of the closet and in the middle of the room. Morris heard his boss hit the ground and turned toward the house. He strode right past Agent Lamphier, who was now up on one knee and trying to get to his feet.

"Do you know who you are dealing with?" the large man yelled as he shoved the door open and stood on the landing. Lamphier had gotten to his feet and was now standing in the doorway, looking dazed but very angry.

In the bedroom, Leanne pointed toward the hall closet and whispered, "All of you get in there, now."

Without question, Will and Nick helped Elder Miles into the closet and closed the door, leaving an inch gap.

Leanne had the .40-caliber pistol in her right hand as the bedroom door flew open; she made no attempt to raise the gun, knowing that there were two men out there, both armed. The pistol dropped to the ground with a thud as she opened her hand.

Looking sternly at Agent Morris, Leanne yelled, "Get out of my house!" Agent Morris stepped up and slapped Leanne across the face with the back of his left hand, knocking her to the ground. Standing over her and looking down the sights of his gun, he said, "Tell me where he is right now."

Agent Lamphier entered the room behind the tall man. Still looking out of sorts, he walked over to the bed and sat down on the side.

"Now, lady, we are not playing." The agent reached up and wiped the blood from his eyebrow with a handkerchief he had pulled from his suit pocket. "I will get that young man one way or the other."

In the closet, Will Black was using all of the restraint he could. Looking through the crack between the jamb and the partially open door, he was trying to decide what to do. William Black had shot plenty of guns. He had killed deer and squirrels, and he had been in fights as a young man, but he had never considered killing another human being. His hands were shaking, and he felt like throwing up. Elder Miles was in the back of closet, sitting on the floor with his back to the wall, and he was smiling. He was praying quietly, yet smiling as if he had no doubts. Everything was under control in the mind of the young Elder Miles. Elder Nick Jones was standing between them, looking at Black as if he would know what to do. He was shaking, and a tear streamed down his cheek.

Morris looked at the closet door and then back at Leanne, "You hiding him in there, lady?" He turned toward the closet door and took a step. William Black stepped back, bumping into Jones, which made a noise as some clothes were knocked off the hanger. He pulled up the pistol and took aim toward the middle of the door. Morris walked up and pushed the door open to see the barrel of a 9mm pointed at him. Morris laughed out loud. "You won't shoot me," he said, as he slowly reached out and grabbed the barrel of the gun.

A loud bang sounded, and Morris looked shocked, as did Will Black. Will Black did not know if he pulled the trigger, or if the agent grabbing the gun had caused it to go off. All he knew was that the gun in his hand just went off, his ears were ringing, and the large man in the suit in front of him was going to die. Agent Morris dropped to one knee. His entire chest was red with blood. He opened his mouth as if he was trying to speak, but only a gurgling sound was made as dark, almost black blood poured from his mouth. He went to the floor face-down. Agent Morris was dead.

William Black was in shock and just stood looking at the dead man at his feet. Across the room, Lamphier had gotten up off the bed and grabbed Leanne. He placed his pistol in her temple.

"Drop the gun, young man," he said. "Drop the gun and she lives. All I want is the boy, the boy who doesn't talk. You know who I am talking about, don't you?"

"Why? Why do you want Elder Miles so bad?" Black was crying. He did not understand why a simple missionary, one like Elder Miles, would be so important. People were dying, and it didn't make sense. "Why," he said again as he lowered the pistol to his side.

"You don't know, do you?" Lamphier looked surprised. "None of you know, do you? If I kill him, the Church dies. Elder Miles is the next President of the Mormon Church." Lamphier laughed a little. "He is your Prophet, and you don't even know it." The agent was now laughing out loud at the irony of the entire situation.

CHAPTER TEN

Back in Salt Lake City, when the LDS Church headquarters was taken, a book had been removed from the President of the Church's office. This notebook had some strange scribblings and personal notes, but most importantly it contained a letter. The letter was included in the notes from a meeting of the Quorum of the Twelve, the governing body of the Church. This handwritten first draft of the letter was written and signed by the President of the Church. To a believing Mormon, this was a letter from a Prophet, and direct prophecy from God. The President of the Church is believed to be a living Prophet.

The initial group that took the Church had orders to keep everyone alive. President Prescott could not afford martyrs, but things went badly. There were a total of seventy-six people killed in the assault. The President of the Church and ten of the twelve were among the dead. Those who survived had only been able to escape when National Guard troops turned on Federal Agents.

This letter, handwritten and later found typed for distribution to all Church members, was dated two weeks prior to the Salt Lake City raid.

I am writing this letter with joy in my heart. In the days to come, much sadness and despair shall come to pass, not unlike the days of our founder Joseph Smith. Persecution and violence will fall on the members of our great church. I am writing to tell you not to despair;

times of change are upon us. I implore you to accept the changes coming to our world and our church. Accept them and prosper in the times to come.

In the days to come, a young man, an Elder and a missionary, shall be called to lead you. Elder David Miles, now serving his mission out of the Olympia Washington Stake, will be called. This calling is beyond that of this earth. As your prophet and leader, I direct you to accept him as your leader into the future.

Soon I and the Quorum of the Twelve shall be gone. We will watch over you from the side of Heavenly Father as you embark on a new journey. Do not mourn those who pass. Follow your new prophet into the future.

The letter was signed:

George L. Ramey,
President

When President Prescott and his Secret Service team saw this letter, they did everything they could to stop it from being published. President Prescott knew that a prophecy and a young new leader would be something people could rally around. He had ordered Lamphier to kill Elder Miles, but only after he found out if word had spread about the letter. Lamphier had had opportunity to kill the young man, yet for some reason he did not understand, he had kept him alive. It could have been curiosity, it could have been his sadistic need to torture, but either way, David Miles was still alive.

President Prescott believed none of the prophecy. His actions were all purely political in his mind. President Prescott never did anything without political motivation. The power of faith is not something he had experienced, or even truly believed in, but it was something he feared. The President knew that a group with a common faith or religious fervor could stop his plans. He was a man of ideology, and he believed his actions were saving his nation, not hurting his people. This man worked toward secular statism with a passion equal to any religious belief. He would save his nation from the evil religious right, and even worse, the cult-like Mormon Church. The President's narcotic belief that he and he alone could save his nation rivaled that of Hitler or Pol Pot. This letter enraged him; it challenged his notion that the Church was nothing more than a cult or political machine.

Few people knew of the letter. Agent Lamphier and a few of the President's trusted advisors knew of it, but that was it. The letter was to die with Elder Miles; at least that was the plan. Lamphier could still kill the young missionary; he could kill his companions and the pretty Mrs. Scott. He could end this and go home. Lamphier was tired. He was ready to go home, and he could see the end in sight.

Chow had driven home and told his wife of the events concerning Elder Miles; he was worried that repercussions would come to his family. Chow had gathered his family and taken them down the street to a neighboring farm that was run by an older, retired woman who lived alone. Mrs. Fisher was a good friend. The Chows had helped her over the years, and now it was time for her to help them. Chow's family would hole up in the Fisher home until things cooled off. Chow then went to Port Smith; he needed to talk the colonel in charge of the military unit stationed there, as he needed to get someone out to the Scott home to check on Elder Miles. All this had gone one while Deputy Miller was taking the long way to the Scott home, trying to avoid attention.

Back in the Scott home, Elder Miles was still sitting with his back to the wall, smiling and looking toward the open closet door. William Black and Nick Jones had come out into the room with their hands raised. Lamphier pushed Leanne toward them and stepped back a little. He was feeling the effect from the impact his head had made on the concrete steps, but he managed to say, "I just want Miles, and then I can leave this godforsaken place." The irony of a man like Lamphier invoking the name of God in any statement seemed to go unnoticed. Elder Miles stood up and walked out of the closet; he stepped over the dead agent on the floor and out into the room. The carpet was soaking wet with blood, and he heard his footsteps make a strange mud-like sound when he walked. The beaten and bruised young man stood tall as he walked toward Agent Lamphier.

"Stop!" blurted out Elder Black.

"No, no one else will die, not for me." Elder Miles spoke clearly without a stutter or hesitation.

"Good, now this can end," Lamphier said as he lifted his revolver and slowly pulled the hammer back. He was taking careful aim at Miles, aiming between his eyes.

It seemed like it took forever to everyone in the room, but it was mere seconds. Elder Miles smiled and looked into the eyes of Lamphier, Elder Jones looked away, and Elder Black tried to jump forward while Leanne pushed herself in front of him. As the hammer on the revolver came back, the sound of a gunshot rang out. Elder Miles never moved, and Lamphier smiled and dropped his gun to the floor. Another gunshot rang out from the front of the house, and Lamphier toppled over. He fell onto the bed and then slowly slid off to the floor. In the doorway was Deputy Miller, on one knee, holding his service pistol, still in the firing position, still aiming at Lamphier as he fell.

Leanne fell to her knees sobbing as Elder William Black and Nick Jones both ran to Elder Miles.

Coming up the cul-de-sac in time to hear the second gunshot was Chow, driving his old truck. Chow had decided to pick up Matt Scott; he wanted Matt with him when he talked to the commanding officer of the marine unit in town. Chow had no idea that Matt had not made it home; he knew nothing of the gun battle at the King home. Chow saw the patrol car with blood smeared on the fender, and he had heard the final shot. He saw the open and damaged front door with the young deputy slouched in the threshold. Chow drove up just in time to see the young deputy kill agent Lamphier.

Matt Scott knew he needed to get to town. He needed to get help to the King family and talk to Chow and the Marine Colonel to report the shooting. Matt stood up and walked to the front door. He picked up his rifle, put on his shoes, and walked across the porch and down the steps. Stepping over a blood-soaked blanket that covered a dead man, he walked toward the Dodge truck parked in the driveway. The keys were in the ignition. Matt climbed in. Laying his rifle on the seat beside him, he started the truck. Matt drove out of the driveway. In the rearview mirror, he could see Mrs. King and her oldest boy standing on the porch watching him drive away. Matt had not said another word to the family. What could he say? Their father was dead, they had watched him kill two men, and the young man had killed two men. This was more trauma than most men see in combat, so what could he say to make things better? The four-wheel-drive Dodge barely lurched as Matt ran over his motorcycle and turned onto the road, tires squealing. He headed for town as fast as he could. Matt wanted to get some help to the King family, he wanted to know if Leanne was okay, and he was worried about the missionaries. Driving at a high speed, Matt started to wonder, would he go to jail? And would he be separated from his wife? Was it all worth it? For a moment Matt thought about turning around to go to his home, to pick up Leanne and run. "I don't want to go to prison," Matt said out loud.

When Matt reached town, he did not slow down. He drove into the twenty-five mile-per-hour zone at over sixty. He was so preoccupied that he did not noticed that most of the town was no longer abandoned—there were people shopping in the stores, the gas stations were open, running on generators, and there were lines of cars at the pumps. Matt drove straight to the City Hall building. The Military had set up an office there to work with the local elected officials, and Matt assumed that is where he would find the Commander.

Pulling up, he drove right up on the sidewalk. Slamming the truck into park, he stepped out, leaving his rifle on the seat.

"Stop!" yelled a young marine, taking aim at Matt with a pump shotgun.

Matt turned and looked at him. "Get me your CO." His emphatic tone and the wild look in his eyes, combined with the blood on his clothing, must have had an effect on the young marine.

"Just don't move!" yelled the marine, his voice shaking a little.

Matt raised his hands above his head. "I need to see the CO."

Before Matt could move, two more Marines were on him. One approached him from behind, pulled his arms down, and had him in handcuffs before he knew it. Matt was tired and his blood sugar was very low. He was stressed and exhausted; there was no fighting back even if he wanted to.

He dropped to his knees. "A family needs your help. People are dying. I need to talk to the CO," Matt said as he felt the handcuffs cut into his wrists.

The double doors to the City Hall opened, and a short, dark-haired woman in camouflage utilities came out. She had silver oak leaves pinned on her hat—a Lieutenant Colonel.

"Now I'm getting somewhere," Matt said, looking at the woman.

"What can I do for you?" she asked in a strong southern drawl.

"Colonel, the King family, they were attacked by some kind of mob. Bishop King is dead." Matt took a deep breath and looked at the woman. "I killed two of them, and two more were killed by one of the King boys."

"Where?" the woman demanded.

"On Lake Road, at the King house," Matt responded.

"Sergeant, you find someone who knows exactly where that is. You take a platoon, and you get out there!" she ordered the man standing by. "Secure the area. We will have no more of this vigilante shit, not on my watch." The look on the female officer's face when Matt used the term *mob* gave him some comfort. It appeared that she had been dealing with this group already, and that possibly Matt would not have to justify his actions. It crossed Matt's mind that they had a common enemy.

Matt had fully expected to be arrested and charged with murder. Matt had no idea that the King house was the third house this mob had hit. They had burned two other homes to the ground. The marines had been looking for this group, and Matt Scott had single-handedly stopped them.

"Can you identify any of them?" she asked as the Colonel gestured to a young Lance Corporal, who quickly came and helped Matt to his feet and removed the handcuffs.

"Maybe." Matt was confused; he was not completely aware of the other incidents, and he did not know that this Colonel had been sent to Port Smith that morning with a Military Police unit to find and stop the mob.

"My wife, I need to see if she is OK." Matt was instantly overtaken with worry.

"Your family Mormon?" she asked.

"No," he said. Then after a pause he asked accusingly, "What the hell does that have to do with anything?"

"If you're not Mormon, how did you find yourself in the middle of this mess?" she asked.

"I will explain after we get help to the Kings and find out if my wife is OK." Matt was frustrated. He was willing to turn himself in and possibly get arrested or worse, just as long as they took care of his family. And now even the Marine Corps seemed to be acting as if being a Mormon was a crime.

"I'm Colonel Phelps. What is your name?" the woman asked.

"I'm Matt Scott. Now can we get going?" asked Matt in an exasperated tone.

"Come with me." The Colonel led Matt toward a waiting Humvee. One of the young marines had retrieved Matt's rifle from the truck and made it safe. Following behind the Colonel and Matt were three young Marines, one of which had Matt's rifle.

"Get in." She gestured towards the Humvee, and then they climbed in the back—Matt and the Colonel and the young Lance Corporal carrying Matt's rifle. The other two climbed in the front.

"Ma'am, we need fuel," the driver said, a bit worried he would upset the officer.

"Then I suggest we get some," she responded as if she were talking to a young child.

The Humvee turned out of the parking lot and drove down the road toward the end of town, but before leaving town they turned left into Matt's shop. Matt had not thought about his business much lately, and it was a shock to see that the vehicles in his parking lot looked like a fleet of military support trucks. Two large tanker trucks were parked on the side of the building. Matt saw Jeremy through the front window of the lobby speaking to a group of three servicemen in coveralls.

"What's all this?" Matt asked.

"The motor pool," answered the driver.

"We contracted with this shop to run our motor pool," the Colonel answered, totally unaware of the fact that the man beside her owned the shop.

"Is that so?" Matt said in a questioning way.

"Is that a problem?" she asked, still totally unaware of Matt's connection to the shop.

"Well, it's just that this is my business." He was trying not to sound offended. Matt felt confident that Jeremy had looked out for Matt's best interests, yet his ego was taking a little hit.

As the Humvee came to a stop and the driver stepped out to talk to a man standing at the end of the fuel truck, Jeremy walked up to the window.

"Matt, is that you? You're OK?" he asked with worry on his face. "God, I heard you had been shot and were maybe even dead!"

"No, it's me. What the hell is all of this?" Jeremy proceeded to explain that the Colonel had come to him looking for a place to service their military vehicles. Jeremy figured it was good business and made a deal. After a few minutes of catch-up, the group was all back in the Humvee, fueled up and ready to go. Jeremy gave his boss a quick hug through the window and told him not to worry about the shop. "I think I found my niche. I should have joined the Army," Jeremy said with a laugh.

The Colonel was talking on a cell phone. "Yes, let me know as soon as you can."

"So, we have a platoon at the King house. They are taking care of things, cleaning up your mess," she added. "Sheriff Chow has been contacted, and he is going to meet us at your house. We are going to get this thing straightened out. Oh, and as far as this," she pulled a copy of the vigilante poster from her inside pocket, "it looks like we have most of the people involved in this in custody. A couple of them turned themselves in after your little episode at the King house. One of them is singing like a bird—names, addresses, the works." She stopped and looked at Matt with a crooked smile. "They thought they had been attacked by one of my teams. You must have made some impression out there."

She paused and changed the subject before Matt could respond. "So let's get out to your place and see what's up. I'm thinking we may find those missionaries there?"

"What about my wife? I need to know if she is OK." Matt's frustration was mounting. Yes, he worried about the missionaries and the Kings. But what about his family? Matt Scott was tired. He wanted, no, needed, his wife. He needed his simple life back.

Colonel Phelps kept talking, ignoring Matt's short outburst. "I have orders to stop two agents, Lamphier and Morris. They were sent to capture or kill your missionary friends."

It was a strange conversation, neither really seemed to be paying attention to the words of the other. Matt Scott wanted answers about his wife, and the Colonel wanted information on the missionaries. It was like they were in two different places. After a few minutes and a few miles, the two finally started listening to each other.

The conversation was taking place as the Humvee sped toward the Scott home. It took a few minutes for Matt to explain his relationship with the Mormon Church and how he had been thrust into the middle of this mess. Apparently, the Commander on site was taken aback by Colonel Phelps's arrival. The female Lt. Colonel had arrived in Port Smith yesterday, with orders signed by Commandant Siebel. She had been briefed on the letter that was found and the state of the Mormon Church headquarters. It was the charge of her unit to secure the missionaries and get any federal agents in the area under control. She had also been given specific orders to kill or detain Agent Lamphier. Upon arrival, the Lt. Colonel learned much about the local area and the happenings over the last week from a group that hung out a local coffee shop. The local Catholic priest had been of great help, and he had encouraged her to find Matthew Scott. To her surprise, Matt Scott had found her.

Matt was continuously looking ahead through the windshield, trying to see; he was very worried about Leanne. As the Humvee rounded the corner toward the Scott house, Matt saw the Tahoe and the patrol car with the open door and what looked like blood on the fender and the ground.

"Secure the area," ordered Colonel Phelps as she picked up her satellite phone and started to talk.

"Get me three fire teams up here right now, and a medical unit. I mean now!" She held the phone away from her ear for a moment and asked Matt, "You have a field or something close? Someplace we can land a helicopter?"

The Scott home was in the midst of several very large trees and the neighborhood and surrounding area was wooded, many of the trees over one hundred feet tall.

"Down the street about half a mile," Matt said, pointing down the hill in the direction they had arrived from. "A playground and a soccer field."

She went back to her phone. The marine in the passenger seat handed her a map, and pointing at a grid area, she spoke clearly in numbers and alphanumeric phrases. "November, niner, foxtrot, three, three. I repeat, November, Niner, foxtrot, three, three." As she spoke, the driver and the marine in the passenger seat got out and took up positions in the front of the Humvee. The marine in the back got out with them, and as he did, he put Matt's rifle on the seat.

Matt reached for it.

"Let us handle it," the marine responded.

"It's my wife." Matt was pulling away when he realized the rifle would do him no good as the young marine had taken the magazine, and he had no ammunition. Matt got out of the Humvee and started to walk quickly toward his broken-down front door. As he did, he could see what looked like blood on the porch.

"Matt, Matt is that you?" He heard Leanne's voice from the house, and his walk turned to a jog, and then a run.

He burst through the doorway and onto the landing and saw his wife sitting on the couch. She had bruises on her face and a black eye. Beside her sat Elder Black, who was tending to her with a damp cloth. Across the room, Elder Jones sat with Elder Miles, tending to the beaten officer. Deputy Miller looked barely alive. His blonde hair was matted with blood, and his eyes were swollen shut. The missionaries both looked up at Matt and instantly got to their feet. Deputy Miller did not even acknowledge anyone in the room. He was in pretty bad shape.

"Leanne, my God. Are you OK?" Matt moved quickly to his wife.

"I'm sorry, Brother Scott, I tried," Elder Black spoke.

"Will did great. He saved my life." She paused then said, "They all saved my life." She looked over at the wounded deputy. Behind Matt, two marines came in. Both had their rifles in a combat-ready position. The sound of helicopters filled the air. The helicopters flew over so low that the windows rattled, and everyone ducked slightly, out of instinct.

"In the bedroom." Leanne pointed toward the closed bedroom door.

One of the marines pushed the door open slowly while the other covered. Inside, they found Agent Lamphier slumped over on his side, dead. Across the room they found Agent Morris, dead on the floor. As they came out of the room, a group of six more came in. These men wore all black and had masks covering their faces. They carried submachine guns, much smaller and more compact than the normal M-4 carbine carried by the other marines. They entered the house in a leapfrog system, going from room to room. Occasionally one would yell out, "Clear!" This process took maybe five minutes, and then one of them walked to the front door and yelled out, "All clear and secure!" followed by a very loud "Corpsman!" Within moments, two medical teams came through the door. Each team of three headed for the living room, one tended to Leanne and the other to the fallen deputy. Deputy Miller was in bad shape; the corpsmen had him stabilized and on a backboard in minutes. They had an IV in and were out the door, heading for the medical helicopter.

"He is a hero. He saved us all." Leanne piped up in a sad tone as if she thought he would die.

Through the commotion, Matt tried to tend to his wife. He wanted to talk to her and make sure she was OK. This was difficult through the work of the Navy corpsmen who were checking her blood pressure, pulse, and looking into her eyes.

"I am OK, just a little beat up." Leanne tried to push them away.

"Let them do their jobs, honey." Matt was genuinely concerned, as he knew Leanne was the type to say she was OK even if she wasn't.

As the commotion slowed, Colonel Phelps came into the room, and with the assistance of the marine who had been riding in the passenger seat, she went methodically to each person, getting written statements.

"Will and Nick were so brave," Leanne told her husband.

"Will and Nick?" Matt was a bit confused.

Elder Miles smiled then and let out a little groan. The smile hurt his bruised face and split lip. This made him laugh, which in turn made him groan. This continued until Will Black, Nick Jones, Leanne, Matt, and Colonel Phelps were laughing.

Through the front door, a marine came in with Sheriff Chow firmly in his grip, his large hand around Chow's left bicep. "Would somebody please tell this guy who I am?" Chow said. Colonel Phelps and Matt spoke simultaneously, "He's OK. It's the sheriff." Instantly the marine let Chow go as he pulled away. "What did I tell you?" Chow scolded the marine, who responded with a look of indifference as he turned to walk back out front.

Silence descended on the room, only to be broken by the words of a corpsman.

"We need to take you in and get you checked out." The corpsman was talking to Elder Miles.

"I am not going back to the hospital," Miles said as he looked at Will Black. "I have work to do at the church." An argument was breaking out between the three missionaries and the corpsman. It was clear that they had no intention of going to any hospital and that they had full intention of getting back to the church as soon as possible. The three missionaries seemed focused on a mission, almost as if none of this had even happened.

Matt was feeling very emotional. Remorseful, happy, and angry—he was not sure what he felt. He was just glad Leanne was OK. There was so much to say. Matt wanted to tell Leanne everything that had happened since he'd left that morning. He wanted to find out what had happened in his absence. Matt looked up as the bedroom door was propped open and two body bags were removed. Leanne started to cry quietly. Suddenly Matt was no longer concerned with his story, or what had happened in their home. Leanne leaned forward and kissed him gently, and then she leaned back and gave him a quick slap across the face. "If you ever leave me again, if you ever sneak out with nothing more than a note, so help me...." She broke down in tears as Matt reached forward and hugged her.

"I am so sorry." Matt held her, tears running down his cheek. Matt had left his wife to fend for herself, his wife and two young missionaries against federal agents, and they came out ahead. Again, the sound of a helicopter rattled the house; it lifted off down the hill and flew directly over the house at high speed. The assault team that had been in earlier was gone, and there was one team of corpsmen left and several marines in the house. Colonel Phelps came over and sat down beside Matt.

"I am going to leave some security and a medical team here. If you need anything, you let that sergeant over there know what you need." She pointed to a very large black man, who was bald and intimidating, "Sergeant Hood will make sure you have whatever you need, won't you, Sergeant?"

Sergeant Hood snapped to attention. "Yes, ma'am."

Matt took a moment to corner Chow and Colonel Phelps. "What about the King house, the shootings?" Matt was not sure what was going to happen. People were dead, families were going to want an answer, and maybe revenge.

Chow looked at Matt. "Self-defense, and defense of another. That's what my report reads."

Colonel Phelps smiled. "Mine too." She paused and looked at Matt only as an officer looks at a soldier or marine in their charge. "I'm proud of you. If you were one of my marines, I would put you up for a medal."

Matt was dumbfounded for a moment. "Don't be proud of me, and don't ever be proud of killing." Matt turned with his head down and walked back to the arms of his wife. He was feeling shame. Matt Scott would never feel good about killing, and the truth was he might never forgive himself.

Colonel Phelps turned and walked out of the room without another word, Chow at her side. The medical team was still trying to convince Elder Miles to take a helicopter ride. Elder Miles was reverting back to his silence, something Matt was realizing might be more of a tool than a condition. Matt and Leanne sat on the couch talking and occasionally hugging and crying. Nick Jones and Will Black were cleaning up, and several of the marines were helping. The blood was wiped up from the hardwood floor, and several people were in the bedroom with towels and bottles of spray cleaner. They were cleaning the carpeted floors. The home was a mess. Blood and carnage filled the true crime scene, but it was still the Scott's home. The corpsmen had made their rounds and checked up on everyone again. Leanne had been given a fresh cold pack and a few butterfly bandages. Both Will Black and Matt were briefed on how to keep an eye on Leanne to be sure she had no serious head injuries and no concussion.

Leanne stood up and looked at Matt with a crooked smile. "Looks like we have a lot of mouths to feed tonight," she said as she let go of his hand and walked to the kitchen. Her makeup had run down her bruised cheek, and her left eye looked terrible, but she was smiling. Matt watched her closely for balance and signs of injury. "You're one tough bird," Matt said with a laugh as he got to his feet and joined his wife in the kitchen.

The couple proceeded to cook—they had to feed three missionaries, three corpsmen, and fifteen or twenty marines. Beat up or not, Leanne Scott was going to take care of those who took care of her family. Chow had disappeared with the Colonel. "Sheriff's work to do," he had said. After thirty minutes or so, there was a large bowl of pasta on the table, loaves of garlic bread, and two huge bowls of green salad. "Good thing Elder Miles didn't give *all* the food away," Leanne said with a smile as she set out stacks of paper plates and silverware. Leanne's need to provide was fueled to an extreme by a house full of young servicemen. She went to the end of the bar with a small plate of pasta, no sauce, just some butter on it, and a side of salad. Besides her plate, Leanne made a plate of pasta with meat sauce and salad; the plate was over-full. It was clear the couple was going to sit and eat together.

"Matt, will you get everyone together, please?" Leanne asked of her husband. Matt went outside and made his way from room to room, gathering marines, corpsman, and young missionaries as he went. Matt returned to his wife's side and placed his arm around her. The room was full of people.

"William, will you lead us in a prayer?" Leanne asked. Matt looked at her and smiled as he opened a bottle of red wine. Matt opened three bottles and put every glass in the house out on the bar.

"Heavenly Father, we give thanks for this meal put before us. We thank You for the strength of faith You provide us, and we thank You for all those You brought to our aid. Father, we ask You to bless the fallen and hold them by Your side." William's voice cracked as a tear ran down his cheek. "Father, give strength to the King family and all those harmed by the deeds of the Adversary." Matt gave the young man a glance, and after a moment of eye contact, he concluded. "I say these things in the name of Your Son, Jesus Christ." The collective "Amen" resonated from each room of the house, from the front porch and even outside the back door, followed by a quick, loud "Uh Rah!" the battle cry of the Marine Corps.

"Eat!" Leanne said as loudly as her bruised body could muster.

Matt poured himself and Leanne a glass of wine, and the two sat down at the bar and drank slowly as they nibbled on their dinners. It had been a long day; it had only been a week since the missionaries had knocked on his door in the middle of the night. The world had changed, but in some ways it was the same, as much as it could be with a house full of hungry marines, corpsman, and missionaries.

That night, the marines and corpsmen left at the Scott house took shifts eating and sleeping on the couch or the floor. Leanne was trying to get the bedroom clean; she had thrown the blood-soaked bedspread away and had laid blankets over the stained carpet. Matt had worked with William Black to repair the front door, again, with what was left of it, and the marines set up watch posts outside the house. They wanted to let Leanne know that she could sleep safely. Never before had Leanne felt so safe. Not only did she have a platoon of Marines protecting her, she had Matt back at her side.

Nick Jones and Elder Miles worked in the spare room to make room for the corpsmen to sleep. The death and destruction of the day seemed to be replaced with a sense of calm. It felt like a big campout. Everyone was doing their part and then some, and the teamwork was natural and efficient.

"We need to sleep. We have church in the morning," Leanne said loudly as an announcement to anyone who could hear.

"Church?" Matt asked.

"I promised Will and Nick we would go to church tomorrow," Leanne answered with a matter-of-fact tone.

Leanne and Matt went to their bedroom and lay down to sleep. With the security of the guards, the comfort of knowing their loved ones were safe, and full bellies, it took only moments for them to fall into a deep sleep. Throughout the night, the marines relieved each other, and they came in and out of the house and took turns eating what was left of dinner. For a young marine who had been in Iraq, Syria, or Afghanistan, this was the most amazing duty. They were treated with respect, given free rein, and fed home-cooked meals. Needless to say, the morale at the Scott house that night was very high.

CHAPTER ELEVEN

Matt woke up to the sound of running water; Leanne had awakened earlier in the morning and had gone to take a shower. She tended to her wounds and worked hard to put on cover-up and makeup for church. Leanne's skill with makeup could cover the bruises but did little to hide the swelling. Matt lay in bed looking out the French doors at the sun gleaming in. For a moment he thought he had been dreaming all of the craziness; it *had* to be a dream. The sound of a helicopter spooling up down the hill and then flying low over his home brought the reality of the situation back. Matt looked out the doors to see a marine leaning on the deck with his m249 machine gun resting on a sandbag as he watched the helicopter fly over.

Matt's attention was broken as Leanne entered the bedroom from the bathroom. She was wearing her big, fluffy purple bathrobe that Matt had always hated, and her hair was up in a towel. Leanne had clearly put cover-up on, trying to cover her injuries from the day before. She saw that Matt was awake and watching her.

"I laid out your blue suit and red tie." Leanne pointed toward an easy chair at the end of the bedroom, a bedroom with blankets on the carpet and bullet holes in the wall. Matt was now feeling like he was in the twilight zone.

"Suit and tie?" Matt questioned.

"Don't you even think you're going to church without a suit and tie," she responded.

"Don't you think this is all a bit much? A tie?" Matt protested as he got up and made his way toward the shower. Matt was joking. The truth was he was feeling good about his wife's desire to get him to go to church. Matt walked into the bathroom and reached in to turn on the shower.

"Make it quick. We have guests who will need hot water," Leanne pointed out. She had no idea if the missionaries were up yet, but they would most likely want a shower, too.

The hot shower felt so good to Matt, while it lasted. It became apparent, when his went cold, that the hot water was being used by the missionaries at the other end of the house. After his shower and shaving with cold water, Matt went out to see if his suit still fit. It had been almost a year since he had put that suit on, and he was sure it would be tight. Too his shock it was actually a tad too big. Maybe the events of this week had taken a couple pounds off.

There was a knock on the bedroom door as Leanne finished her makeup and was heading to the bathroom to do her hair. She opened the door to see Elder Will Black in what looked like a clean suit.

"Let me help you," Will said to Matt, seeing from across the room that he was having issues with his tie. The missionary made quick work of a full Windsor knot.

"It fits," Matt said with surprise in his voice.

"Everyone else is ready," Elder Will Black pointed out.

"Ten minutes. I need ten minutes," Leanne said as she turned the blow dryer on.

Matt was going along with everything else that was happening, yet he kept wondering, *does anyone really remember the last week? The killing, the blood stained carpets, and the President was arrested?* Walking in a state of confusion, Matt made his way to the kitchen and had a cup of coffee; the sight of two marines standing at the bar in full combat gear drinking coffee didn't seem to affect anyone else. The whole thing was a bit like a dream; everyone else was acting as if nothing had happened, like it was normal to have a combat platoon in your kitchen on Sunday morning before church.

"You OK, honey?" Leanne asked as she came out of the bedroom. Maybe this was more of a statement then a question.

For a quick moment, all Matt noticed was her beauty. Yes, she still had traces of a black eye and a split lip, but the makeup covered it well. "Uh, yeah, I think," Matt responded.

"Eat something. You don't want your blood sugar to get low." Leanne went to the refrigerator and pulled out a loaf of whole wheat bread and a jar of peanut butter. "I will make you some toast."

The rest of the house was busy. The three missionaries were all dressed, and Elder Jones had managed to put together a suit from Matt's closet and what was left of his clothes. Elders Black and Miles must have washed and pressed their clothes during the night. Most of the marines had gone outside, and only two remained in the house. Matt could see a group of young marines sitting in a circle on the deck, eating military ready-to-eat meals for breakfast. They were laughing and talking while they ate. The corpsmen were gone, and overall the house looked normal. One of the marines walked over and picked up the remote control to the TV and asked, "May I? We don't get much news on base." Matt recognized the marine's strong east Texas accent. When he was a marine, Matt had a close friend from Marshall, Texas. Corporal Yoder had been killed in a car accident while on leave. Every time he heard that east Texas drawl, Matt remembered his good friend. He missed Corporal Yoder.

"Yeah, yeah, of course," Matt said, again not sure that it even worked. Yesterday they had no power, the country was falling apart, and armed men were having shootouts in the bedroom. Today they had power, hot coffee, satellite dish, and church. Matt was just going with the flow at this point. By now, nothing seemed to surprise him.

The marine had turned the TV to local news. The screen had a KING 5 logo and a cropped view of the announcer. Her words, in white block text lettering, were scrolling across the top of the screen.

"The Provisional Government has announced that local elections will take place on the second Tuesday of next month. Following local elections, a national election will be scheduled for the offices of President and Vice President. Congressional elections for all Senate and House seats will follow." A woman in uniform made the announcement; to Matt it looked like an Air Force uniform, maybe. "To find a list of candidates, measures, and polling places, visit either your local school or post office." Matt was still trying to understand what was going on. Yes, he had been out of the loop for a day or two, but really? Was it possible that the Military could get elections going this fast? It took six years in Iraq.

"Isn't that great?" one of the marines said. "Maybe we can go home soon."

Mathew Scott was standing in his living room in a blue suit with a red tie; he had a cup of coffee in his left hand and a piece of toast with peanut butter on it in his right hand. Two marines in full combat gear, with slung, locked, and loaded rifles stood to his left. Three missionaries were sitting at the kitchen table eating, dressed and ready for church. Leanne Scott was standing to his right, watching the TV, dressed in a dark blue dress that came down past her knees. Her hair was perfect, and she was smiling. The world was OK. Or was it? Was everyone in shock? Was Matt the only one with perspective? The only one that could see the problem?

"Mr. Scott, we are going to leave two marines out front until you get back. The rest of us are out of here. Orders," a tall, bald, black marine said as he put his Kevlar helmet on and set his coffee cup down on the counter. It was the sergeant that Colonel Phelps was speaking to the night before, Sergeant Hood. "If you need anything, anything at all, you let one of my men know, and we will do what we can." Without giving time for a response, the Sergeant Hood left the room. He marched out with conviction as subordinate marines fell in behind him and marched out toward the driveway. Within moments, two of the three Humvees parked out front started and roared away.

"Let's get going," Leanne said loudly.

"Matt, will you get the van? I don't think we will all fit in your car. We're certainly not going to fit in mine," Leanne said with a snicker. Leanne's car, a Mustang convertible, was parked in the garage. Matt grabbed his keys from the key rack beside the refrigerator and made his way out to the van. Bringing the van to the front of the house, Leanne climbed into the passenger seat, and the three missionaries got in the back. "Church, James," Elder Jones said, trying to make a joke. Matt just ignored it.

On the way to Port Smith, there was traffic on the road once again. Matt saw several people out in their yards or on the front porch. It was almost normal until a convoy of military vehicles passed the other way. On the road they saw several burned-out houses and two abandoned pickup trucks, but other than that, the drive was uneventful. The remnants of violence and chaos were everywhere, but people seemed happy and to have a purpose on this sunny morning, a welcome feeling. As they got closer to town, the traffic began to build, and there was actually a small traffic jam as they approached the church building. In the parking lot, not a space was empty. The streets were lined with cars, and across the street and on the lawn of the church were several military vehicles and two County Sheriff's cars. As Matt slowed, he looked toward the entrance. He was scanning for a parking place when he saw Sheriff Chow, in full uniform. Sheriff Chow waved Matt in and directed him up onto the lawn next to a Humvee and his patrol car.

"We have been waiting for you," Chow said to Matt.

"And you, too," he said, looking into the back of the van. Elder Will Black opened the sliding door and stepped out. The three young men got out of the van, each with a Bible in his hand. Sheriff Chow opened Leanne's door and helped her down in a gentlemanly way. "You look beautiful, Mrs. Scott," he complimented.

"Thank you," Leanne said with a smile, which made her wince as it tugged on her split lip.

"Over here," a man dressed in a priest's vestments called as he waved at the three. It was father Flarraty from the Catholic Church in town. He was standing with three other men that Matt recognized—one from the Baptist church, one from the Lutheran church, one was the Mayor, and there was a woman also dressed as a priest. Matt thought she was from the Unitarian church.

Deputy Miller wore a clean-pressed uniform and stood with a cane by the front door. At the other side of the door was a female soldier in full combat gear. Out from the double doors came two men that Matt had recognized from the meeting with Bishop King just five days ago. They hurried to Matt and Leanne. "Come with us," they said as they led the two to the entrance of the church building. They led them to the north entrance, as the south entrance was boarded up.

"Are you OK?" Leanne asked Deputy Miller as she approached him.

"I'll be fine, ma'am." The blond man leaned on his cane and gave a small grimace as he stepped toward the couple. "Mr. Scott," he said reaching to shake Matt's hand.

"Thank you," Matt said as he refused the handshake and hugged the deputy. "Thank you for everything." Matt stepped back from the hug, and Leanne put her hand on Miller's cheek and looked at him. "Thank you," she said in a quiet voice.

The two stepped into the church building. It was crowded with many people Matt knew and many he did not. Matt noticed that more than half of the people he saw were definitely not Mormons; many were not even religious people. The smell of the burned-out office, combined with the noise of the crowd, was giving a sense of chaos. Another uniformed deputy came through the crowd.

"We need to get started," he said as he led them into the chapel and to a waiting pair of seats in the second pew.

On the stage Matt saw the three missionaries, the King family, the priest from earlier, and Colonel Phelps, and somehow Sheriff Chow had made his way up as well. Matt and Leanne found their seats. A stream of men and women, some local church officials, two county commissioners, and a few city council members, made their way to the area behind the priest. The chapel was full beyond capacity. A local National Guard unit had set up a speaker system on the outside of the building, and the parking lot and area surrounding the church building was full of people.

Matt and Leanne had never been to church together, with the exception of the day they were married. Matt reached for his wife's hand; she squeezed his hand and flashed a smile at him. Visible to all sitting and standing near the podium was a wide mix of people. Bishop Riley from the South Ward was standing with Father Flarraty from the Catholic Church. It was a relief to see Bishop Riley, as he and his family had been missing. Maybe they had been in hiding, Matt thought.

"Today's service will be multi-denominational. Before we begin, I would like to ask Elders Miles, Jones, and Black to come forward." The three young men stood and joined the bishop and priest. "Elder Jones, would you open our services with a prayer?" The Bishop stepped back, allowing Nick Jones access to the podium and microphone.

Many in the room stood, some bowed their heads, and some just looked forward. Few seemed to notice the differences, but to Matt it was amazing. He saw a service full of people of different faiths. Matt noticed a group sitting off to his right wearing yarmulkes. At the end of the group of Jews he saw what he thought could only be Orthodox Jews, dressed in traditional dress. Black overcoats and beards with long curls hanging down was not what one would expect to see in a LDS church. All around the room, the differences blended—people of all faiths, races, and economic and social groups.

Elder Jones started to speak, clearly with conviction.

"Heavenly Father, we give thanks for this day. Father, we ask You for Your blessing in the days to come. We ask for Your guidance, and that You endow us with the patience we need as we move forward as a community." He paused and looked around the room, a little unsure of himself and how far he should go. He then concluded. "We ask these things in the name of Your Son, Jesus Christ."

The "Amen" echoed from inside and outside the building and was mixed with words in Hebrew and some Arabic from a group of Muslims in the back of the church building. The use of the words "Your Son, Jesus Christ" left some room for some to be offended, but luckily it was received well by all.

Maybe this is what Church is supposed to be like, Leanne thought as she scanned the room.

After the opening prayer, Sheriff Chow walked to the podium with Colonel Phelps at his side.

"Much has happened over the last week. People have lost their lives, homes have been burned, and a mob has attempted to take control of our town and county. I am here to assure you that, with the help of Colonel Phelps," Chow gestured to the woman at his side in camouflage, "I will bring law and order back to our community. As many of you already know, we have lost Bishop King and several other members of our community to vigilante violence. These events have been, and are continuing to be, investigated. Anyone involved in this group," the Sheriff held up a copy of the anti-Mormon poster, "needs to know it is over. This community will not tolerate mobs or hate groups." The Sheriff stepped back, and Colonel Phelps stepped forward.

"My name is Colonel Marissa Phelps. I am a Lieutenant Colonel in the United States Marine Corps and the Commanding Officer of Military Police in your county. I take my orders from General Siebel and General Siebel only. With that said, I need you to know that we count on you to govern and police your county. We count on you to provide help to those in need and to work together as community. Over the next weeks, you will notice a relaxing of military control in your towns. In the meantime, please work with us. It is our goal to see local control and policing as soon as possible. Our intent is to become a source of support, not a source of authority. We will work in support of Sheriff Chow and local officials." She stepped back a step and put her hand on Sheriff Chow's shoulder. "I will be working directly with Sheriff Chow. If you need help, law enforcement, or public service, I ask that you go to the sheriff. Sheriff Chow Is your elected sheriff, so please do not bring your concerns directly to me or to any of my marines or guardsman." Chow stepped back to the podium.

"Most of you came today to go to church, not to hear me speak, so I will turn this back over to the spiritual leaders of this community," he said, then the two walked back and sat down in the row of seats behind the podium. After sitting, Chow was whispering in the ear of his wife to his left and then to Father Flarraty to his right, continually glancing up to make sure he was not disrespecting the church services.

Bishop Riley came to the podium. "Today we will give time and service to all faiths, and, as this is uncharted territory for me, please be patient." The Bishop shuffled some index cards in front of him and cleared his throat nervously. "Before we start, I would like to say a few words to the King family." He stepped back and turned toward the family seated before him; he swallowed hard and began to speak. "We are here for you. We love you, and we grieve your loss with you." Looking out over the congregation, he continued, "Some of you may not know this, but we lost a great man this week. Bishop King, father, husband, and a leader in this church was taken from us. This family needs our support, and I am sure they are going to get it." This was said with authority, almost as an order.

Over the next hours, Matt and Leanne witnessed a Catholic Mass, Jewish prayers in Hebrew, a Muslim call to prayer, an Evangelist speaking in tongues, and even a Buddhist speaking words of wisdom. Who would have thought there would be such a diverse religious group in a small town like Port Smith? It was strange, but it was something this group needed. As things wrapped up, Bishop Riley returned to the podium.

"During the hour following worship, we will be having a Ward meeting, and following this we will be having a meeting of the high priests. We have some reconstruction and repair business to discuss. We also will be formulating a plan to help with family needs in the community. I thank you of different faiths for your support, and I welcome your leaders to these meetings. The only thing I ask is that our protocol and procedures be followed and respected, as we have much to do in a little time. Food will be served in the common areas and in the picnic area in the back of the property. I ask you all to attend, speak with your neighbors, and enjoy." The Bishop was implying that it was time for the masses to leave. The exodus of the crowd took the better part of forty minutes, with everyone talking and handshaking on their way out. When the chapel was half empty, the public address system was deactivated to give the meetings some level of privacy. As the chapel was clearing down to a usual-sized Sunday crowd, Matt and Leanne were making their way to the door.

"Please stay," the Bishop asked loudly. "Brother and Sister Scott, please stay," he repeated in a louder voice.

Matt stopped and turned. Seeing who was talking to him, Matt gave Leanne a slight tug. They were walking hand in hand. As he got her attention he stopped not just their progress, but also the heavy stream of people moving toward the door.

"We are not members," Matt said. He wanted out. Although this was all great and fun, it was still church, and Matt was ready to go home.

"Stay, Brother Scott," Elder Miles spoke clearly from the side of Bishop Riley.

Leanne turned and faced Matt. "We can stay for a little while." For some reason the sound and tenor of Elder Miles was something that could not be questioned, at least not in the moment.

Matt gave Leanne a jab with his elbow, as she had spoken loud enough that now he had no choice but to comply. The Bishop, Elder Miles, and now his wife all wanted him to stay, so he had no choice.

The couple turned and made their way back toward their seats. As they moved against the tide of people moving in the direction that Matt wanted to go, "Excuse me" was repeated over and over again. After they were seated again, Matt felt fairly uncomfortable, but Leanne sat up proud. The irony of Matt feeling out of place in the chapel and Leanne acting as if she was right at home was not lost on Matt. The doors to the general areas were closed, and the chapel was full of the members and their families, with the exception of the front row, in which sat a priest and several ministers, a rabbi, and of course, the Scott family.

"We will be taking the Sacrament followed by a talk by Elder Black," announced Bishop Riley.

Following the Sacrament, Elder Black took the podium. The Sacrament to a Mormon is an intrinsic part of Sunday services. It is akin to Holy Communion for a Catholic. Leanne very much enjoyed the ritual, as it was something she missed from her days of going to Mass with her mother.

"I have an announcement to make, and it is one of great importance." The young man stood tall and proud. Then he paused for a moment as if he was thinking of exactly what to say. "First, I must explain a little." The young missionary set down his notes; he would speak from the cuff. "Following the retaking of the Temple, and of the Office of the Presidency in Salt Lake, some information has been released." Elder Black motioned to Elder Miles. "We have a successor to the Presidency." He paused dramatically and then smiled. "The leadership of our Church named our new President and Prophet." He took a deep breath and looked skyward for a moment. "Many in our leadership have fallen, died, or gone missing. But before they fell, before they were even attacked, a successor had been named." He paused again in thought, and then continued, "When the offices were retaken, it was found that the Prophet had left us instructions. Notes had been left on the succession of his Office, and specific directions were given in the event of his death. Sadly, the Prophet was killed, and now it is our responsibility to carry out his instructions." There was a general feeling of confusion in the room. Why was an ordinary missionary giving this announcement? And why were nonmembers in the room? There was a general drone of quiet talk amongst the members. Elder Black cleared his throat and placed his hands firmly on the podium.

His actions caught the attention of the crowd, and decorum returned to the room almost instantly.

"Over the past days, we have fought to maintain our Church. We have fought to protect the named successor. And we have fought to save our Country and people. Many have aided in this struggle. Military units, congressmen and women, clergy of many faiths, mosques, and synagogues have come to our aid. In the end our Prophet was saved by the heroic acts of local members and nonmembers." "Elder Will Black looked at Matt and Leanne and then glanced to the back of the room to Sheriff Chow and Deputy Miller. "People with little or no stake in our plight found it within themselves to give shelter, food, and protection at great risk to themselves and their families."

Elder Black then proceeded to tell of the events of the last weeks, how they had gone to the Scotts' home, and how they had received help from the Deputy and the Sheriff. He also told of angry mobs and gun fights and burned-out houses. The narrative went on for the better part of forty minutes. The abridged version as told left out many small details, as one would expect, but the picture Elder Will Black painted with his descriptions kept the crowd's attention. Throughout his explanation, Elder Black left out one key piece of information, which was the most important to most of the people in the room. Who was this new Prophet? It seemed clear that whoever it was, he was in Port Smith. The talk was ending and Elder Black was getting ready to leave the podium when Elder Miles stepped up to his side. Elder Miles stood beside Elder Will Black; he looked at his friend with a different look, more the look of a father looking at a son. The younger Elder Miles smiled as he stepped forward.

"I present to you President Miles," Elder Black said with a smile.

The room went silent, maybe in reverence, maybe in disbelief, but either way the quiet was deafening.

The young Mr. Miles showed no sign of nervousness, not a glimpse of fear or discomfort. He gave a strong air of authority and wisdom.

"I have been called to lead the Mormon Church. Yes, I am young, and yes, you may have many questions. I ask only one thing of you. I ask you to believe in the power of a calling, to believe in the Church, and to believe in our Heavenly Father." Without another word, the young Prophet backed away from the podium and stepped back into the group behind Elder Black. Bishop Riley stepped to the podium, a bit surprised by the quick exit of the Prophet. "I will be giving the closing blessing at this time."

He spoke quickly. The Bishop was going to get to praying before anyone had a chance to respond or question the announcement they had just witnessed.

"Heavenly Father, we ask that You bless our new leader and the restored Church. We ask that You look after those still in need and danger. We ask these things in the name of Your Son, Jesus Christ. Amen." Abrupt and to the point, the Bishop was heading off the possibility of a questioning crowd.

Following the chorus of "Amen," the sound in the room began to elevate. There was a variety of responses to what just happened. Some expressed disbelief or shock and dismay, but the majority of the people in the room were acting as if they had just been introduced to their new Prophet. Most acted with reverence and respect. They believed in the Mormon Church, and now they would follow their Prophet. The noise level was slowly growing; the group on the stage near the podium was milling away toward the Bishop's office. Almost all the people in the room had either gotten to their feet or started to make their way out of the chapel. In the common entryway, on the lawn, and in the picnic area, people from all over were discussing the introduction of the new leader. Elder Miles had been ushered into a back room and was awaiting someone to arrange transportation to Salt Lake City.

Matt and Leanne just wanted to get out, get home, and have some peace and quiet. The couple was feeling some relief from the stress of the last weeks. Leanne had called David's house and talked with both of her children and grandchildren. Matt had received a call from both of his girls, and he knew they were safe. It was time to go home, time to rest and absorb what had been happening. The two of them got to their feet. Matt quickly got a firm grip on Leanne's hand, and he leaned in and spoke into her ear over the noise in the room.

"Can we sneak out of here?"

"You were reading my mind." Leanne had pushed the idea of going to church, but by now she wanted to go home.

The two made their way through the crowd, hearing an occasional "Thank you," and "God bless you." Matt and Leanne both arrived at the van and both entered through the side sliding door. Leanne crawled into the passenger seat, and Matt climbed into the driver's seat. They had gotten away from the crowd without being spotted. In the chaos no one noticed them leaving. The couple looked at each other almost like two high school kids cutting class as they buckled their seatbelts and Matt started the van. After weaving through the maze of parked cars, they left the parking lot and turned toward home. They would have a normal evening—no missionaries, no police, and life as it was, their simple happy life, at least for the night.

Matt awoke early the next morning. He was careful not to close the door too loudly as he walked to the living room to turn on the TV. Returning to the kitchen, Matt made a cup of coffee and put two pieces of bread in the toaster. This morning was like so many before, so much like that morning not so long ago when the world changed. Sitting back on the couch, watching the news and reflecting, a smile cracked across his face. "We are still here," he mumbled to himself. Recent events involved violence and insecurity, the economy had all but totally collapsed, and yet, they are still here, he thought. Never again would things be the same, but they would find a new normal, one that included all of the key parts of life.

Days passed and turned to weeks, then weeks turned to months, and before they knew it, a year had passed since that eventful night with the missionaries at the door. Matt had returned to work; Leanne was helping with several charities and spending time with the church and its administrative needs. Neither Matt nor Leanne ever returned to the Mormon Church or any other church as active members, but they did give time to aid in the works performed by the local churches. Leanne's administrative skills were of great help to the local LDS church. Much of the business of being a church had become more complicated. The Mormon Church was now functioning almost as a government agency of sorts; they distributed food aid as well as provided warehousing and logistics support to local governments.

Back in the little apartment, the storytelling suddenly ground to a stop when the elderly man had another coughing fit. When his wife had tended to him with the nebulizer and a glass of water, she turned and spoke to the missionaries.

"Boys, I think that's enough for tonight." She then turned to her husband and said, "Enough for tonight. It's getting late."

The two young men were standing and getting ready to make their way toward the door when the taller of the two asked. "May we say a prayer?"

"Of course," responded the older man. He stayed seated, as he was clearly tired from the long talk.

"We can finish in the morning," he said, looking up at his wife for approval.

Before she could respond, the missionaries both spoke up in unison. "We can be here at eight."

"Make it nine, boys," the soft voice of a worried wife responded.

The two young missionaries said a prayer and found their way to the door and home. The elderly couple went to bed, knowing the missionaries would be returning in the morning.

"I know this is important, sweetie, but please don't overdo it," Mrs. Scott said to her husband as she prepared his evening medications. The couple was tired, yet they so much enjoyed having the missionaries in their home. The company offered the opportunity to share the events of their lives.

The two young missionaries hurried home to their apartment. They were home in time to check in for curfew by just a few minutes. Normally they would end their evening with a session of planning for the day ahead, but not tonight. After showers and prayers, they retired to the shared bedroom in their little apartment. The two were lying in bed trying to sleep.

"Do you think he is really Matt Scott?" a voice asked out of the dark.

"I'm pretty sure he is." The response came quickly in an excited and happy tone.

The two did not say another word; they just lay in the dark trying to sleep, anticipating the visit they would have in the morning.

When morning came, the two young men were up so early that they had time to clean the small apartment, study scriptures, and even write a letter or two. As they watched the clock, time slowly passed. Finally 8:00 a.m. finally appeared on the clock. The two headed out the door and down the street. They would walk to the Scott's apartment building. As it would only take twenty or thirty minutes, they would be early.

In the Scott's apartment, Mrs. Scott was up early. She had breakfast cooking in anticipation of the morning visit. The young missionaries had brought back fond memories of the young Elders Black, Miles, and Jones. She cooked scrambled eggs, corned beef hash, and French toast, enough food to feed an army.

"My Lord, dear, who's coming to breakfast, the Second Marines?" Asked the elderly Mr. Scott as he slowly made his way down the hall.

Mrs. Scott was setting food out on the table. She turned and smiled, for a minute she was that young woman in Port Smith again, feeding the missionaries. Her smile was all the response her husband needed.

"I love you more every day," he said with a smile as he made his way to the table.

At 8:45 both Mr. and Mrs. Scott sat quietly at the table, waiting for their guests to return. They did not have to wait long. The doorbell rang, and Mr. Scott stood and walked to the door. He unlocked and opened it without thought. On the other side of the threshold stood the two young men, dressed in suites and ties again, Bibles in hand. They had so looked forward to the continuing of their visit that had forgotten it was Monday. Monday was the day off for missionaries, a day known as P day, or personal day, the only day you will find a Mormon missionary not in a suit and tie. But today no jeans and T-shirts. Today they were in their best suits and ties.

As the three entered the room, Mrs. Scott stood with a smile. "Come boys and eat," she said with pride.

Without much discussion—just a short prayer and the clanking of plates was the only sound—the four sat at the table eating.

"Where were we?" asked Mr. Scott.

"Matt and Leanne were back at home," responded the younger missionary.

"It had been a year," offered Mrs. Scott

"Yes, yes, it had been a year," repeated Mr. Scott. He set down his fork and rubbed the whiskers on his chin. "A year later," he repeated.

"You know, things changed a lot back then. Those were different times," he continued.

For the first time his wife interjected. "It wasn't so bad." She paused. "Things were better, I think. Better than before," she said with a smile.

The two looked at each other, smiling. It was clear that they were remembering happy times. They were remembering their younger years.

"You know, life went on," Mr. Scott said. "Life had to go on. We had to move ahead," he concluded as he started back into the storytelling from the day before.

Matt woke like almost every other morning; he tiptoed out, made coffee, and turned on the news. The news anchor was talking about the upcoming elections. The Country had been divided into seven districts, each with a military commander who was charged with not only keeping the peace, but also restoring civilian rule. The debate being levied now was that of division, of a Constitutional Congress, what the United States would look like when all was said and done. Matt was always very patriotic and political, but things were different now. People had learned how to survive on a local level. In the cities things were very hard. Matt and Leanne had taken several trips to Seattle to bring extra food and supplies to Leanne's children. David was working, and things were looking up for the family, but the lower classes were not doing so well. Federal funding did not exist anymore. Local charity was the only hope for people who had received Federal or State aid.

Matt's kids were doing great. Sam and her husband were living in San Diego. The marines had all come home, and they were being used to keep the peace in the homeland. Riana was still at the University of Connecticut. Things were different, but she was still in school. Leanne's job never called back, so she now worked with Matt and Jeremy at the shop when she was not too busy with her charity work. The shop had brought back one of the mechanics who had been laid off before the collapse. Nobody was getting rich, but they kept their families fed. Perspective had changed; it was about helping and surviving, not about getting ahead any more.

The biggest relief for Leanne was that Matt was not charged with any crimes concerning the shootout at the King home. Matt had faced a Military Tribunal and a local Grand Jury following the events of that week. It was determined that he was defending the King family and he was cleared of any wrongdoing. This did not go over well with a select group of people in Port Smith. The Mormon-hating and political battles would go on. Some of these people saw Matt as a murderer, and they wanted him punished. Leanne feared for his safety, as it was not uncommon to hear comments or get harassed when they were in town. In some ways, Matt's life became so much simpler since these events. In other ways it got very complicated. Matt had no fear of these people. "Lots of talk and no action," was what he would tell Leanne. On occasion Sheriff Chow would check in with Matt and Leanne, at first to see if they were OK on a professional level, but in time they became friends. The Chow and Scott family would develop a bond that could only come from hard times.

Within weeks of being cleared of wrongdoing, Matt was approached by a group from the Church.

"We would like you and Leanne to come back to church again." One man spoke for the group that was standing at the Scott's front door.

"I have explained how we feel." Matt was trying to be polite, but all things considered, he just wanted to be left alone. "We have our lives, and we will live them as we see fit," Matt explained as he tipped a cup of coffee in their direction.

Matt and Leanne did make occasional appearances at the church and would help families in the community when needed, but they made a point to make equal appearances at the Catholic Church as well. Leanne put in many hours helping both the LDS and the Catholic Church, but she made an effort to be somewhat secular in her communications and dealings with the members and staff. The Scotts believed in God, and they also believed in the works of the Church. They just did not believe any particular church was the place for them.

There had been a reduction in the numbers of soldiers and marines in the area. Sheriff Chow had taken control of the local law enforcement duties and had six deputies working for him again.

Local government looked much like it did before the collapse; it was just smaller and poorer. The problem was funding, the tax structure had collapsed with the fall of the dollar and Federal Government.

The State tried to step in, but Washington State government had collapsed within days. The Military was managing the primary commodities such as power, water, and fuel. The hospitals were up and running, but there was little in the way of a financial system. There were no banks to withdraw money from, no banks to make payments to. The world's financial system was rebooting. Media survived purely on the handouts from the Military.

The LDS Church took over all food distribution in Region Three—the area including Utah, Montana, Idaho, Oregon, and Washington. This was one of the most stable of the seven regional districts. Most people knew it was due to the rural areas and the ability people had to take care of themselves. The East Coast and Southwest were very different stories. Much of the East Coast survived in a constant state of martial law. The greater Los Angeles area had been abandoned by any form of law enforcement and was being run by a coalition of street gangs. To the surprise of many outside of the Southwest, it was working. The gangs exacted loyalty and rule of law; they used force and violence to keep order, and it worked. The big problem faced by the gangs was a lack of outside help. The gangs had to learn to negotiate with other districts to acquire food, fuel, and water, and many of the farmers of the Midwest had little time or respect for what they saw as "street hoods". Overall the system in LA was far from perfect, but it was working. The gangs looked more like third-world governments than street gangs every day.

People rarely traveled across regions anymore; much of what people knew about the different regions was from the news stations and hearsay. What affected Matt and Leanne was the Pacific Northwest, Region Three. To them the other regions were something they read about in the paper or saw on the news. No longer was there a sense of "One Nation". Region Six was important to Matt—his little girl lived in Region Six—but she was doing OK.

Matt had heard little from Elders Black or Jones. The two had been recalled to Salt Lake with Elder Miles. Elder Miles became President Miles to the dismay of many. Miles was young and inexperienced, and even disabled in his own way. But he had been named the new Prophet not only by the President of the Mormon Church, but also by the surviving apostles. Elder Miles made few public statements or appearances, and many people questioned if he was actually in charge of the Church. But under his leadership much had been accomplished. The Church had taken its position as Food Management and Distribution in Region Three, and was now taking control of two other regions at the request of General Siebel. Some saw this as a bad thing, people who were against any Church control, but others realized that religious organizations were the best equipped to provide the services needed. Similar things had been accomplished through the use of fraternal orders such as the Shriners, or the Elks Lodge. Each organization had been identified for its ability and called upon to provide the services that had gone away with the national collapse.

For the non-religious, or the people who feared too much Church involvement, General Siebel had an answer. "You may not like Mormons, but you don't mind it when they fill your grocery store shelves." The Church had managed to work in a very secular fashion. The missionaries were dispatched to work with the Military and local Law Enforcement to identify people with food needs. The mission moved from proselytizing to feeding the population. The young men in black suits on bicycles, who used to inspire the no-soliciting signs, had a new role. The public now looked at them with respect. Their visits were something to celebrate if one was in need of food or help. They would visit each home and take requests back to their leadership, and the leadership would dispatch food to those deemed unable to fend for themselves. They would provide a source of food to purchase or barter for to the able-bodied, no strings attached. On many occasions they would work with families on techniques for growing and storing food.

This system worked very well in the rural areas, but the cities had a different problem. The missionaries were often attacked, food warehouses had to be guarded by soldiers, and often riots took place in the streets surrounding the buildings. Neither local nor military leadership could seem to solve the problem. It seemed as if the predicament was cultural. General Siebel struggled with the question, "How do you get people to settle for less?" There was less to go around, and rationing was a way of life in the cities. People would need to feel calm and secure before the Military could step down. People needed to find a system to provide for themselves. The urban culture had left a large portion of the population unable or unwilling to fend for themselves, or take responsibility for their own well-being.

The morning passed like every other, but today Matt was wondering how the three young men were doing back in Salt Lake City.

"Why did you let me sleep so late?" Leanne came out of the bedroom rubbing her eyes. She was dressed a fluffy bathrobe, pajamas, and slippers. "Don't we need to get to the shop soon?"

"Jeremy has the morning under control; we can go in later," Matt responded. Work had been slow. Most of the shop had been leased to the Military for a motor pool. Jeremy and Matt had two bays to work with, and they worked on local cars, often for barter. Yesterday Matt and Jeremy had put a clutch in a small pickup; the customer paid them with two apple pies and an IOU. Things had changed. The Military did pay Matt with chits for items such as food, clothes and fuel, which were good at any store that was supported by the Regional System. Matt often worked for other forms of payment, and some people still paid with dollars, yet no one really knew what they were worth anymore.

This morning Matt was tired. "I am beat." Matt did not want to go into work today, but knew he would.

"I'm getting into the shower. I suggest you get ready, Mr. Lazy Bones." Leanne teased Matt, but she had work to do. Leanne was working hard to organize and catalog parts, used and new. Parts had become a problem, and Leanne had somehow found a way to gather used, new, and all sorts of parts. She was actually loving her job and making a difference. Leanne also had set up an office, where she devoted much time to training and helping the local church staffs in bookkeeping and overall office management. Somehow the lack of a paycheck had freed Leanne up to shine. Leanne Scott was the "go-to" lady. If anyone had a management or accounting problem, Leanne was the one to see.

Matt could hear the shower come on. He grumbled a little, topped off his coffee, and headed for the bedroom to get dressed and ready for work. The sound of a car in the driveway caught his attention. One thing that had changed over the last year was the number of cars on the road. People only drove if they had to; fuel was expensive and hard to get.

"Who the hell is that?" he said out loud, his mood becoming more aggravated by the moment. Matt quickly went into the bedroom and put on some jeans and a T-shirt. By this time Matt was feeling generally irritated. He did not want to go to work today, he was generally in a foul mood, and now he had an uninvited visitor. Before the doorbell could ring, he opened the front door. Standing in front of him was a familiar group. Elder William Black and Elder Nick Jones stood on each side of Deputy Miller. Matt's attitude instantly changed. He had not seen these two in a year. They had left suddenly with Elder Miles. The sight of the two missionaries put a huge smile on his face.

Matt threw the door open and said, "Come in, come in!" In a state of astonishment, he led the three toward the kitchen table where they all sat down.

"Honey, who you talking to?" Leanne asked as she came through the door. She saw the young men before Matt could answer. "Will! Nick!" She ran toward the young men and hugged them, the towel falling off her head, wet hair and all.

"Good to see you, too, Mrs. Scott," Will Black squirmed in her embrace and was obviously uncomfortable with her display of affection.

"How many times do I have to tell you, it's Leanne. Mrs. Scott is my mother-in-law's name."

The five of them sat at the table. Deputy Miller was strangely quiet.

"So, what brings you here?" Matt asked.

"Business." Elder Jones had matured quite a lot since they had seen him. He changed his posture slightly, and even his voice took on a serious business-like tone.

"President Miles is asking for your help." The term *president* still seemed strange to both Matt and Leanne. Matt knew the position as president of the Mormon Church and as prophet, but to equate either of those terms with the awkward young man they knew made little sense.

"What does he want from me?" Matt asked.

"Have you heard of the Sons of Nephi?" asked Will Black.

"Sons of Nephi? Is that a gang or something?" Leanne asked.

Matt laughed out loud and said, "That would be a Mormon gang," not realizing that he might offend.

"What's so hard to believe about a Mormon gang?" asked Nick Jones.

Deputy Miller piped up. "Sons of Nephi, they are a group of Mormons working in the cities to feed and help people, kind of like the Guardian Angels. There have been reports that they have turned into some form of vigilante group."

Will Black interrupted. "General Siebel is afraid they may be getting out of control. They started out as a loosely-organized group of missionaries looking for people to help." He stopped talking long enough to throw a dirty look at Deputy Miller. "They have grown into something bigger. President Miles thinks they might be getting a little out of control, as well."

"And what does this have to do with me?" Matt leaned back in his chair with a concerned look, clearly remembering how he was drawn in before.

"General Siebel has asked President Miles to look into these groups, and President Miles wants you to help." Elder Jones had changed his tenor, from friendly and stern to a bit more authoritarian. "We need your help," Elder Black stated simply.

"Why me? What do I have to do with this?"

Before Matt could finish his thought, Leanne stood up. "Haven't we been through enough?" She was visibly shaken, as she knew Matt would not say no. She also knew it would be dangerous.

"Meet with us, that's all we ask. Come to Salt Lake and meet with us."

"Not Salt Lake. How about Miles comes here?" Matt was trying to establish some control.

"You know that won't happen," Will Black said.

"Don't forget, you came to me," Matt pointed out. "Well, I am letting you know that I am not going to Salt Lake." The conversation was quickly leaving the realm of friendly.

"Maybe neutral ground," Elder Jones interjected.

"OK, how about Seattle?" Matt leaned forward with his offer. "I am not going any farther than Seattle."

"I will see what I can do." Will Black stood up from the table and gave Nick Jones a nod.

Nick Jones also stood. "Excuse us. We should get going," he stated.

"I don't think so," Leanne protested. "At least you can come back and have dinner with us, and that goes for you, too, Deputy Miller."

The three men stood up and walked to the front door. "Five o'clock work for you?" Leanne was pushing the issue.

"Yes, five is good" Will Black spoke for all three of them, but no one seemed to be protesting. They all said a quick good-bye and headed out to the street. Matt closed the door and looked at Leanne.

"I know, I know, you're going, aren't you?" Leanne said with a bit of a shake in her voice. "You're going to leave me again, aren't you?" Leanne was remembering the events that had left her beaten, with two dead agents in her home.

"I just want to hear what they have to say," he said.

But Leanne knew better. Matt had that look—a sense of purpose, a sense of calling—and it scared her very much. "You promise me you are coming back in one piece," she implored. It was a forgone conclusion—Matt was going to help, no matter what they needed. It was who he was. Maybe this was part of the mood he had found himself in—maybe Matt needed to matter, to make a difference. It was much like the adrenalin rush needed by returning combat veterans. In his heart Matt wanted a simple life, but things still felt unfinished.

"I didn't sign up for this hero-martyr crap," Leanne said with a break in her voice as she hugged Matt. "Damn you," she blurted out as she released the hug and turned and walked into the kitchen. Pouring a cup of coffee, she took a long drink and looked at Matt. "Damn you," Leanne repeated. The words had some effect on Matt, but the fact that she poured a cup and never offered one to Matt was the telling gesture. Leanne was upset. She was feeling left out, and she did not like it. Matt walked up behind her and hugged her gently. "I love you," he said.

"Prove it by coming home in one piece. Prove it by putting your family before that damn Church for once." Leanne was upset and lashing out. Matt knew it. He knew he had it coming, and he was not about to fight back. Matt just held her as she drank her coffee and tried to calm down.

Matt called Jeremy. "We are not coming in today. No, everything is OK. I may need to take a couple days off, but Leanne will be in when she can." The conversation ended and Matt turned to his wife. "We have the day off," he said in a teasing manner.

"What you will do to get out of going to work," Leanne responded and laughed. She was done being angry for now, and they were going to enjoy their day. Leanne had an amazing way of feeling her emotion, working through it, and moving on—a skill most people would benefit from.

Matt and Leanne spent the day around the house. They cleaned up a little, spent some time in the yard and the garden, and they tried to make the best of every minute. Matt felt like he did as a young marine the day before he was going to get shipped out. They did not speak about the days to come at all; they just enjoyed each other's company. At 4:00 p.m. they started getting dinner ready. Leanne was making her famous manicotti, and Matt was making a large green salad with chopped up vegetables from the garden. There was a somber feeling in the air. When the knock on the door came, Leanne took a deep breath and looked at Matt.

"You going to get that, or just let them stand outside?" Leanne was trying to bring some levity to the situation.

Matt opened the door, and after a quick greeting the three men walked in. "I can't stay," Deputy Miller announced. "I will be back in a couple hours." Without giving anyone a chance to respond, the deputy turned and jogged to his patrol car. He made a three-point turn and took off at a fairly high speed.

"What was that about?" Matt asked.

"Some trouble in town. Seems there was some trouble at the Catholic Church again," Will Black explained with frustration in his voice.

"When are people going to stop blaming the Churches for everything that goes wrong?" Elder Jones wondered.

Over the past year, a small but very vocal group had been protesting all across the country. They protested at churches, military bases, and local government buildings. They had been mostly nonviolent, but on occasion things did get out of hand. The group was a strange mix of Anarchists, Socialists, and Communists—basically a bunch of misfits led by some people who hated organized religion. Matt had had some level of empathy toward them until they got violent. The group burned a few buildings and had started throwing bricks through windows. It reminded Matt of the WTO protests in Seattle. They attacked symbols of what they hated. The problem was most of them were just sheep and had little ability to think for themselves. The group seemed to be clear on what they hated and did not want, but they could never seem to offer any solutions. They protested but could not resolve. Matt felt this was common among the disenfranchised—blame and anger without any ideas or solutions. The deputy was off to keep them under control. He would maybe arrest one or two, but more often than not he would just be a calming presence.

Dinner was uneventful. Will Black said grace. Leanne asked them about their families and how everyone had been doing. Matt was more interested in *what* they had been doing. After getting back to Salt Lake City, Elders Jones and Black had been working with Elder Miles; they were his most trusted advisors. The hierarchy of the Church protested at times, yet the three young men were doing a good job. They worked within the Church as well as with the Military and other organizations.

"You would not believe how well he is doing." Elder Black was referring to Elder Miles. "His presence and his abilities are amazing. It's true he was chosen for a reason."

Matt was having a hard time envisioning Elder Miles as an authority figure, but he would soon find out. Dinner was done, and they all felt like they had eaten too much. Matt and Leanne had a couple of glasses of wine, and now it was time to get to the serious questions.

The four cleared the table and tended to dishes and chores as they had over a year ago; the cooperation was seamless. Matt found it funny that both Will and Nick remembered where all the dishes went. Will dried them and Nick put them away. The four returned to the kitchen table for some conversation.

"So, what's the scoop?" Matt was probing for information.

"It's simple. I talked to the Presidency, and they have agreed to meet in Seattle. Sheriff Chow has talked to Colonel Phelps, and they will provide security and transportation for you and Mrs. Scott."

"Leanne," she interjected, "and I get to go, too?" She seemed very excited.

Elder Black glanced her way and smiled. To Matt he said, "You and Leanne will fly to Seattle tomorrow and meet with General Siebel, President Miller, and a few local officials.

"We will drive ourselves, and Leanne will go visit the kids during the meeting. We make that trip every three or four weeks, so we will be right on schedule. Leanne, would you call the kids and tell them you are coming? I will let Jeremy know you won't be in to work."

"Boeing Field, The Museum of Flight, that's where we will meet at 3:00 p.m. tomorrow." Elder Jones was sounding very calculated.

"Oh, almost forgot, no guns. You will not be let in with guns." Will knew that Matt would want to be armed if he was going into the city.

"No guns in the meeting, deal," he said, making it clear that the rule only applied to the meeting.

There was a knock on the door. When Matt opened it, he saw Sheriff Chow. "Sorry, but Miller is tied up. I am to get these two back to town. After Matt and Leanne offered a short good-bye and hug to each, Sheriff Chow left with the two young men.

"I need a drink," Matt said to Leanne.

"Me too. I thought we were done with this crap," Leanne responded with frustration in her voice.

They spent the evening packing up a care package for the kids and grandkids. Leanne had made some pajamas for the ever-growing grandchildren, and Matt had some toys he had gathered from customers in town.

Matt called Jeremy. "Yeah, going to be gone a couple days at least. You think maybe you could spend a day or two at the house? Just to make it look lived in? Yes, Chow knows where we will be."

The two headed off to bed. It was late, and morning would come before they knew it.

CHAPTER TWELVE

After a normal morning of showers and such, Matt and Leanne loaded the Cadillac, got in, and backed out of the driveway. Driving away from the house, Matt could see Deputy Miller's patrol car parked at the end of the cul-de-sac. He had been watching their house. With the missionaries back in town, Matt figured the deputy was keeping an eye on things to make sure they would be OK.

They drove to Seattle as they had many times before. The tollbooths on the Tacoma Narrows Bridge were open again, and the express lanes were closed. All cars were routed through the tollbooths. This was not a problem as there was little traffic compared to times before the crash. In the days before the economy crashed, it would take Matt three to four hours to get to David's house due to traffic. Now it could be done in two and half hours easy, sometimes less. Traffic jams were a thing from days past. Now it was just poorly maintained roads that slowed people down, along with the occasional checkpoint.

"No toll, just a warning." The attendant in the booth handed a paper to Matt and raised the gate. Matt handed it off to Leanne as he accelerated onto the giant bridge.

"This says to stay in at night and that the city police cannot guarantee safety after dark." Leanne sounded concerned as she read it out loud.

"What city police?" Matt asked.

"Tacoma and Seattle, according to this. David never told me about this." Leanne was now getting worried.

The two made the drive to David's house without any trouble. When they arrived, they parked in the garage and unloaded all of the groceries and gifts they had brought. David had programmed one of the garage door openers in the Cadillac to work on his house. Leaving a car like the Cadillac on the street in Seattle was asking for trouble, even in a safe neighborhood like the one David's family lived in.

The day was full of play with grandchildren and friendly talks with David and Sarah. Sarah was getting some mail from her boyfriend, the children's father, but he had not returned yet from his quest for work. He was working odd jobs making his way back toward Seattle. Sarah seemed OK with this. She was confident he would be home someday, and in the meantime she was just enjoying being a mom. The support she received from her brother David gave Sarah a chance to focus on the children. David's wife had been supportive and present through the entire visit but always seemed to leave space for the family to re-unite.

"Got to get going," Matt said looking at his watch.

"Where're you off to, Dad?" David asked.

"Just a meeting, nothing to worry about," Matt said. But David knew better by the look on his mother's face. Matt walked to the back room with Leanne and gave her a long hug and kiss. "I will be back in a couple hours," he said. Then he turned and walked out to the garage, and he sped away in the black Cadillac.

As Matt approached Boeing Field, the military presence became very large. On two occasions he was stopped and his ID was checked. When Matt was within a block of The Museum of Flight, he was stopped and taken out of the car. Two young soldiers patted him down, and one said, "Come with us. The General is waiting." Matt climbed into a dark green Humvee, leaving his Cadillac sitting with the driver's door open.

"Will you take care of my car?" Matt tossed the keys to a sergeant standing beside the Humvee he had climbed into. "And lock it," he added.

"Yes, sir. Will treat it with kid gloves," the sergeant responded with a grin.

Once he was seated in the Humvee, Matt started to wonder how long this might take. He still did not totally trust the Military.

They drove forward as obstacles were avoided and gates opened until they arrived at the back entrance to The Museum of Flight.

"Come with me, sir," a large sergeant said and escorted Matt toward a door. In the meeting room there was a large oval table. On one side sat several men in uniform and one woman. Matt recognized General Siebel and Colonel Phelps. Standing in the room were Elder Miles, Elder Jones, and Elder Black. Two men in black suits stood by with a menacing presence. Matt guessed they were security for the President of the Mormon Church.

"Sit down." A much-decorated Master Sergeant sitting to the General's left motioned toward a chair. The man had a very scarred face, a shaved head, and looked like the stereotype of the scary marine sergeant. Matt stepped back. He was taken aback by the direct nature of the marines in the room. President Miles, or Elder Miles, as Matt knew him came across the room. Quickly the two security men stepped ahead of him.

"Get out of my way," Miles said, pushing the two aside. To Matt, he said, "Excuse these two. Their intentions are good."

Matt was in shock. Miles was quiet, and he was slow, he thought, but this version of Miles was strong and in charge.

"Brother Scott, I am so glad you came." President Miles said in a very calm and quiet manner.

"I'm not sure I am so glad." Matt was scanning the room. He felt like he was under scrutiny from everyone, each for a different reason and with a different motive. Matt shook Miles's hand. "How about someone fills me in on why I am here."

"Have a seat," the gruff sergeant said again. This time he stood to show respect and spoke in the manner of a request not an order.

"OK..." Matt responded hesitantly.

The table was now full; Matt sat across from General Siebel and beside Miles.

"It's simple. We have a communication problem." Colonel Phelps spoke up.

"Go ahead." The General gave his approval as he leaned back to listen.

"As you may know, we have had a lot of violence in the cities. We have also tasked the Mormon Church with food distribution."

"Go on." General Siebel was hurrying the Colonel along.

"The problem is the Church has taken it upon itself to police the streets," interjected the bald Master Sergeant.

Miles was studying the body language of everyone at the table. He sat back quietly, waiting for the right time to interject.

"A group, calling themselves the Sons of Nephi, they have taken up arms, and we can't have that," the Master Sergeant continued.

Matt noted the actions and reactions of everyone at the table. The two security guards took a very aggressive posture; in a way they reminded him of Agent Morris. The General and Colonel seemed calm. The Master Sergeant looked aggravated. Miles was calm; he had a small smile on his face.

"Our missionaries are like everyone else; they have the right to defend themselves." Miles spoke slowly and deliberately.

"If you could guarantee the safety of food workers, I would think they would not feel it necessary to be defensive," Miles continued.

"Defensive," scoffed the Master Sergeant.

"Excuse me, I did not get your name," said Miles calmly, looking into the eyes of the Sergeant.

"Master Sergeant Crosby."

"Sergeant Crosby, our mission is peaceful, but God helps those who help themselves. We will not let people go hungry, and we will protect the innocent."

"Are you saying we can't do our job?" Matt thought Crosby was obviously looking for a fight.

"No, maybe what I am saying is you *won't* do your job." Miles said it calmly, but it was like pulling the pin on a hand grenade. The Master Sergeant instantly changed his position and attitude.

General Siebel leaned forward, taking control of the conversation; with a glance he demanded quiet and obedience from the outspoken enlisted man.

"President Miles," he diplomatically addressed Miles.

"Sir, I am the President of the Mormon Church. I am not your President. You may address me by my name if you choose—David Miles."

The General stopped for a moment and studied Miles for a reaction. "You will call me General Siebel." He paused. "I am your General."

"Sir, we recognize your authority," Miles responded.

All of the posturing seemed pointless to Matt Scott. "Again, what does this have to do with me?" he asked.

"Well, sir, Mr. Miles seems to think you can work as liaison between this group and our field commanders." General Siebel had a tone of someone not sold on the idea.

"It's only some missionaries; you can't figure it out on your own?" Matt looked at the General and scanned the other marines in the room.

"It's more than a few missionaries. This group has killed several men, and they have looted two warehouses," Sergeant Crosby interjected.

"They have killed in self-defense, and they have recovered stolen and hoarded supplies," Miles responded. "Recovery of property is not looting."

"Call it what you will. They do not have the authority, and we cannot allow them, to take matters into their own hands."

"So, again, what is my place in this?" Matt was becoming agitated. "You took me away from my wife, my business." Matt stood up suddenly, causing the marine guards to shoulder their rifles. "With all due respect, stop wasting my time, arrest me." Glancing at the young marines, he said, "Shoot me, get to the point, or just let me go." Matt was beyond angry. "I don't have time for your blame and politics."

"I would like you to take a representative from the Military out to talk to the Sons of Nephi," Miles said calmly.

"You can't talk to them? Give an edict or something?" Matt asked.

Miles let out a muted laugh. "They don't work for me; I don't even know who they are. I know we have some missionaries in their ranks, but don't kid yourself, they do not work for or answer to the Mormon Church."

"And me? Why me?" Matt asked, hoping that he could make some sense of the situation.

"I trust you. I prayed." He paused, and then said, "It will be you." There was not one ounce of doubt in the young prophet's voice.

Matt sat back down at the table and sighed deeply. What could he do? If the Pope asked, he would do it. If the President asked, he would do it. And now the Prophet of the Mormon Church had asked. He must do what he can.

"I'm listening," Matt said, looking at General Siebel.

"I will send you out with Master Sergeant Crosby and two marines. You will make contact and arrange a sit-down with the group."

"And if they say no, or if I can't make contact?" Matt asked. "Then what?"

"Not an option." The General was speaking with a tone of desperation. "We have enough problems with people hating Mormons, enough violence, it's time to get this under control. There is no plan B. You're it, Mr. Scott."

"I will find them, I will bring them to the table, but I will do it alone." Matt knew if he hit the streets with a group of marines, he would never get inside. "General, if I go out there with this guy at my side, I will never get close." Matt pointed at Crosby. The General thought for a moment

"You're probably right, but we will be watching you," Crosby said.

"Well, if I am going to do this, you need to give me something to work with. Why don't you tell me something about these people, the Sons of Nephi?" Matt turned to Miles. "That name says Mormons to me."

"Well, first of all, we don't know where the name came from—if someone gave it to them or if they named themselves. Hell, we don't even know if they are Mormons." Col. Phelps was taking over the conversation. It was clear from the stack of notes in front of her that she had the intelligence, what little they had.

"So how about you tell me what you do know, not what you don't know," Matt responded sarcastically.

The Colonel ignored his tone and continued. "We know it started in Seattle. Now there are groups in every major city. We know they are challenging the authority of the Military, and we know in Los Angeles the gangs have given them authority and respect. The Crips call them 'The Jesus Team.'"

"So the problem is?" Matt was confused. "Seems like maybe they are not such a bad thing."

"The problem is they are a religion-based group from the Mormon Church, which was in the middle of all of this crap from the beginning.

Perception is everything; we don't need a religious civil war," Phelps responded.

"So the churches are good when they do your bidding, the churches are good when you need something, but they are bad when they defend themselves." Matt was fishing for understanding.

"No, churches are good when they feed people, they are bad when they start to become the government," Phelps said as she leaned forward.

"So I am supposed to do what, again?" Matt was put out by the Colonel's words and attitude.

"Nothing more than get them to the table. We need to talk. We can handle it from there."

"How do you propose I do that? It sounds clear to me that they have good reason not to trust you." Matt was pushing the limits of patience from across the table.

"That question is for you," she said, looking at Miles.

"You will get it done." Miles was very confident

General Siebel piped in. "We know it started here in Seattle; we are pretty sure the leadership is here."

"You think it's that organized?" Matt asked.

"Honestly, we don't know." Phelps answered.

Now in Matt's mind this whole meeting was a silly bit of posturing. The truth was that since the Sons of Nephi had hit the streets, the rioting and looting had almost totally stopped. People were getting food, and life was getting better in the cities. To Matt it seemed that the purpose of the meeting was to find out who these people were and why they were so powerful.

"So if I bring you people, are you going to arrest them? How do I guarantee their safety?"

"You trust us," the General said clearly.

Matt took a deep breath and said, "Take me to my wife and kids. I need to go see them before I give you an answer."

Matt stood up and walked toward the door. Quickly two marines were at his side and walked him out to the waiting Humvee. As he got in, Colonel Phelps handed him a phone; it was a large military satellite phone. "So we can talk," she said.

Matt left the meeting with thoughts running through his head. What was he doing? Thinking of the shooting at the King house, he thought over and over, *Hell, I'm just an auto mechanic.*

"My car?" Matt asked the driver.

"It's at your son's house," he responded. This bothered Matt that this enlisted man would know that David was his son. Matt sat quietly in the back seat waiting to see what would happen.

The Humvee rounded a corner and drove under an overpass. Suddenly there was a huge flash of light and an explosion. The driver slumped over the steering wheel, and they rolled to a stop at the side of the road. Matt was disoriented—ears ringing, vision blurred—when the door beside him opened and someone dragged him out into the street. Across the street he could see the marine who was sitting beside him being hit with his rifle stock. The marine was surrounded by a group of young men; some were wearing what looked like gang clothes, others were dressed in regular street attire, and a few had uniform pants or shirts, either deserters or military "wanna-bes."

"Look for guns and food!" yelled a short black man with gray hair from the sidewalk. Instantly three or four teens started to tear into the Humvee. Matt was still being kicked and hit, and the marine across the street was not looking to good.

"Kill him!" yelled the man as a tall, thin teen raised the rifle to hit the young marine. Matt closed his eyes, and a gunshot rang out. The teen dropped to the ground; half of his head was gone. The three teens beating Matt started to drag him toward a building across the street when more gunshots went off. The muscular Mexican who had a grasp on Matt's right arm slumped to the ground. His shirt was instantly saturated with blood. "Let him go or you all die!" a voice yelled from the overpass. Instantly the majority of the mob took off running. The gray-haired black man yelled. "Stop, get back here and fight them!" Another shot rang out, and the sidewalk beside him exploded from a bullet impact.

"This isn't over!" he yelled as he left with the few remaining teens following close behind. Matt got to his feet and tried to get to the young marine across the street; he needed to help the bleeding marine. He was hurt pretty bad—bleeding from the ears and unconscious. Things were still blurry, and Matt's ears were ringing. The next few minutes went by without Matt knowing exactly what happened. The pain in his head, the blurred vision, and lack of hearing combined to make Matt lose at least five or ten minutes.

Eventually Matt's vision started to clear; his ears were still ringing, but he was able to make out conversations around him. Matt found himself in the back of a suburban. In the second seat a young man was on the satellite phone that Colonel Phelps had given him. "Get a mede-vac now, James St. overpass, one marine dead, two wounded, one serious with head injuries." He turned and looked at Matt and then threw the phone out the window. Matt was not clear-headed, but he could see the hurt marine outside on the sidewalk. Someone was leaning over him and giving him first aid. Matt could see four or maybe five men with rifles on the overpass and on the street. A helicopter arrived, as the suburban driver leaned out the window and yelled, "Now! Now get out of here!" The doors opened, and the suburban was filled to capacity with young men. Most were in street clothes, but three were in black suits and ties. That was the last thing Matt remembered. He must have passed out as the suburban squealed down the side street and drove into a warehouse.

It must have been an hour or two later when Matt came to. He was in a large room lying on a table. It looked like some type of factory, but most of the equipment was gone. Matt could see three young men in black suits talking. One was taller than the rest, and he kept gesturing toward Matt. He looked angry.

"Why did you bring him here?" he kept asking.

"The Prophet, he said we must," responded one of the shorter men; Matt recognized them as missionaries from their posture and way of speaking.

"You don't even know if he is the Prophet or a puppet. Crap, he's a kid."

"President Miller is my Prophet," proclaimed the third. "And he sent a message to bring Brother Mathew Scott into the Sons of Nephi, and I did. Do you have a problem with that?" He leaned in at the tall man as if to say, *Go ahead, hit me.*

Matt was trying to look unaware. He did not want to miss anything, and he did not want them to discover he was awake, but his head hurt so bad that he let out an audible groan.

"He's awake," the tall man said walked toward Matt.

Turning and looking over his shoulder, he said, "Go tell the Bishop. Tell him we have Brother Scott and he is awake."

The two trotted across the expanse of the room to a set of metal stairs. They scurried up two flights of stairs and to a catwalk, where they knocked on an old wooden door with no windows. It opened slowly and they went in. Matt looked at the window beside the door, but the venetian blinds were closed. He saw someone pull the blinds apart and look down at him. Then the door opened again, and out came the two and another man. Matt thought he recognized this person, but he was not sure. Before Matt got a clean look at the new man, everything went dark. The tall man had placed a black cloth bag over Matt's head and sat him up. "You will be quiet. You will listen and do what you're told." He gave a tug on the bag that increased the pain in Matt's head until he almost passed out.

There was no point in fighting back. This was it; this was the Sons of Nephi. Had he already found the leader and would he survive to talk to this person? Matt was running scenarios through his head.

"Get that thing off of him," a familiar voice ordered.

As the bag was pulled off his head, the voice said, "My Lord, someone get him a doctor right now," he ordered. Matt knew this man. He had seen him at the food warehouse in Bremerton, but Matt was groggy and could not remember his name. The man's son, Levi, entered the room. He had an M16 slung over his shoulder and was coming in with a strut and some level of authority.

"Levi, go get Doctor Long right now," the man said sternly.

"Yes, father." He turned and dashed out of the door. This was the last thing that Matt saw. The room started to spin and Matt fell to one side. The tall man caught him and cushioned his fall. Matt was laid down on the table, and the older man gave the tall man a stern look. "You do this?" he questioned.

"No, sir. It was a street gang, the Alki gang, I think. Levi killed two of them."

"God forgive us," the older man said.

Matt Scott was in a makeshift medical facility. The Sons of Nephi had two ambulances parked side by side, and a doctor was attending to Matt as he lay on a gurney.

"Kimball, Earl Kimball," Matt muttered as he came to.

"Get the Bishop," the doc said loudly as he leaned out the door of the ambulance.

Matt sat up. It hurt, but he was not going to show it, at least that was what he thought.

"You have a concussion, and you're pretty bruised up," the doc said as he tried to get Matt to lie back down.

"My head hurts, but I'm OK." Matt's vision had cleared, but his ears were still ringing. He felt his head and noticed he had a bandage wrapped around it; one side was damp with blood. Most of what had happened was still unclear to Matt. How did he get here? How badly was he hurt?

"You took some pretty hard lumps to the head, not to mention the explosion."

"What?"

"Explosion. The Humvee was hit by a roadside bomb. Gangs are making bombs, seems they learned from the Taliban."

"The marines?" Matt asked, remembering the fallen marine on the sidewalk with a great sense of worry and responsibility.

"Not sure, but they medevac'd out."

Matt was hungry and thirsty, his head hurt, and he had an IV in his left arm. Hell, his whole body hurt. Now Matt Scott hated needles, and the IV had not been put in by a gentle nurse. Matt reached for the IV to remove it when Doctor Long stopped him.

"Earl Kimball. I saw him." Matt said.

"The Bishop," responded Doctor Long.

About that time a head peered into the ambulance. "Brother Scott, I see you're feeling a little better." Bishop Kimball was trying to be encouraging, because Matt Scott looked like hell.

"Kimball, you are from Bremerton, right?" Matt questioned, trying to figure out how Bremerton and food stores had anything to do with getting blown up in Seattle. Matt was very confused and trying to piece things together.

"That's me," Kimball said with a grin. "Yup, that's me."

"I thought you and your family were going to Utah." It was coming together for Matt. "What happened?"

"Well, we didn't get past Seattle. Gangs attacked and took our food and van." He paused and then said in a broken voice, "They killed my wife." Bishop Kimball stopped and looked at the floor. The pain of losing his wife was still very fresh, and Matt felt sickened by the sorrow he saw on the Bishop's face.

"I'm sorry." What else could he say? *What a stupid thing to say,* Matt thought. *Say something else,* he thought. But no words came out.

"Your wife, the pretty redhead, she OK?" Kimball looked at Matt. Kimball was smiling, but the tears had already welled up in his eyes. Matt could see he was hurting. Men often don't know how to react in such a situation. Women, they comfort, they nurture, and Matt felt lost and clueless.

"Yes." Matt smiled. "She's good. Do you know why I am here?" Matt questioned.

"Because we wanted you here," the Bishop responded in a bit of a cocky manner.

"Because you want me here?" questioned Matt. "What is that supposed to mean?"

"We did save your life and bring you in." Kimball looked sternly at his injured guest. "You were sent by whom?" Kimball asked.

"True, I was sent by..." Matt started to reply.

Bishop Kimball interrupted, "I know, Colonel Phelps and General Siebel, right?"

"No, I would not have come for them. I was sent by Elder Miles." In Matt's mind Miles was still an awkward missionary. "Yes, the marines asked, but I came at Miles's request."

"You mean President Miles," a voice piped up from outside the ambulance. It was Levi. Levi's tone was that of a call for respect.

"Yeah, the whole thing is confusing to me; he was just an awkward kid, now he is the head of the Mormon Church." Matt's words were more of a question than a judgment.

"He is our Prophet," Levi said out loud. Levi was clearly a true believer when it came to Elder Miles, or President Miles, as his title defined him.

"Some claim he is an imposter, placed by the military," Bishop Kimball said.

"Well, I don't know about him being a prophet or not. I will promise you that he was not put in by the military. They don't like him much," Matt retorted.

"Enough politics, we need to get you some food and some rest. I will have one of the men get word to your wife that you are OK." He paused and smiled. "You're in good hands now," Kimball reassured.

"She's at…" Matt was trying to give directions, but before he could complete his thought, the Bishop interrupted. "We know. We have been watching you. We will let her know and keep an eye on your family."

The thought of being watched by this group made Matt uneasy, the thought of his wife, kids, and grandkids being watched gave him mixed feelings. Would Kimball's group keep them safe or attract trouble? Matt wondered.

Matt and the Bishop got out of the ambulance and walked slowly across the warehouse floor. Matt was still a bit wobbly and walked very slow. They made their way to the stairs at the end of the building.

"Let me get you some help," Kimball offered.

"No, I'll manage. It's just a bump on the head." Matt was being stubborn.

The ringing in Matt's ears had let up a little, and his vision was clearing, but his headache had not changed much. It took almost ten minutes to get up the stairs, but Matt made it. He stepped up one step at a time and then would stop and gather his balance. They arrived at the office on the third floor and went in. Matt sat down in an armchair as the Bishop poured him a glass of water from the water cooler. The door then opened behind them, and a young man handed Matt a plate. It had what looked like a warmed-up TV dinner on it.

"MREs, they're not too bad," he said as he left the room. Matt was pretty sure the young man was being sarcastic; the food looked terrible. Matt had a memory of eating military "meals ready-to-eat" as a young marine. Matt and his buddies thought the acronym should have meant "meals rejected-from-Ethiopia."

Matt slowly ate the food. He was not sure if the meat was pork, beef, or what, but he was hungry, so he ate everything on the plate. Putting the food on a plate did make it more palatable. It was better than Matt remembered. As a marine, he ate his MREs out of the brown plastic bag they came in. After he drank two glasses of water with his food, Matt was feeling much better. The headache was now a dull pain, and his ears were not ringing so badly. The entire time Matt was eating, Earl Kimball was talking with the tall young man from before. Matt watched out of the corner of his eye as he saw what looked like an argument that turned into a scolding.

"So it's pretty simple. They just want to meet," Matt blurted out, interrupting the secretive conversation in the corner.

"That's not so simple," replied Earl Kimball, looking back over his shoulder with a glare.

"Why?" Matt responded.

"Who are they going to meet with?" asked Earl.

"Well, you, I guess. This is group seems to be your baby," Matt responded.

"*My* group, what do you mean? Yes, these young men look to me for guidance, but that's as far as it goes." Kimball was clearly trying to diminish his role in the Sons of Nephi.

"What about the rest of them?" Matt asked.

"What do you mean?" Kimball asked.

"The other groups—the Sons of Nephi in Los Angeles and New York. You know, the others." Matt was confused.

"They have nothing to do with us," Kimball said. "Not sure what you are talking about." Kimball looked baffled and totally out of the loop.

Kimball's reaction caught Matt a little off guard; it was becoming apparent that this was not the organized group that the Military thought it was.

"But, they are in every region now. Who do they answer to?" Matt asked Kimball, though at this point he did not expect an answer.

The Bishop smiled. "God, I guess. They must answer to God." Kimball seemed a little smug with the idea of Sons of Nephi across the nation.

"Oh, shit." Matt slumped down in his chair. How was he going to bring in the leader when they did not have one? He began to realize that if there was not an organization to pull together, maybe there was no one for the Military to talk too. Then what? All of this ran through Matt's head in an instant.

"Besides, some of my men are Catholics, some are Jews. This is not a church-based group. My position as a Bishop has no real authority here." Again Kimball was trying to diminish his authority. Matt was starting to feel like he was not being told the entire truth.

"The name, Sons of Nephi; the missionaries are giving orders and carrying guns." Pointing out the obvious, Matt was calling Kimball on his obtuse way of redirecting.

The Bishop smiled. "The missionaries were tasked with distributing food in our district. When I was attacked, a group of boys from the seminary helped us. When Catholics needed help, I made sure that they got food and medical supplies. We are just a group of people helping each other."

"The name—why the Sons of Nephi?" Matt asked the question without expecting an answer.

"Sons of Nephi, it was a joke. When we took back the SODO district food warehouse from a gang of Bloods (SODO was the slang name given to South Seattle), they asked who we were, what was our gang. Levi yelled out, 'Sons of Nephi,' you know, Nephi in the Book of Mormon. I guess it stuck. Funny, as there is no reference to the Sons of Nephi in the book of Mormon at all," he continued. "Later, Levi told me of some missionaries who helped a young girl and her babies called themselves the Sons of Nephi, too."

"Stuck." Matt was shaking his head. "Do you know how many of you there are? Sons of Nephi, that is? Do you have any idea how big the Sons of Nephi is?"

"No, not really," Kimball responded.

"Well they are present in every major city, in all seven regions. In Los Angeles, the Sons of Nephi have taken control from the gangs. You people scare the shit out of the military command. They think you are going to turn the country into a Mormon Theocracy." Matt was trying hard to get Kimball to understand the scope of the movement.

"That's ridiculous," Kimball said. He paused, and then stated, "This is not a religious group. We are religious men, yes, but we are not trying to create a church state. That's what started this whole mess."

"That's why I am here. You all need to talk, and you need to work together. I think General Siebel is afraid we are going to have a religious war on our hands." Matt was trying to stress the danger of the situation. "I'm afraid that things are much larger then you intended. I guarantee you don't want to fight General Siebel and the US Marine Corps," Matt finished.

"The Sons of Nephi, we are not that organized." Kimball actually had a tone of worry in his voice.

Elmer Kimball was looking distressed. Matt could sense that for the first time, Kimball was mentally leaving his little world, the streets of Seattle. Matt wondered if Kimball's mission of taking back the city kept his mind off his wife, the love of his life who had died. Kimball's children had become soldiers.

"What have I done?" Kimball sat back in his chair and clasped his hands together. Resting his head back on the headrest, he said, "God, forgive me."

The Sons of Nephi had grown. Some sects were nonviolent and concentrated their efforts on feeding people and providing medical care. Some had become quite violent and had asserted themselves as peacekeepers.

"I was just trying to help." Kimball looked up as if he was talking directly to God.

"You did. You fed people, and you saved lives. No one wants to punish you; they just want to talk to you," Matt reassured.

Levi had entered the room. "Don't trust them, Dad. They just want to lock us up."

Matt turned in his chair to face Levi. "Not so. It was Miles, President Miles, who asked me to come, not the Military." Matt had made a point of showing Miles the respect that Levi felt Miles deserved. "Besides, if General Siebel wanted you locked up, he would have rolled in a division of marines and either locked you up or killed you already." Matt was trying to put some reality into the young man's head.

"The Prophet?" Levi said. "You met the Prophet?" He didn't seem to hear a word about the marines.

"Well, yeah. I took care of him last year when things started." Matt was shocked by Levi's blind faith in a young missionary with Asperger's.

Matt Scott was still having a hard time seeing Elder Miles as any type of leader or inspiration, but it was clear that Levi Kimball would lay down his life for Miles.

"The Prophet promised me that no one would be hurt or arrested," Matt continued.

"What did he say? What exactly did he say?" Levi demanded.

"He wants us all to talk, to find a way to work together and stop the violence." Matt looked directly at Levi. "I know him well; he does not want anyone else to get hurt."

The meeting had degraded to Matt explaining himself, Levi being flash-blinded by the thought of the Prophet, and Bishop Kimball being unsure of what to do.

"You have no choice, you know" Matt was explaining. "We work together or a civil war starts. And you will lose. We will all lose."

The Bishop sat down. "I need to pray on this and ponder my options. Please leave me alone." He waved his hand toward the door. Bishop Kimball had a way of talking very directly and very much to the point. It would be easy for people to be offended by him or possibly even feel insulted. But the truth was Bishop Kimball was much like Elder Miles—not so socially skilled. Often people with high levels of intelligence lacked that certain ability to know what to say, or more importantly how to say it. Both Matt and Levi were very aware of this by this time and took no offense as they hurried out of the room.

Matt and Levi found the tall man standing outside the room. "Let's get some rest," Levi said to the tall man as the three of them made their way down the expanded steel steps. Every step seemed louder and louder in Matt's head. When they got to the bottom, Doctor Long approached them. "How are you feeling?" Before Matt could answer, Doctor Long turned to Levi. "You wake him up every hour and check on him. If he acts out of the ordinary, come get me." The thought of being awakened every hour was miserable, but Matt was not in charge right now. And rest, even interrupted rest, sounded great. He was exhausted. The high carbohydrate meal combined with the injuries and stress of the last day left Matt ready for any form of rest. The three men went across the warehouse into a room with a line of cots in it.

"Get some sleep," Levi said, pointed to a cot with a white blanket and pillow folded up at the end of the bed. The two went to the end of the room and knelt in prayer. Then Levi left the room, and the tall man stripped down to his underwear and climbed into bed. Matt's first thought climbing into his bed was, *there is no way I am going to sleep.* His head was throbbing as he laid it on the pillow. His next thought was, *why you are waking me,* as Levi shook him. "Look at me. Come on, let me see your eyes." Matt was so tired, but he opened his eyes and looked at the young man. "OK, you look OK. Back to sleep." Matt was so tired that he was instantly snoring again. It had been a long time since Matt was so tired that pain, worry, or comfort had no bearing on sleep. Exhaustion is real, and few men ever hit that point in their lives. It was something that Matt had experienced in the Marine Corps, something he had hoped he would never face again, much like the feeling he had when he had to kill. Over the past year, Matt had been forced to return to a time in his life that was long forgotten, a time he had hoped he would never revisit.

Back at David's house, Leanne awoke. Not knowing were Matt was, she was worried, but she knew he could take care of himself. Leanne had been sleeping in her grandson's room. She lay in bed thinking about Matt and where he was. The quiet was broken when she heard some talking downstairs. Her son David was speaking to someone at the front door. Leanne put on a bathrobe and ran down the stairs.

"Is it Matt?" Leanne asked as she rounded the corner at the top of the stairs.

"No, Mom. But come down, please" Leanne's heart sunk in her chest. For a moment she could not breathe. Was this news? Was Matt hurt or dead? Hesitating, Leanne stopped on the stairs and took a deep breath. When she started moving again, her pace was slow and deliberate. Leanne saw two men in black suits. The red tie and blue tie gave her a clue they were not Feds. Maybe they were missionaries, but why were they here? Had Matt sent them? All of this was running through her mind. The entire time she did not breathe in fear of crying out.

"These men need to see you." David was not so sure he was going to allow it; the protective son was showing his colors.

"Ma'am, are you Mrs. Scott?" Leanne was frozen in her steps and not breathing. The man who was speaking must have seen her fear because he quickly assured her, "He is OK."

"Thank God," she said, letting out a gasp of air. "Where is he?"

"I can't tell you, but I will promise that he is safe. We have also been asked to watch over you and your family. We will be watching your house, just in case."

"In case of what?" David was angry and worried. He turned to his mother. "Mom, what is it that you and Matt are involved in?" He paused and turned back toward the men at the door. "Who or what are you supposed to be protecting us from?"

"I can't say, just know you will be safe," he replied.

David did not do well with authority and seemed very upset by the lack of answers.

Leanne hurried to her son's side. "David, trust them for me," she said. Leanne was watching the two as she talked to her son. The two men said good-bye and left the house. They made their way to a dark suburban parked across the street. Leanne and David watched as the two climbed in and closed the doors. The suburban did not move. They were staying, as they said, to watch over the family. This annoyed David as much as it made Leanne happy. "They are good men. Matt would not have sent them if they weren't." The mother and son walked to the kitchen to start breakfast for the rest of the family.

As morning came in Seattle, the streets were filling with protestors. Many carried signs calling for the arrest of General Siebel. Some supported him, and others showed pictures of President Prescott converted to an image of Hitler. The general feeling of the protests was much like those back in the 1990s. The WTO, it was chaos and mayhem. Few knew what they were mad about; they just were mad and getting violent. Storefronts were damaged, cars were rolled over, and the streets of downtown had become a war zone.

This was going on across the nation, with the exception of District Six, which included Los Angeles. The cities were falling into anarchy more and more every day. Los Angeles was under control, as an iron fist was being applied by a coalition of the Sons of Nephi, the Cripps, the Bloods, and the Mexican Mafia. The gangs did not like each other, but they did learn to work together. The unholy alliance was working, peace was rarely interrupted, and when an occasional public protest or outburst occurred, it was quickly and violently put down. If protestors started to get violent or even confronted the rules put in place by the gangs, then heads rolled. The gangs were released in incremental waves, starting with pushing back the crowds and ending with open gunfire. The cities like Los Angeles had strict gun laws prior to the fall of the economy, so the general population was unarmed. Any resistance to the heavily armed gangs was suicide.

General Siebel had given control to these gangs; he watched from a distance and was always ready to send in the Marines if things got out of control. To the surprise of many, the gangs were keeping the peace for now. The peace kept may resemble the iron curtain in the 1980s, but there was order. The fear, the concern that General Siebel and others shared, was that the gangs would not relinquish power when the day came. But that battle or even war was for the future. General Siebel had bigger fish to fry right now.

General Siebel was meeting with his advisors and several Representatives; the meeting was taking place in Seattle at the Boeing Museum of Flight. Seattle was going to be the start of a new campaign. It was clear that something had to be done before the violence in the cities became irreversible.

"Why don't we just put more marines and soldiers in the streets?" Congressman Hobson asked, looking at General Siebel.

"We are not going to do it. I am telling you that even one more set of boots in the city and we are the enemy, if we are not already. Didn't you learn anything from Afghanistan and Iraq? We need to take away the reason they are mad, not beat them into submission." The General was getting tired of the elected officials looking to him for political answers. The truth was that fighting a war of insurgency was the last thing the General wanted.

"We can force short-term peace in the moment, but we cannot force long-term peace. That's your job." General Siebel had been considering resigning or maybe just calling for all-out military coups. "Sometimes I wonder if by getting rid of Prescott we just traded one despot for another." Seibel was frustrated because civilians had attacked his troops daily. Policing the American people was not why he became a marine. "My job, my oath, is to protect the American people, not go to war with them." He did not feel good about much these days and was letting the politicians know it.

"We have called out the Church of Jesus Christ of Latter-day Saints. We are going to get the Sons of Nephi under control, or I am going to order you to take them out," Congressman Hobson stated emphatically.

"With all due respect, Congressman, I don't take orders from you, and be careful what you ask for. Don't think for a moment that a United States Marine is going to obey orders to kill American citizens, whether you like them or not." General Siebel paused for a moment and then added, "You know you don't sound much better than Prescott at this point." General Siebel got up and walked out of the room. As he reached the door, he stopped and turned around. "I will give you two days to get a plan together. If you can't, I will be meeting with the rest of the Commanders, and we will solve these problems ourselves." The General looked at the Congressman and the other men and women in the room; he scanned from one to the other, left to right, in a very deliberate way. "We took Prescott out of power; it would be dangerous to think you are immune to such events." General Siebel was threatening his civilian leaders, a dangerous thing to do, but he felt he had no choice.

"I will not allow you to pull an *Animal Farm* revolution," Siebel concluded.

In the history of modern government and revolution the story had often been the same. The revolution happened, the new government was worse than the old and was followed by a military coup. The pattern could be seen in the history of every continent, every political system, and every philosophy. General Siebel believed that Orwell got it right.

Seibel returned to the table. "*Animal Farm*, not on my watch," he said quietly under his breath as he gathered the papers in front of him and put them in a leather satchel, preparing to leave the meeting.

The General had a plan. He used the events of the Iraq war as an example. After nearly ten years of fighting, the Commander in the field went against President Prescott's orders and started to work with local militia and clans. Iraqis did a much better job keeping the peace than some American soldier who was ten thousand miles from home. General Siebel studied what was going on in Los Angeles. He did not trust any one of the groups alone, yet together he saw a model that worked. The General had one shot—he needed the Sons of Nephi, and he needed their support. He knew that if he could get the key players together—the churches, the fraternal orders, the local governments, and even the gangs—he could stop the decline toward anarchy. Siebel had never wanted to be a politician, but the truth was that anyone that made it to his level of success was a politician whether he admitted or not.

General Siebel and his entourage left the museum and sped away toward Fort Lewis, nearly a seventy-mile drive. The streets of Seattle had become unsafe even for him, maybe *especially* for him. The group was made up of Humvees and Striker assault vehicles. They moved quickly, using tactics learned in Iraq. Yes, Seattle was a combat zone much like Baghdad was in the years of the Iraq war. People would avoid the convoys of military vehicles running through the streets. Seattle or Baghdad, these were still Marines, not Seattle Police. The Marines did not react with rubber bullets or tear gas. If someone threatened a convoy in any way he was dead. The General and his group sped through the city without a single event. Guns at the ready, they made their way to Joint Base Lewis McCord in Tacoma.

Back in a warehouse in South Seattle, Matt woke up. He sat up slowly and looked over to see Levi Kimball. Levi was sitting up in a chair with his head leaned back against the wall, sound asleep. Matt considered his options. Should he run, or should he wake the young man up? He was exactly where he needed to be to complete his mission, but then again he had no plan, so maybe escape would be the best idea. All of this was running through Matt's head. His head still hurt, but the blinding headache was gone. Levi stirred a little, re-gripping the rifle in his lap.

"Hey, wake up," Matt called to him in a whispered voice.

Levi stirred, and Matt said, "You don't want to get caught sleeping on the job." Levi sat up quickly, blinking and rubbing the sleep out of his eyes. Before Levi could thank him, Elmer Kimball came in the room.

"You are feeling better?" Kimball asked Matt.

"Yes. You think I could get a cup of coffee?" Matt asked. Knowing he was talking to a Mormon Bishop and the founder of the Sons of Nephi, he asked with a bit of reservation, not wanting to offend.

"I will get one of our NM's in here. One of them will find you some coffee." Matt assumed this meant non-Mormons or maybe nonmembers. The Bishop paused and looked at Levi; he knew his son had been asleep. Elmer cracked a smile at Levi. "Son, you go get some rest." Elmer Kimball had one regret even bigger than that of losing his wife: Levi Kimball, the mild-mannered stock boy, the basketball star at the local high school, had become a warrior. Levi would never be the same, and Elmer Kimball knew it. Levi Kimball had lost the innocence that every soldier or marine loses in combat, and this broke his father's heart.

"Yes, Father." Levi looked at Matt and mouthed a quick thank you.

"Make sure someone gets Brother Scott a cup of coffee on your way out," Kimball ordered. Then he turned to Matt Scott and asked, "So what's next?"

"We need to go meet the General and Elder Miles," Matt answered. His tone made it clear that it was the only option on the table.

Matt took a long pause, and then changing the subject, he asked, "How did this happen? Who put this together?"

"What do you mean?" Kimball said.

"The Sons of Nephi, you, Levi with a gun. What happened?" After a brief pause he continued, "From Bishop and stock boy to General and soldier. How and why?"

"Maybe we should get you that cup of coffee now," Kimball replied. He turned toward the door. "I will do my best to explain." Elmer Kimball's voice was cracking a little. The thought of talking about the death of his wife, or his son becoming a killer, was almost more than he could bear.

Elmer Kimball and Matt Scott made their way down the metal stairs. At the bottom they met a young man. He had a large cup of coffee in a Starbucks to-go cup. The coffee was steaming from the small hole in the lid.

"It's hot, sir. Be careful," he said as he handed it over to Matt Scott.

"Wouldn't want a McDonald's law suit," Matt said jokingly. The humor was lost on the young man, obviously too young to know of the event Matt was referring to. The young man gave Matt that *whatever* look that only a teenager could pull off and walked away. The two men walked to a table in corner of the room and sat down. Elmer Kimball told the story of how he came to be in this place, of why his son was carrying a gun, and of the events that occurred since the first time Matt and Leanne had met the Kimballs.

The Bishop explained that after Matt and Leanne had left Elmer Kimball and Levi at the warehouse, the Kimball men had returned to their family. They had loaded a van and a pickup truck with family and supplies and were heading for places safer, ideally Utah. The family was traveling through the south end of Seattle toward highway 18 when they encountered a roadblock. A group of younger men and women had blocked the road with a makeshift barricade, one made of an old truck and some railroad ties. Two of the group—a young Goth-looking girl and a tall black man—were armed with pistols.

Elmer Kimball stepped out of the truck he was driving. The pickup was leading the way, and he had his son Levi with him. The van behind him was driven by his wife and had the rest of his family in it.

"We don't want any trouble; we just want to head east," Elmer said to the group.

"You Mormons?" the Goth girl asked. "Food-hoarding Mormons?"

"We only have enough for our family. We are not hoarders," responded the senior Kimball. During this time several people had surrounded the van.

"We don't want trouble; we just want to pass through," Kimball restated.

"You've got trouble," said the young girl. "I think you are Mormons." She was waving the pistol in the air. "You damn Mormons, you and your Nephi missionaries or whatever you call them, you think you control the food." She was ranting and pacing. "Who controls the food now?" she yelled, waving the pistol in the air and pointing it at the van and then back in the face of Elmer Kimball.

Levi Kimball was trying to get back to the truck slowly. He had a pistol in the glove box, and he knew that if he could get to it, maybe he could save his family. Levi was taking slow, small steps backwards toward the open door of the truck.

"Where are you going?" yelled the tall black man as he pointed a large revolver at Levi.

"What do you want?" asked Elmer Kimball, trying to distract attention from his son.

The young girl laughed out loud. "Your food, maybe that van, and whatever else we find."

Across the street, a small group of young men had gathered in an ally. They were a group of Mormon missionaries and a few others who had joined their ranks. The missionaries had been tasked with rationing and supplying food to the city. When the food ran out, they had been attacked by a mob, and these were the ones that got away. They were watching and listening. They were armed, but not violent by choice. This group was unnoticed by the attackers but had caught the attention of Elmer Kimball.

The young girl walked over to the van and opened the driver-side door. She grabbed Mrs. Kimball by the arm and pulled her out of the van and onto the ground. The young Kimball girls in the van screamed. Levi ran toward his mother, and Elmer Kimball reached for him. The Goth girl laughed out loud, pointed her pistol at Mrs. Kimball, and shot her in the head. From this point much of what happened was speculation. The group across the street charged into the crowd. The tall black man was shot; no one really knew who pulled the trigger. The shot came from across the street. He fell forward; Elmer Kimball grabbed the revolver from his hand as he fell.

"Get down!" he yelled as loud as he could. Levi went face down on the ground; his sisters ducked down in the van. Elmer Kimball then took deliberate aim at the Goth girl.

She turned and looked at him with a twisted smile on her face. "You won't shoot me. God would never forgive you," she said in a sadistic voice.

Elmer Kimball did not hesitate. There was a loud report from the revolver, and the left side of the girl's head exploded. She stood for a second as if her body did not know she was dead yet. Then she fell backwards into a puddle of blood. Elmer Kimball spun around and pointed the revolver at a young man in a black suit; he was carrying a hunting rifle.

"Wait," we are with you; we are from the Tacoma Stake." The missionary knew Kimball; he had met him at an event at the temple in Bellevue.

Kimball lowered his gun and turned to run toward his wife. Mrs. Kimball was dead.

Through the sound of crying children and fighting, the missionaries took charge. They got the Kimball family loaded back into the van and Levi on his feet.

"We have to get out of here," the young missionary said. "Now!" He was pushing people into the van. "There will be more of them very soon."

During this most of the original mob had run off. A few tried to fight, but the group of seven missionaries and four volunteers took control of the intersection. There was no further gunfire. Unarmed and leaderless, the remains of the mob scattered in all directions.

A young man in a dirty black suit took charge.

"Davis, you drive the van; Reed you drive the truck; someone get the Bishop's wife in the truck." He was standing in the center of the commotion. "Move it now!" This young missionary was a natural leader, the kind of young man who wins medals in war.

The group had managed to get the Kimball family loaded, and they sped out of the neighborhood toward West Seattle. They had a warehouse in South Seattle, one that had been a food distribution center, and they would all go there.

After getting everyone to safety, they explained to Elmer Kimball how they had lost all control of the food distribution center in Seattle. Street gangs, combined with groups of Anarchists from surrounding cities, had converged on the missionary food stores. They targeted South Downtown and the commercial area. Several young missionaries were killed; there was an active list of missing. Much like the days of the WTO riots, groups bussed in from Portland and Vancouver to strengthen the Anarchy Movement in Seattle. Seattle had become one of the key battlefields for the Movement. Anarchists had created chaos in San Francisco, Minneapolis, and Tampa, Florida, and of course, Seattle. In most of the country the Anarchists were quickly put down by Military, Prescott supporters, or rival street gangs, such as Crips, Bloods, and the Mexican Mafia. But in Seattle the Anarchists had been gaining a foothold, at least up until this point.

The remaining Anarchists in Seattle felt cornered; it was their last stand, the Anarchy Alamo of sorts. The idea of a leader in such a movement seemed ironic, but the one known only as Naomi had become the icon of the Seattle Anarchy Movement. Naomi was not mentally stable, she was a sociopath, and she killed for fun. Naomi ordered the burning of the food that her group could not eat. She ordered the killing of anyone who professed any form of religious beliefs or affiliation. Naomi had a special hatred for Mormons and Jews. Most of this was unknown to Kimball and the Sons of Nephi at the time she was killed. Elmer Kimball had created a martyr for killers and social misfits after most of the food and supplies had been ransacked and taken.

Groups of Anarchists merged with small neighborhood street gangs, much like the one they had just encountered. This new alliance had taken control of the streets; they were looting, killing, and leaving the city in a general state of chaos. The Marines and National Guard had managed to take back most of the residential areas, yet they showed little interest in the commercial districts. The churches and other groups worked with the Military to establish a supply chain for the populations in the suburbs. The gangs were forced into the industrial part of town and south downtown; these areas became a no-man's land. The Kimballs were in the wrong place at the wrong time. Elmer Kimball explained to Matt that if it had not been for the young missionaries who had stayed to find several lost missionaries, the entire Kimball family would have been killed. They believed that some of the missing may be alive and in hiding. The truth was they were either dead or had made their way to a safe neighborhood. Kimball's rescuers were the last of the missionaries left in South Seattle, and several young men from the Kings Cross Academy had joined them.

When Earl Kimball asked them why they were still in the area and so heavily armed, he always got the same response. "We are not a gang. We are trying to help. We are just outnumbered." This was the justification for the fighting from the position of a young missionary. The truth was that the conviction of these young men, combined with the immaturity, had created a very dangerous situation. The Sons of Nephi needed a leader, they needed direction, and they needed a man like Elmer Kimball, an experienced man to guide them. Elmer Kimball also needed a mission, he needed something to focus on, a battle to avenge the death of his wife. This became Elmer Kimball's calling instantly, even though he was somewhat unaware of how vested he was in the beginning.

God had led him to this place; God had taken his wife home and left him with a mission only he could carry out. For a man like Elmer Kimball, opting out was not an option. He believed in the power of prayer and the calling of the Lord, so there was no option but to follow. To many this may have seemed extreme, but to Elmer Kimball it was the key to his faith. Elmer Kimball could not leave; he could not abandon his post. Only a release from the Prophet, the President of his Church, would allow him to take his family east to live in peace.

Matt learned much about this man and his actions from their talk. Bishop Elmer Kimball also learned much about the outside world's perception of the group he was leading. The Sons of Nephi had a reputation—much of it was fiction, and much of it was exaggerated exploits. The Sons of Nephi had become larger than life. The talk on the streets, and the word getting to the Military, was that of a well-organized militia. The truth was it was a group of frightened yet angry young men who needed leadership and structure to keep them from turning into just another gang. Elmer Kimball was now their leader. He had been accused of being their founder, but that was far from the truth. The Kimball family was rescued by this ragtag group. The Kimball family gave this group structure and direction. With the help of Elmer Kimball and some contacts he had with the Mormon Church, the Sons of Nephi grew not only in numbers, but also in strength and conviction. The Sons of Nephi were now near two hundred strong in South Seattle. To some degree what others thought was true—the ragtag group had turned into an organized militia with the leadership of Bishop Kimball and the young Levi Kimball. The group only used violence or force when they had no other choice. They spent most of their efforts locating locked-in families and the elderly so they could provide them with food or transportation out of the areas with no law enforcement. The Sons of Nephi became the law in no-man's land. Their presence, their exploits, and their accomplishments had become urban legend.

Some in the military wrongly believed that they took orders from the Mormon Church. It was true that they received some support in equipment and information when possible. But Elmer Kimball explained, "We take our direction from God," which was a dangerous thought to some. But after the long discussion, Matt knew their intentions, and he understood that they had no desire for power. Elmer

Kimball admitted that the Sons of Nephi might have been more powerful than he intended. The truth was that they wanted to help, and most did not want to fight.

If this conversation had been recorded or witnessed, it may have sounded like religious fanaticism to many. Matt Scott knew and understood the Mormon belief system. The statement from Elmer Kimball that he answered to God gave Matt some sense of relief. Knowing that the leadership of the Sons of Nephi felt a degree of humility to God or to the leader of the Mormon Church assured Matt Scott that they would not become another cult or street gang. Yet the fact was that this was the leader of the Seattle-area group, not of a national movement. The question was, who was in charge of the other groups? Were they coordinated? And if not, would the other groups step in line? What would stop them from getting out of control? The big picture was not Matt's mission, yet somehow he knew that General Siebel was counting on a national solution.

Even after hearing from Elmer Kimball, Matt still had some feeling that Elder, or now President Miles, may have more control of this movement than Matt was being led to believe. Maybe this was wishful thinking, but either way it did not affect his mission. Matt Scott needed to get this group to the table, and then he could go home to his wife. Thinking about national movements and problems in other cities would just get in the way. Seattle, the Sons of Nephi, and General Siebel was all that mattered. All of this was running through Matt's head while he listened to Elmer Kimball's explanation of how things came to be. Matt told himself not to overcomplicate matters. When it came to this group, Elmer Kimball was now their leader. The irony of the whole situation was that as far as Matt could tell, none of the Sons of Nephi knew how feared and respected they had become. Elmer Kimball knew that the Mormon Church was aware of the group. He had sent some of his young men into the areas controlled by the Church for information and supplies. Even Elmer Kimball had no idea of the reputation they had earned. Much of the community saw them as heroes. Many in the group had been marked for assassination by the street gangs. What was happening outside of his family and Sons of Nephi was not part of Elmer Kimball's reality. This was clear to Matt after the long conversation.

Matt learned that the death of the young Goth woman was a tip-ping point. She was an icon in the Anarchy Movement, part of a group that came up from Portland. The death of Naomi, as she was known, galvanized many of the gangs against the Sons of Nephi. Naomi was a mystery to the Military, to the reforming government, to the gangs, and even to her Movement. Few knew where she actually came from. Naomi was a thin woman in her mid-twenties. Much like Elder Miles, Naomi seemed to arise from nowhere with a huge amount of influence and power.

Some of the more religiously minded members of the Sons of Nephi, primarily the Catholics, thought of Naomi as the Anti-Christ. The truth was that Naomi was from Portland, Oregon, she was ex-tremely political, and a staunch Anarchist. She had dropped out of college after being arrested for assaulting a young Jewish man at a pro-Palestinian rally. Naomi had no love for the Palestinians; she just had a deep hate for Israel.

Why she turned out this way was unknown and made little sense. Her parents were average—her father was uneducated and worked at a paper mill, and her mother clerked at a grocery store. Neither parent was political or religious. Naomi started to act out in high school. She attended protests as often as possible. Naomi envisioned herself as the next great revolutionary. Following a hard break up in college, her life took a major shift. She left college, dropped out of society, and lived on the streets. During this time she became engrossed in the concept of Anarchy. The drug scene, the streets, and maybe some mental instabil-ity left this smart young woman nothing more than a fanatical killer. If left to her ways, Naomi would have the world dominated by violence and brute force. A strange thought from a small, thin, frail-looking young woman, but frail she was not.

Elmer Kimball explained that Naomi was dead, but what she represented was not. Her body disappeared after that day when Elmer Kimball avenged the death of his wife. Many in the movement claimed she was still alive. Sightings were reported and her legacy lived on in a violent way. It was not uncommon to see the Anarchy symbol painted on a building or a bridge with a large "N" painted beside it. Elmer Kimball and several others knew that she was dead; there was no doubt. If her body had been found, nothing would have changed. A martyr, dead or alive, is still a martyr. Elmer Kimball had found a way to arm his missionaries; he gave them basic tactical training, and they showed great discipline. This was necessary as they were targeted by so many. They were also being called on by many others for help. The killing of Naomi, right or wrong, was the event that turned the Sons of Nephi from a ragtag group into what they had become.

The tide was turning, and the street gangs had grown weaker and more desperate. Many left and headed back to Portland or north to Vancouver. The remaining Anarchists and gangs were very militant, and the situation was that of civil war on the streets. The gangs had little discipline and often fought amongst themselves. They were no match for the Sons of Nephi. Both tactically and strategically, they would lose. But in the process, they were dangerous not only to the Sons of Nephi, but to any civilian they came across. It was a sad fact, but the gangs would have to be destroyed. Their members would have to be killed in large part, and that job, for some reason, at least in Seattle, was left to a group made up of volunteers, missionaries, and family men—the Sons of Nephi.

The more Matt learned from Elmer Kimball, the less he trusted Colonel Phelps and General Siebel. Matt was starting to believe that the Military was letting this group do their dirty work. Matt wondered how long it would be before the military would target the Sons of Nephi.

Elmer explained that the battles were usually short. Often a quick skirmish would lead to a retreat by the gangs. The killing of one or two of the gang members would cause panic and retreat.

Elmer Kimball stopped speaking for a moment; he stopped explaining and justifying.

Leaning forward, he looked at Matt. "I have not become Kurtz, have I?" Elmer Kimball was referring to the character in Joseph Conrad's *Heart of Darkness,* or maybe to Marlin Brando in *Apocalypse Now.*

Matt smiled. "No, you just did what you had to do." He paused, thinking this break in Elmer Kimball's narrative might be an opportunity.

"What matters is what we do now," Matt pointed out. "We can stop the violence now."

The Sons of Nephi had intended to be nonviolent, but the truth was that when they fought back, or struck out, the casualties were heavy. The lack of military rules of engagement, combined with a dedication beyond that of any draftee or career military man made them effective, brutally effective. Matt was very aware of this. This group was not much different from the groups Matt fought as a young marine. Although Elmer Kimball spoke of an attempt to be nonviolent, Matt was sure that his most difficult task was that of minimizing the devastation. Years later Matt would learn that Levi Kimball had earned a reputation. When Levi led a group on a mission, the casualties on the other side were total. Levi saw every Anarchist, every gangbanger, every looter or common thug, as the one who killed his mother. Levi would lead an engagement with the words, "Mercy and judgment is for God to give, and it is our job to arrange the meeting."

Elmer worried for his son. When peace came again, would Levi Kimball be able to function? Had he lost his son to the dark side of revenge?

"It has gotten out of hand," Elmer Kimball told Matt. "Too much killing." Elmer Kimball had a tear in his eye.

Matt stood and looked directly into the eyes of the leader. Matt was reliving the shootings at the King home. He was remembering the feeling of killing. Most men couldn't kill; some enjoyed killing. Men like Matt and Elmer were forced to kill, and it haunted them for the rest of their lives. Matt's chin was shaking, like it would when he was a little boy and he was trying not to cry. In this moment the gravity of the past week's events was hitting him. So much had happened. He feared for his wife, for his children, and for the missionaries he had been so close to. Matt was doing the best he could, but for the first time in his life, Matt was afraid for his eternal soul. Everything—the worry, the guilt, the anger, and the empathy—was coming down on this man all at once. And right now was not a good time for a breakdown. Matt could mask it as effects from the blast, or maybe even missing his wife, but it was bigger than that.

"God will forgive us?" Matt asked Elmer Kimball, his statement was clearly a desperate question.

"I don't know," responded the man who was a Bishop, a Stake President, and now the leader of what had become a militia. "I don't know," he repeated as only a truly remorseful man could.

"Elder Miles, he is in charge of the Church now," Elmer Kimball stated. "The Church, it will help stop this." He paused, and then added, "President Miles, he will help stop this." He was looking for some reassurances from Matt.

"I don't know. But I do know that the Military seems to think they need you and the Church to get things under control." Matt wanted it all to end as much as Elmer Kimball did. "I do know we have to try, and it's the only option we have." Matt was going to get this done; he was missing Leanne and his old life.

"Well then, we will give them what they need," Kimball stated with conviction. "We will, and I want to bring a few NMs with us, and I mean non-Mormons. We need to show that the Sons of Nephi is more than a group of missionaries run amok."

A tall man in a black suit walked in with a cup of coffee in a large Starbucks cup. It was an insulated travel mug with a green Starbucks logo stenciled on its stainless-steel side.

"Black OK?" he asked.

"Great, thank you, but I already have one." Matt pointed at the near-empty paper cup on the table.

"This one is for the road," he responded, as if he knew they would be heading out soon.

Matt reached for the coffee and took a sip without taking his eyes off this man. "Do I know you?" Matt asked.

"I don't think so," replied the tall man.

"Yes, you were there. You were the one helping the Marine. Is he OK?"

"He should be. They airlifted him out right away." Matt noticed what looked like a crucifix around the man's neck. The cross was visible through the dingy white dress shirt he was wearing. "You're not LDS?"

"No, sir, Catholic. I was raised Catholic at least. Went to Catholic school, but never went to church much.

That statement froze Matt for a moment. He closed his eyes. He could see Leanne, and for a moment his heart broke. The gravity of things seemed to be setting in even deeper. Matt just wanted to go home to his wife. This was a feeling every married soldier or marine got, a gut-wrenching fear combined with guilt. *I should be home*, Matt was thinking.

"You OK?" Elmer Kimball asked.

"Yes. What he said just reminded me of someone," Matt responded without thinking.

"Your wife is Catholic, isn't she?" Kimball saw the worry in his face.

Matt had a rush of emotion. He felt a sickening feeling of regret. He had left the love of his life, and he had not heard anything from his children in days. And this was a big mistake. All of these thoughts where rushing through Matt's head. He had to stop this; if he wanted any chance of ever seeing Leanne again, he had to keep his head clear.

"She understands," the tall Catholic man said. "If she is half the woman you think she is, she understands."

This did not help much, but Matt had to focus on the task at hand. Having no idea what was going to come of it, Matt's job was simply get the parties to the table. After that he could go home to his family, live his life, and be left alone. Matt took a deep breath and centered himself. He then took another sip of the hot coffee. *After this the answer will be no*, Matt said to himself. *We have given enough.* Despite all the internal dialogue, all Elmer Kimball saw was Matt staring off into space for a moment.

"You OK?" he asked, worried about a possible head injury still.

"Yeah, just thinking," Matt responded.

"I can't call in. Your man tossed my phone out the window," Matt pointed out. His voice had changed, and focus was back. *The meeting, the mission, that is what matters right now*, he repeated in his thoughts.

"Who were you supposed to call?" Kimball asked.

"A colonel, a female colonel, Lieutenant Colonel Phelps, a Marine." He paused. "She was in Port Smith, but I don't know where she is now."

Elmer Kimball gave the tall man a quick glance. "Yes, sir, I will get word to her," he said and left the room in a rush.

Matt was feeling out of the loop. Why did they need him? Did they know the Colonel? And if so, why could they not just talk to each other?

"What are you thinking?" Kimball asked Matt.

"Why? Why me? You have the contacts, maybe more than anyone realized. What do you need me for?" He hesitated. "You know what to do. What do you need me for?" he repeated with frustration and anger in his voice.

"Everyone trusts you. The Prophet said you are the Messenger. You are our Moroni." Kimball was referring to a Mormon Scripture, one that would make no sense to anyone who was either not Mormon or had not read the teachings and history of the Mormon Church.

"Why?" Matt questioned. "I am not a Prophet, and I am definitely not a modern-day Moroni." In Mormon teachings, the angel Moroni was God's messenger. Most faiths had their own Moroni, Abraham, Moses, and Muhammad.

"It really doesn't matter; it's bigger than us." Elmer Kimball had a way stating things, a way that seemed profound and did not allow questions. "Let's finish this over breakfast."

Matt had finished his second cup coffee. "This is amazing coffee," he said with a smile.

"So I have been told. Brother Casio owned a Starbucks before the crash," Kimball said.

"Is that his name—the Catholic, the man from the road?" Matt was trying to keep track of the names and faces.

"Yes," Kimball replied.

The two walked out and across the main warehouse area into another corner. There were a few tables where four or five were eating breakfast— eggs and pancakes with peanut butter and jelly.

"Fancy." Matt was a bit taken aback by the spread and teased Elmer Kimball a little.

"Well, a man has to eat," Kimball replied.

"Tell me, who does all of this? Who cooks? The doctor, the coffee, the guns, the cars, who put this together?" Matt was feeling kept in the dark. The stories of the ragtag group were not fitting with the organization he saw.

"The trick is putting organizations together, not starting over." Kimball pointed across the table at two men sitting and talking. "Davis and Thompson, they are from the Christian mission downtown; they provide food and cooking resources. Over there," he pointed at a doctor and what could only be described as a large orderly, "Doc, he is from Doctors Without Borders; he was stranded at the airport when he came to us for help. The guns, well, we have a member who owned a gun shop in Federal Way. Should I go on?

Matt was tired and did not need any more details. "I get the picture. Just like having the LDS Church handle food distribution in the region. They have the resources and the know-how." Matt hesitated and then said, "You, that's what you do. You put things and people together." Matt looked at the Bishop. "A real leader." This was truly meant as a compliment.

Kimball laughed. "You, Matt. You are putting people together; that's your calling." He paused. "I guess that makes us the same in some ways. That's it. The problem is so many people don't trust motives. They question everyone's motive. Sometimes when we go to deliver food, the families refuse it because it came from a church. We try to explain that we just delivered it and that there are no strings attached. Then others accuse us of holding out on non-Mormons. People are a pain." Elmer Kimball was starting to show some emotion. "People can be very irrational."

"Maybe that's why so many push for a secular solution, a secular government." Matt was being devil's advocate with a very religious man.

"Well, I say as long as we have a freedom of religion, I don't care who is in charge." Not the answer Matt was expecting. "Honestly, I am tired and just want to go home." Elmer Kimball was exhausted in all ways. Elmer Kimball was good at covering up his emotions with his family and his men; with Matt he was letting go a little. Matt Scott could see the cracks in his armor and felt empathy for him. He had lost his wife, his entire life was turned upside down, and now people were asking more and more from him. Matt genuinely felt for him.

The two men walked towards the table. At the end of the table they picked up a plate and silverware and made their way down to a row of tinfoil-covered chafing dishes. Matt had a couple of pancakes and a large scoop of scrambled eggs. He found a place to sit and placed his plate only to return to refill his empty coffee cup at an airpot stationed at the end of the table. As he sat he looked at Kimball with a smile. "Never thought I would see the day when I would have a cup of coffee at breakfast with a Mormon Bishop." Both men smiled. "A lot of things have happened that I never would have imagined," replied Kimball.

CHAPTER THIRTEEN

After breakfast Matt Scott and Elmer Kimball walked out front and joined Casio and one other man at the side entrance to the warehouse. They got into the back of a gunmetal gray Chevy Tahoe and started to drive out toward the edge of town.

"Aren't you worried about ambush?" Matt asked.

"They don't mess with us much anymore. They fear us," Casio said from the front seat. There was a cocky arrogance in his voice.

Matt was perplexed by the answer, but what did he have to lose? He leaned back and rested his head as they sped south down Martin Luther King Jr. Drive. Soon they would be at the Boeing Museum of Flight. For a few moments it was quiet. Matt had a full belly, but sure would love a shower, or maybe some time in the hot tub. His head still hurt, he noticed that he smelled a bit fowl, and his face had gone from stubble to a patchy gray beard. Overall Matt looked and felt like shit. How much he would give for a shower, a shave, and his recliner right about now.

As they arrived it was much like before. The guards at the gate stopped them, and Casio rolled down his window. "I was told to tell you that I am bringing Matt Scott." The guard peered in, and Matt gave a small wave. The guard looked at Matt and back to a photograph he held in his right hand.

"Go ahead. Drive slowly to the main entrance and leave the car there." Casio rolled up the window and chirped the tires as he pulled out—his way of defying authority.

"No need for the theatrics," Kimball scolded Casio.

As they rounded the corner, two armed guards guided them into a roped-off parking area. Once the car was parked, they all were escorted into the same meeting room as the last time. This time they were the only ones in the room, with the exception of two armed guards. The four men sat and looked at each other, not saying a word. The big double doors suddenly opened and Colonel Phelps walked in beside General Seibel, and the Master Sergeant from before was following behind. They entered the room and closed the door behind them.

"You two," the Master Sergeant looked at the guards, "out." He pointed toward the door. The two guards quickly complied and left the room in a hurry.

"Where is the Prophet?" asked Kimball in an accusatory fashion.

"He will be here soon," Colonel Phelps said as she walked up to Matt. Seeing his bruised face, she commented, "Well done. I see you decided on the hard way?" She had a snicker in her voice.

"The marines, did they make it out OK?" Matt was still worried for the young men that fell in the firefight.

"We lost one, but thanks to your friends here, two were saved." The Colonel was not going to sugarcoat anything. She spoke like the combat veteran she was. Most likely Colonel Phelps earned her knocks in Iraq. For the first time many female soldiers and marines found themselves in combat. In a society that has no value for women, it was twice as hard. Matt respected any woman who could make it as a marine, but to lead men in combat and to do it in a Muslim country was something that warranted the upmost respect. It was clear that Colonel Phelps was battle-experienced and highly respected by her peers.

The General and the Master Sergeant had sat down, and Phelps made her way over to sit to the General's left.

"You're him?" The general said to Kimball.

"I'm just me," Kimball said with a twisted smile.

Before they could continue, the doors opened without a knock and Elder Miles entered with his two guards, one at each side. He stopped and gave each a look. "Leave this to me; you two wait outside." As Miles came into the room, Kimball, Casio, and the other man who came with them stood quickly. The meeting was to begin. Matt had done his part—he put the parties together as he was asked.

He had no idea how this would end, and, honestly, he did not even care. Matt Scott was done. He wanted to go home, and he wanted to see his wife.

"I have done what you asked of me. Can you please take me to my wife? I would like to go home now!" Matt was speaking to Colonel Phelps, the only one he knew he could trust at this point, and deliberately avoiding speaking to or toward anyone else in the room.

"You are welcome to stay," General Siebel said.

"No disrespect, gentleman, and lady, but I couldn't care less what you have to discuss. I have done what I was asked, and I would like to get to my family." Matt turned to the General this time. He still made an effort to avoid looking at Elder Miles. The thought of the young, awkward, sometimes annoying missionary being the President of the entire Mormon Church and a Prophet just had not sunk in.

The world had changed, but in some ways nothing had changed. A year ago, President Prescott suspended an election and shut down the government to avoid the chance of a theocracy. Now a Marine General was meeting with the President of the same Church, telling him to stand down and stop his people from defending themselves. Many things were the same, just in different wrappers. Mathew Scott was beyond skeptical, and it was clear to those around him.

"You have a problem, Mr. Scott?" the General asked.

"No problem," Matt said with disgust in his voice.

"No, you speak your mind. You've earned it," Colonel Phelps said.

Matt got to his feet. "Excuse me, but you can drive me to my family, or I can walk, but either way I am done."

"Not so fast. If you would please give us just a few more minutes," Colonel Phelps asked.

"Honestly, Colonel, I am not so sure that I trust any of you anymore. Looks to me like we got rid of one corrupt government for another. I am sitting here watching negotiations between the Military and the Church. Do any of you see how ridiculous this is?"

"Please, Matt, sit, just a little longer." The General was speaking with a calm voice. "We have all been through a lot. Please give it just a bit more time."

Matt turned and looked at Miles. Miles and Casio had both sat back down at the table and were listening.

"So, the truth, we need the real reason we are here." Miles said to the General.

Matt sat back down. He could stay for a minute, as he was very curious to hear what Miles would have to say. Again the thought of Miles being a leader, icon, or prophet seemed so unbelievable that Matt was willing to sit and watch and listen for a few minutes. If for no other reason, curiosity had gotten the better of him.

The General spoke after a large sigh. "In a nutshell, it's Prescott. President Prescott is back on the scene. He has quite the following in Regions One and Two. He is calling our region a Mormon Theocracy. It's worse than that. He has some support in the Military, and we have lost several bases and units on the East Coast to his control. We could be looking at a civil war." After a pause, he continued, "Not between civilians, a civil war within the Military."

"And you're blaming the Sons of Nephi?" asked Kimball.

"Not blaming," interjected the colonel, "it is politically..." She paused. "Let me try to explain. When a group of Mormon missionaries, or a group that is named after a Mormon or looks like Mormons, takes control, it looks bad." She stopped and looked around the table. "Prescott is making points. He has demonized the LDS Church, and a large number of Americans are going to follow him if we are not careful."

"We are just asking for restraint," interjected the general.

"Restraint?" Kimball stood and raised his voice. "We did not start this; we only fought back when no one else would. For God's sake, they killed my wife!" yelled Kimball. He looked at Miles. "They killed the Prophet."

"It's bigger than us," said Miles unexpectedly in a soft but commanding voice.

Kimball was visibly shaken, but he sat down. "I am sorry," he said to Miles.

"No, I am sorry for your loss," Miles responded.

Matt thought it was strange listening to Miles speak. The awkward young man who would not or could not put a sentence together just months ago was speaking clearly and definitively. Matt wondered if the old Miles was a ruse or if there was something to this Prophet thing. It seemed like Miles was a different man—a calm, articulate, wise man, not a young, lost, disabled missionary.

"So how does this work? What is the response to Prescott?" Matt asked. He was now intrigued and not pushing to leave so quickly.

"Elections," General Siebel stated. "We are going to announce elections, and following the presidential election, we are going to convene a Constitutional Congress. We need to move before Prescott becomes too strong."

"So you are asking us to lie low?" asked Kimball.

"More than that, I need you and the Mormon Church to stand up and ask all of the groups to stand down, to give the elections a chance." General Siebel sat quietly for a moment. "That's where you come in, Mr. Scott; you will go on a series of public announcements with Mr. Miles and Mr. Kimball."

"And say what?" Matt was a bit taken aback by what seemed like an amateurish political move by the General. It was poly science 101—have your advisory join you, the old keep-your-enemies-close thing.

"You will ask all of the Sons of Nephi to step down and turn in their weapons, across the country—the three of you," the General said.

"I won't do that. I will go on and explain who and what they are, I will even ask them to stand down, but I will never ask them to give up their guns. Do you know Mormon history?" Matt looked at the General with distain. "You realize they will become targets. You are asking these men to surrender to a vengeful enemy."

"Wait a minute, all over the country, what do you mean by that?" asked Kimball.

Elmer Kimball had no idea how the Sons of Nephi had grown in reputation and in size. He had heard what Matt Scott had told him earlier, but he never totally grasped the scope of the group. Sons of Nephi had started up all across the nation. At the rate they were going, it would not be long before every Mormon ward in the nation had a Sons of Nephi group. Matt Scott had told Kimball of other groups, yet it really had not sunk in. In Elmer Kimball's mind, there were a few copycat groups, but the only real Sons of Nephi were in Seattle, and he knew them all.

"We estimate about forty thousand Sons of Nephi currently, at the rate of growth we could see a half million by year's end," the Master Sergeant interjected.

Kimball, Matt and Casio sat back in shock. "Wait a minute, did you say forty thousand?" asked Kimball.

"Maybe more," responded the General.

"We are starting to lose soldiers and marines. The Mormons are deserting and joining your groups, and they are taking their weapons with them," the gruff old sergeant interjected. This time he spoke with respect.

There was a moment of silence in the room. Could it be that this little group of missionaries and a few volunteers started something as big as this? How did it happen? Matt was wondering.

"How?" asked Matt, verbalizing some of his thoughts.

"Does it matter?" Colonel Phelps answered. "What matters is we have a possible civil war on our hands." She leaned forward toward Matt, Miles, and the others. "You may not have asked for this, you may not have started it, but if you don't help stop it, a lot of people are going to die." The Colonel was very clear with her tone; this was not a game. "A lot of your people are going to die," she continued.

Miles stood up. "We will do it. I will give a public decree to stand down, no violence. I will decree that all Mormons are to support free and open elections." Miles stood for a moment, looking upward. "We are a peaceful religion, and I will remind the world of this. I will publish an edict to support the elections." He stopped and looked at Elmer Kimball. "We can call in the Catholics to help us," he finished.

Matt looked at the two, General Siebel and President Miles. "They burned the temples, they killed Bishop King, and they tried to outlaw the practice of your faith. My God, you were there. How can you trust them?"

"It is not the Military, or President Prescott, or the Sons of Nephi that I trust, Brother Scott. It is my faith. I trust in God, and I will do what it takes to make this a free nation again." Elder Miles spoke sternly to the group. "We will turn the other cheek."

"Brother Scott, we will survive. If we are right in our beliefs, we will withstand the onslaught of President Prescott and his supporters. If we fall doing the right thing, then so be it. We shall drop our arms and depend on the grace of God. If we fall, we will fall righteously." President Miles was quiet but stern in his words.

"Will they listen?" asked General Siebel.

"They will," Casio responded.

"All we can do is ask. Bishop Kimball, you will support this, won't you?" asked Miles.

"Yes." Elmer Kimball had a tear in his eye. "It's time the killing stopped." He was thinking of his son, Levi.

"Well, let's get down to business, then. Mr. Scott are you on board?" asked General Siebel.

Matt nodded yes without saying a word. The gravity of the statement made by Miles had left him speechless.

The meeting progressed with a lot of discussion on how this was going to take place. There would be posters, TV, and radio announcements. There would be a series of edicts from every major church supporting the free elections and the Constitutional Congress. The outcome was far from certain, but it was time to end the chaos. General Siebel ensured everyone that similar meetings were going on with the Catholic Diocese, as well as leaders in every religious group in the country.

When the meeting ended, all stood together and walked out to the parking area, where a group of marines and soldiers waited. Miles approached Matt Scott as he stood talking with Kimball and Colonel Phelps.

"God bless you, Brother Scott. To you we all owe a great debt." President Miles than grabbed Matt Scott's right hand and held it for a moment. "You go back to Leanne. Go home, and be happy." The words and tone spoken by this young man were those of an old soul. Matt felt humbled in his presence.

"Thank you, and God bless you," was all he could say in response.

After some brief discussion of upcoming work to be done, Matt made his way to a Humvee, where two marines waited for him. Matt was guided into the back seat as the two climbed up front. A convoy of armored Humvees sped out of the guarded parking lot and onto Martin Luther King Jr. drive. They were taking Matt to David's house, to his wife, Leanne.

Leanne and David were sitting on the front porch talking when the sound of a convoy filled the air. Humvee after Humvee pulled up in front of the house. David and Leanne stood up, and neither said a word. By the time the last vehicle in the convoy pulled up, there were seven Humvees and a Striker parked in the grass, on the sidewalk, and in the street surrounding David's house. The mother and son stood watching as a back door opened on one of the Humvees. Out stepped Matt, his face bruised and a little swollen still, and covered with gray and brown whiskers. Matt stood tall and walked toward the front porch with a slight limp. Leanne broke out into tears as she ran down the stairs and into her husband's arms.

"I love you so much," Matt said as he wiped the tears from Leanne's cheek.

As the couple reunited, the convoy backed out onto the road and sped away without a word said. Leanne had been strong. She had convinced herself that Matt was indestructible, but now that he was home, now they were safe, she could let go with her emotions.

"I thought you were dead," Leanne said. "I thought you were dead."

The reunited couple walked to the front door and into the house. Matt rested at David's house for a couple days before they drove back to their home and to the lives they missed so much. A week after they got home, Colonel Phelps contacted them. It was time to get to work. Matt and Leanne returned to Seattle; this time they did not stay at David's house. Colonel Phelps had put them in a suite at the Silver Cloud Hotel. Matt Scott, Leanne Scott, and Elder Kimball worked on public statements, they had reporters writing the story of Port Smith, the King family killing, and the rescue of Elder Miles. Much was embellished, much was diminished, and much of it was just propaganda. Miles, Casio, Kimball, and the Scott family reviewed ads, articles, and TV interviews. After weeks of intensive work, Matt and Leanne were on their way home. Leanne had gotten word that she was to get some part-time work back at the insurance office, organizing for a post-election opening. The next year was not easy; there were flare-ups of violence every now and then. There was a lot of nasty campaigning going on, but every day the world became a little more civil again. Every day it seemed like normalcy would possibly return.

CHAPTER FOURTEEN

*B*ack in the little apartment, one of the missionaries looked at Mr. Scott. "The way you tell the story, that's not what we were taught." He was perplexed.

"Son, the truth was adjusted." He paused, and then added, "People could not have handled the truth. We needed peace," Mr. Scott explained.

The other missionary looked even more confused. "The prophet, he lied?" he asked.

"Never. He never lied," Mr. Scott responded sternly. "The prophet helped save his people."

Mrs. Scott had cleared the plates hours ago, and the four were still seated at the table. While the old man got up for a bathroom break, his wife brought more food and drink to the table.

"Leanne, is it lunchtime already?" he asked as he returned to the room.

"Well past," she responded as she set out crackers and cheese for the young men.

Thinking the missionaries may be bored with the ramblings of an old man, Mr. Scott sat down in his recliner instead of at the table.

The two missionaries ignored the food and got up and moved into the living area and sat on the couch. Clearly they wanted to hear how it ended.

Leaning back in his Chair Mr. Scott continued.

It had been over a year since the day a bloody missionary had knocked on the Scott door. Many wounds had healed, and many still had a ways to go. Port Smith was a town again, no more tanks or marines on the streets. There were still harsh words at the coffee shop on occasion. Matt still felt guilt and pain for the men he had killed. The King family would continue to mourn their father. Elmer Kimball and his family had moved to Salt Lake City. President Miles had moved the Kimballs into a home near the center of the LDS Church. Sarah had returned to Portland to marry her boyfriend and raise their children. Riana was going to grad school, and she would stay on the East Coast. David and his family were doing well and visited Leanne and Matt often. And Sam and her husband were in California. She never left camp Pendleton, and her marine husband came home to her and was now working security in San Diego.

Matt was sitting on the couch; he had a glass of scotch in his right hand, and Leanne sat at his side. Across the room were Nick Jones and Will Black. They were standing with Sheriff Chow. The TV was on, and everyone was waiting with bated breath.

"This is a public service announcement," a voice from the TV pronounced.

On the screen were Matt, Elder Miles, and Kimball. "We are the Sons of Nephi," Elder Kimball said. "We are regular men, fathers, husbands, and neighbors," Matt said. "I am the President of the Church of Jesus Christ of Latter-day Saints," announced Miles. "And we are standing together to call for peace." The camera scanned to Matt. "Over the next month, elections will be held in each region. Following the elections, a Constitutional Convention will be held in Kansas City. We implore you to allow the people to speak their will. It is time for peace, time for our country to return to its glory." Kimball stepped forward, "Sons of Nephi, stand down." Elder Miles stepped forward. "All Latter-day Saints, I remind you that our faith is one of peace." The screen faded, and the commercial ended. This was the last of a series of announcements, articles, ads, and other media bits put out since that meeting at the Boeing Museum of Flight.

"You're a movie star," Leanne teased as she hugged Matt.

Before this ad hit every airway there were posters, short stories in paperback form, social networking, and blogs. The story of Port Smith was made into a short, tell-all documentary, and the public was being informed, maybe even manipulated by General Siebel and Colonel Phelps. They had used their experience in nation-building to try to save their own country.

Some of the cities had incidents of riots and violence, but overall the process was peaceful. In the end, President Prescott won the election in three of the regions. The Northeast refused to be part of the convention, and the United States split into two separate nations. Regions One, Two, and Three became the Eastern Democratic States, and Regions Four through Seven became the Republic of the United States.

After the Constitutional Congress, a new capital was formed for the Republic in Casper, Wyoming, of all places. The next few years were not easy for anyone. There was a lot of infighting, and many families moved from one region to another. Many moved from the Republic to the EDS, as it became known, but in time things settled out. The Republic maintained a majority of the remaining military, much of which was disbanded and put into mothballs. The attempt at a common currency failed as the Republic went to the gold standard and the EDS went to the new Euro. Prescott was elected president of EDS, and a little-known congressman from southern California was elected president of the Republic. In time life returned to normal for most. Within a few years, the accounts of the Sons of Nephi fighting in the streets were only told by old men.

Matt and Leanne Scott sold their business to Jeremy and retired. Leanne never returned to her office, and the Scotts spent their aging years traveling. Matt would often say, "We have a whole new nation to discover." The Scott children did well in life. Matt's son-in-law became a master sergeant in the Marine Corps before he retired. His daughter Sam worked with the Red Cross. Riana only returned to the west to visit. She was married and stayed in Connecticut to work as a teacher. Riana would often tell her students of Port Smith. The events of Port Smith were interpreted a little differently in the EDS, but Riana often corrected her students. "My father, he was no Prophet, and he was no terrorist. He was just a man, a man who fought for what he believed in."

Leanne's son, David, and his wife lived in Seattle and raised five adopted children with their son and daughter.

Elder Miles went on to be a much-respected President of the LDS Church. Many bridges between faiths opened under his leadership. Miles was known as "The Great Uniter", and some called for him to run for President in later years. He always laughed and declined. "I am just a missionary, doing God's work, not a politician," was always his answer.

Port Smith, Washington, became a very busy tourist town. Many came to see were the Battle of Bishop King took place. Monuments were put in to commemorate the fallen on both sides. The Republic was a new nation, a young nation, but it was one that already had great history.

Many years later, in a small apartment, lived an elderly couple. When there was knock on the door, two young Mormon missionaries stood waiting for someone to answer. A slow-moving old man with bad knees made his way to the door. Setting his cane aside, he opened to door to greet the young men.

"Hello, sirs, we are missionaries from the Church of Jesus Christ of Latter-day Saints. Have you heard of the Book of Mormon?"

The old man snickered a little. "You can tell me about the Book of Mormon, and I will tell you about the Sons of Nephi," he replied as he turned and walked with his cane toward his chair.

Mr. Matthew Scott then snickered a little more and looked at the two young men.

"You boys come back next week, and I will tell you all about our travels around this great nation."

The next day came and went. The missionaries were too busy to stop by, and by week's end they received the news. Matthew Scott had died. There would be a simple funeral, a small funeral at the LDS chapel. In attendance were family, a few missionaries, and the Prophet, one Elder Miles.

Leanne Scott lived only a few more months. She had moved in with her son in Seattle. Some say Leanne died of a broken heart. Elder Miles knew she died happy; she needed to be with her husband, and together they would spend eternity. This was the one tenet of the Mormon faith both Matthew and Leanne Scott believed with all of their hearts. Theirs was an eternal marriage, and they would reunite in death.

THE END

Mark DuMond is proud to be a father, stepfather, grandfather and husband. Along with a stint in the Marine Corps, Mark has made raising children and running a small business on the Olympic Peninsula in Washington State his life's work thus far. With the encouragement of his loving wife, Mark has moved toward his lifelong ambition of writing. Though the first in print, Sons of Nephi is one of several of his works, and only one of the genres in which Mark has written. Family, travel, and many more adventures are in Mark's future, along with new and exciting stories to share with readers.

Made in the USA
San Bernardino, CA
20 March 2018